Mariana

Also by Katherine Vaz

Fado & Other Stories
Saudade

Mariana

Katherine Vaz

ALIFORM PUBLISHING
MINNEAPOLIS

ALIFORM PUBLISHING
is part of The Aliform Group
117 Warwick Street SE   Minneapolis, MN USA 55414
612-379-7639 information@aliformgroup.com
www.aliformgroup.com

Mariana was originally published in 1997 in the United Kingdom
by Flamingo, an imprint of HarperCollins Publishers

First published in the United States of America by
Aliform Publishing, 2004
© 2004

Library of Congress Control Number
2003115205

ISBN 0-9707652-9-0

Set in Times New Roman

Cover art by Marco Lamoyi: *En el despuntar de la noche y el otoño, no
muy lejos del río que divide la ciudad de la selva* (detail)
Cover design by Carolyn M. Fox

I would have had no hesitations, God knows, in following you...to the flames of Hell...I beg you, think what you owe me, give ear to my pleas, and I will finish a long letter with a brief ending: farewell, my only love.

from a letter of Héloïse to Abelard

The way I read a Letter's — this —
'Tis first — I lock the Door —
And push it with my fingers — next —
For transport it be sure —
Emily Dickinson

Part 1

WHEN MARIANA was too restless, she counted angels. Her father taught her that all the children in Portugal were learning to do this.

"These are dangerous times," Papa warned. "The angels will watch over you during the hours when I cannot. You worry about the next world, and leave this one to me."

When her father was away, Mariana counted the hours, which were round and the color of air, like invisible clocks. When they looked unbearably faceless, she pretended she could string them together, into necklaces made of sky.

Sometimes Mariana would shout, "Speak! Tell me about the war!"

The hours would elongate into the shape of bared teeth, in order to answer, "The war has jagged edges, and it is eating us alive."

The sky was helpless to resist responding to Mariana, who possessed eyes the color of leaves just thrust out from a bough, that green, the intensification of green, that enraptures anyone who sees it. Her limbs were thin and a sapling-brown. Her hair was long and dark, and she twisted it around her fist if any locks got in her way. She had pronounced biceps and thighs, and a wide forehead and wide cheekbones and wide, set lips, geranium-red, which made her a child of unusual definition.

One afternoon, when she discovered some boys teasing her little brother, Baltazar, because she and her family supported the fight for freedom, she grabbed a lute that her parents kept in the parlor and raced out to attack the boys.

"Leave my brother alone! Leave him alone!" she screamed. At first they were too surprised to react, and she clouted them with the instrument over and over until she broke it on the back of the largest tormentor, and even then did not stop until the strings tangled with the ruined soundboard in her hands. The boys ran away, and when they called her rude names over their shoulders, she laughed at their inability to see that their bravado made them not merely defeated but absurd.

When her mother asked why she had broken the lute and not used one of the sticks in the yard, she explained that a lute was beautiful and a stick was nothing, and Baltazar had to be defended by a beautiful weapon.

To her mother's mild "Perhaps we can find someone to put it back like new," Mariana replied by stamping and storming about the lute being better as wreckage, because now it bore the visible proof of her caring for her brother.

She *would not permit* its repair.

Its silence and mangled shape also served as a fitting homage to the War of Independence, which often seemed as quiet and invisible as the clock-shaped hours. Papa would say to Mariana, "Wait. Watch." Spain had been ruling Portugal for sixty years, and now that the Spanish were fighting their Thirty Years War with France, Portugal had taken hold of the chance to declare her independence from Spain. Papa had persuaded many local nobles to support the appointing of one of their own as a rebel king. The Spanish king was an imposter. "Wait," Papa would say, fiercely, as if waiting had to be a ruthless and not a patient act. "It's calm at the moment, but when the Spanish tire of combat with France, they'll turn their attention to crushing us. A man who plans to win – and I plan to win – has to think far ahead and have everything in place, before the final battles." Everyone's fortune was uneasy, but the war required every man to do what he could.

Papa rode everywhere, inspecting the lands of the Portuguese rebel crown. The wheat crop was a miracle, and Papa arranged for it to be transported to the millstones he ordered set up along the Guadiana River, running south along the Spanish border, where the wheat was ground into biscuits to feed Portuguese soldiers.

He negotiated for the best stud horses to be sent to the farmlands that the rebel Portuguese king had presented to him, in thanksgiving for his urgent valor. Portuguese soldiers needed the best horses in Europe.

No worker was beaten who did not deserve it.

Nothing would stop him from creating his own *morgadio,* or entailment – what Mariana described as a "little kingdom."

She would stand on the family estate and consider the plans of her father until she exhaled her own heated thoughts.

He kept records of every transaction, account, or proposal, signing them "Francisco da Costa Alcoforado," with the initial of his given name entwined, as custom dictated, with the initial of his wife's name, Leonor. Together the letters F and L formed a single flourish that looked like ironwork. She was caught up in his every signature. How thrilling, what a marvel, that writing could contain a beloved one!

The most magnificent parties in the city of Beja were the work of Papa. Mariana adored, *adored* the smell of lime waters, pomades, and garlic (especially garlic, strong enough to speak through her skin for days after being consumed), and she thrived upon the high tenor of agitation. Many noblemen arrived at these feasts, saying that they were content declaring themselves to be Spanish and had already learned the language of the powerful Castilian nobility. They would leave the parties full of Papa's brandy, saying that they were ready to die to save their occupied country.

Watching their drunken steps caused Mariana to reel herself, from her sheer love of parties. She would stumble dizzily to her room, where she was free to wonder so much about so many things that she forgot what she was thinking about, and fell inside wonder itself. That was when troops of angels were likely to invade her room, including the ones whose gauze skirts had been slashed by Spanish soldiers. Some of these angels were vengeful, because they had wandered into battles and come out with missing arms, or holes for stomachs, but Mariana was not afraid of them. She considered this war as hers. It was now ten years old, and so was she, both of them born in 1640. At her baptism, the priest had signed a cross of chrism on the back of her neck to protect her from evil, and if the angels frightened her, she would roll over and pull aside her long brown hair, so that whatever remained of the oily cross on her neck would dazzle the wounded angels away.

Go bother *her,* Mariana would tell them, pointing to her older sister, Ana Maria, snoring through her big nose in the bed nearby.

Go swim in her chamber pot, for all I care.

Little Catarina was two, and slept like the dead, like peace. Mariana did not have much use for her, though she admired how untroubled Catarina seemed, neither kicking nor squawking at the night.

Baltazar slept in a room off the middle of the hall, next to their baby brother, Miguel. Once a week, the servants opened the thick green hulls of the unripe walnuts that had fallen in the yard and rubbed the stain from the hulls on the wooden panels of the hallway. Baltazar was only five years old, but loved to help the servants redouble the darknesses of the wood so that the corridor shone with the tones, wet darkness upon dry darkness, like the ones in the Velásquez painting, Papa's joy, that had once hung there. Now, because of the war, he had taken it down. A man doing the bidding of the insurgent Portuguese court could not have a Spanish painting, even a prized one, hanging in his house.

If you scare Baltazar, she told the bitter angels, I will stab you myself.

Their grandmother, in a canopied bed in the enormous room at the end of the hall, would know what to do if trouble came to her in the night. She would tell the ragged angels to go away, and they would. If she ordered them to come nearer to give her a better look, they would do that, too. Sometimes it was so intolerable to be apart from her grandmother for even the space of a night that Mariana would feel her way down the hall, slip into her grandmother's room, and brush her white hair into a smooth, soft fan on her pillow as she slept. "You're so gorgeous, Vovó," Mariana would murmur. And to the angels, she would say, "Do you see my Vovó's hair? It is more beautiful than your skirts will ever be."

Before the angels left in shame, Mariana would ask if they, like everyone else in her city of Beja, were going off to report their dealings to her father. She would say, Tell him that you are supposed to watch over us, and instead you are horrible. Tell him I know he wants to make a sealed world where we will be safe, but the war has gone into our dreams.

*

Late one afternoon, Mariana and her grandmother decided to go on a forbidden walk. Mariana's parents refused to give them permission to leave the estate, and Vovó enjoyed disobeying anyone who told her what to do. As Mariana stole into the kitchen to wrap cheesecloth around some cakes made of ground almonds and egg yolks, she whispered happily at Vovó, "We're going to get in trouble!"

"Yes," said Vovó, trembling with excitement. She was short and heavy and liked to show that having a large bosom meant that she could stick it into crowds as a lever. Where her breasts intruded, the rest of her body would follow, and soon, before people could guess that they were backing away, she would be at the front of the lines in the market when the men brought in the brittle shingles of dried codfish from the coast.

Instead of helping pack the cakes, Vovó began to boast once again about her huge breasts being a superior weapon in getting what she wanted.

"Shh, hurry," said Mariana, who did not want to be caught without having done anything daring.

"I cannot go anywhere without my jewelry," announced Vovó, refusing to lower her voice. She had worn black since the death of her husband, Mama's father, the only detail to suggest that Vovó might have loved him, especially since she was bold enough to dress up her black mantua, a loose gown with a black sash beneath the bosom, with a fanciful leaf-pin of pearls.

Vovó's fingers were too swollen to fasten the pin, and Mariana set down the almond cakes to attach it onto her grandmother's front. It floated there like a sparkling leaf on a black mountain.

Vovó clapped her hands together as a child would and said, "Eyes up, and keep walking."

At the wrought iron gate, Vovó removed the key hidden in her sash and opened the lock. She spat onto the earth in the direction she believed Holland to be, as she did every morning now that the Dutch were taking advantage of Portugal's troubles and seizing the Portuguese trade routes and outposts. She and Mariana glanced back at the house, high, square, plain-faced, and with dentils, like a yellowing fort. Verandas on both the higher and lower stories allowed the family to stare from various heights into the distant plains, where soldiers were said to be camped, biding time, occasionally skirmishing.

As Mariana and her grandmother struck out for the road, they passed the sign with bold, black letters that read "Alcoforado." Papa had ordered it because he wanted his own official carriage stop, to be set near the platform where his friends arrived from their visits to Lisbon and Versailles.

Mariana asked, "Are we going to visit the souls?"

"Yes! They need to be fed!" said Vovó. "So do I!" She tore open the cheesecloth around the cakes that Mariana was carrying and ate one of them, and insisted that Mariana have one. She did, and the pleasure on her tongue spread outward, and down her throat.

The sun was hot and falling closer to them, and their feet slapped powdery dust. They were scarcely halfway to the shrine for the souls-not-at-rest when a group of four Spanish soldiers came out of nowhere and walked slowly towards them. Vovó told Mariana to remember the lesson of wild creatures: a bigger animal will retreat if the smaller, threatened animal stares into its opponent's eyes. Such fearlessness will cause the attacker to back away. This was how a dog might defeat a wolf. Since the Spanish had been among them for over half a century, their presence was nothing new. The change was in everyone's attitudes, in everyone's insides. The soldiers drew nearer. Their leather boots widened upward from their ankles to their knees, their spurs were downward-pointing stars, their gold sashes were dirty. One of them had lost the feather from his hat, and his garter rosettes were frayed. Another, despite the heat, wore his embroidered gauntlets. When they were close, Mariana could see the tears in the loops of stitching.

"Senhora!" said the one with the gauntlets, bowing to Vovó and winking. The soldiers jostled one another, hoping that an old woman and a young girl might be undone at the barest gesture of love.

Mariana was unable to make them fall over dead by staring into their eyes, though to her shock one soldier glanced away. "Huh," said Vovó, blowing them kisses. They laughed, but did not steal Vovó's pearl leaf, or grab the cakes, or commit murder. Mariana tried to register everything, to tell Baltazar later, but nothing else happened. The men kept walking, their swords dragging like loose spines at their sides. Smoke from faraway camps threw fading pokers into the sky. Vovó explained that since the war had been going on for a decade, the soldiers were losing their urge to fight and were spending their time looking for places to get drunk. This war might die of its own waiting to conclude itself.

Vovó's stoutness prevented both of them from walking fast, and sweat wrapped them in a close, watery lace. Mariana's white bonnet and white linen dress seemed woven from pure glare. "What is it that we kiss, but never adore, Mariana?" asked Vovó.

"Spanish soldiers!" said Mariana.

"No."

"Tell me."

"No, my One More Than Everything. It's a riddle. You have to guess."

"I give up."

Vovó said, "Don't be so impatient, Mariana."

Not far from the shrine for the souls-not-at-rest, they stopped at a well and lowered its wooden bucket down into the black water and raised its heaviness up. When they used the dipper tied to the bucket, the sunlight converted the pane of water in the dipper into a mirror that shone so brightly they had to drink quickly, Vovó first, at Mariana's insistence, and then Mariana, before it hurt their eyes. They drank several dipperfuls. Mariana kept a lookout for more soldiers, but none appeared. She was disappointed. Around them were the cork oaks, the bark curling white away from where knives had sliced out the hidden hard sponge. Near one of these trees was a wooden stand with a sheltered platform high off the ground, like a bird house with legs. Someone had built it for the souls of people who died before finishing their obligations on earth. They belonged nowhere. Though no longer alive, they could not gain admittance into the tranquility of the other world. They might have betrayed a friend, or committed some other unforgivable act that prevented their souls from being free. Perhaps they had not used a talent to its fullest, or had debts, or had not loved someone enough, or had died with a surplus of unanswered questions. Mariana was sorry that these souls were condemned to search for shrines where they could drink the holy water and eat the food that people left for them.

Some roses were frying from the heat inside the shrine, and Vovó dashed them onto the ground, grumbling that this was another sign of her country falling apart, and maybe the Spaniards should be kept as leaders.

Mariana set the remaining cakes in the shrine. "Is it the souls-not-at-rest that we kiss, but never adore, Vovó?" she asked.

"No," said her grandmother

"Vovó," said Mariana, "who dies with everything finished? Aren't we all going to be souls-not-at-rest?"

"I plan to die with everything finished," said her grandmother, arranging some wild flowers in the shrine. "I'm not going to crowd in here with these idiots."

"If they're idiots, why are we being nice to them?" Mariana asked, and giggled.

"I have a certain compassion for their weariness," said Vovó.

The sugar dusting the almond cakes was already melting. Mariana understood that it would be soldiers who would come along and fight over the sweets, but whether it would be souls, men, or birds, it was worth every risk to be out here in the open air with Vovó. Mariana would go for walks whenever she wanted! One day she would visit the court of Louis XIV, as Papa's friends did. Wearing taffeta, she would attend masked balls. If a marquis annoyed her, she would tug the ear wires that made his ringlets stick out from his head! During her travels in Goa and Macau, she would inhale spices. She was not the godchild of the great-grandson of the explorer Vasco da Gama for nothing!

The best way to avoid being a soul-without-rest would be to exist within a love where ordinary mortal rules did not apply. She must be like Inês. Inês de Castro, Inês the Beautiful. Possessor of the most exalted romance in the universe. Almost three hundred years ago, Inês secretly married Pedro, the son of the Portuguese king. Not knowing about his son's marriage to her, the king believed the nobles who hissed that she was a spy. He ordered his men to cut her throat. When Pedro ascended the throne two years later, after the death of his father, he hunted down her murderers and killed them, and then he ripped out and ate their hearts. He commanded that the body of Inês be dug up from her grave. After placing her on the throne next to his, he made everyone in the court kiss her rotting hand and call her his queen.

To this day, by his decree, Pedro lay in his sarcophagus facing the one carved for Inês. When they arise during the resurrection of bodies on the last day, she will be the first creature he will behold. Until then, they will serenely endure the entire history of man and the languid times of God.

Mariana trembled every time she recalled the story of Inês and Pedro, because it was not a fairy tale. It was real.

She would soon be eleven, and it was not too early to plan for her future. She had no choice but to be a reborn Inês. If one had to live, why not be worshipped beyond the flesh shrinking off one's bones, why not rise up at world's end to own heaven itself? Yes, absolutely! Mariana rocked back and forth on her heels at the thought of such triumph, such defeat of the normal rules governing human existence. She would have to find someone whose soul, like hers, could only achieve rest by reclining upon the vastness of their love.

She had chosen him already. Rui de Melo Lôbo. Papa would approve. Rui was from the oldest noble house in Beja, and his family's headstrong courage was legendary. The Lôbo brothers were leaders in the fight for independence. Papa was always declaring that they had the raw energy and fever that might save everyone. Rui was bold enough to wear his passion on his body, with that gash on his chin, barely covered by his red beard, and that limp from being stabbed in his thigh during a battle. People said that he was ugly, but Mariana saw him as radiant with the fineness of wearing wounds and not being hurt by them. Rui loved to sing, gamble, and tell stories about the war. He tore life open as if it were a wrapped parcel he could not bother to approach cautiously. One of his ancestors had sent someone the head of a king as a gift.

Rui was more than twice her age, but she would convince Papa that no one braver could be at her side, and there was no better way to join the two finest houses in their city – one of them ancient and impetuous, the other new and disciplined but no less exuberant.

As if reading Mariana's dream, Vovó sang:

> *Considera, meu bem,*
> *Considera,*
> *Considera, considera bem . . .*
>
> *Consider, my love,*
> *Consider,*
> *Regard, consider well. . .*

They decided to attempt the journey into town, to the market. Vovó liked the marketplace so much that she would stand before it for long minutes in glad astonishment before entering, bosom first. Mariana was hoping that Papa would again discover her missing and ride out looking for her, to see how brave she was, staring right into the eyes of Spanish soldiers. He would report to Rui that this was a girl worthy of his awe. But instead she heard the familiar gallop of the horse belonging to Luís, Papa's servant, coming to collect them, and it put an abrupt end to the day's adventure.

At home, Mama was waiting. Mariana was unsettled to notice a white pouring of pain in her mother, like a hot milk flowing right below the skin. Everyone was in the kitchen except Papa. Ana Maria was kneading bread dough, Catarina was playing on the floor with a marionette, Miguel was tottering from table leg to table leg, and when Baltazar threw his arms around Mariana, she buried her face in the top of his black, wavy hair, ashamed that she had worried him.

Mama and Vovó started to argue, but they quarreled so often that none of the children bothered to listen.

"Everyone thinks you have a giant brain, but you're stupid," said Ana Maria, taking her hands out of the bread dough to jab them in Mariana's direction. "Some day I hope you get run through, right through your stupid heart."

"Do you know why they named me 'Mariana'? Because 'Ana Maria' is mixed up and spelled backward, and Mama and Papa had to have me on account of you being such a fat mistake," said Mariana, but a worse offense than her older sister came into view. Dinner was going to be the platter of *migas* on the counter. *Migas*! What torture! Mariana hated the stale bread soaked in lard lurking beneath slabs of pork and despised the bloated look of it, the taste, and the fact that it meant Papa, who hated it too, would not be there for dinner. Papa allowed Mariana and her brothers and sisters to sit with him and Mama at the table. He called them his own true nation, and permitted them to speak if they put down their silver and asked permission.

"You are not to leave the house again, Mother," Mama called out as Vovó escaped, her feet thudding harshly, then faintly, as she returned to her room. Mariana laughed, picturing Vovó using her bosom as a wedge to get past Mama, to go outside whenever she pleased.

"Mariana," said Mama, picking up Miguel. "What am I going to do with you?"

"We went to feed the souls."

"She's practicing to be Joan of Arc," said Ana Maria. "She hears voices and is going to save us."

"Shut up, melonhead," said Mariana.

"I will not have this kind of barbaric talk," said Mama. Catarina was crying, and Mama, still holding Miguel, gathered her up as well. Mama's spine curved to manage the weight of both children. She would have grabbed up her two other daughters and Baltazar if that were possible, until Mariana would need to cry, Unclasp us, Mama! We're killing you!

Is it our parents that we kiss, but never adore? Mariana would later ask Vovó.

No, my One More Than Everything. Guess again, Vovó would reply. But it was such a good answer that Vovó needed to consider it well.

If I wait long enough, the answer to every riddle will come to me, Mariana told herself. She was sitting alone at the dinner table because Mama had forbidden her to move until she finished her serving of *migas*. She glared at the wet bread and wished she had struck it hard enough with her fist to splatter it on Ana Maria's smirking face. Everyone had eaten and gone to bed. Vovó was not coming to her rescue. Papa could be anywhere. The night was casting itself through the windows, sheets of black sky and sheets of white starlight. Angels crowded at the windows, waiting to be counted to put her to sleep, but she told them to go away. Had Inês tolerated this kind of interference? Had Inês ever been forced to eat *migas*? Mariana prayed that the Spanish would catapult some flaming rags onto their roof, as they once did to the Almeidas' house, but there was not much of that these days during this sagging part of the war. She would outlast hunger. The moon could go up and down one thousand times, and she would be sitting here as the *migas* hardened on her plate, then shriveled from old age. All of this was training for being Inês and waiting for God to dispense with eternity.

Mariana practiced a defiant stare at her plate. If only Papa would free her. But there was no stirring until after midnight, when Baltazar, his night shirt trailing on the floor, sleepwalked into the dining room.

"Baltazar!" she said.

"Lift me up," he said.

"Of course," she said, and put him on her lap. Mariana liked to picture him as a baby, when he had been the right size for her to encompass him in her arms and pretend that he was hers. She could not explain why she did not see Miguel or Catarina like this. She felt what she felt. Because Baltazar had been so small at birth, his gold baby ring had to be tied onto his middle finger with ribbons that ended in a bow around his wrist.

If she told him to, Baltazar would come live with her in the house she would own with Rui, her great love.

"Can't you sleep?" she asked.

"No. Bicho-Papão is going to eat me."

"No, he isn't. I'll scare him away for you."

"Then he'll eat you."

"I'm skin and bones. He'll spit me out." Mariana made gagging noises.

"He'll get you, and I'll have to kill him," said Baltazar.

"Ah ha, then you're not afraid of him."

He smiled and put his head on her chest.

"Who told you about Bicho-Papão?" asked Mariana.

"Ana Maria."

"And what did she say?"

"That he's the monster on the roof who swings inside houses to eat children. He gobbles them up inside the pouch he has under his mouth."

"Did she tell you that he only eats wicked girls named Ana Maria?"

"I don't want him to get her either!" shouted Baltazar.

"Shh, I won't let him get any of us," said Mariana. "We'll feed him something else." She shaped the *migas* into a bread-person, and threw it out the window. "There," she said. "That will stick in Bicho-Papão's throat, and he'll choke to death. No one can swallow that poison."

Baltazar smothered his laugh with both his hands over his mouth.

She carried him back to his room, down the hallway that smelled of walnut juice. Miguel, a year old, was sleeping in the bed next to Baltazar's. The blue and white azulejo tiles showing rolling plains and fountains on their bedroom walls were covered with hair-sized cracks and fractures the shape of lightning bolts. It looked to her like a nervous frozen storm across a lovely scene.

Baltazar fell asleep as she sat with him, and though she wanted to hurry back to the kitchen – it would be tragic if Mama were to wander in and think that Mariana had surrendered and eaten her dinner – she took up some stray threads from Baltazar's bedclothes and used a touch of saliva on her finger to glue them to his forehead. She did the same to Miguel. Vovó had done that to them when they were infants, so that Bicho-Papão would think her grandchildren were too gruesome and stringy to chew or kidnap.

Mariana returned to the kitchen and filled her plate with more *migas*. She commanded her heavy eyelids to stay open, but could not decide whether she preferred time to stand still or speed up.

Mama, in a wrinkled gown, looked in on her and said, "I can't sleep either."

"Oh?" said Mariana, coldly.

"I worry about you."

Mariana was silent as her mother sat next to her and said, "Shall we toss this to the pigs and not tell anyone?"

"That won't be necessary. I don't think the pigs want to eat their cousins."

"Mariana, please. Do you know how tired I am?"

"I am sorry that your thinking of me has kept you awake. Is Papa home? I want to talk to him."

"I haven't looked in his room. I don't know where he is," said Mama.

"Goodnight, then. I'll be fine here."

Looking into Mariana's face, Leonor craved to be dressed in one of her blouses with the extra buttons that she had sewn onto the sleeves along the underside of the arms, the full tender length, there for all to see. She had added the buttons so that the emptiness would not be as terrible when she was not carrying any children against her breasts. Weights, light as coins, might stave off the ache. A nightgown by itself was weightless as a ghost. Mariana was the most difficult of her children, but nothing could stop Leonor from adoring her babies, every one of them. Having them was like pushing her own heart out from between her legs, and she feared being too old to have more of them – hearts, children. Her legs were crossed with blue and green veins from the weight of bearing her children, a body that erupted in sea colors, and still she would not stop giving birth. She even loved José, the boy that her husband, Francisco, had had with another woman, years before Leonor married him. Nice-tempered José brought chestnuts and figs to the children at Christmas. At a young age, he had joined the priory of Our Lady of the Snows without protest and was now a monk. He had never seen snow and naturally never would, and he said it made his dwelling sound exotic, a palace of imaginary crystals. A bastard son of Francisco da Costa Alcoforado never need be ashamed and would be welcomed as family, but neither would he insist that any part of the Alcoforado *morgadio* should be his. Being a holy brother of magical winters could be a fine destiny, and Francisco da Costa Alcoforado donated a stipend every year to Our Lady of the Snows to cover José's needs. Leonor yearned to steal some of José's agreeableness and wreathe it around Mariana, whose eyes had a vehemence that allowed them to devour the books, one after the other, that her father kept in his solarium. Look at her earnestness. Now that Baltazar and Miguel were born, maybe Francisco would stop treating Mariana as a son.

"Tell me, Mama," Mariana burst out, "what do you think of the Lôbo family?"

Solely one detail about the Lôbos pleased Leonor. They were fearless, and would collapse backward onto the gates of hell protecting anyone they decided was their own. Although she abhorred the notion, Leonor knew that Francisco was seriously considering the idea of marrying one of her precious girls to one of those marauders. She would have to repeat to herself: safety, protection, wealth, land. A swordsman would be a good defender. The Lôbos were noblemen, though they did not act like ones. Their wives would be well provided for, well-guarded, but she preferred to pretend that such a marriage would never happen. She said, "I think you're tougher than any of them, my Mariana," and took the plate of *migas* to the scraping pail. Mariana threw her arms fiercely around her mother, a death-clutch. Leonor, alarmed at her daughter's fervor, kissed her once, twice, before watching her run off to bed, hoping that the kisses asked, "What was that about? Can you do nothing softly, for heaven's sake?"

Mariana went to her room, but could not sleep. Her nerves jumped like living whips. Ana Maria was slumbering loudly in the adjacent bed, but Mariana decided not to loathe her. Mama had more or less agreed that Rui was a good match, and Mariana was overcome with the image of him with his fiery skin and red hair, Rui, who once was telling a story and had to stop and dance, not heeding his bad leg, because his emotions were running too high to settle down into words, who once showed her how to spit the husks of dried fava beans over a wall, who once opened a box and said that inside was pulverized indigo, mankind's most expensive dye. It was the richest blue, purple-blue, black-blue, jeweled as sugar, that Mariana had ever seen. How rare blue was! She almost fainted when Rui said it was hers, and put it into her hands. From that moment on, she did not care that she lived in the interior and had never seen the ocean; Rui had given her a box of ocean. She traced his initial entwined with hers onto the blue surface, and treasured her blue fingertip. Men who understood her could sense how thirsty she was for all shades of it. Her bedspread was blue, allowing her to sleep beneath the tone of her love for Rui, although it was her godfather, Dom Francisco da Gama, the great-grandson of Vasco da Gama, who brought this bedspread as a birthday gift from Macau. Red Chinese letters were sewn into the blue, and Mariana ran her fingers over them for good luck.

Blue would be the daring color of the walls of Mariana's future home, blue furniture, blue linens to lie upon with Rui. Scandalous thought! Alarming color. They would live a ceaseless feast, enveloped by the ornate costumes of guests, exotic plants, story-crammed tapestries. Rui would shock the guests by waltzing with her without any musicians playing, guided by the sounds radiating from brightly-hued objects.

Mariana leapt from her bed, as if she needed to begin at once to undertake her plans. What to do first? Assign the importation of fish, fatten the animals with chestnuts, mend the tablecloths. The weight of the details caused her to swoon in her dark bedroom, from the sheer effort of imagining what might be required to live to the fullness of her wishes. She lay on the floor and moaned as everything spun around. A voice whispered, "That's what you get, for wanting to organize the things of this world!" Opening before her, as she panted from the fear that she could not make everything as perfectly appointed as she wanted, came a vision of age. Guests at her party grew old and disintegrated, leaving their clothing in frayed heaps. Rui was nowhere to be found. Flies attacked the buffet tables and maggots chewed whatever clung to bones until Mariana whimpered and did not see how she could possibly rise off her bedroom floor.

How did Mama know to come for her?

Mama arrived to sing to her, and did not think her strange. She bent over her daughter, and kept her melody low.

This music cured Mariana of her whirling illness, and allowed her to sleep.

The first rooster's crow startled her awake. She dressed as the dawn said to her, Find your father! Tell him your plan of being a wartime bride! There is no reason to wait upon love, when you know whom you love.

She walked down the hallway and proceeded through the kitchen and past the parlor and music rooms. She stopped at the entrance to the solarium in the east wing, where her father often read or met with friends in the early morning. He referred to this as his calling the day to order.

There he was, at the far end of the immense room. Papa. Several of his friends – she recognized the Marquês de Niza, Portugal's ambassador to France, and Dom Joaquim Ferreira de Fontes, who ran a *morgadio* of his own – were seated at the walnut table, and Papa was standing at the head of it and speaking to them so intently that he had not yet noticed her lingering near the bookcases at the solarium's entrance. The sun's giant hands were squeezing the domed ceiling of the solarium to create a sphere of light. Papa was soaked with the rays. Unfurled bolts of sunlight draped themselves over the ceiling-high bookshelves and the gold-backed spines of the books. Prominent on the wall was the Tablet of Privileges carved into chestnut wood by the order of King Dom João IV, the rebel king of Portugal, that named Francisco da Costa Alcoforado as "perpetually a noble Christian." The Alcoforado escutcheon, with its eagle over a checkered blue and silver pattern, was over the tablet. A salver of oranges sat out of everyone's reach as a centerpiece.

He was dressed in black like the Ministers of the Crown of France, with black lace across his doublet. Out of its cut-open sleeves, his white shirt billowed like cold visible air. He was handsome, in a severe way. He was almost fifty, with a bold nose and sharp profile. Even at this distance, she could smell – or could sense in her nostrils what would be there to smell, if she were closer – Papa's tobacco and moustache wax. His shining black hair fell to his shoulders. His one imperfection was a deep line across his forehead. Some day he would invite her to grasp both his temples near the crease and lift off the top of his head and look inside to read his thoughts. A lot of men wanted to do that, and they would be jealous of her. She looked forward to that moment. First, Marquês de Niza and these other grim-faced men needed to go away, and then Papa would call to her.

Luís, the servant, was offering the men pigs'-ear fritters from a silver tray, along with coffee from Brazil and tea from Ceylon. He had a devil's frightening blue eyes but also a good sense of humor. His serving coat was a long-sleeved tunic with elaborate frogging down the front, which he called his Chinese Roman look. He set a porcelain cup on its saucer, poured some coffee for her father, and held a lump of cane sugar with silver tongs at the coffee's surface, so that the sugar would drift evenly through the cup and not sit in a dissolving heap on the bottom. Papa hated that. Luís returned to stand near the lowboy and winked at Mariana. Papa would see her any second now.

Instead it was Dom Joaquim Ferreira de Fontes who noticed Mariana, and warbled, "*O, menina, menina, pequininha!*"

Oh, little girl, little girl, little little girl.

My God, thought Mariana. With a brain like that, I hope Papa is not expecting him to think up any war plans.

Francisco da Costa Alcoforado lifted his head and dark eyes in her direction. His gaze braided with hers. He owned every motion he made, each one effortlessly imperial. *Papa,* spoke her nerves, nothing else but *Papa.* She never asked if he preferred her to Ana Maria. She figured that he did. Look how the men were staring, wanting him to dismiss her!

"*Meu bem,*" he announced.

Worth the disruption! Worth the sleepless night! She understood how much was in those two words:

My dear. Or, My love. My best treasure, I'll be with you in a moment. Stay. Wait. Watch.

She picked a book off the shelf to show him that although her tutor, Senhora Néné, had fled to the kingdom of the Algarve in the south, she would continue studying her French. She worshipped books – the cream-colored pages, the crackling of thanks a book gave when she opened it wide. Papa had ignored those who said that teaching his daughters to read was worthless. She smiled as he returned to his meeting. Let this conference last for weeks, now that Papa was hers. The torture of waiting was one matter, but the pleasure of anticipating that she would soon be her father's sole audience was another.

The Marquês saw that he would have to pretend that she was invisible, and said, "We have to ask ourselves what's in it for the French if they send troops to help us, when they're still fighting Spain. I've heard that the French people won't agree to expanding their war."

"They'll agree to anything that kicks Spain," said another man. "They don't want a united Spanish peninsula right below them."

"We can't depend on the French or anyone else to fight for us and not want half of Brazil for their services," said the Marquês de Niza.

Mariana strained a bit to hear Dom Joaquim Ferreira de Fontes say, "Better half a kingdom than nothing. So what if we have to pay the French? The way we're going, we'll disappear by the end of the century. Or decade."

Mariana tried to imagine a whole nation – hers – disappearing.

"We need the French here. At once," said Francisco da Costa Alcoforado.

"Dom Francisco," said the Marquês, "the French are – I'm sorry, but they're extravagant, and they prefer to run everything. There's not enough money in the whole of Europe to persuade them that if we're the ones paying, we're the ones in charge."

"Our own people are going to be upset when they find out that their taxes are being used to bribe the court of Louis XIV," said one of the men.

"Look," said the Marquês, "we've always had trouble with Spain. We'll keep having it. We should relax and learn Spanish."

"Do you think that?" said Francisco da Costa Alcoforado.

The edge in his voice made Mariana look up from her book.

The Marquês hesitated. Everyone was watching him. "Yes," he said.

"Let me tell you something," said Francisco. "The Spanish are fortifying their garrisons along our border and catching their breaths. They're fighting us in a few places, to stay in practice. It's been a dull war, and they think we'll forget about it."

"Maybe that's what we should do, if it will mean peace," said the Marquês. "The French people themselves are tired of –"

"The French people will do what their king tells them to do!"

Mariana stared as her Papa's voice rose until he was shouting.

"Have you been drinking too much of their wine?" he thundered. "I'll tell you what you can count on. Treaties can go to hell. You can count on the French to know after they win their war with Spain – and they will win it – that if those Spanish sons of bitches push *us* into the ocean, they'll keep marching north again, treaty with France or not, until they have bulls running through the gardens of Versailles!"

"But the money – " said the Marquês.

"Do I have to do everything? Tell the French agents what we need, then give them what they want. Pay them, and hand them a bottle of port. Too bad Cardinal Richelieu is dead. Empty the best bottle onto his tomb. Just make sure we get some French troops in here before every coward afraid to die is speaking Castilian." He ordered Luís to fetch his seal, ink, and parchment paper. "As alderman I have the right to order the tax collector to divert funds to the war effort. If it lines the pockets of some sympathetic French politicians, I don't care. If Spain succeeds this time, no one will have to worry about losing anything, because everything will be gone. Do you understand?" he said.

"I hope we win," said Dom Joaquim Ferreira de Fontes.

"I never hope. I know," said Francisco. He preferred Chinese ink, in a solid stick, so that his writing smelled like the Orient. Mariana loved inhaling her father's writing. She pretended she could smell the ink from where she waited as Luís rubbed the Chinese stick on a piece of slate and dropped water from a spoon to form a black pool.

She enjoyed how much she was still trembling from her father's shouts, and to steady herself she selected another book from his library as her father wrote his orders to the tax collector. Her favorite book had a blue back. It was Cervantes. According to Vovó, Cervantes once said that the Portuguese die of love. It was a pity that he had not written about Pedro and Inês, and a shame he had died decades ago and would not write about Mariana and Rui. She should conceal the book. Papa must have forgotten to hide his Spanish authors. She tucked it behind a Shakespeare that was filled with watercolors of noblemen and clowns. The English language was difficult, but Papa said that the English people would be allies some day, despite their naval attacks. It was really the Spanish with whom the English quarreled.

Luís stepped in to blot the letter, fold it, and put it in an envelope. He lit a red stick of sealing wax, holding it so that the flame tilted away from Francisco. Red tears fell. The brass seal was handed over for Francisco to center his coat of arms in the hot red flower of wax.

If only Mariana could see the *L* for Leonor that Papa would tie into his signature. The French would obey her father. Her heart pounded as Papa placed the letter in a velvet pouch and handed it to the Marquês de Niza to deliver. He dismissed the men with a half-wave of his hand. As if they were flies. This was magnificent!

She flinched when the Marquês, carrying the letter wrapped in velvet, attempted to pinch her face as they left. She was not a baby.

"Can you keep all our secrets, eh, *menina?*" he said.

The other officials filed out solemnly, hardly glancing at her. Luís attended to clearing cups and plates off the table. At last she was alone with her father!

"Papa!" she said.

"My angel," he said. A sheen of sweat aged him, as if he had gone out to battle the gargantuan plains – the air itself. Her father was from the mountainous north, and she recognized how that stayed in his blood. Whenever he looked out over the plains of Beja, he had to fight the urge to command them to buckle, rise up. He told her once that it was a great moment when he realized that the plains, slow as eternity, seeming never to change, were teaching him how to perceive the subtlest of changes.

"Papa, I have to talk to you."

"More business?" He knelt, and as she hugged him, his black lace jabbed into her mouth. "Haven't I had enough business for one morning?"

"No," she said.

"All right. Would you like a new doll?"

"No," she said, standing away from his embrace to show him she was angry. A new doll would be very welcome, though, and she was regretting her haste in refusing it.

"Why are you awake so early?" he asked.

"To visit you."

He was amused. "Is that so?"

"Papa! You're so suspicious." She walked over to sit at the table, and her father took his place in the high-backed chair.

"I know my angel," he said.

"You don't!"

"I never listen to what people say to me, you know that, angel. I listen to their insides." His finger pointed to her chest. He had taught her the saying, *Boca de mel, coração de fel* – mouth of honey, heart of bile.

"May I have some coffee, Papa?"

Francisco Costa da Alcoforado held up his hand, and Luís poured a cup for Mariana.

"Thank you, Luís," she said.

Her father frowned. No one should be thanked for doing his job.

"Papa," said Mariana, sipping her coffee, "I want to get married."

Her father laughed. "You do, do you?"

"Yes."

"Do you have someone in mind?"

The instant had arrived to say Rui's name, but the idea of him had become so large, so much a feeling and not a word, that expelling even a syllable would be a defilement. She sat radiating him. Papa could read minds. He would know the person she went to bed with at night and woke up dreaming of every morning. "The name isn't important, Papa," she said.

"The name," he said, "is very important. Does your mother know about this?"

"Of course not," said Mariana.

"You will speak with respect about your mother."

"Yes, Papa."

"Does your grandmother know? This sounds like one of her ideas."

"No, Papa. Vovó doesn't know."

"You can wait a few years," said her father.

"I'll do that," said Mariana. "I can have a three-year engagement. We can have parties, until I'm ready. I mean, until you say I'm ready."

Her father's eyes looked like spots of fire that had dropped onto his papery face. "Do you know that the Spanish have been here a long time, to make us part of Spain?" he asked. "Do you understand that we had the largest empire in the world, we sailed places where no European had ever been, and now everyone is tearing away pieces of us?"

"Yes."

"Do you know why France and Spain are fighting?"

"Senhora Néné explained everything to me, and so have you. Both of them want to be the King of Europe, but what they truly want is to run all the trade in Asia and the New World."

"You're a clever girl, Mariana. Do you know what I think? You should either rule the world, or never bother with it. You're like me. Nothing in between will ever be good enough."

"Thank you, Papa." The coffee was painting her stomach with black flames. She was the happiest girl ever born.

"Do you understand how much danger we're in?"

"You know I know all that. I need to get married so my husband can guard me."

"I'll be the one to guard you, Mariana. Any husband who's old enough to guard you is old enough to fight to free his country."

"I'll wait for him."

"You might be an old woman by the time he gets home."

"I'll wait for him."

Rui was swelling like a vine inside her. The vine was blue, dark blue, indigo, the color of the ocean she had never seen, that he had given to her. Parts of it were red, flowering red, the shade of his hair and beard and the gashes where he had risked death. If she did not speak, utter something, the vine would burst past her lips and wrap around her father. "You know him, Papa!" she shouted. "If anything happens to your land, he'll get it back for you!"

Francisco stood, his fury contained. She understood why the workmen obeyed him, and the ambassadors called at the house for advice, and King Dom João IV kept him in charge of the storehouse's treasury in Beja. His will was the strongest in the land. "The day some boy has to do my fighting for me is the day I perish. What I have will stay intact, Mariana. Remember that. It will *always* stay intact."

"Papa," she said, in a tone that said she was sorry.

Luís gave a grimace of sympathy from where he stood by the silver, but he could not interfere.

Papa walked over to his library to locate a book. As Mariana got up to leave, he said, his back to her, "I'll have to decide what to do, if this nonsense is going to start. Ana Maria is older than you, and I'll have to consider her also." He stayed engrossed in what he was reading, but added, "See if your mother needs help, Mariana. She hasn't been well."

She did not, as she fled the solarium, search for Mama. What a futile, pointless day. Tasks, food. She was going to die from glaring with hatred at Ana Maria. Vovó's invitation to sneak out to the road did not interest her. She hid in her room, studying the *Mudéjar* tiles on the wall. She liked to sense what her feelings were in a room at a given moment, and also tried her best to let the feelings of other people enter like pins through her flesh. The strain of comprehending these left her shaking. The entirety of the feelings over time, from her and from others, could be compiled into the history of a room. Today her feeling was one of being in an ocean of dust. Examining the tiles might pass some moments in this miserable day.

Mariana awoke in the stillness of night, in her bed. Mama must have tucked her in. Look at Ana Maria, her arms at her sides, practicing being a corpse. Who is going to wed her? No one. She eats fruit without peeling it. She is fat. Fat! Her godfather was a nobody. Alas for poor Catarina, having to wait forever for her two older sisters to be married.

After leaping up and grabbing a pair of shears, Mariana cut off Ana Maria's shoulder-length black hair. Ana Maria did not feel a thing. See? She was dead. Since she was too round to get a husband, some missing hair was not going to matter.

Mariana looked at her hand. Standing on the cold floor, holding Ana Maria's hair in the dark, she was swept over by queasiness. What had possessed her? Her sister's hair looked like a little unwoven rug in her fist, and she threw it under Ana Maria's bed.

Before she could count any passage of time, she awoke from a darkly water-dreamed sleep to see Ana Maria and Mama standing over her, with Catarina fussing behind them.

Leonor, her daughters in an uproar around her, thought her insides were going to push to the outside of her body. She hurt everywhere. How laughable, whenever people announced, "I rested today." During a war? During peace? (Had such an era existed?) Was there ever any minute, in war or peace, when the pain of love ceased, when one's sentiments stopped functioning? When a family needed no protection?

"Cut off hers!" Ana Maria shouted.

"I didn't do anything," said Mariana, clutching her blue bedspread.

"Please do not lie, Mariana," said Mama.

"Yes, Mama. Sorry, Mama."

"Say you're sorry to me," said Ana Maria.

"I'm not sorry about you. I'll never be sorry."

"Mariana!" said Mama.

"Mama!" Ana Maria was weeping, and Catarina started to wail.

"I didn't do anything terrible," said Mariana. "It'll grow again."

"Cut off hers, Mama. Or I will," said Ana Maria, sobbing and pulling at the uneven tufts at her crown.

"I dare you to try," said Mariana.

"Tell me what I should do with you, Mariana," said Mama.

"You should reward me. She looks much better," said Mariana, but her voice faltered. Why had she done such a stupid thing? From the sound of what Papa had said, she would have to wait for Ana Maria to marry first, and making her uglier would not hurry anything. For the first time, Mariana somewhat pitied her older sister.

Ana Maria flew at her, slapping her face, before Mama managed to pull her away. Catarina, crying, collapsed onto the floor. Mama said that she was sorry, but Mariana would have to be punished. She was to be restricted to her bedroom the entire day.

Groaning, Mama bent down to pick up Catarina, and led Ana Maria towards the hallway.

I was feeling sorry for you, you bald pig, until you slapped me, thought Mariana.

She pictured the news of her captivity spreading through Beja. Soldiers of the resistance would cast lots to see who would rescue her, but it would be Rui who would tie a ladder out of cork-tree bark and climb to her. Flinging her arms around him, she would bury her face in his beard.

A minute passed. Two. Nothing. How would she last a day? She appreciated why people said they were dying for something when they meant they were waiting. To want something enough was to die for it. Should she escape? A Lôbo would not remain a captive! She went to the window. Baltazar, collecting walnuts in the yard, looked up and waved.

"Baltazar!" she called out. "Find someone to get me out of here!"

He waved again, not understanding that she was trapped.

"Listen! You're not listening!" she said. Where was Vovó, when Mariana needed her?

Instead of being a Lôbo, it would be more picturesque to be Saint Barbara, who had commanded a sumptuous view after her father locked her inside a palace tower to hide her beauty. Poets, philosophers, and wise men came to stand in the manicured gardens and report to her the secrets of the universe. When the prefect had Saint Barbara tortured to the point of death for her faith, her father stepped in to behead his daughter, a blow of mercy. It confused Mariana why Saint Barbara's father had not prevented the torture in the first place. Maybe the government was too strong. Mariana had been in trouble once with her tutor, Senhora Néné, for asking why, if the saints were the anointed of God, He put them through such anguish. Néné said that everyone asked that, and no one could say why God's methods were puzzling. This vague reply did not prevent Mariana from venerating the saints, particularly the ones who levitated, like Saint John of the Cross and Saint Teresa of Avila, though they were Spaniards. Mariana wished to be chosen like Saint Teresa, who suffered agonies for thirty years before heaven rewarded her with a life in ecstasy. Imagine being swallowed inside magic and love, and melting into a star. Mariana told God that He could please send her a vision now, and she would be grateful. She was tired of being in her room.

She wished so hard her skull throbbed. No vision arrived.

Inside Ana Maria's escritoire were a quill pen and paper. Mariana wallowed in the urge to chop off the bothersome feathers as she wrote:

Baltazar, dearest,

Do not forsake me here. You must persuade Mama, Papa, or Vovó to free me. The next time we have roasted pig, I will give you the skin.

Love, forever, your imprisoned sister, M.

She pitched her message into the garden, but her words sailed away on the wind, and Baltazar, playing busily, saw nothing.

Suddenly everything in the world and every feeling in the room were altered, because Mariana looked over at Ana Maria's needlework on the floor, knocked there during their scuffle. It lay in a heap, murdered. Tendrils of yarn hung from the underside. The scene was of a mountainside and wild flowers, and Ana Maria was stitching the dull brown mountains to save the desirable parts for last, the opposite of what Mariana would have done. Ana Maria's timidness, her holding back from the green, sky-blue, and rose-colored strings, was shabby and sad. Mariana ached as if she had cut open her sister and spilled out her drab, duty-bound sorrows, mountainous sorrows that said, With so much yearning inside you, Mariana, can you not direct any towards us? Towards your sister?

One morning, Ana Maria looked at her legs and said, "I stand with them together, and I can feel air blowing between them in places!"

She was moving the fat out of her legs and up into her breasts. It was rising from her face into her butchered hair, making it longer and richer. A new gloss gave life to her fingernails. Fat was melting from her arms, making her touch smooth and oiled. Her voice no longer creaked. Each morning, Mariana looked over at her awakening sister to see what was new. They spoke together, and Ana Maria laughed at Mariana's jokes. Mariana tied a green ribbon around Ana Maria's hair, when enough of it grew back. Ana Maria, surprised, patted the ribbon and thanked her.

"I know what we should do," said Mariana.

Ana Maria leaned her forehead against her sister's. They were doubly on fire. "Yes?"

"It's time to bury Saint Anthony," said Mariana, and Ana Maria nodded.

They would dig him up once he did his job as the patron of lovers. After stealing the statue from Vovó's room, they went to the garden, to the bed of the lilies-of-the-Nile. Saint Anthony, in Mariana's hand, looked impassively at both girls. Caked, dried paint was chipping off him. Over the years of her marriage, Vovó had painted yellow robes, scarlet capes, and flowered tunics onto Saint Anthony as a gift, to persuade him to intercede for her when she felt unloved. When he did not respond, she would hang him by his neck with a rope in her closet. If he answered her, she would set him on her dresser and use her ancient paintbrush to smear fresh clothing onto him in gratitude, directly over the old painted out-fits, not noticing how thick and grey the layers were becoming. Mama said that she used to gauge how her parents were getting along according to the condition of the statue of Saint Anthony.

Ana Maria hesitated. "Won't he be angry if we bury him?" she said.

"No," said Mariana. "Vovó says that as long as he's rewarded after he helps out, he won't mind. We have to be extreme to get heaven's attention. She and Saint Anthony are the best of friends."

"Then do you think it's right to steal him from her?"

Mariana rolled her eyes upward, nostalgic for the days when Ana Maria was her enemy. "He's not going to be in the ground for long. When he finds love for us, we'll unbury him and give him new clothes and repaint his face. We're borrowing him. Vovó isn't going to mind."

"Shouldn't we wrap him up first?"

"No," said Mariana. This was getting annoying. "He goes in head first. The blood will rush there, and he'll think faster. Go ahead and dig the hole."

"You do it."

"No, you. You're older, and he has to take care of you first," said Mariana. She folded her arms and watched as Ana Maria dug the hole, put Saint Anthony in head first, covered him, and patted down the dirt. "Sorry," Ana Maria whispered to him.

"Don't apologize. We're just asking him to do his job and be quick about it," said Mariana, though questions plagued her as she sat back on her heels alongside her sister. What was Saint Anthony supposed to do, if two women prayed for the same man?

"Have you ever heard Vovó's riddle about the things we kiss but never adore?" said Mariana. The answer might be the saints.

"No," said Ana Maria. "She doesn't confide in me, Mariana. No one does. Maybe you."

"Of course I do," said Mariana, resting her head on her sister's shoulder, because Ana Maria's loneliness was terrible to look upon. They debated how Saint Anthony was going to bring them love. Vovó said that love was not a "him" as much as an "it." Once someone found love, it would never leave, because it would not know how. When Ana Maria said that she could think of no one to love, Mariana hesitated. Should she tell Ana Maria that it was simply a matter of opening her heart and seeing who was concealed there? Should she tell her about Rui? The chance to reveal his name again came, and moved on, and left her silent.

"Don't worry. It's Saint Anthony's job to arrange the details," Mariana said, pointing to the fresh grave.

Should a waiting person pray for swiftness, changes in a flash? Or should that person say that God is slow, and leaves us to recognize the endless variations in a single moment?

Ana Maria and Mariana, in the thrall of Saint Anthony, peered through the keyhole of the dining room door at their parents' dinner. Mama was in a white silk dress, with flowers on it like bouquets on a white bed, and her skin was liquid as olive oil under the flickering lights from the candelabrum. Her black hair was tied up, but curls were springing loose. Ana Maria and Mariana pushed against one another for a better view. "Leonor," Papa said, and stroked her throat. "Oh!" said Ana Maria. She covered her face with her hands and let Mariana have the keyhole, and Mariana could not stop watching. Papa lowered his hand onto Mama's belly, and she placed her hand on his. Mama's babies had made her stomach pushed-out and hard. She and Papa were holding fast to a globe they had created under flower-scattered white.

"Mariana!" said Ana Maria, pulling at her and saying that they should go outside and stare upward and hope that heaven dropped something into their eyes. *To erase a sight not meant for us,* she considered adding, but did not, for fear of Mariana scoffing.

"Yes!" said Mariana. *To burn a picture of love onto our brains!* she wanted to bellow.

Outside was black, punctured with stars. Perhaps swiftness and slowness together formed the best of all worlds, and a star was its sign: starlight sometimes exploded and raced across the sky, or it hung above, never moving.

"It's Rui," said Mariana, surprised at herself. "I love Rui de Melo Lôbo."

"He's –" Ana Maria wished Mariana could be sensible, for once. "He's a bit rough, don't you think, Mariana?"

"I'll never, not ever, never think that," said Mariana. She would write the history of her great love starting from this night, when his name rang out as high as the stars. Her story would begin, "One night, my sister and I witnessed the mystery of our parents. Mama's stomach sticks out like a globe from her having four children. Papa loves it." If Papa were to write a story of his family, he might start out by saying, "Once upon a time, as the planet was destroying itself, the Alcoforados had a globe that was theirs alone."

Maria Alves hunted everywhere for her leaf-pin of pearls. Had Mariana borrowed it again? She did not want to ask, dreading that this was another of those episodes, more frequent of late, in which she misplaced something and blamed someone else. Last week, she had accused Leonor of taking her gold queen's-style earrings, until Leonor pointed out that Maria Alves was wearing them. Maria reflected that she had never been an ideal mother, she was too quarrelsome, and that could prove her undoing if she expected her soul to be at rest after she died. Nor was she at peace about her deceased husband, Francisco. A strange fate, to have a Francisco for a husband and one for a son-in-law, both of them with iron wills that she admired but hated. Everyone she knew was so unwilling to end feuds. She included herself in this judgment. She had never broken the wish to avenge herself upon her husband because of his affairs.

She tore through her closet searching for her Saint Anthony. If she wanted to avoid an afterlife in draughty shrines, she would need to forgive her husband, and the assistance of the guardian of love was urgent. Where was he?

She would have to wear herself out trying to conjure some forgiveness on her own. She shrouded herself in sympathetic memories: When that kidney stone was torturing him, her reaction had been uncompromised. She had invoked Saint Benedict, the patron invoked against bodily stones, asking him to attach the pain onto her. When her husband passed the stone, she was appalled at how tiny it was, a hard fleck, and her love for him staggered her, because he was no different from anyone else for whom an imbedded speck of a thing can bring the worst of agonies.

Maria might forgive her husband if she strained her feelings to the breaking point. He had been fond enough of his daughter, Leonor, to put her in charge of the books for their Eastern-imports company before he died. That was something – a girl, in charge of books!

Oh! Ai, ai, ai, her heart was a cannonball. Saint Anthony, she mumbled, Did I bury you and forget? You're at work on me, old friend, I can feel it, I must have put you upside down somewhere and asked you to turn me upside down, and oh, it hurts. I'm exhausted. I love you, Saint Anthony, better than I ever loved my husband because as you know women love the abstraction of men but cannot love them for who they are. I gave money so that four Masses would be prayed every year for as long as the world shall last – one for my father's soul, one for my mother's, one for the souls in Purgatory, and one for mine – none for my husband! What shall these Masses merit me, if I cannot forgive him?

I found him with that woman and I burned her clothing. The smoke rose into the sky and tormented me by hanging in the shape of her lace, stretched out for everyone to see.

I said once, "What are you thinking of?" He said, "Nothing." But I was watching another woman dancing on the tops of his eyes, so alive were the pictures of her in his daydreams.

Maria Alves, who feared that she was suffocating, called for Saint Anthony to stop this, please, she would prefer to be a soul-not-at-rest. Finding reasons to absolve her husband would not suffice. Love was a sensation, not a reason or revision, and if her long-hardened emotions were to change, it was going to rob her of the last of her strength. She would not be able to move or eat or lift her arms over her head. She would have to give up pushing herself to the front of crowds. Most of all, she would miss stealing away with her granddaughter, Mariana. Maria Alves stretched out on her bed, already spent. She scolded her heart, telling it to soften, but it was stubborn. Her limbs grew heavy from the hardness they were drawing out of her heart. Alas, life, goodbye! she said. I am too old and fat to manage both living and forgiveness at once.

She lacked the strength to do more than lie there and watch as the warring feelings within her, of love and hate, of forgiveness and pride, took possession of her body and prepared to battle each other to the death. When her daughter Leonor and her grand-daughter Mariana came into her room, she did not have the stamina to speak, though she wanted to tell them not to fret, that it was quite amusing to watch feelings using her as a field of war. How sad Leonor looked! She kept saying, "Mother, speak to us. We're going to have a party in two days. Mother?"

Maria Alves mouthed, "Aren't I being a good mother now? No trouble to you," but exhaustion prevented her from releasing the words.

Mariana was shaking her grandmother's arm and saying, "Vovó? Why are you staring like that? Are you ill? Papa says there's going to be an enormous party, and a wedding is going to be announced. A wedding!"

Maria Alves closed her eyes. A wedding? How wearying to hear of the start of love. She sensed Leonor putting her under the covers. The strain of attempting to forgive her husband plunged Maria Alves into a coma. She heard the voice of her One More Than Everything pleading, "Vovó?" Maria reached towards Leonor's hand, and Mariana's, and that mere mortal effort caused the collapse of all her physical reserves. Though she was not dead, her active engagement with the world was over, and her mind was forced to bid farewell to it, without wasted sentiment.

The road was empty as Mariana and Ana Maria headed for the center of Beja. It had taken Mariana hours to persuade Ana Maria to escape with her. No one could wake Vovó from her strange sleep. Mariana had remained at her grandmother's bedside throughout the previous night, talking to her, calling her to the surface. Vovó must attend the party! Mama had confided that Mariana must have prompted her father to recognize that his girls were getting older. He had mentioned that it was time to think of marriages, vows, and futures, before the war roused itself to its finish. It was impossible to sit still! Saint Anthony was working so swiftly it was stunning. The Lôbo brothers were to come to the party, and Mariana was certain that Papa, who could read minds, would offer Rui her hand, after taking care of Ana Maria by giving her hand to Bartolomeu or Cristóvão, one of the older Lôbo brothers.

She and Ana Maria halted. Not far from the castle, some Portuguese soldiers were sharing a bottle of *bagaceira,* its medicinal scent merging with the smoke from scattered camp fires. The girls glanced with pleasurable horror at the holes in the castle hold, through which boiling oil was poured onto invaders in ancient times. A toothless dog was choking on a bird. Soldiers, with women lounging next to them, laughed at it. Mariana led Ana Maria east on the Street of the White Crest, past the Church of Santa Maria, where they had been baptized, and into the square in front of the Royal Convent of Conceição, where Rui's sister, Leonor Henriques, lived. Sloping downward from that was the marketplace, built like an Italian loggia, with amber bottles, *carapau* fish, olives, and jade-colored chard for sale. Loquat flowers were displayed on the upper gallery. Mariana suffered pangs for Vovó, who thrived on the bounty of the market.

Steers and cows rested nearby, in the middle of the square. Men and women were sticking paper flowers and streamers onto the livestock with dots of tar. Women with baskets wandered among the groups of soldiers, selling raw pork and curved roof tiles to cook the pork over the camp fires. Everything was dun-colored or red, not green. The sky was blue, to remind Mariana of Rui, but an air of uneasiness hung about.

Spaniards were encamped at the farthest point of their eyesight, out towards the plains. If Mariana could see them, then so could the Portuguese soldiers. The Spanish were also in Mértola, a full afternoon's carriage ride to the south. But motion had died. From the convent's balcony, some nuns watched. Soldiers stood guard around the convent, since it was the richest in the country and under royal protection.

Mariana had to keep moving until the time for the party. She was going to rise into the air!

They heard guitar music, and applause, and joined a crowd watching a gypsy woman dancing, though it was difficult to push to the front without Vovó wedging forward with her breasts. The dancer's shoes struck the flagstones in time with the notes, and she was in such a trance that the spectators and guitarist rode the melody along with her, gliding into the rhythm. Mariana was enthralled at the vigor pouring out of the dancer, so pure an effort of the body that the body all but disappeared.

Ana Maria said, "Let's go home, Mariana."

"*Duende!*" someone shouted.

A general roar swallowed the square. No one minded exclaiming a Spanish idea.

"*Duende!*" a woman shouted, clapping her hands over her head.

"*Duende! Duende! Duende!*" a man affirmed as the dancer kept on, leading the music now. The Spanish brought this notion of *duende* across their border, and Mariana reflected, disloyally, glad that her father was not there to read her thoughts, that it was a shame that the Portuguese could not choose whatever Spanishness they wanted to keep, and expand their own definition of *duende,* which also meant a hobgoblin or spirit, to include this Spanish sense that people could be so utterly in love with a motion or idea, or music, or love itself, that they could actually become it. They could change into white heat. That was the perilous part, erasing mind and body so that the goblins might enter and take over forever.

The dancer could not stop.

Nuns on the balcony of the convent were extending their arms, to grasp the dangerous, exhilarating sounds of *duende.* The sun cut patterns of light onto their black veils, changing them into mantillas.

"Mariana, please," said Ana Maria. "We're supposed to be helping Bastiana prepare for the party."

A few Spanish soldiers, drawn to the music, wandered in from the encampment. Some milled around the livestock, slicing the paper streamers off the cows' hides with their swords. The men and women who had been decorating the animals were backing away. A soldier grabbed a bucket of tar and threw a burning stream at them, and screams and the laughter of the Spaniards pierced the flamenco music, which abruptly stopped. The dancer's body forced her spirit to end its whirling. The guards leaning against the outer walls of the convent stood up straight.

A Spanish soldier, surrounded by his friends, strolled to the front of the crowd, brandished his sword, and ordered the guitarist to continue.

"Dance for me," he said to the gypsy woman.

The spectators edged away as the guitarist began plucking strings, and the dancer went through the motions as a few more Spanish soldiers gathered, pulsing their lower bodies towards the dancer in a way that made Mariana stare. The Portuguese soldiers from the castle, drunk on *bagaceira,* staggered towards the commotion as people tried to flee. The convent's guards approached, swords ready. Mariana was having no success staring into the eyes of the Spanish soldiers to defeat them. She took Ana Maria's hand and they were running when they heard a Portuguese soldier, waving his bottle in the air, yell, "Don't any of you know how to get rid of Spaniards? Trample them with cows on fire!"

"Yes! Set the tails of the animals on fire!" shouted the soldier's companions as the cows, their paper flowers in tatters, stomped around, already maddened. The guitarist and dancer used the distraction to vanish, and the Spanish drew their swords and banded together to retreat to their camp. A nun marching along the balcony pushed the other nuns inside the convent.

Portuguese soldiers seized buckets of tar and grabbed at the cows and steers, who lowed and moaned as their tails were clotted with tar, and failed to shake it off as they tore circles in the dust with their hoofs.

"Time to get to work!" said a soldier, slapping the flanks of an animal. "Hurry! Hurry!"

"Nice cow!" sang a soldier, kissing its nose. "Will you marry me?"

"Fire! Who's got some fire?" someone called out.

A soldier lowered his sword into one of the camp fires, and touched it to a tail. It burst into flame. The cow's tongue rolled out, bleating. Other swords were lowered into fire, and an army of fiery cows was set loose. But instead of knowing that they were supposed to trample Spaniards, the cows and steers raged in every direction and kicked through the camp fires before falling onto their sides to writhe and bellow. People were screaming and stumbling under a shower of sparks. Mariana's ribs dissolved and flowed into her stomach, where they sprouted into ribs again. Ana Maria clung to her. Someone yelled that the Spanish soldiers were retreating towards the plains, and it was the people of Beja who were going to die.

A man tossed a bucket of water over a cow, but rivulets ran uselessly over its back. Blood poured from another man's leg and he clutched it, his face tightening. A steer rammed another man against a tree, then pitched forward harder, slamming into him so that the tree shook. Mariana stopped and would not allow Ana

Maria to keep pulling her towards the road home. They had to rescue that man. Someone outraced them to him and grabbed the base of the steer's flaming tail. The battered man's face was purple and smashed, and he dodged another cow as he ran from sight.

A woman's hand was scarlet from holding it over a man's torn ear, and he was too dazed to respond to her plea that he stand up.

A cow was bearing towards Mariana and Ana Maria, its eyes like blood puddings, dark and wet. To Mariana's shock, before she could react, Ana Maria pitched herself onto her sister. They fell to the ground, and although Ana Maria had lost weight Mariana could not push her off. Ana Maria lay upward on Mariana's back, using Vovó's lesson about smaller animals offering their vulnerable parts to a stronger wild creature, and stared into the eyes of the beast that wanted to trample them.

Ana Maria thrust her belly out farther towards the cow, which had stopped, its pupils bulging towards her. She connected her own pupils with the cow's. Courage was a small thing, really, a minute gesture. A trip of the feet, a lying on a sister's back. Mariana was crying, "Ana Maria!" and struggling to get out from under her, but Ana Maria only smiled. A picture of herself, her arms spread outward, was imprinted upside down on the animal's eyes, and its thick meat eyelids went up and down over her reversed reflection. The cow reared back, and cantered off. Never, not once, had she heard Mariana crying her name, never before had Ana Maria saved her sister, and as she stood and received Mariana flying into her arms, Ana Maria no longer dreamed of being someone else.

Mariana thought, You covered me with your body, Ana Maria. I am yours for life.

Francisco da Costa Alcoforado galloped through the embers and howls, straight for his daughters. A man who could not control his family controlled nothing. He would carry his daughters to safety and speak his mind to them. They would agree that his mind was theirs.

Mariana saw him coming for them. "Look at the fire in Papa," she whispered to Ana Maria. "He's thinking that his daughters are so brave they deserve to marry soldiers."

Bastiana poured boiled sugar over curved sheets of dough to harden them into the dessert called *rasquilha branca*. After a few hours, she poured another coat, and waited, and then poured another, and waited, until the dough turned into brittle white shells that could hold red wine. A vat of pigs' blood was in the cauldron over the fire, for black sausages. A plucked chicken and rabbit sat in ceramic pots, getting jugged with brandy, white wine, and laurel leaves. On various trays, Ana Maria arranged honey cakes and the sweet known as Eat-and-Cry-for-More, bought from the convent of Conceição, and tarts of ewe's milk cheese. Luís slaughtered a turkey that he had tenderized by feeding it *aguardente* over several days, so that execution would come in a daze. ("My drinking pal," he had said slyly to Mariana.) Mariana's task was to slice and arrange tomatoes like butterfly wings, but in her impatience they came out like wet red stones.

Hours before the party, she changed into her white lace dress. Everything inside her was rioting. She did not comprehend why Ana Maria was still helping in the kitchen and not worrying about getting dressed. Mariana looked in on Vovó, who refused to wake up. Mama said that this could be one of Vovó's tricks, making everyone guess what was wrong. "Worry about yourself tonight, Mariana. We'll whisper into Vovó's ear what happens, when it's over." She had not looked content when she said that, probably because of her concern about Vovó, and because it would be like Mama to be already missing her daughters.

Father José, from Our Lady of the Snows, came early, while Mariana, anxious to the point of sickness, sat in her room. He went to her and said, "Mariana. You're more beautiful than usual, I see."

"And I see that you're barefoot!" she said.

They had a ceremony they both rejoiced in. José loved to touch his naked soles to the blue of her bedspread. She would take off her own shoes and join him. Together they did a dance of pretending to walk on water.

"Your father is going to persuade the French to help us," he said. "Now he just has to convince the other local nobles to stop saying they're Spanish. I assume that's what this party is for." Mariana regarded José fondly. She knew about the French. Yes, this party was for politics, but it was for her, too; to announce love. And it was for Ana Maria. José had sad eyes, uncombed hair, and a childlike manner of tilting his head, as if that improved his hearing.

He was so polite that he never referred to Papa as his own father nor to Mariana as his half-sister.

Baltazar ran in and hurled himself onto the bedspread, and Mariana tickled him with her feet before holding him up to the window to see the Chinese lanterns strung between the walnut trees. Bastiana and Luís had set up a buffet table outside, and guests were arriving and gathering around it. A woman with a gorgeously cinched waist appeared. Mariana was eager to hear the voice that might rise out of such a waist. A man could link his two hands around it and hold the center of a woman.

"Mariana," said Baltazar, and opened his fist. He pushed some stolen almonds into her mouth. They were sweaty from his hands, and she was glad that from then on, almonds would taste to her like Baltazar.

"None for me?" asked Father José, in mock-sadness.

When Baltazar looked stricken, José took him from Mariana to hold him at the window. "Do you see that food down there, on the table?" José waited until Baltazar nodded. "You and I are going to eat until we fall down. People are going to ask, 'Are those two kings or two hogs?'"

Baltazar snorted with amusement.

Dom Joaquim Ferreira de Fontes and his wife entered the yard, and so did some nobles from Vila Viçosa. The chatter climbed wild and high; they had to be discussing the cow riot. Usually the Marquês de Niza attended Papa's celebrations, but he was en route to France. A buzzing settled over the party as the guests awaited the arrival of the Lôbos.

Bartolomeu Lôbo, their father, now dead, remained infamous. When a monk had kept him waiting one day and refused to apologize, Bartolomeu thrashed him until he was dead. When escorted to the tower, Bartolomeu, his broad-brimmed hat majestic on his head, stared down haughtily at the townspeople who came to gawk at their leading nobleman held against his will. No one was surprised that he never stood trial.

His sons were also held in awe. Gil Vaz Lôbo, the youngest, died as a soldier of fortune in India, and another, called Bartolomeu after the father, was an infantryman on the frontier and had spent time in the Limeiro prison in Lisbon. But the most notorious was Cristóvão Pantoja Lôbo, who had recently been released from the stocks. He was always getting locked up for quarreling and threatening everyone, including the local magistrate, and then he would be released because he was the fiercest soldier in the army. He once heard someone comment that "only a field general could tame Cristóvão Pantoja," and promptly slashed his way through half an enemy regiment before stabbing a Spanish Field General. No one had ever see one soldier kill so many men so fast merely to prove that what was said as a tribute was actually an insult. Cristóvão considered himself invincible. The Field General who could tame him would never be born.

The Lôbos also had a sister, Leonor Henriques, a nun in the Franciscan order of the Poor Clares in the Royal Convent of Conceição. There was also Rui, a fierce soldier who had committed no crimes.

Mariana was dying to see him. She drew in her breath. She had glanced away for a second, and the world had altered. There, standing and waiting for people to come to them, assessing what was going on, were the Lôbo brothers – Bartolomeu, Cristóvão, and her Rui. Her stomach lurched to see his shining boots and fine dress, scarlet and green, the colors of an independent Portugal. "Look! Look!" she said to Baltazar and José. She wanted to shriek until her lungs flattened.

"That knave is certainly dressed up," said Father José. He frowned as he studied Mariana's eyes. "I wouldn't trust him to be up to any good. Are you listening, Mariana?"

"Listening?" She faced her half-brother. "No, I'm sorry, I have a party to attend. Come with me!" Without waiting for a response, she hurtled towards the outside, to go to Rui.

Leonor watched everyone drinking. The Lôbos were swaggering, as usual. Their finery did not fool her. She had argued with Francisco that four people died in that cow riot, their own daughters might have died, and they should be in a chapel somewhere, praying for an end to madness. Instead, they were perpetrating more of it. Francisco was determined to unite their house with the Lôbos, who had the most impressive *morgadio* in Beja and no notion of what to do with it. But why did one of her daughters have to be sacrificed for it? At least she had successfully argued that those two criminals, Bartolomeu and Cristóvão, would marry into the Alcoforado house over her dead body.

Very well, my dear, Francisco had said. I shall not violate your wishes in that particular.

But nothing was as she wished. What was Mariana doing, running, knocking into people, to get to the Lôbos? Good God. She was putting her hands into Rui's fat paws, as if to welcome him to the family, as if sensing what her father had willed.

Ana Maria, in purple velvet, was thunderstruck when Papa told her to be ready to have her hand given in marriage. She went to stand on the churned patch over Saint Anthony, muttering, "I take my wish for love back. It was Mariana's idea, not mine. Tell heaven I made a mistake, will you? Please." She got herself a plate of turkey and peas with fried eggs but was unable to eat it, and broke the food into pieces to feed Miguel, who was crawling on the lawn. She sat down, hoping it would smudge her dress so that no one would have her, and set Miguel on her lap, as a shield. She was going to be thirteen soon. Too young for this kind of shock. There was no man at this party she cared for, even remotely. She noticed Mariana looking happy with Rui, and was glad that Saint Anthony was unerring for one of them.

Black light, starlight. Cut into darkly yellowed shapes in the openings of the lanterns. Mariana almost burst with, Oh, to own the night! To own Night itself streaked full with every coming day.

She was gazing into Rui's face. His presence, strong as it was, was subsumed by an overpowering maleness and rigid military arrogance in front of her, smelling of *bagaceira* and ringing with battle stories. A sense of blueness, of blue gifts, set her trembling, and their words hung in the blue-black air of night.

What does Papa have planned? she teased.

He has strange ideas about calming me down, eh, sweet thing.

Calm? I despise calmness, don't you, Rui?

You know me that well, Mariana.

Have you eaten? Are you warm? Are we safe tonight?

From the Spanish, yes, for tonight, at least. The night of my fate. We're safe unless Cristóvão has too much to drink again.

Then you'll protect me.

To the death I'll protect my new family.

When did she float away from him and their soaring voices?

Papa, calling for quiet, stood in front of the buffet table with Rui. Their heads were bright as full moons. Papa said to everyone assembled, "It is my pleasure to bless the three-year engagement of my future son-in-law, Rui de Melo Lôbo, to my eldest daughter, Ana Maria. May the house of Alcoforado and the house of Lôbo live long and prosper as one." He held out his arm towards Ana Maria, who sat stunned, clutching Miguel in her lap.

She called out, heartstricken, "Mariana? Mariana?"

Mariana waited for Papa to realize his error. He was supposed to give Rui to her, after announcing the betrothal of Ana Maria to someone else. Apparently Ana Maria thought the same. She was staring at Mariana and at Mama, who had to look away. Mariana watched Ana Maria, panicked, leave Miguel and walk on wooden legs to the front of the assembly as they toasted her and applauded. She could not glance at Rui. Any moment now, this nightmare would correct itself. But it did not. Ana Maria stared at her feet, Rui drifted away to his brothers, and Papa and Mama received congratulations. When Ana Maria looked up, it was towards Mariana, who could not move.

Mariana whispered into her grandmother's ear, "Tell me what to do, Vovó. My love was taken from me tonight, but my love is greater than ever."

Vovó slept.

"Will you talk to Saint Anthony and explain the mistake?" Mariana asked. Vovó's hair was a white blossom on her pillow.

When Ana Maria, her face smeared with tears, came into their grandmother's room, she said, "What should we do, Mariana?"

"What Papa wants, I suppose."

Ana Maria said, "Please hate me, Mariana, don't be so calm. Hate Papa. Something. I'll tell Rui it's you who loves him, not me."

"I don't hate you at all," said Mariana, "and clearly Rui is not meant for me." She sat with her spine like a spire. A magnificent contentment swathed her. Pride would always get the better of her sorrow. She could be as masterful as Papa in that.

And yet after tucking Ana Maria in and telling her that she wished her happiness, Mariana hurried into the cold yard, and alone with the darkened lanterns and debris from the party, she was convulsed with illness. She imagined herself retching out everything she had ever eaten, until she saw Baltazar padding across the lawn to her.

He put his hand on her forehead and said, "I could feel you were sad and I couldn't stay in bed, Mariana."

In Mama's arms, Mama's arms studded with extra sewn-on buttons, Mariana listened to her mother cooing that it was the age of miracles. God was behind everything that occurred, and everything, by that definition, was good, even if it did not seem so at first glance. It was a matter of reading God's surprises as roads to better fortunes. If God destroyed the crops, it was a *milagro,* a miracle. God was saying, "Do not plant barley, but wheat." If God permitted the crops to thrive, He was saying, "I give you the miracle of abundance." *Milagrismo,* the notion that everything had a direct divine intent, was an appropriate impulse to thrive during war. No need to call these days fatal. God shall unfurl His strange pathways.

But Mariana could not see how this turn of events was miraculous. She waited months for Papa to realize his mistake, for Rui to free her from her room. Not long after her eleventh birthday, she decided that love was meant to surprise her, and that if she gave herself over to a belief in *milagrismo,* then a love grander than Rui, as unfathomable as that was, existed in the unknown for her. She must go and claim it. She spent two hours hammering at the lock on the gate with a rock before the catch broke, and she set out, so that her future would not have to waste time trying to locate her. She got as far as the shrines for the souls-not-at-rest before Luís found her and said he was sorry, but she must come home. The next morning, she broke the lock that he had repaired and marched out again, swinging her arms and keeping her eyes up, as Vovó had taught her. This time she traveled a very short while before Luís rode up to take her home.

Mama said at their next breakfast, "Mariana? Are you going to behave today?"

"Yes," said Mariana, and went into the yard, broke out, and headed onto the road.

On the tenth day of Luís being sent to fetch her, she walked harder and faster as he called to her from his horse. "Mariana," he said, galloping forward and then slowing his horse to trot alongside her. "Aren't you going to say hello?"

"Hello," she said, increasing her stride.

"Are you going to stop this nonsense?" he said. He dismounted and held his horse by its reins as he walked with Mariana.

She did not answer.

"Mariana," said Luís, grabbing her shoulder. "You're going to get hurt."

"I don't care," she said, pressing onward.

"There are more soldiers in town these days."

"I don't plan to stop in town. I plan to walk to Évora." The capital city of the province was more vast than Beja, and it was there that she would find another destiny.

"Mariana, do you think you can walk to Évora? It's too far."

She stopped and looked at him. "If I take one step and then another and keep walking, eventually I'll be there."

"Are you mad?"

"No." He was starting to bother her.

"Look, Mariana, I'm supposed to bring you home," he said, sighing. "Are you going to make it easy for me?"

"No," she said. After he carried her for a while, her eyes shut and her muscles tight in protest, she felt sorry for her friend and told him to put her down. She would walk the rest of the way home.

Her new fate was indeed awaiting her. Papa was at the broken gate to greet her. He gave a brief speech about the convent of Nossa Senhora da Conceição, where many girls her age, or younger, were going. The convent, over two centuries old, was loved by the crown and showered with gifts. The royal guard made it one of the safest places in the province, with many noble women taking refuge until the war ended. Though conditions were crowded, Abbess Maria de Mendonça had agreed to shelter Mariana and arrange for tutoring. Mama, coming outside, close to weeping, said that Mariana would finally have friends and be on her own, as it seemed she wanted. It was the only place where a girl like Mariana could read, study her precious books, learn Latin, and sing to the heavens.

The ribcage of Maria Alves vibrated with forgiveness and glowed like a strange tiara. But the organs beneath it remained unyielding, and they throbbed with the goodbye she had received from her favorite granddaughter. Curse this work of forgiveness. Her bosom was a useless mountain range, crushing her. When Mariana had said, "Goodbye, Vovó, my One More Than Everything. Someday I'll guess the riddle," Maria Alves tried to shout, "Your father is saying that the convent is safe in time of war, that you can study there, but he wants to protect his holdings from too many sons-in-law. Of course you are the one who must go, Mariana, because Ana Maria is docile and perfect for marriage." But no sound came from her. She forced the tiara of her ribs to open, so that whatever heat was stored inside her would be sent Mariana's way.

Francisco da Costa Alcoforado, in formal regalia, led Mariana to the convent of Conceição. Luís followed her, carrying her parcels. A party was going on within the convent, and they entered the locutory, where visitors were feasting. The front door facing the plaza was wide open and unattended. Townspeople, men and women, were having their run of the place. A lay woman with a thin, white towel around her head carried a tray of egg sweets and chestnuts and offered some to Mariana and her father. She said that the Abbess was expecting them. Some novices in white veils chased one another through the locutory, although when they saw Francisco glaring at them, they crept away.

Abbess Dona Maria de Mendonça, a breathless, elderly nun, greeted Francisco with a bow. She took Mariana's face in her hands and said, "Such a beauty. I'll be happy to be your mother."

"You aren't my mother at all," said Mariana.

"Mariana," said her father.

"I shall be, if you'll allow it," said the Abbess. "I've fixed your room to welcome you. I think you'll like it."

"I'm sure I won't."

The Abbess knelt and peered at Mariana and said, "I love candid hearts, and therefore I suspect I shall love you wonderfully."

"Where is the scribe?" asked Francisco da Costa Alcoforado.

The Vice-Abbess, Sister Maria Madalena, entered the locutory, as if Francisco's wishes were meant to materialize at once. Along with her came the scribe, Sister Brites de Brito, a young nun carrying a huge book with a stained cover and parchment pages. She set the book on a table covered in old damask. Francisco gestured for a drunken visitor to remove himself from a chair of Russian leather, high-backed and inlaid with damascene. Francisco sat there as the scribe opened the book to the year 1651 and entered Mariana's name.

Francisco took a document from his doublet and read it aloud to the Abbess. He would provide 300,000 *réis* as a stipend for the convent in exchange for them sheltering Mariana. He would also donate a parcel of a wheat field, with the provision that it feed the convent, provide Mariana with an additional fee to cover her expenses, and then become the property of the convent upon the death of his daughter. Other pledges would be given to the convent at the time of her profession. Mariana Alcoforado was to renounce all rights to inherit anything from her mother or father, except what she might wish to donate as an offering to the evangelistic saints.

The Abbess was shocked that he had written everything down, and more disturbed that he was reading it in front of his child. It was an incredibly generous agreement, but voicing it was insensitive.

"I'd like a receipt, Abbess Dona Maria de Mendonça," he said.

"A receipt?" She had never heard of such a demand. Sisters Brites de Brito and Maria Madalena blushed. Everyone knew that a nun could not inherit anything directly from her parents. The Abbess put her hands on Mariana's shoulders. Odd that the little girl did not act distressed or frightened, but impervious. Above everything. The Abbess wondered if Mariana could appreciate the politics involved. It had taken the Abbess, a noblewoman herself, years to recognize that her own parents had put her into the convent in order to keep the line of inheritance to their *morgadio* clean and uncomplicated, and to keep the country's political systems unfractured, with undivided properties. The Alcoforados had so many daughters that they would have to do the same.

Francisco da Costa told her that no soldiers would harm her here. She was too smart for him to let her be anyone's wife.

Abbess Maria de Mendonça nodded. Living in a dominion of women had its merits. In time, Mariana would see that.

"Goodbye, dearest," he said in a loud whisper, reaching down to kiss her goodbye.

Mariana was hit by the scent of his hair — oranges and ashes — and she said, "You can't leave me here, Papa," and she dug her fingers into his doublet and held on, refusing to cry, and it took both the Abbess and Vice-Abbess and her own mighty father to pry her loose, and again she clutched onto him, and again they grabbed her fingers one by one to release him. A jolt went through him at his daughter's astonishing vigor. Waves of it were thrusting through her and into him.

As he left the Abbess and Vice-Abbess to restrain her, she called out, "Papa!" once more, a last lance thrown straight for his heart.

"Come see your precious room," begged the Abbess.

A note of welcome from Sister Leonor Henriques, Rui's sister, was in the apartment that was to be Mariana's. A pillow embroidered with roses dressed up her large teakwood bed, and she ran her fingers over the "JMJ" for Jesus, Mary, and Joseph carved inside a heart on the headboard.

The Abbess pointed to the flowers on a lacquered chest. "From me," she said. "Do you like them?"

"No," said Mariana. "They stink."

"You're very sensitive, then!" said the Abbess. "Those flowers have no odor. Ah! Was that a smile I saw?"

"No. I'm wondering what good they are, if I can't smell them."

"We shall have many fine philosophical discussions. I'm to be your teacher, you know."

Mariana turned to her and said, "Then I beg your forgiveness. I worship tutors." Her mouth pulsed with discomfort.

"Worship? No," said the Abbess, and took Mariana's hands before saying, "I should be overjoyed if I end up learning from you, and I suspect I might. Shall I leave you to get accustomed to your new apartment?"

"Don't leave me," said Mariana.

"Shall this be our first lesson, learning how to feel the presence of those we love even when they are not materially in front of us?"

"Yes," said Mariana, realizing that Abbess Maria de Mendonça had trapped her into pledging love to her superior. She grinned for the first time that day. "I enjoy tests. I shall conquer any test you give me."

"Very good," said the Abbess. "Until we meet again."

Mariana practiced feeling the presence of her family — and the Abbess — within the pictures on the wall, next to the crucifix. She tried to sense them dancing on the esparto grass rug decorating the floor, or tossing the bouquet of boxwood twigs set over her holy water font. She explored the rest of her new home. A polished wardrobe was set against one wall, and on her nightstand was a breviary and a lantern. Her walnut writing desk had many drawers.

Two little chairs of mat rush and two larger ones of chestnut were in the corners. Mama had informed her that the daughters of nobles received the rooms in the new dormitory like this one, called "little houses" because they were *so* huge, while other nuns and homeless refugees, and some married women whose spouses were often away on war business, were crammed into the cells in the regular dormitory. Two hundred and eleven women and girls lived at Conceição, over fifty more than the usual number. In the short time she had been downstairs with her father, she had seen men — workers, artisans, soldiers, and husbands — milling in and out of the locutory, bringing gossip from their homes, the streets, and the battlegrounds, or a piece of jewelry or basket of food. Apparently the portress let in anyone who was not a Spanish soldier.

Mariana sank onto the bed in her "little house," exhausted with trying to feel the presence of people who were not there. Why should she? Why was suffering supposed to be a game? She wanted some real, living company now. She waited for her father to correct his mistake in bringing her here. The Abbess did not return, nor did Sister Leonor Henriques arrive. Mariana took off her coat and folded it and looked at the habit of rough white cloth she was expected to put on.

She reminded herself, *I shall endure this. I shall enjoy a worse wait, if it means future glory.*

Her first guests before dinnertime were Mama, and Ana Maria carrying Miguel, and Baltazar holding Catarina's hand. Mama gave Mariana a box of buttons and said, "I cut them off my blouses. I'd rather feel my arms empty, if you cannot be in them, Mariana."

Ana Maria said, "I shall visit like a madwoman, do you hear me, Mariana?"

Baltazar said, "I hate convents," and Mama told him not to be blasphemous.

At night, alone, Mariana shook the box of buttons and informed herself that they were Mama's arms singing. She took this with her as she attempted to leave the convent, but a soldier of the garrison caught her and sent her back to her room.

She remained sleepless. Towards dawn, another girl was drawn to Mariana still shaking music out of Mama's buttons. She introduced herself as Dona Brites de Freire, a novice, and said that she was thirteen.

"I'm Mariana Alcoforado," said Mariana.

"From *the* Alcoforados?"

Mariana shrugged.

Dona Brites de Freire jumped onto Mariana's bed and leaned back against the wall. "Did you see what the Marquêsa Dona Fernandes was wearing at Mass this morning? Diamonds! I'm surprised some Spaniards didn't charge in and snatch them off her. I certainly wanted to."

"I was too far back."

Brites de Freire laughed. "It does get crowded in there. The rich townspeople get the best seats. Oh – sorry. I meant no offense."

Mariana said, "I want to go home."

"Listen, it isn't so bad here," said Brites de Freire, taking Mariana's hand. When Mariana was paying attention, Brites said, "You know the good thing about veils and habits? They make the face stand out. Have you noticed how the faces of nuns float, pure and pretty? You have brown eyes that speak and speak, and I wish my nose were small like yours. And something talks under your skin. An interesting sadness is in your forehead. I'm guessing one of your parents is dark and one is light, and you're in between. You have the bones of an animal without them being too big, which is grand, because most women have the bones of birds. I do."

"No you don't," said Mariana. "Though I wish you did, so that you could fly me out of here."

"My father says that out there is no place for a girl to be."

"Why? Because we might fall in love with a Spaniard?"

They giggled, and Mariana saw, in a flash of knowing herself, that she could not survive without conspiracies.

"Let's go exploring!" said Brites de Freire. The Abbess never bothered with head counts at bedtime or at the reciting of the Hours in the chapel, nor did she lock the door to the dormitories. Even if she had been young and energetic, the number of residents in the convent was unwieldy.

Mariana and Brites de Freire slipped down to the kitchen, where the cooks were busy. They worked through the night, so that the delicacies they would sell to townspeople appeared as if by magic at sunrise. Egg whites were used to starch everyone's habits and wimples, which left so many yolks that they had to invent yolk-rich desserts to avoid the sin of wastefulness. In the cooks' struggle to dream up new things from the same old substance, they had to rely on humor, giving their creations names such as Nuns' Bellies, Angels' Breasts, Abbots' Ears. Mariana and Brites de Freire were enthralled by this frieze from time immemorial, with women awake before daylight, working, inventing, amusing themselves.

The actions of the pastry inventors were as slow and careful as a grace that chanted, God? God? Where are You, God? Let me see You.

I am the fire so hot it cannot be seen. You would die to see Me, God warned.

Make ecstasy kinder, God, so that we can look upon You and live, replied every laboring soul.

The women worked on, with clouds of flour ascending. Inside themselves, since it was the time of the Grand Silence, the refrain continued, God? God? until to quiet them He dropped some sheddings of stars into their eyes. Who could bear more than tiny reflections of His fire? Their eyes gleamed in pain, and from the anguish of not daring to ask for anything more burning.

Mariana and Brites de Freire standing together was not so different a picture from the one that occurred on the night that Mariana and Ana Maria had looked up at the stars over their home. Mariana's mind was speaking along with the inner chorus sent up by the working nuns, God? God? God? What is any lifetime, but a waiting for You?

On the work table rested a basin of egg yolks, like suns breaking one against the other. Altogether, they were the color that Mariana, in the company of her new friend, in wonder, chose as the shade of an almighty fire. Next to this basin rested another enormous one, and it was filled with egg whites, the jellied mass of them looking like the humor from the backs of the eyes of God.

50

Part 2

A PARTIAL ROSTER OF THE NUNS
AT THE ROYAL CONVENT OF CONCEIÇÃO

FRANCISCA FREIRE: mistress of the scriptorium. "She with the Heart of a Dove."

BEATRIZ MARIA DE RESENDE: a singer since childhood; knowledgeable about organ music; lost her sight from so much dedication.

BRITES DE BRITO: when elected Abbess, she ruled with a fine disposition, and had a glorious death. Former mistress of the Forty Hours.

MARIA DE SANTIAGO: gave the example of freeing herself from all scurrilous and unnecessary correspondence.

BRITES FRANCISCA DE NORONHA: always lived in the greatest fear of God.

MICHAELLA DOS ANJOS: ruined herself with abstinences and, according to nuns who assisted at her death, her body repeatedly went rigid, then limp.

IGNEZ DE SÃO JOSÉ: entered the convent as a very young child; in her girlhood, she was always sick. Had a love of gardens.

MARIA DOS SERAFINS: stayed in mental prayer almost until dawn.

BRITES DOS SERAFINS: acted superior to Our Lady, and was therefore punished.

. . . and also among those in the convent:

SISTER DOLORES: mistress of the choir.

SISTER ANGELICA DE NORONHA: mistress of the kitchen.

SISTER JULIANA DE MATOS: mistress of the infirmary.

SISTER MARIA DE CASTRO: a youthful friend of Mariana; ordered to study her lessons in the choir loft, to contain her tendency towards high spirits.

SISTER BRITES DE FREIRE: confidante of Mariana, also a noblewoman, also placed in the convent at a very young age.

SISTER MARIA DE SÃO FRANCISCO: rebellious in her youth, she was later reformed by the strength of an inner sensation.

SISTER MARIA DE MENDONÇA: loving and wise mistress of novices, and first teacher to Mariana in the convent. A former Abbess.

SISTER GENEBRA NOGUEIRA: a "New Christian" (of a Jewish family forced by the Inquisition to convert to Christianity). During most of the war, the portress of the convent.

SISTER LEONOR HENRIQUES: of the infamous and wealthy Lôbo family of Beja. Cristóvão Pantoja, Rui de Melo, Bartolomeu, and Gil Vaz (who died young in India) were her brothers. Devoted to Mariana.

SISTER MARIA MADALENA DE CASTRO PEREIRA: a very old noblewoman, Abbess during the riot against the English soldiers in 1662, and then again at the very end of the war, after her sister Isabel's death; considered modest and sweet, but also decrepit and incompetent.

SISTER ISABEL PEREIRA: blood-sister to Maria Madalena de Castro. Abbess briefly during the time of the Love Letters; did not live to complete her term.

SISTER JOANA DE LACERDA: another Abbess during the war; of a noble family; extremely old. Nothing at the convent remained within her control

RIVERS OF GOLD flowed into the convent. Golden wheat, the fleece of sun-embossed sheep, coins like the loosened eyes of angels: Fear of dying made people generous with gifts. They wanted the nuns to pray for them, or to record their belongings as given to God before the Spanish seized them. Sister Mariana Alcoforado noted every dowry offering or donation in a massive accounting book during her daily hours in the scriptorium. With each entry, a sensation hit her full force, as if these golden rivers, studded with money and animals, smashed down the door to the office and flooded over her. Despite this violence, the rivers traveled through her arms calmly and emerged in fluid writing. She knew from her father (if only he would visit, she could report to him all she had learned!) that the one with the key to the records of an estate was its master, and it surprised her that so few of the other nuns took any pleasure in capturing the history of their days, especially days such as these. Sometimes she pretended that her sums were an army of angels under her command. "I I I" were three columns of seraphim in the midst of this fortress of women, which was in the middle of Beja, which was in turn in the dead center of the pincer claws lately formed by Spanish troops. During the last decade, they had bled across various points along the Guadiana River and into border towns in the east, north, and south of the province. They were awaiting the right moment to snap the pincers shut and slice through the interior, with Beja in its marrow, cutting the country roughly in half. The Spanish army could then sweep west towards the ocean, to destroy Lisbon. If Évora, the capital of the province to the north, continued to withstand the pressure, as it was now doing, barely, the pincers could be kept propped open. If Évora collapsed, Beja would be next, which was why English soldiers had been garrisoned here for such a long time as allies. They, like everyone else, were growing tense with waiting. So many complaints were being lodged about the English carousing, stealing, or sleeping in doorways that the people of Beja were forgetting that the English were on their side. It was the twenty-second year of the war that Mariana considered hers. Believing that Beja could be anyone's idea of a strategic point was as diffi-cult for her as recognizing herself as an adult, and a nun for the last six years, since taking her vows at sixteen. Part of her was still waiting for Papa to come and free her, so that her true life could commence. Oh, how would she survive, how would she amuse herself without her folly?

Today it was impossible for her not to rise from the long oak writing table and stare out the window overlooking the courtyard edged on its four sides by the cloistered walkways. The wind was rustling the laurel trees and the marsh mallow plants and maiden-hair ferns around the cistern. Her friends, Sister Brites de Freire and Sister Maria de Castro, liked to tell her that she worried too much. But that wasn't it, not at all; it was, she told them, that her skin opened and strained outward, like a coat of ears. Postulants, novices, nuns, lay sisters, and refugees were crowding around the shrine to Saint John the Baptist in the cloister — ten deep, twenty deep — and mourning their dead. "Something terrible is about to happen," said Sister Mariana.

"Your sister is going to have another set of twins?" teased Sister Francisca Freire, in her forties and Mariana's superior in the scriptorium. They were supposed to be working in silence, but everyone was breaking the rules. Sister Francisca, like Mariana, also sensed something very wrong, but preferred to make the moment light rather than see Mariana troubled.

"Yes, that's it," said Mariana, and smiled. She always guessed when her older friend was in sympathy with her.

"Or perhaps the English soldiers have invaded the refectory?"

"Then we won't be able to find them," said Mariana, and they both laughed, though nervously. With so many women and girls packed into the convent, the refectory doubled as a sleeping quarters and its tenants were quarrelsome about protecting their nests. Mealtimes were uncomfortable, with many nuns forced to stand crushed against one another. It was so bad that some of the rich ones who lived in the New Dormitory seldom left their "little houses," and their parents sent servants to care for them. Sister Brites de Freire, who worked in the kitchen, reported almost striking those servants who claimed the right to plunder the larder as they pleased.

"The noise today is enough to rupture the ground," said Sister Francisca, leading Mariana from the window. Seeing her like that reminded Sister Francisca of little Mariana when she was first here, acutely waiting for someone in her family to visit. Ana Maria was the most faithful of callers, but with four children already, including twins born two years ago, venturing out was difficult, and anyone who crossed town ran a gauntlet of drunken English soldiers. Mariana's mother had new babies of her own to care for, and the Alcoforado patriarch was busy with plans to build a mint. Baltazar had been put into a priory in Beringel, over an hour's carriage ride away, and Mariana once said that she was going to explode from trying to dream up what he might look like by now.

Her arm around Mariana, Sister Francisca suggested that they continue with their daily work. Fulfilling an accounting task might seem unimportant in wartime, but any ordinary act was a form of singing defiantly on the way to one's execution.

Mariana resumed documenting the donation of one hundred crates of tallow soaps from a local merchant. Many of the numbers she wrote were fat, swollen with howls.

Some numbers were stretched-out and thin, as if attempting to peer over the convent's walls and describe the trouble before it hit.

Sister Francisca was impressed. What was written by Mariana's hands was always, always Mariana, taking the shape of the given hour and the hour's ruling sensation.

Sometimes the numbers were Mariana herself, tall and strong-boned, with intense, wide features.

The Abbess at the time of Mariana's arrival, Maria de Mendonça, had heralded Mariana as an astonishing pupil, exceptionally meticulous and obsessive with details and yet capable of draping a gorgeous veil of mystery over her work. She was sent to the scriptorium to continue her studies under Sister Francisca Freire.

59

Besides excelling in her Latin, Greek, scriptures and theology, philosophy, history, and calligraphy, Mariana was a brilliant accountant, and was soon the youngest member of the administrative council and finance committee.

In the beginning, Sister Francisca Freire would inspect Mariana's entries and occasionally remark, "No. I feel nothing as I look at your work. Begin again." The sum totals would be correct, or an obituary accurately written, but Sister Francisca would be unsatisfied. She would say, "Your heart must bleed upon the page, Sister Mariana. Even a mere numeral is concerned with life and death, and the life and death of this very day, and I must tremble to behold it."

Mariana would reply, "Yes, Sister Francisca. Pardon me."

Sister Francisca Freire's nickname was "She with the Dove's Heart," and Mariana held her in awe. The marriage of Sister Francisca's parents was a scandal. Her father, a nobleman, married for love and did not care when his family disinherited him because of it. His wife was the daughter of a Bejense surgeon of modest means. Being raised in a tender household left Francisca with a hugely robust and sensitive soul that caused her to decide that the only possible love greater than that of her parents would be a love of God. She entered the convent of her own will, unlike most of the others at Conceição.

Sister Francisca once said that some of the yellowed, crumbling folios, the archives on the careers of the early, long-forgotten Abbesses, were not creased by time, but were tinted and furrowed by the stars.

She had been delighted to inform Mariana that her work bore no traces of *Gongorismo*, that affected, sentimental style named after the Spanish poet Góngora y Argote, as cheaply seeded as morning-glories and therefore popular all over Europe. Flowery words did not drain the emotions to read or to write, and Sister Francisca was gratified that her pupil instinctively abjured such silly ease. Every comma or dot went onto Mariana's pages like an incision and showed up as almost a mirror incision on her. Sister Francisca marveled that the young woman did not repeatedly faint. Never had she witnessed anyone with such a zeal for keeping books, which made it curious that Mariana continued to be anxious for her approval.

On the morning they both knew that a tragic storm was gathering, Sister Francisca said, "Sister Mariana, you are pressing so hard with your ink and quill that you are piercing the paper."

"Oh," said Sister Mariana, and held a page up to the light. The groans of the women in mourning floated through the cuts of the letters and numbers. Her writing was actually crying out. Such surprises, out of nowhere. This day she would remember as the one on which she wrote, emphatically wrote, on the air.

"Ah!" said Sister Francisca. Ah, an accountant's dream, to leave scratchings upon the sky!

Dear Baltazar,

You lazy fellow! You do me the gravest of disservices! I have heard that you have time to gather up your bird dogs with the monks and local dukes and go hunting, yet it is the rare occasion on which you write me a letter. I feel wary today, and no matter where you are, I would expect you to be able to detect my state. How else am I to know you, since we must be apart? When are you to take your religious vows? I am deprived of watching you enter adulthood, having seen precious little of you in the last eleven years, and nothing in the last two, since the arrival of the English. Do you speak like Papa now? (Does Papa ever visit you? If he does, please inform him that I must speak to him.) What do you look like, my brother? Do you have a moustache? Are you finally taller than your forlorn sister?

Baltazar, if you have any wise words for your poor Mariana, if you have learned anything in your priory to convince me that your destiny and mine, though separate, are blessed with a loftier purpose than my ignorance has yet perceived, then your counsel will be received with gratitude.

I hear that the Prussian we have hired to lead our army, General Schomberg, is doing a good job, but the outcome of the war is uncertain. I had so hoped that the war would end before you were grown.

Please live forever.

With infinite embraces, from your constant
Mariana

On the veranda at the end of the New Dormitory, near the chapel to Our Lady of the Angels and the window facing the gate that marked the road towards Mértola, Sister Mariana conducted a tea party. Catarina of Bragança, the daughter of deceased King Dom João IV, was celebrating her second year of marriage to King Charles II of England. Queen Catarina had taken the tea that Portugal was accustomed to getting from the trade routes to the East and brought it with her to England. The English were becoming mad for tea, thanks to their Portuguese Queen.

Brites did as Mariana asked and stole some puff pastries, baked with orange juice and the fat from around pork kidneys, from the kitchen for their tea party, so that she, Mariana, Ignez de São José, and Maria de Castro could practice being fancy ladies.

"I hear it's so cold in England that they wear coats indoors," said Sister Maria de Castro, using her black scapular to wipe sugar from her mouth. She referred to herself and the rest of the nuns as bell-heads, because of the way their veils sloped to their shoulders. She worked in the laundry, and called her job bell-washing. In her early days at Conceição, she and Mariana had stabbed their thumbs to mingle their blood.

"They wear fur coats, mostly," said Sister Brites, her voice brimming with authority.

"They're Protestants, and it's a big mistake having them here, even if they help us win the war," said Sister Ignez de São José. "They've already stolen tea from us, and Bombay and Tangiers."

"They're welcome to Bombay. I'll never get there," said Sister Maria de Castro.

"Catarina introduced tea to the English. They didn't steal it," said Mariana, "and giving them some property was part of the agreement. I think we should toast the English, and Schomberg." They agreed that Portugal must end the war so that they could begin their lives before they were old women, even if it meant buying assistance with all that remained in the Indies or Brazil. Even if it meant being beholden later on to England or France or Prussia.

"Easy for an Alcoforado to say," said Brites.

"Oh, hush," said Mariana.

They toasted Mariana's father for engineering the building of a mint. Holding glasses of tea, crowding along the balcony, they peered down at the English troops milling around the convent.

Mariana dipped her hand into her tea as if it were holy water and shook it over their heads. Her friends followed her example. Maria de Castro poured it straight from her glass. Startled to find this taste of home, and these nuns throwing festive rain onto them, the English soldiers looked upward. The sun on their faces was blinding, the tea was familiar, and everyone felt transported elsewhere, if only for a moment.

Sister Francisca suggested that it was a fine paradox in convents that regimenting the hours towards a surpassing daily sameness produced the sort of trance of mind, body, and soul during which ecstasy was most likely to strike. As if reducing every hour to ordinary routine might efface ordinariness, or a focus on time might render time meaningless.

Mariana regarded the canonical hours as ladders with vividly marked rungs, on which many women and girls scampered up and down.

The first rung — the Grand Silence. Silence was supposed to commence at bedtime, at seven in the evening, but this was violated over and over. Senhora Alexandra Texeira Bettencourt, who wore frocks with galloons at the hem and wide pagoda sleeves, wanted to hide her ruby ring in the cloister and announce a treasure hunt among the nuns. It was worth the price of a gem to get some attention.

But everyone was quaking and timid. All because that troublemaker Mariana was spreading alarm, saying that a cataclysm was on its way. Did Mariana think she had direct contact with God, just because she was an Alcoforado?

Matins & Lauds, the next rung of the ladder – *You shall draw water with joy out of the fountains of the Savior*, recited half of the nuns in the midnight darkness of the Main Chapel. *Drop down dew, Oh heavens, from above, and let the clouds rain upon the just one*, swelled forth the antiphonal response from the other half of the chapel.

Sister Maria de Mendonça left the infirmary to recite Matins. She could not rid herself of a bad premonition about the English soldiers in town, though this could be a remnant of the shock that had not released her since the Holy Father turned his back on her country. He listened to the Spanish Jesuits who told him that Portugal was merely an extension of Spain. Singing of water at midnight soothed her illness about the Pope's abandonment, as did the sight of her former pupil, Mariana, who never failed to wave at her before Matins. As if to say, I started at the convent with you, and even now I start every day with you, Sister Maria de Mendonça.

One day after Spain captured the eastern frontier, Mariana had broken out in red blotches over her entire body.

Today one of Mariana's arms was solid red.

After Matins, Maria de Mendonça went with her thoughts momentarily brimming with water and coolness to see if she could touch away the anguish staining her young friend's arm.

"You understand me as if I dreamed you," said Mariana, watching some of the redness fade under the hand of her former teacher.

Sleep — another set of hours. Abbess Maria Madalena Pereira was consumed with vertigo. In the center of the spinning was a memory she prized. She had been a young nun, sweeping a floor. Suddenly, what felt like an envelope of gummy light surrounded her, enfolded her. She was a letter inside it. Then the light was gone. That feeling had never returned. But it told her, and she had never forgotten, that all that was written inside her was precious to someone she could call God.

She was at peace, despite thinking that Sister Mariana was right. The hour of judgment could well be upon them.

First diurnal hour — Prime & Dawn Mass. Sister Maria de Castro chanted from her Psalter, *The star of morn to night succeeds*. She was sick on almond-stuffed figs stolen from the kitchen, but was alert as Sister Beatriz Maria de Resende sang the "Tantum Ergo." What a conquering voice! Though scarcely into her twenties, Sister Beatriz Maria de Resende was losing her eyesight. She was a singer of such magnitude that her organ-playing and her voice made listeners want to prostrate themselves and never rise again.

Sister Maria de Castro never did anything so lofty. She was recently caught overturning the apothecary's jar of leeches in the infirmary, and could not look at Sister Juliana de Matos, the infirmarian. Sister Maria de Castro had shouted at the leeches, "Hurry! Run! We're in trouble now!" She found this hysterically funny, but the infirmarian did not. Sister Maria de Castro wore a silk tunic beneath her habit, and did not care that her punishment should be two years of no one being allowed to speak to her.

Look at Abbess Maria Madalena Pereira. She could hardly stay awake, much less maintain order. The nuns were supposed to stay behind the grilles separating the upper and lower choirs from the main body of the church, where townspeople and soldiers, French and Portuguese and even a few English, filled the pews, but the nuns spilled out of their confinement. There was no order.

What was that? Yells, clanging of metal?

"I hear noises outside!" shouted Sister Maria de Castro, interrupting the Consecration of the Mass.

The congregation turned to stare at her, and a rumble of speculation arose. So those sounds of terror were not merely inside their heads?

The priest offering the Mass called out, "Sisters! Brethren! Mind why you are here! Pray against fearful noises."

We Offer Up Our Daily Tasks. Sister Mariana Alcoforado, unnerved by her friend's outburst at Mass, proceeded to the scriptorium, with its aroma of the paste binding spines together. Out of the massive stacks of books came a smell of boiled animals that transported her back to Papa's solarium. She loved the Song of Songs asking, *Whither goest my love? Where is he?* But today she was frightened. Her numerals were looking like many-legged insects. She waited for Manuel, the convent's procurer of supplies, to bring her news about the outside.

Manuel entered the convent, as usual, through the front door, but today his pace was swift, although the crate of fruit he was carrying was heavy. He was glad to be away from the town center. With a ruffian like Cristóvão Pantoja Lôbo as the governor of Beja, the surprise was that there had not been any upheavals before this.

It had long ago stopped occurring to Manuel that he was quite casual about entering the cloisters. No one ever prevented him — or any other man, as far as he could see — from wandering about at will. It would be a sad day when life here reverted to normal, because he enjoyed working with Sister Mariana, who was a genius at moving around funds. (An odd thing about her was that she often said "for the nuns," as if she were not one herself.) Because she had illegally transferred an allotment for cleaning the kitchen tiles into the food account, he had been able to buy pears at a special rate from an Englishman in town. Mariana was wild for pears, but today she said, "Forget the pears. I can read a story clouding over your face."

"An Englishman set fire to the blacksmith's house when he wouldn't give him a drink," said Manuel, sinking into a chair that Mariana offered and setting the crate of pears on the floor. "They put out the flames and arrested the Englishman, but then those miserable Lôbos showed up. Cristóvão forced Dom Lourenço, who's supposed to be the overseer of the English troops, to escort the arsonist out of the jail. Cristóvão whipped the prisoner in the public square, and then the Lôbo brothers went hunting."

"Is the prisoner alive?"

"Barely," said Manuel. "He's lying in the street. Now Sergeant-Major Dom Miguel is demanding that Dom Lourenço explain why he obeyed a Lôbo instead of consulting him for any matters of military discipline. They're yelling, and a crowd is watching and shouting."

"We've been hearing terrible noises all morning."

"Let's hope it won't be for long. Dom Miguel and Dom Lourenço can go on and on, but they should be finished screaming soon. Shall we have some of these pears, Sister Mariana?"

"I could not possibly do anything so divine right now," she said.

Another rung of the daily ladder of hours — Terce. Nine in the morning.

The nuns chanted, *For You Oh Lord have rescued me from all distress, and my eyes have seen the downfall of my foes*. They filed past Our Lady of the Milk on the staircase leading to the upper choir loft, where chairs were linked and built into the wall. A chubby oak angel had a navel sloppily filled with gilt. Probably the work of the Marquêsa Dona Fernandes.

"Something has gone wrong with the English soldiers, and the Lôbos are in the middle of it," whispered Sister Maria de Santiago to Sister Brites de Freire, and the undertone of the hymns became "gone wrong, gone wrong" as the message was passed from sopranos to mezzo-sopranos to contraltos.

Sister Maria de Mendonça had to excuse herself. She stumbled through the cloister back to the infirmary, certain that more bad news would kill her. She had, thus far, hidden her malady, vague and unnamable, from most of the nuns. She had not been well for three years, not since 1659, when the Peace of the Pyrenees Treaty was arranged. That was when France won the Thirty Years War against Spain but agreed to let Spain do as she pleased with Portugal.

It was an insult to be thrown as a concession to the loser. Nor did she understand why France should immediately ignore the treaty by sending French troops here and helping Portugal acquire General Schomberg. The war was utter perfidy on every side.

The bells in the city's tower were ringing. Sister Maria de Mendonça heard an outburst of tumult, and ran to find Mariana. Her impulse to hide would never overrule her need to protect her favorite former student. Where was she? The nuns and refugees, and a few men, were running through the cloisters and corridors, hurrying onto the balconies and verandas to see what was happening. Sister Maria de Mendonça almost fainted in the pack of women and girls gaping at the people of Beja, including children, which made this worse than the cow riot of a decade ago because this time the innocent young had gone mad, everyone, men, women, children, were chasing English soldiers and beating them in the street. They were being dragged out of doorways, out of homes, and hit with sticks, with poles, bricks, shoes. Baskets of lemons and dried codfish were flung, and bottles were broken and thrown. Dogs snapped, leaped. The loggia of the marketplace was open-eyed, open-mouthed. Sister Michaella dos Anjos was reciting the rosary in the midst of the jostling on the veranda, and Sister Dolores, the choir leader, was screaming out to the mass of people to stop, please stop. The Portuguese garrison around the convent was indifferent, though stones and rubbish flew high near the verandas, causing the nuns to scream and step on one another's feet. A woman — was that the chandler's wife, grown ancient and hateful? — dragged an English soldier by the hair over the cobblestones. Sister Maria de Mendonça tried to call out to her, but her voice was swallowed by the shrieking, so she shouted, "Sister

Mariana! Are you here? Sister Mariana!" until she must have passed out and been carried to the infirmary, where she awoke in pain. The clamor of the riot answered her before growing fainter, until the sounds echoed in her head, then died.

Mariana had been on the veranda and seen a postulant of no more than ten arrested with such fear that Mariana grabbed her and pressed her to the black cloth of her scapular and brought the girl to the safety of her "little house," where the faintness of the din resounded in the stones.

"Are we going to die?" the girl had asked.

"I don't know what's going on," said Mariana, receiving the girl in an embrace. "All I can tell you is that you are to stay with me until this nightmare quits, and if death comes, then you and I will die together. I would never leave anyone who needed me."

We Once Again Offer Up Our Work to the Praise and Glory of His Name. Sister Leonor Henriques heard the rumor that her brothers were involved in the riot. And yet they expected her to choose one of them as the recipient of her wheat fields after she died. Before this, she had been merely bored with their obvious attempts to win her affection. Now she was furious. She dipped her branches of boxwood into the holy water font over her bed and shook this dripping aspergillum over herself.

The holy marking of the hours did not stop for tragedy — Sext, noon, the hour of Christ's Passion. Sing *O Sacred Head Surrounded/ By Crowns of Piercing Thorns*. The nuns were to think of betrayal, agony, death.

They did, in their separate cells and "little houses." No one attended the divine offices except the Abbess, who wept at her inability to keep the convent on schedule.

Beatific rung of the day – Dinner (in silence), followed by Study & Meditation Time. Nones, 3 p.m., the time of Christ's death. Study, Choir, Classes.

No one ate or studied. The nuns meditated, as they were bound to do, upon death. Mariana watched over the postulant sleeping.

An important rung of the ladder of the day – Our Daily Meeting in the Chapter Room to Discuss the Temporal and Spiritual Business of Our Community. The ten nuns in attendance, ignoring the Abbess's calls for quiet, talked about the two English soldiers murdered in the riot. As a result, the English garrisons had withdrawn from the city.

With these allies gone, Beja was more than ever open to invasion.

Vespers, followed by Collation, the light meal – Maria de Mendonça sat up in the infirmary to see Mariana with a tray of Abbots' Ears. The women joked that these egg sweets might give them bigger ears and better hearing before the next uprising.

Relaxation, followed by Compline — only a few dozen nuns showed up to recite Psalm 90: *A thousand may fall at your side, ten thousand fall at your right; the terror of the night will never approach you.*

Sister Leonor Henriques daydreamed about the roses embroidered on Mariana's pillow, which were wearing thin. This meant that Mariana must be wearing them on the back of her head. Let the English go wild, let the French fail them, let Schomberg's reputation crash, let the Spanish come. Let her brothers joust over that wheat field. She must follow Mariana's example and wear invisible roses.

The Grand Silence once again — Sister Brites de Brito, in a cell with three others in the Old Dormitory, could not sleep. She was deciding that Sister Mariana must take over the Forty Hours. So much had gone on during the riot that Sister Brites de Brito felt defeated. The compiler of the Forty Hours had to record everything in a forty-hour period in the convent, with the thoughts and actions of every nun or lay sister rounding each moment to near-breaking fullness. Sister Brites de Brito had never persuaded anyone to take over this tradition, since it required an aptitude for writing symphonies and a faith in the minutiae of history. Mariana could do it. The problem might be that Mariana would attempt to include everyone and everything that occurred within a forty-hour period, and her frustration would turn every line into a cacophony.

Was the Grand Silence the bottom rung of the previous day, or the top one of the next ladder for Mariana to climb? The ladders would seem to create a never-changing present, but today was proof that all could change in an instant. She used to envision that the ladders of the hours were vertically attached, one to the next, skyward and ever higher, until at one point she might be able to scale the walls, grab Baltazar from his priory in Beringel, and climb past the moon with him, but that was not true. The hours, the days, lay horizontally on her chest, in stacks that were crushing her.

Her prayer that night was, I shall pass this test, and all tests. Nothing – being a nun, being incarcerated, living through a war – nothing shall keep me from the life of my heart. Send me every strife You can imagine, God, and I and my longing can endure still more.

Those Englishmen did not have to die, God. I believe You know that.

"Mama!" Mariana cried, gripping her side of the grille meant to separate the nuns from their callers. Everyone ignored this propriety, visitors wandered into the cloistered areas and nuns strolled out, but her mother would not approve. Mama had braved the blood and wreckage in the street to come visit!

"My baby," said Mama. "Will you forgive me for not coming sooner? Oh, if anything were to happen to you!"

"I'm fine, Mama," said Mariana, "but you shouldn't have gone out. It's not safe."

"It's unsafe everywhere. Even at home," Mama said, and began to rant. Mariana's father was charging Ana Maria and Rui for household expenses, saying that as long as Rui lived under their roof he would contribute before he gambled everything into ruin. Then Rui would call him a miser. The disaster with the English had redoubled their quarrels.

Mariana's father had ridden into town at the height of the riot. Clutching his sword in the wreckage of the square, he ordered the rioters to go home and think of how they had opened the door to calamity. "Your father dispersed the mob," said Mama, "but the Lôbos started everything."

Mariana tried to ask what exactly the Lôbos had done, but Mama was distracted.

"One more thing," said Mama. "I had a baby who died."

Baby Filipa. Mariana regarded this Filipa as a white-hot plum, short-lived. Was it wrong to be jealous to think that although Filipa never had to do a single thing to earn love, Mama might love her better than the rest of them?

"I'm sorry, Mama," said Mariana.

"You are saved from knowing such sorrow," said Mama when she stood to take her leave. She could not be long away from the house. It was impossible to promise when they would see each other again. Mama's grey hair was sticking needle-like from her head, and her eyes were circled with purple. They kissed whatever flesh of their faces could be pressed against the grille.

Mariana guarded her thoughts to keep the visit gentle, but her departing mother left her throbbing with, How could you love me so much, Mama, and be so mistaken about me? I do know sorrow.

Mama had other new children. Ana Maria had sons named Francisco de Melo and Luís, and daughters named Inês and Caetana. Strange to recall what it was like to hear of her own mother and sister in childbed during the same months, attended to by a half-grown Catarina. Whatever happened to Mariana's time, Mariana's chance for love and children?

She was also grief-stricken at having missed the chance to call to her father as he rode through town. *Papa, the world was in flames, I was a breath away. Why did you not rescue me? Why do you trust royal soldiers to defend me, when I cannot imagine anyone but you saving my life?*

She cried so loudly for her mother and father that the postulant whom she had comforted earlier entered Mariana's "little house."

"Don't be scared, Sister Mariana. I was in my cell, but I could sense you crying," said the girl, and held Mariana's head to her chest, as Mariana had done to her. My ribs are feeble, my body thin, the girl's frame seemed to say. Not big enough to comfort you, but all I have.

Sister Leonor Henriques, at the sight of her brother Rui in the locutory, wasted no time in saying, "What did you have to do with the trouble?"

Mariana, returning some repaired missals to the chapel, observed his grin with distaste.

"Is that any way to greet me?" he said.

"I'll greet you as I please," said Sister Leonor Henriques.

"I see!" said Rui. "I suppose it is irrelevant to you that a Count of Chamilly, one of the finest leaders in the French army, has voiced his wish to meet the brothers who are the bravest soldiers in the Portuguese army."

"That means nothing to me," said Sister Leonor Henriques.

Rui turned to Mariana and said, "You care, don't you?"

Mariana said, "I care that we're completely vulnerable now."

"You worry too much, sweet thing! My brothers and I will protect you and my furious sister here."

"Rui," said Sister Leonor Henriques, "I asked you to explain yourself."

Mariana hardly listened as Rui said that Leonor Henriques should be lecturing Cristóvão, that good old bastard Cristóvão, who did not deserve to inherit from her that nice piece of property, that it was Rui whom she should remember in her will, because when he and Cristóvão and Bartolomeu rode back into town after hunting, Dom Miguel and Dom Lourenço were still arguing, those hotheads, and Dom Miguel called Cristóvão a coward for riding off, which was the worst thing anyone could call a Lôbo. Cristóvão picked up a whip to confront Dom Miguel, and accidentally slashed Dom Lourenço's face. Someone in the crowd shouted that they should not be shedding their own blood, but the blood of the English soldiers who had turned into a nuisance.

"You are amused by death," said Sister Leonor Henriques.

"Then why do I have so many children? Life is what amuses me," said Rui, and laughed.

Mariana fled from the locutory. How dare he speak so lightly of burdening Ana Maria! What confounded Mariana, struck her, whenever she saw Rui during his boastful visits? That it was not within his powers to give a woman a moment's peace, and this type of tumult could never resemble the tumult of love. How heavy and frantic Ana Maria had become. Had Mariana said, standing with her sister and staring up to read the light-writing of the night, that she would love him always? No, the idea of him had seduced her. A black cloth was draped over the portrait of Rui that she carried within herself. He remained there because she could never go back upon using the word "always," though she had been a child when she uttered it. But his portrait was concealed with mourning colors within her, gone except for its muffled shape, so that even the fiery redness of his hair was put out.

"Mariana!"

The sound of her name hurled around the quadrants forming the sheltered walkways of the cloister, the Quadra of Saint John the Baptist; the Quadra of the Portaria, near the front entrance; the Quadra of Saint John the Evangelist; the Quadra of the Rosary, where the bodies of deceased nuns lay below unmarked flagstones. Through the central courtyard, the fury resounded, "Mariana! Mariana!" It echoed in the cistern and off the metal dipper attached to the bucket. It slammed against the walls of the prison room at the west end of the Old Dormitory, long unused, where punished nuns were supposed to be confined. A cry of "Mariana" rattled the blue bottles in the infirmary, and the oaken cups — held against a sick person's skin to draw out bad humors — clattered with music.

It was a man's cry.

"Mariana! Mariana! Mariana!" The bellowing reached her in the scriptorium, and she said to Sister Francisca, "Do you hear what I hear? What is it?" But her pulse had quickened; she knew, she knew.

Sister Francisca got up to inspect Mariana's accounting book. She was recording a gift of linens, and the writing was as vibrant as ink siphoned from sunlight. All moments were vital, but some, such as this one, required a person to hold them tightly.

"You are being summoned. Go at once," said Sister Francisca

Mariana ran from the scriptorium, through the Quadra of the Rosary and the door that led into the main body of the church. She would recognize that voice no matter what, no matter how long she would have to wait between the spells of letting it bathe, glut, bless her ears. Standing in the nave, his fists pounding his knees from the work of screeching her name, making the tabernacle and the statues quaver, his body wrenched, screaming without stopping "Mariana! Mariana!" until she reached him, not caring that some nuns were hissing, "Tss! Tss!" there he was, dressed not in monk's robes but in regular doublet, knee-breeches, and cloak, there he was, Baltazar, blood flushing through his face as if his burst heart was sending a fountain up through the inside of his head.

"I knew it. I knew it was you," said Mariana, and her feet left the ground as she flew to him. He whirled her around as he danced towards the altar, almost tripping over the stone positioned there to remind the nuns that no one must throw stones at anyone's faults, and her feet rose in an arc and knocked down a candlestick. When he set her down, they were both breathless, as if she, too, had been screaming his name loud and long. She put her hands on either side of his face, to hold him engraved in her mind, to be conjured after he was gone. He was very tall and broad shouldered. His face had become wild; Papa's mountain looks. His eyes held darts of fire. How could they patiently read scriptures?

"Baltazar," she said, as if the clarity of his name could hold him there.

"When I received your letter, I felt guilty, Mariana, and then there was that business with the English, and you can't imagine how worried I've been about you, so here I am! Humble servant, Baltazar, in person. I stole a horse and some clothes from the Duke of Sidónia. No one saw me escape from the priory. I don't need to tell you how impossible it is trying to go anywhere."

"If we step outside, even on an errand, we get excommunicated. You and your hunting friends at the priory get away with every-thing, I think."

"Let them excommunicate me! Hurrah if they do!"

"Baltazar! What would Papa say?"

"I would give him an earful back, Mariana, the way Rui does. I'm seventeen now, and I can do as I please."

"I won't listen to you say such things." She pressed her palms over the veil covering her ears.

He grasped her by the elbows and lifted her, until she giggled and begged him to set her down. Sister Michaella dos Anjos was glaring and slamming down hymnals in the lower choir, but Mariana ignored her.

"It's true, Mariana. He wants me to behave like a man, but only if I'm concerned with what he wants me to do, and what kind of man would I be then? I'd be like him. Haven't you heard about that business with the convent at Santa Clara? They're going to appeal to the magistrate against Papa. He bought their property at an absurd price and won't sell it back."

"Why should he? Why are we speaking about this?"

"Everyone says he forced them into something they didn't want to do. The way he forced me to live in the priory because he's decided I'm not strong enough to run his precious estate. I'm the eldest son, and I have to stand up for my rights."

"Where did you learn to talk like this?"

"In the priory. This is what comes of all that reading, though it's becoming dull. Come to think of it, I should thank Papa for sending me there. Then I'll tell him I quit, before I'm forced to take my holy orders. Everyone's saying that with the English gone, we have to be ready for what's next. I want to join the army with Rui, Cristóvão, and Bartolomeu as soon as they'll take me along."

"You'll do no such thing. I couldn't bear it."

"How proud would you be of me if I let everyone else do the fighting?"

"You don't have to do anything for me to be proud of you. Can we please talk about something else? How's Mama? And Ana Maria and Catarina and Miguel and Vovó, and the babies?" This conversation had not a flicker of resemblance to the one she had been rehearsing for years. Their embrace had been as she had dreamed it, but the words were decidedly not. Nor was his stance, more gangly and swaggering than she would have guessed. He still seemed to her a child, only larger and older.

"There's a splendid French cavalry captain who insisted upon meeting the Lôbos," Baltazar continued, not noticing her expression. "I was with them when he arrived at their tent! I tell you, I've never been so impressed in my life. He was grand."

"I'm glad for you, I think," she said, her voice faltering.

"Mariana," he said. "Please. I can't stand to see you sad." He took a pomegranate from his satchel, and sliced it open it for her with his knife. The wet red seeds stood out in the white flesh, and he pried a few up with the tip of the blade. "Good?" he said, feeding his sister.

"You remembered how I love them," she said. Inside her mouth, the seeds were staining her tongue. She bowed her head. "You remembered how I love you."

"I don't have to remember what never leaves my mind," he said.

Lovely Baltazar, so good at reading her — who else would have the instinct for bringing a pomegranate? She admired the sweet perversion of a fruit that required so much work to yield such tiny spots of taste and color, deliriously wonderful, imbedded in extraneous, bitter matter. This visit from Baltazar was brilliant red within the pith of her pointless years in the convent, luminous red, the shade of Baltazar, who risked everything to come to her.

"I couldn't bring myself to defy Papa and the monks and come to you when I was younger, but now I'm old enough not to care. It may be a while between visits" — and he did not add that it would be because he was about to join the army — "but I won't stop coming to see you. Not ever. I don't care if they chain me inside my cell and throw away the key. I don't care how many rules you and I break. Do you hear?"

"Yes," she said.

He lifted her face. Her eyes were gleaming. "If you can think of a place where I could bring you, and you could live happily, will you tell me?" he said.

"There isn't such a place," she said. "But you're a dear to want one for me. I know you must go."

"I'd better, before they find me gone, but I won't say goodbye," he said.

"No. Don't say goodbye."

Baltazar kissed her, walked quickly away, and was outside the convent when Mariana rushed to the main door and, leaning against the restraining arm of the portress, Sister Genebra, she shouted past the royal soldiers turning to stare, "This chapel is a happy place for me now, Baltazar! It had you in it!"

"Then everywhere is happy for me," he shouted back, strolling backward to look at her as long as sight allowed, "because I can't go anywhere without seeing you beside me."

She did not attend any of the Hours for the rest of the day. When Brites and Maria de Castro tried to get her to leave her "little house," she refused and locked her door. Shortly before the Grand Silence, a hand on the outer knob snapped her door open, and there stood Sister Maria de Mendonça, fragile, hunched, and wrinkled, her skin the color of a bruised fruit. She said, "Sister Mariana, I do believe I have injured my hand, thanks to your obtuse self-pity."

"How did you snap the lock? Brites was trying, and couldn't do it."

Sister Maria de Mendonça looked pleased. "My wish to see you must have made me a death-defying new woman. Alas, the change will not be permanent. May I sit?" Without waiting for an invitation, she pulled out the chair to Mariana's writing desk and eased herself onto it.

"You didn't see me at Vespers or in the refectory, and now here you are," said Mariana, who had never lost her aptitude for playing guess-the-answer games with the nun who had been her first teacher in the convent.

"Don't be absurd, Sister," said Maria de Mendonça, feeling a touch grey from the flare of strength it had taken to snap a lock. "One could not find Hannibal riding an elephant in the midst of the disorder in this convent. I heard that you saw Baltazar today. I thought you would be hiding. I am correct, I see."

"I shall die if anything happens to my brother."

"Sister, do you hear that noise? It is the sound of women sobbing. They are your sisters. Their brothers, uncles, and fathers — and for some of them, their husbands and sons — are dying. The end will be coming for many more of them. They are your brothers as well. I do not like that you are here brooding exclusively upon yourself and your family."

"I am not thinking of myself," said Mariana. "I am wishing that all of us could live somewhere else, far away."

"I suspect your father would not care to hear you speak like that."

"I cannot recall the last time my father was here to see me."

"I assume he is busy working to save this country you are so eager to flee."

"I have island fever. I want to go everywhere."

"If you desire to go everywhere, then you do not have island fever, not yet, my dearest."

"I do."

"You do not. You do not understand what island fever is, if that is how you define it. One day you will recognize what it is, and you will know if you have it or not. I must have been a poor teacher. Was I, Sister Mariana?"

Maria de Mendonça walked over to sit next to Mariana on the edge of her bed. Mariana flung her arms around her and muttered, "You're still a wonderful teacher. But it's true, what I said. I'm sorry if I sound selfish. If my brother dies, I shall have no reason to live."

Maria de Mendonça, with Mariana's head resting against her, smoothed down the black veil, as if patting Mariana's hair. "You do not need reasons. You need only to live, and that is homage to God. You are too luminous not to live, and I'm sorry, but you are too bright and you care too deeply not to exist in pain." She could feel Mariana's grin against her neck. "Will you sleep in peace tonight, Sister Mariana? Will you do as my mother used to advise me, and count angels?"

"I don't believe I've ever slept in peace."

It was Maria de Mendonça's turn to smile. "If I tell you I shall worry, if I think you are restless and unwell?"

"Then for you I shall sleep as if I am resting on the bottom of the blue ocean."

"Good heavens." Maria de Mendonça kissed the top of Mariana's head. "You are a vivid child. Knowing you has been the single most delightful surprise of my old age."

"May I call you Mother?"

"Though I am no longer the Abbess?"

"You are my second mother. Always."

"Then I shall be honored to break the rules with you. Good night, Sister Mariana. Our prayers must shout down the danger that is to come."

"Good night, Mother," said Mariana. "God, I promise you, shall hear my shouts."

How quickly the terror of the riot receded, and how swiftly the women settled back into their likes and dislikes, their ladder-climbing of the hours for each day.

Sister Angelica was outraged. If only that doddering Abbess would address the troubles here! The prefect, after his annual inspection, had issued a statement declaring, "This is not a convent, it is a grand concourse! Workmen coming and going, and constant visitors! The Franciscan nuns at Conceição do not remain behind the grille, nor pass messages through the stone round in the wall, but wander into the locutory. An unseemly number of soldiers come here for the food and drink, with which the kitchen seems quite ready to ply them."

As mistress of the kitchen, Sister Angelica de Noronha remained stung. Preventing people from raiding the pantry or preparing food in the "little houses"and carrying it out to guests was impossible. Manuel was far too bold about acquiring things for the nuns with handsome allowances.

Sister Ignez de São José looked over at the Palace of the Founders. A passageway connected the convent's upper choir with the locked-up palace, where the Dukes of Beja had resided for the last two hundred years, since the deaths of the king and queen who had established the convent and lived in the palace. The Queen would come from her house into the upper choir through her special corridor, to hear the music. When her husband died, she joined the Order.

Sister Ignez de São José, embarrassed to be entertaining such a frivolous thought in the aftermath of a riot, thought it a pity that the convent of Conceição could not acquire that property from the current Duke of Beja and fix his shabby garden. The convent's courtyard garden hardly existed. Shame on you! she scolded herself. After what has gone on in our midst! We are going to be overrun by Spanish soldiers anyway.

The next time she was in the main chapel, she focused on the *talhas*, the gilt-painted wood in twisted designs forming the reredos behind the altar. The *talhas* looked like golden iron. (Or heaven's idea of a garden trellis? Listen to her! She would perish for a fine garden.)

General Schomberg was pacing, his jaw jutting out with impatience as his friend Captain Salomon offered words to calm him. But who could be calm when this most recent trip to the palace in Lisbon had put maneuvers seriously behind schedule? The Spanish were poised to take Évora, and he was trying to cut them off, but it was going to be close.

He seethed to recall how this latest summons to Lisbon had also included Queen Mother Luisa ordering him to confront, face to face there in the throne room, the Portuguese generals who wanted to argue over protocol. The one from Beja, Diogo Gomes de Figueiredo, had been vocal in his insistence that since this was Portugal's war, a Portuguese commander had to have the last word.

Thank God for Captain Salomon, who had pointed out that volunteers were flooding in from as far as Italy for a chance to serve with Schomberg, and that this constant posturing and countermanding by the Portuguese generals, merely to show who was in charge, could be fatal to the war effort. The crown (or the Count of Castelo Melhor, who had declared himself the new Prime Minister — who could keep them all clear in one's mind?) should decide if they were serious about winning the war. They had to stop calling Schomberg into the palace to settle petty disputes.

Diogo Gomes de Figueiredo had sputtered about his opinion being anything but petty, but the Count of Castelo Melhor had indeed given full authority to Schomberg as supreme commander, and had pacified the Portuguese generals with new titles.

Such foolishness had taken up precious time. Schomberg and Captain Salomon had been forced to ride through the night and the entire next day and evening to return to their bivouac in the northwest of the Alentejan province. Schomberg fumed while walking back and forth in his tent. Nearby, his elite guardsmen slept in their blue jackets to facilitate dressing when called.

As often was the case, Captain Salomon was astounded by his friend's restless energy. "You think we'll win?"

Schomberg laughed. "I have no idea. I'm nearing the end of my career, my dear fellow, and I want a challenge."

The Captain drank water from a clay jug and passed some to Schomberg. "Sit down and relax, Frederic. You should remind me why we're bothering."

"Have you ever saved an entire country before? I have done many things, especially for France, but not that," said Schomberg. He drank a sizable draught, and drops stood round and tense on his moustache.

"You think the French King wants to invade this country? He wishes us to preserve the weakness of Portugal?"

"He refuses to let this territory stay Spanish. That is the entirety of my problem, and it is enough."

"Ludicrous Portuguese King. Did you glance into the room where they'd locked him up? Poor ghastly fool."

Schomberg waved his hand. "He's not even a figurehead. He won't interfere. It's that General Gomes de Figu— what was his name? I can't pronounce it. We'll be hearing from him again."

The Captain was surprised. "He won't obey the direct orders of his own throne?"

"He'll try to. But these people have a passion for their passion. They're known for it. His feelings will get the better of him. Then he and I will spar again, and I shall win, and what will his passion do? Increase. Now! I won't keep you long on these plains, dear fellow."

"Shouldn't we sleep?" asked Captain Salomon. Right now his wife would be dozing in their bed in Prussia.

"Sleep? Get out the maps, if you please."

They traced their fingers along the areas penetrated by the Spanish. If the Spanish flooded through Évora, the capital of the Alentejo, they would continue down through Beja and be positioned to sever the country in half. If they got through Beja, the war was lost. Schomberg and his army were trapped in the upper part of the Alentejan province and needed to start a dart-like march before dawn, with full artillery, to block the enemy at Évora. If the Spanish could not be stopped there, Schomberg would have to swing a net to the south of them, fanning out to break up the assault that was going to tighten in a circle around the throat of the nation. If the Spanish completed this stranglehold, they would pour west from Beja, in a flow like blood out of the conquered country's neck, to chop the crown off Lisbon's lifeless head. Captain Salomon commented that the stars were seldom as blazing as they were on this night, and it might be a good sign if one were inclined to superstition.

Nothing in the stars indicated that many months of thrust and parry, without resolution, were ahead of them.

"You plan never to speak to me again?" Francisco da Costa Alcoforado asked his wife.

Leonor shook her head to indicate that no, she meant every word of her lecture, especially her final statement that from this moment forward, she would neither address him nor any soul on the earth — not anyone — until he relented from his insistence that their own daughter pay for household goods. She refused to allow Ana Maria to suffer any more than necessary. Being married to Rui de Melo Lôbo was trial enough. Leonor had been secretly giving money to Ana Maria for months, and Francisco had found out. His objection was pronounced, and Leonor recognized that her only chance of winning would be to use the tactics of her native plains — silence. She knew that he wanted to cut a hole in Rui's coin purse and start a trickle that would divest him until he was worthless. Certainly she did not object to that. What she would not tolerate was the effect this was having on Ana Maria. With the wolves of war scrabbling about, a battle over the cost of flour and oil was madness.

"This will tax you more than me," said Francisco.

Tax indeed. She admired his cleverness in tossing out a money word, and regretted that she could not congratulate his skill.

"I'm going to the mint. The presses are coming in today," he said.

She nodded. She kissed him, and put her weight into a joyful wave as he left. Though hardly anyone believed it, she loved him fantastically. It made sense that their disagreements should assume large proportions.

Bastiana was in the kitchen, her hands in some clabber from ewe's milk, pressing the curds and letting the whey seep between her fingers. Leonor turned aside. If anything could be said to look like nausea turned into an action, it was the handling of whey, sickly-colored, gruel-thin. She was certain she had developed this notion from doing so much cheese-making (that unconquerable urge to mold food out of nothing and store it ready for the young) whenever she was pregnant. An artificial bloom of morning sickness terrorized her. Her childbearing years were over, and sometimes (quite a lot lately) she was shaken by the feel of the early days of carrying a child, a false chill blown in her direction from the land of the dead. Bastiana was peering at her, asking if the Senhora needed to sit down.

She shook her head at Bastiana. No thank you. Bastiana was the sort who would understand a comment like "Whey looks like nausea" and Leonor was angry at herself for vowing to swallow every single word to everyone in order to win an argument about household money.

She walked down the hallway to her mother's bedroom and entered with her feet loudly hitting the floor, not giving up the hope of waking her mother out of her coma. Air went in and out of the dormant lungs of Maria Alves. Leonor kept a shawl around her mother's shoulders, and often grasped both ends and pulled Maria Alves into a sitting posture to prevent her insides from flattening into a map, though she remained so fat that Leonor would laugh to herself — *she's as gigantic as the landscape*. Knocked-out like the spent country we live in.

Now that Leonor was sworn to silence, there was an entire litany that she could think to (was bursting to) tell this breathing shape of her mother.

I got my stubbornness from you, mused Leonor. It looks as if I'll be mute forever. Yes, Mama, I'm blaming you. Do please wake up and crow. Do you remember that hideous conversation we had almost half a century ago? I've decided that you thought you were doing me a kindness.

I think you wanted to make me fearless, and I am.

When Leonor was five, her mother had instructed her to begin at once to take care to make her mind clear, because she must have her life in order before she died.

"I'm not going to die," Leonor had said.

"I'm sorry to disappoint you while you're young," Maria Alves replied. "But yes, you will. Everyone does."

"I'm me, Mama. I'm not everyone."

"You're my angel, my acorn, my baby bird, my darling, my One More Than Everything. But you're going to die. I don't believe in lying to children about that. You won't have to worry about it for a long time, though. I'll lead the way."

Leonor recalled thinking, rather guiltily, that her mother could do as she pleased (she always did), but Leonor should be permitted to make up her own mind about this death business. She would have none of it, especially not if it entailed following her bossy mother's lead.

Not long afterwards, a chest with goods from India was delivered to her parents' warehouse in Beja, and her mother shrieked that no one was to spring the catch. According to a story going around, a Lisbon merchant who dealt in Indian cloth had recently unlocked a chest with bolts of fabric from Calcutta, and the air from inside the chest killed him instantly. The theory was that the exotic vapors had become concentrated in the chest during the overseas journey, with fatal results. Leonor's parents decided to face their dilemma by opening the chest in stages, allowing any poisoned air to dissipate in measured exhalations. A calculated risk was worth it. A fortune was waiting to be made in these imported silks. Each day over a two-week span, Leonor's mother or father braced the lid of the chest one degree higher, using different-sized wedges. At last they removed cloth so smooth and glorious that Leonor gasped. It looked like painted water.

Hundreds of chests later, as her parents grew wealthy, Leonor heard an increasing number of comments about death, as in, "Huh! That Mendes family thinks it's going to live forever," or "I wouldn't want to have to talk my way into heaven with that much money sewn into my hem." She asked her older brother and sister for the truth about dying, but they were not giving her the answers she wanted. It occurred to Leonor that no one was one thousand years old. This pointed to her mother being right, which made her almost as sad as having to die and make room for new people.

The logical solution was to deal with the inevitable at once. Five years alive was about as good as fifty. If she had to die, it was a good plan to be killed by exoticism and beauty. When the next chest from India was delivered, she waited until her father left it with a tooth-sized wedge in its opening. She threw open the lid, and inhaled deeply. Nothing. She got out a bolt of scarlet cloth, pressed it to her nose, and waited. The lushness of India continued to spare her. She spread the silk on the floor and writhed on it, flailing her arms and legs to stir up the vapors. Nothing. Instead of death, a remarkable happiness was allowing her to fly on a carpet of color. She imagined the hooking smoke of frankincense tickling her skin, and ivory-hued oxen bringing this cloth to market. Rapture overwhelmed her. Her mother had warned her about death, but not that a deliberate act of defying it might invite unspeakable joy.

As a grown woman, she lay upon white cloth for her husband, and thought — happiness. Oh, it is the easiest thing in the world to be miserable, and I'm equal to the infinitely more demanding task of being happy.

Today Leonor found a sheet of white silk to slip beneath her mother, and she thought, Happiness, Mama. Why don't we melt ourselves down to this one word? We never got along, but can we agree upon this?

"Well!" A voice she hated interrupted her reverie. "The grand ladies of the house."

Leonor eased her mother back down and faced Rui, his scarred face wrinkled in a grin. "You plan to roll her up in a sheet and drag her to the party tonight?"

She glared at him. Her vow not to speak might rupture her insides.

"Let's see. What have I done this time? I didn't come home last night. Is that why I'm getting the silent treatment? I'm used to it from my wife. This her idea?"

Bastard. My daughter is in bed because you've made her pregnant again. Can you read my face? thought Leonor. Of course you can't. Murderous bastard. Old-looking, too.

"Don't think I don't know you're on his side. You want money from me?" He took some coins from his pocket and cast them at Leonor's feet. "Go ahead. Pick them up. Still won't speak? Think that'll drive me mad, and I'll leave? I like women who know how to shut up. By the way, the coins are from the new mint. Your husband's. That's right, I stole them. You think I don't know that you and he want me to get killed, so that you can pocket what I have? What my father set up for me? I'm entitled to a few of your crumbs."

Even if she allowed herself to speak, Leonor would not inform him that he was mistaken, that she was speechless to force Francisco to be more benign to Ana Maria (and, by default, Rui, but that part of it couldn't be helped). Ingrate. She picked up the coins, and slid them inside the mule slipper that she removed from her foot. She stood up to her full height and threw the weighted mule as hard as she could at Rui's skull. It hit him on the wounded side of his face.

"God! Jesus! You mad woman!" he yelled.

The shoe clattered to the floor, and the coins spilled out around him. While he stormed off muttering curses, Leonor could have sworn that the features of her comatose mother lightened.

When the hour arrived for the party to celebrate the opening of the mint, Leonor showed Luís and Bastiana how to convey her mother to the carriage that would bring them into town. Leonor was busy corralling her children and grandchildren, and wrapping Ana Maria in blankets while indicating, silently, that some air would do her good and be salutary for the new baby inside her. Ana Maria, holding her gut, looking at her swollen legs, asked her mother what she and Papa were fighting about this time. Leonor regretted that she could not explain.

The townspeople gathered — no one was going to violate Francisco's orders to appear — but they were subdued. The ceremony involved all of them constructing the final wall of the mint. Frightened and wanting to hide, they milled around, awaiting directions. Though almost a year had passed since the trouble with the English, they had never recovered. They were like fowls, with one feather plucked out every day for months, giving them a tortured, gradual sense of exposure. Francisco was determined that when the Spanish invaded (no one said "if" anymore, but "when"), they should find the citizens of Beja bustling about, not cowering and waiting to be slaughtered in their beds, but with a mint in spasms of production, flooding the landscape with the coin of rebellion. Victory was in the details, he was fond of saying – good horses, good biscuits, well-made ladders, Eastern gunpowder, swords polished and blessed, fine clothing to raise their moods, parties, their own coinage, plans. They must live as victors. He was getting tired of telling them the obvious. Where were their guitars? He called out orders about finishing the wall and hammered a plaque to the front of the mint that said "AD 1663 Beja/Pax Vobiscum/Ora Pro Nobis."

Barrels of olive oil, crowned with flames, gave off light and heat. Everyone handed around skins of wine and wide trays of roast pork. Leonor inclined her head and nodded when she was greeted. She ignored people saying, "Wonder what Francisco and she are arguing about now." Evening was upon her. God, wild as a child and with a child's enchantment with repetition, was painting His prompt black line to trace the evening contour of trees, arches, berths, and subjects. Everything else He filled in with bruise-colors, or orange.

Leonor settled onto the ground next to her mother and Ana Maria. Ana Maria's children, eight-year-old Inês, seven-year-old Luís, and her three-year-old twins, Caetana and Francisco de Melo, were doing their best to carry stones to their proper places in the wall. They tended to be confused children, and it made them earnest and given to nightmare. Leonor's youngest, three-year-old Maria Peregrina, was dipping a ladle into a water pail to bring drinks to her father, and Leonor was pleased to see that he would stop and drink, and pick her up and proclaim, "She's the best worker here!" Peregrina was delighted with herself. Francisco da Costa – Leonor allowed herself a moment of purely gazing at him – was over sixty, and a miracle to behold, killing himself to appear certain of victory. She knew he was more troubled than he appeared. She pushed aside a regret about their silent battle. The fact that he was anxious did not mean that she should not fight for her daughter. But she looked at him with compassion. He often sat in his solarium with a brush swollen with Chinese ink held over a page. He was waiting for God to send him a drawing. He could not force it; his hand would have to move without him controlling it. He was hoping for a divine diagram on how to end the war before Portugal ran out of money.

Since God had not sent a revelation about this, her husband had decided that he himself would paint the countryside with new money. There was not sufficient time to wait for God.

The Marquês de Niza and Dom Joaquim Ferreira de Fontes were issuing instructions on applying mortar, urging everyone to hurry so that they could be done and drink into the night. When someone underscored the pointlessness of building a wall that was going to get broken with a cannonball, or manufacturing money they would not live to use, the Marquês sentenced them to hoisting a double load of stones.

Peregrina dipped the ladle into the water pail again and raced it to her brother Miguel, who was trying to give orders like his father. He told Peregrina to stop bothering him. Leonor's face contorted. Fourteen, tall, rope-like — but stern. Francisco the Younger was eight, almost as competent, but without the hard edge. When Peregrina brought the ladle to him, the water spilled out, but Francisco knelt, pretended to drink the water out of the dust, and made Peregrina laugh. Peregrina — the Pilgrim. If Leonor and her husband were taken prisoner, they would not survive, but Peregrina might be spared long enough to feel the inspiration of her name, and escape, and roam.

Catarina and Bastiana were preparing cauldrons of stew. Adorable, forgotten (by almost everyone, but not by Leonor), ebullient Catarina. She had taken such good care of Leonor and Ana Maria when they were both in bed, Leonor expecting Peregrina and Ana Maria waiting for her twins. A less remarkable girl than Catarina would have become drab. She knew how to make every motion, the simplest, most forgettable of motions, bend instinctively towards ceremony. On the dinner trays for her bedridden mother and sister, she would set serviettes folded in the shapes of swans. She checked their hair for lice and soothed almond oil onto their foreheads. Catarina's own hair was light and messy. She did good imitations of Dom Joaquim Ferreira de Fontes and, though she was barely fifteen, had managed the cleaning of linens, the supervising of meals, and the butchering of hogs. She cared for the horses and the garden without appearing aggrieved or saintly. She recognized that the times were not conducive and her father was not receptive to the idea of her being married, though she was at the proper age to expect a future. Yet her eyes did not narrow piggishly from trying to guess what he had in mind for her. Catarina was not waiting for anything in order to define her existence. That was how rare she was.

Some hours before the wall's completion, Leonor felt a heaviness in her middle. The words she had swallowed up to now were gestating inside her like a final, impossible child, one formed out of her unspoken sentences. Words made flesh. The noises of the stones piling up grew far away. Ana Maria, bundled next to her, was dreaming, and Leonor decided to join her. That was the gift that the mind gave to women who were with child, a bizarre whirl of fantasies and wishes that descended out of nowhere and ordered the body to submit. The Portuguese language was generous in supplying a single word for such a condition — *entojo*.

She heard the crick-crick of frogs. They were saying, Why are you indulging in the fantasies of *entojo*, Leonor Mendes? You will have no more children.

My children are eternal, she informed the frogs.

She opened her eyes to see Rui, drunk, holding a struggling cat by its neck. "I'll make a deal with you, grand lady. If you speak, I won't do anything to this tiger here," he said.

Ana Maria, awakening, sat up and said, "Rui. Put that cat down."

Catarina slapped his arm. "Leave that animal alone. Rui!"

"I'll leave it alone when your mother talks. I want to hear her say, 'You're right, Rui. You're welcome to everything in our household, including our daughter.'"

Ana Maria struggled up, tried to pull the cat out of his arms.

"Rui, Rui! Stop it!" Her punches made him laugh.

Leonor did not move. She kept her stare steady and gestured at her daughters to stop doing exactly what the beast wanted. She was going to teach this man a lesson about what she and her children were made of.

"Say, 'I hate you, Rui.' I'll even take that," he said. He grabbed the cat's tail and swung it overhead. Ana Maria screamed.

Leonor stared.

"I'm going to get Papa," said Catarina.

Leonor shook her head, No. This one is mine.

Rui threw the cat up in the air and caught it. Its fur stood in bristled ruffs, and Leonor refused to move. Ana Maria begged Rui to put the animal down. They went back and forth, with Catarina grabbing at the cat, Ana Maria crying, Caetana stamping her feet, and Rui saying, Talk, talk, talk, and flinging the animal, while Leonor stared through him, until the cat screeched in the air and landed, its neck broken, in Rui's arms.

The next day, Rui brought Leonor a bouquet of azaleas. He set a prized bottle of port outside her room. He was struck dumb around her. You see, Leonor hoped she had said to her daughters, I'm not sentimental about an animal. I reduced the famously brave Rui to a buffoon. Oh, brave man, animal killer. It was worth seeing him disgusted with himself, watching him learn that we shall never, never do anything by his command. That is my gift to my husband. We have now taken over the Lôbos' power. Should Rui dare attempt to break any of you when I am not there to protect you, merely hiss in his ear, "The cat."

People spoke in low voices of Leonor's victory. She might as well have said, I'm the only one to call a Lôbo a coward and survive, and I didn't even bother with words to do it. I'm tougher than anyone here. That's why I'm married to Francisco da Costa Alcoforado, who rode down out of the mountains of the north, the man I began to search for from my childhood, without even knowing it, the man who has dedicated his every breath to the plotting of a way to live forever.

Mariana leaned out a window in the convent, straining to hear the distant party to celebrate the mint. A mist bathed her face, and she whispered, "Vovó, wake up! It's the kind of night you love, full of the ripped clothing of ghosts. Can you hear me? What is it that we kiss, but never adore? Is it our fates, Vovó?"

She recalled the arguments that her father and grandmother would have about where the future of the country rested – with noblemen like him, or with merchants like Vovó and her husband, who became rich as middlemen with imported goods, lacquered chests, spices, elixirs from China, cloth and gems from India. It was the businessmen, not the nobles who built fancy monasteries, who would became wealthy in days to come, Vovó maintained, but she never pushed Mariana's father too far.

"Wake up, Vovó," prayed Mariana. "Wake up and argue with him some more. He pretended you made him angry, but he loved your debates. You and Saint Clare are my heroines of the night."

Saint Clare, the founder of the Order, was locked into a room by her father but clawed her way out one night to run to Saint Francis, her inspiration. He and his followers met her with torches to celebrate the night and her devotion. Mariana adored this story. She imagined Vovó awake, wearing her leaf-pin of pearls, bearing fire, and removing a key from her sash while saying, "Come, my One More Than Everything. Now is your time of escape and riddles."

A tremor shook Maria Alves, and some knots in her spine loosened, the last spots where her muscles refused to forgive her husband. Where had the last year gone? How had 1662 dissolved into 1663? Six pinpricks of malice towards him remained in her white hair. Her work was nearly finished.

Who was invading her room? It was her daughter Leonor, with Peregrina clinging to her nightgown. Catarina, Ana Maria, and Francisco the Younger were behind her, and Miguel, demanding to know why they had to participate in a worthless game. Inês, Caetana, Francisco de Melo, and Luís, Ana Maria's children, tagged along. A midnight mist was rolling in. They crowded around the window to watch it. Ana Maria said, "It's Sebastião weather, Vovó!" No wonder Maria Alves felt gladdened. She was a devoted Sebastianite. Every good mourner for King Dom Sebastião longed for the watery shroud of mist. Over a century ago, at the battle of Alcácer-Quibir, young King Sebastião led a march in which thousands of Portuguese died. His own body was never found. Two years later, Spain took over Portugal. Now Sebastianism was a conspiracy of memory. People prayed that the King, the ultimate soul-not-at-rest, would ride in on the mist, returning to save them. His folly had wasted money and enabled Spain to come in. He had fashioned himself as an intolerant leader with his anti-Moorish war-making, but that was forgotten. Most Sebastianites – wistful, sad, delighted for an excuse to go outdoors and drink – would be out in force in this mist, awaiting a vision.

"May we go back to bed now?" asked Miguel.

"Mama," said Catarina, "is King Sebastião going to come? I can't see him."

"Another one of our stupid legends," said Miguel.

"Move your elbow, idiot," said Francisco the Younger.

"Shush," said Inês.

It was murdering Leonor not to speak to her children. She wanted to proclaim, Look at the night! It's a shame we have to sleep, and miss any night. Sebastião, I know that we call you The Longed-For. I do believe that your mist is concealing my Mariana and Baltazar from harm. Soothe my husband's brow. Here are my mother, my children, my grandchildren. Our freedom might end tomorrow, but tonight we exist as we wish. In all my life I have seldom felt, as I do tonight, that all I have longed for is mine.

What arrived when the mist lifted by morning was not the vision of a savior King, but a half-starved messenger riding into town, carrying the banner of the King of Spain. Most of Beja was asleep after laboring at the mint, although Francisco da Costa Alcoforado was at his alderman's office in town, seeing to the transfer of livestock to feed the troops.

The messenger rode through the square without incident. He had no trouble finding Francisco, nor in knowing that this was the man he sought. The messenger took pride in his instincts. Look how this white-templed man was staring at him, as if he knew that the future contained nothing but ambush.

"I come with a message from the King of Spain," began the boy.

"I did not give you permission to speak," said Francisco.

"The King of Spain gives me permission."

"I do not see him here."

"You shall, sir. Or rather you shall see his men. We have seized Évora, and the King commands you to hand over the keys to your city. It's best to surrender, sir. We have the capital of your province. It is impossible that you shall not fall even more swiftly."

Francisco did not change expression. He had been negotiating for a year to bring the English troops back, to protect against this moment. He was alone with this disgusting boy, whose officers lacked the courtesy of bothering to write down the terms of surrender. They had seen no need to send a General or the King and his guard. Francisco was gravely offended. "I have a message for you now," he said, and pulled his dagger from his boot and his sword from his scabbard. With an agility that shocked the messenger, he leaped forward and pinned him to the wall with both points of steel.

"We treat our prisoners well, sir," said the frightened emissary, his back rigid against the wall, his chin flattening into his neck.

"Ride back and tell your King to come in person to claim the keys to my city!" Francisco shouted. "Beja will not be delivered without combat. Your King will have to pry the keys out of my cold, dead fist." He pulled the dagger and sword out of the wall, and the boy ran to his horse and hurried towards the plains.

Francisco rode to the mint and found Rui snoring in a corner. A woman was sleeping with him. Francisco kicked him hard on his thigh, and when Rui reached for his sword and sat bolt upright, Francisco said, "Évora has fallen."

Rui was on his feet, racing to where his brothers, Cristóvão and Bartolomeu, had passed out on the floor. He kicked them, and when they saw his face and noticed Francisco uncovering the crates of gunpowder stored under straw piles, they knew that history had turned. Within moments, everyone in Beja heard the news. Francisco's son Miguel wanted to ring the bells in the tower, but his father said there was no time for anything but following the plan of action. The soap-maker and his wife carried a stockpile of muskets out of their attic and into the street. The butcher rolled a cannon out of his house. Women pulled bandages from their cupboards and drew water out of wells. The Lôbos rode through the byways, crying for everyone to bring the swords and pikes they had been hiding to the north wall of the city, by order of Francisco da Costa Alcoforado, where they were going to stand, and wait, and fight, and die. Francisco chose the exact center of the parapet on the top of the north wall, facing the route the Spanish would take.

Cartloads of munitions were brought to the bulwark. Rui, Cristóvão, and Bartolomeu flanked Francisco, staring with him into the horizon. Leonor was at the foot of the north wall, right below her husband like a sentinel on the parapet. She wrapped her cape around Peregrina and Francisco the Younger. Ana Maria and Catarina huddled near her, along with their slumbering Vovó. They watched over Inês, Luís, Caetana, and the littlest Francisco. The entire town was arrayed from the inside of the wall outward, filling the square. Miguel climbed onto the wall to be with his father, despite his mother's gestures that he stay with her. She would not break her vow of silence. If anything, now was a time beyond speech. Every time her husband told her to take a carriage back to their estate, she shook her head no. If they were going to die, they must not die apart.

Before the assembly, as the wind snapped his cape, Francisco beheld his wife and said, "Leonor, I do not believe we shall win. Therefore I would like some victory to be awarded to one of us. You. It is futile to promise this now, but I absolve my daughter and son-in-law of any household expenses. No point in paying my corpse. You win. I would concede everything to hear your lovely voice before I die."

She lifted her chin towards him, shocked that he had relented. This was unexpected. Words stuck in her throat, and as the town watched, what emerged from her was a whimper for Mariana.

Francisco said that she was safer where she was, and besides, knowing Mariana as he did, he pitied any soldier who tried to harm her.

When she said that Beringel was not far enough to protect Baltazar, Francisco said, "Baltazar is a fool, and God watches after fools."

"He is beloved of my heart!" Leonor shouted.

"I am the beloved of your heart!" roared Francisco.

"Yes, you are," she called out, and did not care that everyone in town could hear. "Yes, Francisco! You are the beloved of my heart."

Now it did not matter if the world should fall asunder.

As evening approached, neither he nor the Lôbos moved. They never sat. When Ana Maria brought them food, they refused it. Mutterings about surrender could be heard. Why did they have to die, because the Alcoforados and the Lôbos were headstrong? Who cared if they became Spanish? Who had a stomach for food?

When this murmur reached the top of the wall, Rui bellowed, "I'll personally run through anyone who wants to surrender and toss his worthless body to the dogs."

"Hurry up and bring out the wine!" called Francisco. "You're not dead yet."

When the townspeople were slow to obey, he shouted, "Let them find you celebrating! Hurry up! Prepare to live your last moment as free men and women."

A few people ate, and some danced, but Francisco did not alter his stance. Rui's jaw was set. Leonor was singing to her children so that they would not die in terror. She was free to pour out words. How glorious words and sounds became, released from vows of silence.

Sister Ignez de São José was gazing out from the balcony near the window that faced the road to Mértola when the blacksmith dashed through the square and called the alarm up to her. The soldiers guarding the convent jumped to attention and rolled catapults into place.

Sister Angelica de Noronha, cutting fringe borders on tissue paper squares to set below cheese tarts, heard the cry, "Évora is gone!" and grabbed the tile counter to steady herself. Sister Brites de Freire, witnessing this, noted that it was a pity they were about to be massacred now that she found herself somewhat liking her superior.

Sister Beatriz Maria de Resende ran from her cell to the choir. Although the pages were milky under her failing eyes, she forced them to guide her in playing the "Ave Maria" on the organ. May the music hover in the air over what would soon be the slain bodies of the nuns, her friends.

Sister Mariana, upon hearing that her father was stationed on the parapet of the city, was seized with such a confusion of emptiness, pride, and longing for her mother that she went searching for Sister Maria de Mendonça and found her in the infirmary. "Mother? You're here again? Why haven't you made clear how sick you've been?"

Maria de Mendonça was unable to push herself upright in bed, but insisted that Mariana sit with her. "I would have had to confess, as I am doing now —" she bent her head forward so that

Sister Juliana de Matos, the infirmarian, could not hear "– that I am afraid." The admission made her cough. Mariana held out a handkerchief to catch the blood.

"My. By the time the Spanish arrive to cut my throat, I won't have any blood left. I am not afraid of dying," said Maria de Mendonça. "I am afraid of leaving when there is much more to be done. Isn't that arrogant of me to judge myself indispensable?"

Sister Juliana de Matos came to her bedside. "Sister Mariana, leave this woman in peace. You should be in the chapel, praying the last rites and taking Viaticum."

"Let her pray with me," said Maria de Mendonça. "Father confessor came and went before I could admit to him my selfishness in wanting company. Shall we call it my final wish?"

Though Sister Juliana de Matos made it clear that she did not approve, she left them alone.

"Did I ever explain the term *mouvement* to you, Sister Mariana?" asked Maria de Mendonça.

"Mother, Sister Juliana is right. You need to rest."

"I need to teach you the things I forgot to mention. The word is French. I know your French is fair, Mariana. Can you guess the meaning of *mouvement*? No? It describes the automatic raptures that escape the control of our will and consciousness. Such a holy notion."

"It is, Mother."

"It is the single best word I know of in the universe," said Maria de Mendonça. "Motion and emotion sweeping someone away. Ecstasy unplanned for. I feel a touch better, do you know? I've explained a beautiful word. I'm trying to remember everything I've ever meant to teach you. I had meant to wait for the right time to teach you such a word, and – oh, I don't know what 'right time' means anymore."

Mariana wiped the blood from Maria de Mendonça's mouth. "I treasure every word from you. You must be well, and give me many more."

Maria de Mendonça nodded, and lay back on her pillow. Giving Mariana a conspirator's look, she said, "Thanks to you, I can consider myself a good teacher. You made me that. I am lucky."

Mariana heard distress echo through the convent. She had seen nuns arrayed along the balcony, waiting for death. Where was

Baltazar? How perfect it would be if he rode in to save her. But he did not.

Then — nothing. Nothing happened. Into the hollow of tremendous waiting — nothing. Night, and night's end.

Night losing out to morning.

Mariana awoke, startled. She saw Sister Juliana washing Maria de Mendonça and saying that it looked as if she had died to cheat the Spanish. Mariana said no, Sister Maria de Mendonça was alive. Sister Juliana stared at Mariana, took Mariana's hands, folded them over her chest, and said, "She lives in there, in you, yes. That is all that remains, I'm afraid."

Mariana walked from the infirmary with her hands arrested in that position and went to the balcony on the upper story. With her hands remaining crossed over her chest, she looked towards the empty plains. The breeze was supremely ordinary. *Mouvement*? Mother, I forgot to ask how a bloody world can sustain any beautiful words at all.

Brites found her and exclaimed that she had been searching everywhere to bring her the wonderful news. General Schomberg's compatriot, the Count of Vila Flor, had stormed into Ameixal and defeated the Spanish in a tumultuous battle. They had been stopped in the last possible town before they would have marched in to take Beja.

"Your father is still standing on the wall," said Brites. "But now it isn't because he was going to be the first to face the enemy. It's because everyone is cheering him. Mariana, are you listening?" Brites was shocked to discover that her friend's hands were folded like welded iron over her chest and that she was trembling. A shower of tears was arrested on her face, suspended, as if exhausted with natural laws.

Leonor was surprised that she could feel serene while waiting for Beja to be destroyed, only to collapse afterwards. Her city and family were saved, at least for now, but her womb closed, her arms and legs stiffened, and the hinges on her eyelids broke. She was almost fifty. Was her body hardening from the sorrow of not being able to have any more children, or from having had them? She fought an urge to cry out for her mother. People suggested that her husband did not understand her, but she knew otherwise. Once while his ink-swollen brush was poised over a page as he waited for God to send him a picture, he had entered her bedroom with a drawing of her lying naked on cloth and said, "Nothing was sent, so I painted a picture of you." That was the night they conceived Baltazar.

Tonight he came into her room holding the pages of her updated will, completed the day before, and said, "What is the meaning of this? Do you think we survived the threat of a massacre for you to give up?"

"I was prepared to die then," said Leonor. "I'm not afraid of the peace of heaven now."

"I forbid you to die."

She laughed, and so did he, but the effort not to weep made the lines stand out on his forehead. When they were first married, he brushed her hair every night. He had not done it in years, but now he took her brush and combed upward along her neck and to the scalp, across the grain, then with it. Lulled, she put her head on his chest. It had been forever since she had done that, too. It seemed a gesture for the young and the old, overlooked during the years between, that amazement when one listened profoundly, head on chest, to rhythmic breathing, to serenity, and thought, *bound to you, bound to you, to you.* If she lay back and was still, she might grow thin and with as many landmarks as a country. Leonor as the plains. Leonor writhing on the silken earth. Her shining, brushed hair was smooth as a river. She could lie earthbound and look up and see her husband fighting for her, and her children racing across the terrain of her, saying, "Don't worry, Mama. We're going to go exploring in the grove, and we'll come back!" If she were their country, they could not leave her. Her chest heaved up with a ferocity that almost cured her when Francisco said, "With all my heart and all my soul, I love you. Don't surrender. Don't give up now. Peace is almost with us."

She had been hearing that rumor for half her life. She was a country, and exhausted, and she could no longer wait to be at peace.

It would have been fitting had she left the world upon hearing Francisco finally reiterate that he loved her, but the modern age had ruined the niceties of timing. She lived several more days. Though he attended her faithfully, he was not with her in her last moment. Some people remarked that Leonor did her best, out of instinct, to ensure that her beloved Mariana, in losing both her first mother at the convent and her real mother at about the same time, would be inconsolable for one era instead of two. Others said that Francisco da Costa Alcoforado was doing everything so that he and his family lived forever and was angry that his wife would not comply. Shame on you, replied others. He stood on the wall, and in front of countless witnesses allowed her to win an argument. Call him what you like. His loves are too fierce for most of us to understand.

He was off receiving a royal letter commending Beja's resistance and promising fortifications when Leonor rose from her bed and went to lie next to her mother. "Mama, stay here longer and rest," she whispered, "but allow me to do you a favor. For once, I'll lead the way for you."

Mariana took a step backward. "Catarina?" she said. "When did you grow up?"

"Mariana," said a girl in a blue, ankle-length skirt and a neat blue bodice. She carried a green reed basket covered with a white cloth. The sky-blue bonnet on her head framed her round face. Her skin was as fair as Papa's, and her hair was light brown. She was holding the hand of a little girl in a bright red coat and flat calf-toned boots that she was testing for sound against the tiled floor of the locutory. The fingers of her free hand were in her mouth. "Peregrina, say hello to your older sister. Do you remember that I told you her name is Mariana?" said Catarina.

The little girl stared.

"She's afraid of nuns, but don't worry," said Catarina.

"Nun?" said Mariana. Was that what she looked like?

Catarina drew aside the cloth over the basket and offered Mariana an almond cake. "Have you eaten?" she asked softly.

Mariana fled. No one gave anyone bad news without first inquiring if that person had a full stomach. She crawled into bed in her "little house." Workmen outside were dragging blocks of stones to build a new wing. The hours passed but hung before her. Light taps and heavy thuds combined into an odd music coaxed from the stones, with bass grunts and sighs from the men heaving them into place, that would not allow her to sleep, and hunger started up inside her, first as a trickling of want and then with a raw gushing need. Running into Catarina in the refectory could be risked. It was a challenge to locate a particular person there. Like looking for a nun in a nun-stew, Brites once remarked.

The smoking torches high inside the refectory sent black curls, like a disappearing ink, around the nuns jammed in at the long tables. Mariana glanced about and did not see Catarina.

Sister Angelica de Noronha scowled at Mariana's lateness while dishing up some bread soup for her and jabbing into it a crust of corn-and-wheat bread to use as a spoon. Crisp pieces of *encharcada* – egg yolks enriched with sugar and cinnamon – waited on plates for the nuns who were finished.

Mariana wedged herself along the east wall, between Sister Dolores and Sister Maria de São Francisco, when she spotted her sister Catarina, in the white habit without scapulars given to postulants and novices, seated at a table with Peregrina on her lap. Catarina was guiding Peregrina in using the bread-spoon while also gazing at Mariana, as she probably had been from the moment Mariana entered the refectory. Mariana glared at her, sticking the corn-and-wheat bread paddle into the gruel to say, My stomach is empty. Don't bring me any grief.

Catarina gestured in a way that said, Eat. Eat, Mariana. Please. Is it my fault that I have to tell you something? Then she reached up and slowly drew the fingers of both hands downward, the length of her face, leaving her eyes shut in their wake.

A death mask.

Nautilus shapes were carved through the air as sleeves swooped and gestures passed the wordless gossip that the Alcoforado sisters were silently speaking. Someone had died.

Sister Francisca Freire signaled Mariana with a thump to her chest that said, Eat, Mariana. Have courage. Find out the truth.

Mariana chewed and swallowed some bread, set her soup bowl on the floor, and gestured in front of her breasts, pretending they were gigantic, signifying, Is it Vovó?

Catarina shook her head, and they instantly covered their mouths to keep from laughing. The legend of Vovó's bosom wedge lived on.

The lips of Sister Michaella dos Anjos flattened in disapproval. Here and there, nuns put down their bowls and watched.

Abbess Joana de Lacerda clapped her hands. She was not unkind, but she had that brand of weariness that made a person collapse into a chair for no discernible reason, crying, "Ai, life! Ai, my God!" as if she had scaled a mountain. So hard to do anything in this country! So much dust of the past like invisible clods on our shoulders!

The Abbess made a spooning gesture with one hand and pointed to Catarina and Mariana, to indicate that they should be eating, nothing else. Pantomimes *were not* the same as silence.

The gaze between Mariana and Catarina transmitted an agreement that they must wait for these others to go back to their supper.

They waited.

Quaking with fear, Mariana touched her side, then pulled a clenched fist to her breast-level. Papa, drawing his sword.

Catarina made her eyes go from side to side, as a head might do to indicate, No, not Papa.

I can't do this, said Mariana's imploring look. I can't.

Catarina cupped her hands around Peregrina's head and turned it gently to face Mariana.

No. Mariana's teeth ground at the insides of her cheeks until she tasted blood. No.

Catarina's lip shook, but she held Peregrina's face towards Mariana, who looked towards the Abbess, hoping she would clap again, clap this away and denounce Catarina as a liar.

Peregrina had Mama's eyes, Mama's hair, Mama's engaged look. It was Mama. Catarina was telling her that Mama was dead. Mama had shrunk to the size of a baby, a new life, as if to say, Here's a baby who's my double to start over for me, I myself won't outlive this war. Goodbye, Mariana! Goodbye! Goodbye! Your Mama sends kisses up one of your arms and down the other. Do you remember at parties how you and I overdid the powdering of our faces and said we were turning into ghosts? It is not so difficult to be one. Be as strong as you always are, Mariana.

Before the Grand Silence that evening, Sister Leonor Henriques explained to Mariana that the Order had agreed to take not only Catarina but Peregrina, though she required a special dispensation because of her age. Ana Maria had offered to take care of everyone and run the house, but that was too much since the arrival of her fifth child. The noise of stones that Mariana heard was the building of an addition commissioned by her father to honor her mother, lovely apartments, where his girls were to be housed. Peregrina would stay in one of them with Catarina, next to the "little house" that Mariana would have by herself – even nicer than the one she had now. "Your Mama would want all of you together in such an impressive new place," said Sister Leonor Henriques. The Abbess would choose other nuns from noble families for the remaining places.

Dear Ana Maria,

I cannot bring myself to pick up Peregrina. She looks so like Mama! I walk away when she cries. It is a relief that many of the nuns treat her as they would a doll and carry her everywhere. Catarina gives her child-sized tasks as they work in the garden, where she is assigned. This is not as idyllic as it sounds; the garden has never been well tended.

What do you remember of Mama? All at once, it is the unknown that I long for. How life storms on, with no heed to any of my desires!

I am sorry to hear that matters between Rui and Papa are as bad as ever. Congratulations on the birth of little Bartolomeu. I hope he brings you the comfort you have grievously earned. Please cease condemning yourself for not visiting of late.

One thousand embraces, from your constant
Mariana

Catarina Alcoforado possessed a vegetable patience. She was able to draw water out of the well and stare at its coin-like surface in the bucket as the red silt sank to the bottom, leaving clear water to splash around the onion and bitter greens patch. Mariana was incapable of waiting for the red to settle; she would carry the bucket immediately, letting the silt and water churn into a thin blood siphoned from the earth. Catarina would steal spoons from the kitchen – she was an Alcoforado, and when she wanted something, she took it – and used them to dole water, drop by drop, into the cracks in the dry, red-clay ground, suturing them closed, a surgery for the garden. She had the overwhelming tolerance of nothing happening, which was required of a true gardener, and the faith of a true gardener that blooms would appear. When Catarina talked Mariana into planting the seeds for an orange tree in the courtyard, and Mariana complained that they would not see it full-grown in their lifetimes, Catarina said, "But we'll see it as grown as it will get while we're here, Mariana."

The stone dormitories commissioned by Papa blossomed almost overnight. As the Abbess promised, Catarina and Peregrina were given the "little house" next to Mariana's. Mariana was allowed to move her furniture — bed, writing desk, mats, crucifix, and chairs — into her new place. It was like having her own tiny kingdom. (To her, a kingdom was a place to hide. To someone like Papa, a kingdom must allow one to range over it with a horse.)

Matins.

The choir practiced a "Hosanna" in Gregorian chant. Sister Dolores was teaching the principle of reiterative style, which blurred and diffused the melodic line. She called it "oriental." The older nuns grumbled that it sounded like a blatant disregard for clarity.

The Marquêsa Dona Fernandes, who liked choir practice, pretended to limp to imitate their nineteen-year-old King, Dom Afonso VI, crippled and insane, locked up in a room by his ambitious brother.

Brites giggled, but Mariana nudged her to stop. She feared it was a terrible omen to have taken her vows the same year that the noble, original King of the war, her war, Dom João IV, died. She took her vows the year that idiocy began its reign.

We Offer Up Our Daily Tasks.

Sister Michaella dos Anjos was cleaning the baronial shields in the convent's Room of Escutcheons and spat on the blue-and-silver Alcoforado emblem. She blamed Francisco da Costa Alcoforado for the foreigners here, who had come for their own gain. That Mariana strutted about like a queen. Sister Michaella dos Anjos despised the Lôbo shield as well. That Rui thought he was so smart, swaggering into the locutory with his soldier friends whenever he wanted, plaguing his sister Leonor Henriques about her property. The nuns sat there with their mouths open wide enough to catch flies while Rui talked about battlefields. Oh, Sister Michaella dos Anjos could see through them all!

She turned and saw Catarina and Peregrina studying her. Had they seen her spit on their father's shield?

"Well now," said Catarina with a smile. "You donated a part of your own body to make my family shine. You're much too generous."

Terce.

While reviewing the Rules of Saint Clare, a passage sprang out at Sister Leonor Henriques: "The Sisters shall appropriate nothing unto themselves, neither house, nor place, nor anything, but they shall be pilgrims and strangers in this world..." Has Peregrina, the Pilgrim, been sent to remind them of this?

Dona Antónío Sofia Baptista d'Almeida, a nun transferred from besieged Évora, complained of the cold. Everyone told her it was sweltering, and that she was being absurd. But Catarina Alcoforado not only brought her extra blankets, she agreed with her. Brr. Cold. This constituted an act of compassion that warmed Sister António Sofia Baptista d'Almeida.

All sang the "Stabat Mater." The "Ave Verum." Catarina Alcoforado had such an exuberant, awful alto voice that Sister Dolores said, "Dear, please make your joyful noise unto the Lord more subdued." Catarina said, "I thought I had to be loud enough to reach heaven, and that's a long way from here." Sister Maria de Castro choked with laughter. Sister Dolores thought, This lively girl is wrong. Heaven is where she is.

Sister Brites de Freire learned how to fold serviettes into the shape of birds. Catarina admitted that this had been her favorite part of caring for her mother and sister when they were in childbed — seeing how to take the ordinary and find something in it to bring them joy.

Despite Sister Ignez de São José's dream of gardens, she had never planted anything. She assumed it would be a waste, with everyone trooping over the ground. But Catarina planted, replanted when a seedling was stomped upon, laughed, weeded, yelled at passersby to get off her plants. Seeing Sister Ignez de São José looking on,

Catarina invited her to train a tomato vine onto the wall. Sister Ignez de São José's envy vanished.

Sister Maria de São Francisco kidnapped Peregrina one day. Catarina, frantic, found them in the moldy prison room. If the room were to hold everyone who deserved to be in confinement for a violation, the walls would collapse. Sister Maria de São Francisco liked to hide in this empty room because no one ever looked in, and because she imagined the cries of the long-ago imprisoned still reverberating off the walls, which fueled certain rages in her soul. Sister Maria de São Francisco thought, Leave it to Catarina to be able to track down the heartbeat of her baby sister. There's no hiding place from her. Aloud she said, "You didn't think she could get out of the convent somehow, did you?" When she looked at these Alcoforado girls, the fires of rebellion leapt inside Sister Maria de São Francisco, the desire to do bold things. She loved how their fearless example raised the temperature of her blood to levels of vibrant discomfort.

Sext.
  Sister Brites de Freire scolded Mariana for avoiding Catarina and Peregrina. (It was not often that she felt superior to Mariana.)

In the dark, Sister Michaella dos Anjos looked upon the altar at the statue of Saint George, wearing armor and seated on his white horse, and found herself having an unlikely musing, Is this the sort of toy that young Peregrina Alcoforado must settle for?

Sister Maria de Santiago was caught dressing Peregrina and putting rouge on her face, using her as a living Vanity Doll.
  Sister Maria de Santiago admitted to an urge to pretend that Peregrina was her own child, to which Catarina replied, "She is your child. You don't have to pretend."

Study & Meditation Time.
  Sister Mariana Alcoforado hardly ventured from the scriptorium. Sister Brites de Brito had given her the job of reviving the Forty Hours, and it was difficult to know what was worthy of being written down. What were the finest things that had happened in

the last forty hours, what deserved to be written into history? She included Abbess Joana de Lacerda's lecture about the rumors regarding the unrest among the white-veiled Carmelites in Beja's convent of Esperança. The Abbess declared that the authenticity of the ecstasies being recorded in that convent by Sister Mariana da Purificação was an issue to be settled by the church's spiritual fathers. The desire for relief from these troubled times might have unduly influenced this young nun and driven her to mild hysteria.

Mariana felt a kinship with this nun she had never met, who shared her name. The Marquêsa Dona Fernandes found a copy of Sister Mariana da Purificação's writing, and was circulating the forbidden words (voices hushed, hand to hand) at the convent of Conceição. In the Forty Hours, Mariana dared to write some passages from Sister Mariana da Purificação:

Where does the place exist where I can live only with my Love, utterly removed from the workings of worldly creatures? For I dwell with my Heavenly Spouse, and I am never alone; always He comes to me, in loving transports, making me wish to forsake all others, and go with my Beloved into the desert.

What ecstasy grips me! I t makes my heart burst from me, to fly where it desires, proving that it cannot live within me, but only with my Divine Spouse. He joins me in my bed, and I pass all night in this union with my Love, so sweet it is that sometimes it lifts me upward, enwrapped in the force of Love, as if He is calling me to Him.

Such things come to me, things that human voice cannot utter! I well know I cannot be free from this, and when I am in such throes, I cannot hear nor see any other; He opens His arms to me, an ardent fire. I t comes to me without warning. Last night I lived in this fire from dinnertime to nine at night; the divine burning never ceased. Who in the history of mankind can relate such revelations? My sisters, I feel so much love that I must spread it across the world, though my pain when I am without my Love, and even when I am consumed, is too terrible to relate.

What could Mariana write in the Forty Hours after this? What comparable majesty presented itself? Nothing was apparent but the unusable, the mundane. From the window of the scriptorium, she could see Catarina with Peregrina in the courtyard's garden.

105

They drew a pail of water from the well. When the head cook, Sister Angelica de Noronha — that ogre — appeared, Catarina grabbed one side of the pail's handle, and Sister Angelica de Noronha took hold of the other. They paused while Peregrina curled her fingers around the pail's lip, to pretend that she was helping them carry the water. This could have been done much more quickly, and without thought, by one person, but they made a pageant of it. They brought the pail to the back door of the kitchen, which Sister Brites opened to receive the fresh water and pour it into a cauldron. A curious scene then went into play. After assisting Peregrina with climbing into the damp, emptied pail, Catarina and Sister Angelica carried the baby back to where they started. At intervals, they set down the pail to catch their breaths, while Peregrina clapped her hands in amusement. All of them were laughing.

Mariana had been in the convent for over thirteen years, and had never seen Sister Angelica de Noronha laughing before.

Did this belong in the Forty Hours?

Mariana omitted it, but that evening, she ran into her sisters as they retired to their "little house" next to hers.

Why that time-waster, that nonsense, in the garden? Mariana asked Catarina, not looking at Peregrina. Why with the cantankerous Sister Angelica de Noronha?

It was very simple, Catarina said, to wait at twilight for Sister Angelica de Noronha to finish her kitchen chores and come out to carry some water and play with Peregrina. Sister Angelica used to perform water-carrying chores when she was a child, and they made her less homesick. Surely Mariana, who had been here a long time, had discovered this about Sister Angelica de Noronha? Perhaps Peregrina reminded her of a younger sister she had not seen in decades.

"She's really delightful, don't you think, Mariana?" asked Catarina.

What? Sister Angelica de Noronha? Mariana did not reply. The first notion to take hold of her was that her sister, having lived her entire life saddled with domestic chores, had a genius for not making them tedious.

The second notion was that within a short amount of time, Catarina had discovered something about Sister Angelica that made her seem human (somewhat).

"Will you visit me tomorrow in the scriptorium?" Mariana asked. "I'm sorry I haven't shared my work with you yet. Will you show me your garden?"

Catarina answered that tomorrow would be glorious.

Our Daily Meeting to Discuss the Temporal and Spiritual Business of Our Community.

The Abbess droned on with her warning that the violations in dress must cease, and that the cavalry officers who wandered in must not be asked to deliver letters. Such communications with the outside were rife here, but against the rules. Were they aware that the French were in the habit of reading personal letters aloud to one another in salons? Did the nuns wish to have their idle words thus exposed?

The Chapter Room was gorgeous, drunkenly-coated with *Mudéjar* tiles that made Mariana want to cry out across the room, "Like the ones at home, Catarina!" It was difficult to keep still, to stop herself from pointing out all the deliberate errors in the tiles that dare not flaunt perfection before the faultless Allah.

If only the Abbess would stop. Mariana wanted to tell Catarina that they should ride the curves of blue in the tiles and fly away. Blue crowns, blue darts, blue daggers, blue pools. Blue eyes, blue script.

The Abbess was lecturing about the austerity of Saint Clare, in contrast to the disobedience and extravagance of this community. The war was not an excuse.

Endless, endless hour.

When Mariana arrived in the scriptorium for her work the next day, she found Catarina, who had not dared intrude upon Mariana's domain until an invitation was extended, already awaiting her. A book was open in front of her at one of the long tables, and Peregrina was asleep on her lap. Mariana still could not look at the baby, but said to Catarina, "I didn't think you could read."

"I can't," said Catarina, whispering over Peregrina, with her face of Mama, squashed, small, at rest. "But I recognize the letters in your name, Mariana. You wrote them down for me one day when we all lived at home. I kept the paper. You were being a show-off, but I didn't mind. Very much, anyway."

"You were a baby. You couldn't have been older than —" Mariana pointed at Peregrina, unable to touch any of her, including her name.

"I know it," said Catarina. "Look. I've found an 'a' here, and here's an 'i,' and over here, an 'm.'"

"No, that's an 'n.'"

Catarina's round face fairly glowed. "An 'n'! Really? Today is the day of finally understanding 'n.'"

They shared a love of saints. They agreed that Maria of Villani was remarkable in saying that her heart was pierced with a spiritual sword. After her death, the autopsy proved that her heart had a wound cauterized in the shape of a kiss, as she had described it. Catarina liked Fiacre, the patron of gardeners, and Mariana liked Edith, who lived in a cloister but loved fine clothes and still got to be a saint. They agreed on Anthony, in charge of watching over lovers and Portugal, whose tongue had never decomposed after he died. ("Ai, tongue sandwich," said Catarina.) Archangel Raphael could be asked to bless happy meetings. ("Yes!" Mariana. "Yes!" said Catarina.) There was much to commend in Christina the Astonishing, who levitated to get away from the stench of people. ("She must have lived a while in a crowded convent," said Mariana, and Catarina laughed so loudly that she almost woke Peregrina.)

Think of fifteenth-century Saint Catherine of Bologna, from the order of Poor Clares who, like them, had illustrated a breviary. Monks were not the sole illuminators and artists.

"I'll show you my favorite book. You must promise to keep it a secret," Mariana said.

"I promise you," said Catarina.

Behind a hidden panel at the back of a brazilwood armoire was a notebook, dry as a leaf, that Sister Francisca Freire once showed to Mariana. It contained the records of nuns at Conceição who had experienced the miraculous. Mariana read to her sister about:

Sister Maria de Assunção, devoted to the rosary. While attending the burial of another nun, the rosary in the hand of Sister Maria de Assunção bleached itself white.

Sister Catarina do Espírito Santo told her parents she preferred Jesus to the husband they had chosen for her, and at the hour of her death in the cloister, her body was consumed in a divine fire.

Sister Helena de Jesús one night described the saints marching through the claustral arcades.

Stars appeared around Sister Catarina de Aragão, who had continuously fasted and performed penances, as she was buried.

Sister Guiomar de Jesús, devoted to choir and the Divine Office, was sick in bed and could not attend Matins. She dragged herself to the choir loft, where she fell down, but recited, alone, the office she had missed. A nun in the lower choir reported that she heard ethereal voices accompanying Sister Guiomar de Jesús.

"Oh, my," breathed Catarina.

"I want to be chosen for a miracle," confided Mariana. "Don't you?" To her, the saints were the ones tapped by God, the chosen, the famous, the ones cloaked in glory.

"Is that why you like the saints?" asked Catarina. Peregrina was coming drowsily awake on Catarina's lap.

"Isn't that why everyone likes them?" said Mariana. "They were proclaimed as special, and they get remembered."

"They got suffering in daily life," said Catarina. "Saint Teresa would hold onto grates when she levitated, begging for that power to go away. The saints are terribly ordinary, don't you think, Mariana? Miracles come out of plain things. Think about the women in your notebook. Someone praying a rosary, someone fasting."

"What about the ones with a vision of the dead?"

Catarina considered this, bounced Peregrina on her knee. "Since death comes to us all, shouldn't a vision of it be the most ordinary thing in the world? I think it's just a matter of allowing it. It's like a memory, except brighter. I see Mama all the time, and I'm sure that you do, too." Mariana admitted this was so. Catarina said that this was enough theology for today. The sun was out. Why didn't they steal some wine out of the storehouse, and Catarina would show Mariana some parts in the garden — unless they were trampled — where green heads were pushing through. "Another ordinary, garden-variety miracle," she said, and grinned. "Come?"

"Yes," said Mariana. "I'm right behind you."

That night, Catarina heard Senhora Dutra, a refugee, sobbing in the "little house" down the hall in their building. Senhora Dutra's husband had died on a battlefield.

Catarina knocked on Mariana's door, held out Peregrina, and said, "Take care of her while I go see Senhora Dutra."

Mariana set Peregrina in a corner of her room and said, "Go to sleep." Turning over on her bed, Mariana tried to rest, but could feel the baby staring at her back. She sat up on one elbow and said, "Come here, and keep quiet. If you cry, I'll put you back in the corner." The baby toddled over to her sister, climbed onto the bed, and stayed at the far end, and seemed to know better than to speak, or kiss her, or reach for her.

> Dear Baltazar,
>
> It is all I can do not to scold you severely for being swayed by Rui about the splendors of combat. As much pleasure as it gave me (and Catarina and Peregrina) to embrace you today, I remain in shock from seeing you in uniform. My sole consolation is your mentioning that Papa said he was proud of you and might change his notions about your future. I imagined that he would never allow you to leave the priory, but it appears that your impetuousness has won out.
>
> No — forgive me. When you spoke once again of meeting many of the French officers beginning to camp in our area, and of your hope of someday encountering Schomberg, you were so vibrant that I must find it within myself to allow you to go. Yet you sounded so ingenuous that you must not blame me for fearing for you. Forgive me!
>
> Do be careful. Take heart, take heart, take mine.
>
> As ever, much love,
> Your Mariana

When Catarina ran the Alcoforado household, her chores taught her how to enter the farthest reaches of silence. Leaning into the quiet helped her glide through dull tasks. Her ears would be soothed by hearing, from several rooms away, the hushed singing of Mama. Catarina taught Mariana how to train her ears to detect what went on beyond the cloister's walls, by leaning so headlong into silence that one fell inside it and was transported. Mama's song was not to be found, but Mariana listened for Baltazar's breathing, to assure herself that beyond her, somewhere out there, he was alive. She would be able to gauge, by the rush or slowness of his breathing, whether or not he was in panic. Overwrought with the desire to hear, her imagination invented the sounds of ripping skin, clanging swords, muskets firing, and horses screeching, and she would cover her ears in alarm.

Catarina suggested that she lie next to Mariana, and that they travel together. It might be less disconcerting. They should hold hands, stretch out and be exceptionally still, and see where silence took them.

Mariana's spirit lifted past the cork trees of the Alentejo, their bare branches like white-stockinged legs in the air, and their bodies, red and stripped, stuck head first into the ground. The legs of the trees forked open, unprotected. Baltazar? she called, roaming over the military camps. Why were there no sweets in the shrines to the souls-not-at-rest?

She traveled to the manor across the square, where she and Ana Maria had been born before Papa moved them to the estate on the outskirts of town. Seeing it from anywhere in the convent was impossible, and she longed to glimpse the bull that Papa had carved onto the manor's side. The house once belonged to Vovó, but Papa had claimed it from her, saying that it was his birthright as a noble-man and as an outsider from the Trãs-Os-Montes area in the north to establish himself in the middle of the affairs of his new province. Now it was empty, but Papa refused to sell what was his. The street was called the Rua do Touro, or Street of the Bull, to honor the animal that supremely owns the land it roams upon. Mariana flew there and caressed the bull carved by her father.

Why not, under cover of night, slip inside one of the bedrooms in Beja and watch? Senhora Ferreira de Fontes was being undressed by a boy who was not her husband. She caressed the top of his head as he bent to unlace her shoes.

Ana Maria, married lady. Her colicky babies crying. Vovó lying there, not hearing Mariana say, Vovó, come with us. Come away.

Why not go to the ocean? (No, she could not see the water, that thick, bluest dream, without Baltazar.) How unfair, how terrible, to have been born in Portugal! Why not fly to Madrid, and stare up at the spires? Why not venture into the salons of France, where the women adjusted their headdresses and bustles? She would go to the rooms where men undressed, and she would stare.

She journeyed to the Convent of Esperança, to visit Sister Mariana de Purificação, and waited for the Divine Spouse to enter her bed. And waited.

"Mariana," whispered Catarina. "Come back now, and tell me where you went."

Mariana opened her eyes and recited parts of her voyage, leaving out the men. "And you?" she asked Catarina.

Catarina squeezed Mariana's hand. "Nowhere," said Catarina. "When were we last together, just you and me, and when like right now? All I did was fall in love with how you breathe. I've never spent such an unbroken time with you beside me, Mariana."

Scaly bodies with saber-like fingernails, twisting in the fires of hell, were carved into the arch outside the Chapter Room. On the arch's keystone was the mystical rose of heaven. Between the scaly bodies and the mystical rose was a snail with its head hidden.

"I can see heaven and hell very clearly," said Catarina, "but I have to admit that snail confuses me."

"Sister Maria de Mendonça explained it to me when I first came here," said Mariana, who hated admitting to Catarina that there was once something that she, too, had not known. "She said that failure of the imagination was one of the greatest evils of mankind. Inactivity was death. Better that the snail look and stretch about and declare what is heaven, in every manifestation it can envision, and what is hell."

"Better to be alive, seeing and imagining the best and worst of everything, than to be a coward? Better to have one's whole mind and being venture to extremes?"

"Yes."

"Mariana!" said Catarina, laughing. "Do you mean I'll have to give up hating the snails for eating my plants?"

"Thank them for teaching you to be active and extreme, and then crush them underfoot."

Some beliefs voiced by Catarina Alcoforado as she prepared to take her vows as a Franciscan, of the Order of the Poor Clares:

It is the job of nuns to sorrow for creation, to sing to it, to atone for it. This is not withdrawal from the world, but a commitment to nourishing it.

It is the job of nuns to fight the impulse to use prayers as a list of demands. (Mariana's days were a pursuit of accomplishments, written pages, correct numbers, and prayers that were forms of begging. She was astonished to discover that Catarina asked for nothing when she prayed.)

Prayer was attention in its purest form. It was a prayer when Catarina discovered that the bottles in the infirmary enchanted Peregrina, and took her there to gaze at them.

It was a prayer when Catarina sang so loudly off-key in the choir that everyone admitted to being amused and inspired for an hour afterwards, including Sister Beatriz Maria de Resende, whose voice was as lovely as Catarina's was terrible.

Catarina adored the system of the Four Waters of Saint Teresa. The first level, or water, consisted of the will. A person declared herself in charge of her own fate. That took some strength, but was the easiest stage. The second water was the state of allowing inspiration to enter in. Sometimes artists could accomplish that. The third water was being utterly possessed, completely losing one's own will. (Sister Mariana de Purificação?) It was the realm of geniuses and grand lovers.

The fourth water was known to only a few people in the history of the world — mystics, saints. Perhaps also Inês the Beautiful. It was the searing ecstasy of actual heaven.

When someone had asked Saint Teresa why she called these phases "waters," she had replied, "Because I love water."

Catarina suggested that gardening could fall somewhere between the second and third waters. She loved her water-soaked patches. And everyone, especially Mariana, loved her for this, and for everything else that Catarina thought and did.

Mariana ran to tell Catarina that she had sat admiring Our Lady of the Milk so intently that it felt like a prayer, the first ever in her life that was not a request made of heaven. She had thought, *Milk, lady, abundance, feed one and all . . . Catarina.* That was the prayer.

Because she could not wait, she burst into the room with the wash basin, needing to speak to Catarina at once. Mariana saw a red animal the size of a fist bulging out of her sister's breast, as if she were delivering her heart out of her body.

Mariana screamed.

"Shh, shh, Mariana," said Catarina, covering herself. "I didn't want to tell you, for fear you would make a fuss."

Mariana pulled off her veil and tore at her hair and garments as Catarina went to calm her. Mariana screamed again, "Yes, I shall make a fuss! Like none that anyone in this convent has ever heard."

On the morning that Catarina was scheduled to take her vows — to lie beneath a white sheet at the foot of the altar and proclaim herself dead to the world — she was beneath a white sheet in the infirmary, her breast in such ruins that a hand held above it, an arrested touch, made her wince. Sister Mariana was in her "little house," writing a letter:

> Dear Holy Ghost,
>
> If You could find it within Your munificence to restore to complete vigor one of Your prized children, Catarina Alcoforado, I shall never ask anything more of You. Please tell our buried Saint Anthony that he need not trouble himself anymore with me. (Not that he's done so much, I fear it is only fair to add.) I no longer wish to be Inês. I am loathe to prevail upon You in these disastrous times, but I do hope You noticed that I whipped my back until it bled in the hope that You might, in Your infinite mercy, lance the swelling that has devastated my sister. It must be an agony. Otherwise she would never ignore her garden.
>
> I must request that though I do not wish You to turn Your Ear from the land of my fathers as the war's crescendo comes to shrill possession of us, all of You, entire, must pour into Catarina.
>
> I am hoping that a letter is a more eloquent offering than the prayer I constantly recite within myself. Catarina would scold me for making a prayer yet another wish. Punish my impudence and forget my earlier selfish requests. Do what You will, but spare her. She is only fifteen.
>
> Your servant,
>
> Sister Dona Mariana Alcoforado,
>
> of the Order of Poor Clares of Saint Francis, Beja, AD 1665

Mariana set her letter on fire, so that it could float upward and reach heaven. Heaven incensed. She and Brites helped a distraught Sister Angelica de Noronha fix Catarina a tureen of jugged rabbit, with brandy, port, and wine poured over the meat, packed in with onions, garlic, tomatoes, parsley, and the end off a ham, a deep rose with age. Mariana took it to the infirmary, and tore thick parts off the haunches, where its tenderness was melting off the bone, and blew on it to cool it and feed it to Catarina. Mariana discovered that the meat was too rich for her sister, and ate some herself, three tears of the flesh to every one for Catarina, so that they could finish sooner and hold hands. When nuns visited, Mariana shouted at them to leave, that she and she alone knew how to care for her.

Sister Ignez de São José came with daily reports on the progress of the garden, with special mention of the orange tree, now a shoot half the height of a girl. She kept Peregrina under her wing. The nuns debated whether Peregrina should observe Catarina's condition. Mariana screamed that Peregrina should be taken away.

Abbess Joana de Lacerda prayed, "Remind me, God, that she is going closer to You − a moment devoutly to be wished for, for her and each of us." She considered reprimanding Mariana for an excessive number of hours in the infirmary. Every nun must love her sisters no more and no less than any other, and certainly not to the shunning of her duties. Her standing lecture to give this brash Alcoforado girl was, "As the years wear onward, I trust you will stop squeezing life with your bare hands and let it come to you, like grace." But she told herself that she was a bad Abbess, the convent was poorly run, and now was not the time to put it harshly aright.

Sister Francisca Freire, She with the Dove's Heart, asked Catarina to caress the pages of the record books with her sweating hands. Sister Francisca thanked her profusely for changing the records into a ribboned smear of young life. She slept at the foot of the sick girl's bed, as if struck herself with illness, and kept no records of Mariana's absences from her work in the scriptorium.

Tears stitched salt through the crevices of Sister Angelica de Noronha's face as she recited, "Better a short time with her, than not to have had her at all." She repeated it but could not force herself to believe it. She prayed, "God, remove the ailment from the body of the only person to befriend me. I am old. Give her ailment to me."

It was Mariana who was always with Catarina, whenever she awoke, throughout the time she slept, and was there to feed her and change the linens. Sisters Brites de Freire and Maria de Castro worked with Mariana to roll Catarina onto her side and remove the sheet below her, clean it with water from the well, and hang it to dry in the moonlight. The exhalations from Catarina's plants lightly made the linens sway. Mariana believed that the influence of the garden might restore Catarina, that moon, water, and green stems would effect a cure. When the night was chilled, she and her friends fanned the linens with their hands for hours to hasten the drying, past Matins, hands moving, waving, without ceasing until Prime. At dawn, not having slept, they would bring the sheets back and work them underneath Catarina. The three of them, and Sister Juliana de Matos and Sister Ignez de São José, with five-year-old Peregrina playing on the floor when Mariana did not order her to be taken elsewhere, would lift Catarina's skeletal arms and legs, thin as grasses, one at a time, so that her limbs would feel the lightness of the breezes.

Alone with Catarina and clutching Catarina's thin hands in her own, Mariana commanded the power of all that was within her to penetrate her sister's weakening flesh, to expand inside her in a flush of health. Mariana shook Catarina's hands in hers. She squeezed them harder. *Take my strength, take it, take all of it, drink it out of me*, said her mind, until her pulse submitted to the rhythm of that refrain.

"You're wishing so hard you're hurting me," said Catarina.

"Tell me what I can do for you," said Mariana.

"I have everything I want," said Catarina. "I have you."

"Yes! Take the strength out of me and use it," said Mariana.

"Please save some for Peregrina. Will you care for her?"

"I'm going to care for you until you're well."

"Mariana."

"Look how strong I am. Can you feel it? Take some of it. I don't need it all for myself. It's too much for me alone."

"Mariana, Mariana," said Catarina. "I refuse to leave you weak and drained."

"I'm never weak," said Mariana. "Never worry about me."

Catarina smiled. "You sound like Papa."

"I sound like Mariana, and I'm here now telling you what to do." She pressed harder on her sister's hands. "Take my strength, please," she said, "take it right out of me. I have more than I know what to do with. Take all of it!" she shouted. "My God, I don't need it!"

"Oh, Mariana, I never thought I would be the one to go on an adventure. Farther than silence. Imagine! Me."

Mariana was not listening. Force and desire were pumping through her veins and out of her mind and into her sister, with Mariana pleading without end, "Take me, all of me, please. Catarina! Take what you need of me!"

A last surge of strength seemed to issue from Catarina, a pushing back, a resistance, remarkably mild but insistent that Mariana's strength must save itself, save life for the living. It was a last gift from Catarina to Mariana.

Francisco da Costa Alcoforado, for the first time since the beginning of the war, thought not only that he might not live to see its end, now that he was in his mid-sixties, but that he no longer cared with the same fire about the outcome. He shared this heresy with no one. He could stand the idea of losing a son in battle, since that would transfigure into honor, but to lose Leonor and now Catarina was too much. It was harder to justify making a world unassailable for his family if everyone in it died out. In the old days, he managed to find incentive even in tragedy for working harder. Now he was not sure. His own son, Baltazar, spoke to him with insolence. So did Rui. Francisco was often locked in contests of will with both of them. The one thing he could not stand was to turn into a mocked old man.

No. That was not true. That was what he would have said a year ago. What he could not stand was being incapable of preventing his family from being destroyed. He selected a white burial gown for his daughter.

When he was in the convent, pressing Catarina's lifeless head to his chest, he said, "I brought you the gown with lace." This struck him as so futile a detail that an unearthly cry issued from him, the one he had not known he had been saving since the death of Leonor.

He had a vague memory later of his daughter Mariana asking him to take her home. He had roared that she was at home, she was a nun, for God's sake, and no Alcoforado ever broke a vow. When she said, absurdly, that he could change that for her, if he wanted, had he shouted that if he could fix anything, it would be to bring his wife and daughter back to life?

He sent Mariana a letter saying that he loved her, that he was upset by recent events. Though he could not apologize for saying what was true, he wished he had said it with the elegance that a nun like Mariana deserved. A day later, a messenger delivered the letter back to him, ripped to shreds, though Mariana had taken care not to destroy the initial of his name, the one that he still entwined with an *L* for Leonor.

Sister Ignez de São José, eager to get out of the cell she shared with two other nuns in the Old Dormitory, agreed to move into the "little house" next to Mariana's and watch over Peregrina. This, Mariana realized, was not exactly what Catarina had in mind when she requested that Mariana care for the little girl, but it was the best she could manage for now. There was no love left in her, no desire for it, for anyone. She was twenty-five, and that was too old for love. All she wanted now was for Baltazar to survive the war, and her own life to proceed uneventfully as she worked in the scriptorium. Baltazar was bad about writing, but she wrote daily, demanding that he let her know how he was. A French officer was good about circumventing the rules (he had a taste for the convent's brandy) and picking up letters to be delivered to the front, and he and Mariana often chatted. Not since her childhood, working with Senhora Néné, her tutor, had the chance presented itself for her to practice her French.

While working on a Forty Hours entry, attempting to make a reasonable presentation about a set period of time, Mariana developed a distaste for her own story. To have lost a mother, to have had similar deathbed scenes with Sister Maria de Mendonça and then Catarina – too many tragedies or coincidences made one's life incredible. For what listener would not remark, A better story would be one loss that all of us can feel at undiluted strength. Enough with loss upon loss, even in wartime!

But history never bothered to notice the human need for symmetry and sensible timing.

She recorded a donation of corn. Most of the nuns could not bring themselves to eat this strange crop from the Americas. They fed it to the pigs. Mariana thought that corn scraped off its cob looked like yellowed or blackened teeth, teeth of the dead.

Her numerals were fat and square, like tombstones.

When she turned in her day's work, Sister Francisca's eyes flooded with tears, and she said, "I have never seen numbers that hurt as these do. I would say that time will heal all grief and rifts, Sister Mariana, but you are too smart to believe that."

All at once, Mariana cried out. She was able to dream up an idea, she was able to lift her arms and record numbers, which meant that she had some strength left. She had not given everything to Catarina. She was a failure, a phony, a coward, she had not loved her sister strongly enough. If she had, she would have no arms. She should not be alive.

When the battle of Montes Claros was described as the meeting of so many thousands of men on both sides that its outcome contained the future, Sister Beatriz Maria de Resende refused to stop singing. She said that she would stay in the choir with her music until the battle ended, to sing some sense at the world. When her eyes strained terribly, she ran her finger over the pages of music, her breath obeying the touch she gathered out of the measures of the songs. She played the organ, and when the keys blurred into a gaping lion's mouth, she was not afraid to run her hands over its teeth, playing by feel as her eyes grew sore. Her feet worked the pedals until she began to wince from the cramping in her legs.

At the tenth hour, the Abbess told her to rest. Sister Beatriz Maria de Resende said that when she went completely blind, she would continue, singing what she knew from memory. What were her eyes, compared to the deaths that were occurring? God might take her eyes and spare, in exchange, two men, or two battalions.

Baltazar was in the battle, taken to the front by Rui, Cristóvão, and Bartolomeu. Mariana leaned into the silence, listening for the sound of his boot securely finding the footholds in a trench wall. An involuntary clamping of the muscles in her back came in cadence with the music from Sister Beatriz Maria de Resende, as if Mariana were bending to offer her joined hands for his foot, to boost him upward if he needed to flee from the trenches. She slept on the choir loft's floor, because the music drowned out the sounds in her head that were like the fuses of hackbuts being lit, the clang of swords on breastplates and armored helmets, the rattling and screeching of horses overheating with their blood splattered finery that ran from the cruppers to the reins. Crests and banners would be chopped out of the hands of boys, and the mere thought of that made her fingers go into spasms. Sister Beatriz Maria de Resende refused food and drink from Sister Brites de Freire but allowed Sister Maria de Castro to mop her brow. As she sang, sweat coursed through her saturated veil and dripped in an even rainfall from the ends of the cloth.

She sang Alleluia choruses and a psalm from the Hour of the Angelus, directing this downward, towards the floor of the church, where the notes could flood through the doors and windows leading to the outside.

When she sang "Elevatis oculis in coelum," and a "Kyrie Eleison," Sister Dolores directed other sopranos and altos to join her, and stepped in to direct everyone in a "Dies Irae."

After twelve hours of singing, most of the nuns had to leave the choir loft and rest, but not Sister Beatriz Maria de Resende.

When the throat of Sister Beatriz Maria de Resende became hoarse, Sister Mariana said, "Sister, let me help you." They continued singing together, with Mariana projecting her voice with a loudness inspired by memories of Catarina. Sisters Brites de Freire, Maria de Castro, Angelica de Noronha, and Ignez de São José with Peregrina at her side stayed with them, and far into the night and morning of the next day, they sang so that God would listen to them and end the fighting. He must hear Sister Beatriz Maria de Resende and judge that some of creation was wondrous, and not all of it need be destroyed.

The battle of Montes Claros ended on the third day after it began. By then, every nun except Mariana and Sister Beatriz Maria de Resende had needed to eat or sleep. Sister Beatriz Maria de Resende was scraping her vocal cords for the last of their musical notes.

Mariana figured that God must have said, *I shall end the largest battle in the history of this war, and take in payment the eyesight of my beloved servant, Sister Beatriz Maria de Resende*, because when Mariana passed a hand in front of her face, she saw that the most talented artist in their convent had at last gone blind from her efforts to make the ugliness of war kneel down and surrender beneath the beauty of what she could do with music. She was moving her jaws and mouth, but the sound was thoroughly wrenched out of her.

Mariana kissed her hand, and touched her throat, and said that Sister Beatriz Maria de Resende had given everything — given it so hard and far that she had used up her most precious abilities and pleasures forever — and now she must stop.

"I'm so sorry you can't see,"said Sister Mariana.

Sister Beatriz Maria de Resende, her blind eyes as black as the dome of the night, could not speak above a rasping, but it came out as, "The concert of my life. You, Sister Mariana, stayed with me to the end."

God did not take as payment one Baltazar Alcoforado, who sent word to Mariana that he had been spared. He sounded invigorated by the battle. God permitted a victory to the combined forces fighting on Portugal's behalf — the Spanish losses were put at four thousand dead and five thousand more taken prisoner — but He did not, for reasons that Mariana had trouble fathoming, cause this massive destruction to end the war.

> Dear Papa,
>
> We are so much alike. I have not been quite right since returning your letter to you in such an angry manner. Papa, you and I are both prideful. Please, won't you take this letter and send it back in shreds to me, so that I know that neither of us will have to feel sorely the advantage of the other, and wait upon the other to surrender.
>
> Then we shall be able to go on. I do not need to see you in person, Papa, nor even hear from you ever again, if that is not to be, but my very existence depends upon knowing that you do not despise me.
>
> I have heard that Baltazar survived another huge battle, the one at Alcaria de la Puebla. He wrote to tell me that he was inspired by fighting alongside the French.
>
> No day passes that I do not think upon those of us who have thus far survived, and those of us who have died.
>
> Your loving daughter,
> Sister Mariana Alcoforado
> in the service of God

A messenger brought, by return mail, her letter to her father in shreds, but within the envelope was a pressed iris from the

Alcoforado estate. When she pieced the fragments of the letter back together — as her father knew she would — she found, entwined in the initial of her name, an *L* and an *F*, like traces of both her parents, the dead and the living.

"You never write love letters, Frederic?" asked Captain Salomon.

"No time, no time," said General Schomberg.

Schomberg's exasperation amused the Captain. He mentioned this as he wrote to his wife, telling her that they kept winning what should have been called the final battle of the war. He included a few comments on his admiration for the French. He himself had advised Schomberg to promote Noel Bouton, a Count of Chamilly, to the rank of Captain of a cavalry. Bouton had earned it on the battlefield at Montes Claros, and after three years in this war could communicate well with the Portuguese soldiers, who greatly admired him.

The Captain concluded his letter by saying, Is the forest sublime? He found it impossible to tell his wife he loved her, but she would understand. They had once made love in the forest near their home, and any reference to it was their private code for affection.

He passed the letter along to an officer who would be riding north through the Low Countries, where it could be sent on to Prussia. Schomberg and Captain Salomon saddled up, took along three thousand foot soldiers and fifteen hundred cavalry, and crossed the Guadiana River into the border towns of Spain. The mayors of the towns heard that Schomberg himself was going to ride through, raised white flags in the town square, and fled, leaving the citizens to fend for themselves.

The small town of Paymogo was deserted. Captain Salomon requested permission to stop for a day or two and rest. He would catch up with the army later.

"I think they've finally got the message. Take a week," said General Schomberg. "A pity the entire war wasn't this easy."

The Captain, invigorated, bid his friend goodbye. He and some guards stationed at the Paymogo fort raided a warehouse and arranged a banquet.

The night watchman dozed off, a soldier later reported to Schomberg, and by the time they realized that they were under attack, it was too late. Some Spanish patriots broke into the fort, and Captain Salomon was among those killed.

Schomberg inquired of the messenger if he continued standing there because he thought he might see General Schomberg weep like a woman.

"No, sir," said the messenger.

"Then get out of my tent," said Schomberg.

As he went over his maps, he pinpointed how his troops would have to spread out in a web across the Alentejo province. He would tell Colonel Briquemault to bring his cavalry regiments to Campo Maior, a short distance north of Beja. Other troops would be stationed west and south of that city, and some within the city walls. The Spanish might aim for it in a last defiant push. Twenty-six years into the war, it was more than ever the point of convergence. He would lead a triumphal march through Beja, which was his right as the victor of the last few major battles, another show of force, but he would never again let down his guard, not until a bell tolled at the signing of a treaty. Maybe then the world would allow him to stop and mourn his murdered friend.

Sister Mariana stayed in the scriptorium, alongside Sister Francisca Freire. Since the death of Catarina the year before, Mariana was spending all of the time in her "little house" or here, tending to her work. She did not chat much with her friends. They understood, and left her alone. She tried to find her usual comfort in the scriptorium's library, in the magnificent tome of the *Rules of the Order of Saint Clare*, the copy of the *Flos Sanctorum*, and the record books of decades of transactions, professions, deaths. Mariana found comfort in paging through the treatise on the essays of Francis Bacon and a study on the war between Mary of Scotland's House of Stuart and Elizabeth of England. She stayed late, missing the Divine Offices, in order to compare Bibles in French, Latin, and Greek as well as Portuguese. The works of Saints Teresa of Avila and John of the Cross, and the famous Father António Vieira, renewed her fervor about God sending her a miracle. She never wanted to leave this room! High shelves held parchment scrolls of sermons tied with iron-colored ribbons. Illuminated missals proffered fleurs-de-lys, elves (somehow they reminded her of Baltazar), and blue dragons torturing the occasional capital letter into beauty. In the brazilwood armoires that consisted of thin, catalogued drawers were the folios creased by many, many stars.

She had these old folios of deceased Abbesses to restore, and told her friends that her tasks were keeping her occupied.

But one day Sister Brites raced by the scriptorium, shouting that the French had arrived. A glorious parade of soldiers was headed through the town square and past the convent, to celebrate a victory at San Lucar.

"Mariana? Are you listening?" said Brites.

"Hmm," said Mariana, not glancing up from her record books.

Brites had to repeat herself, and tempt her by saying that the horses were gorgeous and the French finely dressed, to force Mariana at least to look in her direction.

"Come along, Mariana!" said Brites. Sisters Brites de Brito and Maria de Castro, and Sister Juliana de Matos holding Peregrina's hand, and Sister Dolores holding blind Sister Beatriz Maria de Resende's hand, dashed past, some of them pausing to look into the scriptorium to shout, "Hurry! You'll miss them!"

"Mariana, come on," said Brites.

"You go along without me," said Mariana, returning to her page.

Sister Francisca Freire looked up and said, "You've been here for hours, Sister. Go and watch the parade. Your brother and brother-in-law might be among those riding past."

Mariana considered this. She completed her thought, finished the line she had been writing, and blotted the page. She blew on the ink.

"Mariana!" said Brites. "Hurry up!"

She lagged behind Brites through the cloister and up to the New Dormitory as nuns, girls, and noblewomen ran up the stairs to collect along the upper balconies and verandas. Mariana was staring at her feet, letting Brites pull her up the stairs towards the window of Mértola with its cross worked into the iron grid. A whoosh of clamor and dirt swirled in through the window as it burst open, and Mariana began to lift her head, and she walked slowly but without pausing towards the veranda. Her step was calm, but the tumult around her was shooting through her feet, and it put a faster cant into her step, and the others, including Brites, stood aside, opening a path for her.

As she stepped onto the veranda, she began to raise her head and look straight down onto the street, where everything on all sides of her fell away except for a French Captain who was twisting his horse around, and in the exact moment her head was entirely lifted her eyes caught his and his locked into hers, as if he had been waiting for her. All around her, nuns and the soldiers guarding the convent and townspeople were waving white handkerchiefs, partly to welcome the troops, partly to wave away the tremendous clouds of dust.

Mariana did not blink, did not move. When the Captain pulled his reins and lifted his horse from the ground and had the animal perform a perilous gavotte, her hand flew over her heart. His gaze was consuming her, and no one else. Columns of flag bearers and men in green and red uniforms streamed past, thick columns of waving soldiers, but they fell away; he was the one who saw the openings where he could make his horse charge, pull up fast, dance around again.

"Look at that animal flying!" said Sister Maria de São Francisco.

How infinite the sky, a bowl turned upside down in front of Mariana, pouring its stunning blueness onto her, through her.

It was not in Mariana's power to stay away from the uproar that night in the locutory, where soldiers were visiting, drinking, speaking loudly of their adventures. Sister Genebra Nogueira was waving them in. The crowd once again parted for Mariana when she entered. She knew he was in there somewhere, come for her.

There he was. She did not know his name. He was a shape in the night. It was clear that he had been searching for her. Stepping forward in the same moment that he did, her hands lifted to meet his. His peruke had every curl and hair in place. His array of ribbons was the maddest dash of colors she had ever beheld. He placed a medal in her hands, Saint Christopher, the traveler. The medal he gave her was burning. He kissed her hand. Soon she would be back in her bed, twisting around, finding it impossible to sleep, unable to stand being within her own skin.

Catarina? she almost cried. Catarina? Is this a joke from you, you who told me that my will was the poorest of impulses, nothing compared to the surprises to which an open life is heir? You, who once smeared a line in the record books with your fever? Is this your doing, to urge me not to close myself down?

She could see Catarina above, chipping away at stars so that white flaming dots could fall from them into Mariana's eyes. That was how a painter brought a portrait to life − a dot of white, a white star, or small cluster of star-points, within the dead, black, lifeless pupils.

The burning of the star fragments bringing her to life made her close her eyes in agony.

Back in her room, with the medal that was as warm as a hand pressed to another hand, she rewrote his words not in her mind but along the fast-roaring currents of her blood, a hot rush of what she remembered of their conversation: ". . . the most beautiful oasis, most beautiful woman, most beautiful, you alone, beautiful, that I have seen . . ." Had he said that to her? Had she dreamed it? No, she had as proof the Saint Christopher medal to clutch, hard enough to draw bright roses to the top of her skin. Oh, flowering blood! Wait! She had made no plans! No plans with him! Where had he gone? She forgot to ask his name. What had she said in reply? Had she spoken? Who had seen her? She wanted everyone to be her witness, but no one to watch. He was gone now; not a name, but a force. "I desire . . . I wish for. . ." What had he said? Or had that come from her? From both of them, at once? She was by herself in her "little house," her little kingdom, and her body was breaking out into a mottling of roses as she played over the words that had in their utterance delivered her now to this stage: *You alone, you alone, you alone.*

Part 3

O HE IS THE GRAND HERO whose praises they are singing! Nuns and townspeople, men and women, altogether everyone is singing like angels about him and his heroism. People are chatting and flapping about, making the air alive and full as if filaments are being shed from wildly fluttering wings.

One can inhale the excitement.

In the locutory, the soldiers eat and drink and the hum is incredible, and when it reaches Mariana, she covers her ears with both hands but all that does is confirm for her, she can feel and hear it, how fast her heart is beating, saying, Come alive, come alive, whether you want to or not. You have no say in the matter.

The leader of the cavalry ...Noel, his name is Noel Bouton, a Captain, a Count of Chamilly...the hum keeps saying, Mariana, change your life, change life itself ... the moment you saw him you gave away sleep, you gave away tranquility, you gave away peace, you said, "Where am I? What was I before this sleeplessness?"

Working in the scriptorium, she saw herself floating above the dead husk of the person she had been. She thought, How has it happened that during the first twenty-six years of my life I never guessed that love would have nothing to do with choice?

Sister Brites de Freire put a hand on her arm and Mariana jumped, yelled out of nowhere. She threw her arms around Brites, who said, "You've been looking at that page and writing nothing? That's not like you," and her voice shook, because Mariana was trembling as if she had been swept up into the arms of the world and shaken, shaken.

"Tell me why everyone is speaking so well of that French officer, the one named Noel," said Mariana and could not hear the reply because she was drowning in that distant hum. *It's the chorus of praise of him, it's his soul and flesh calling to me, I can hear it. When I stretch out a hand, I find that the words about him form a wall that steadies me in my strange new illness. When Sister Maria de Castro said yesterday, "Did you hear of his heroism at Alcaria de la Puebla?" and when Sister Genebra said, "Ribbons, such ribbons he wears, and the Portuguese soldiers adore him, how well he treats them," my hand went out as if to find him and hold all that he is, and these words remain as another wall to hold me upright, to lift me trembling from my chair.*

And I say, Words of him, take me blind down the corridor you're forming, take me to him and I will say, "I'm awake now, and I don't know why I had to pass through death to be so violently shaken alive."

Sister Brites said, "Mariana, are you drunk?"

She said, "Yes, I'm discovering religion."

Here is the treaty to which I shall hold: If I go to the locutory and you are there, it is because you are waiting for me. If you are not there, I have been dreaming, and bless you for such a dream.

He was waiting. He was large and ornate in a crowd of plain soldiers, and Sister Angelica de Noronha was laughing at something he was saying.

And Captain Noel Bouton saw Mariana and — what was it, this state Mariana had never seen before that was beyond him smiling at her? Everyone else, all else, was dismissed, though he kept speaking out of politeness to the others. Look how triumphantly he managed that! She had allowed her skin to answer his. He was awaiting her. No, it was beyond any waiting she had ever done or witnessed. It was *knowing*.

Knowing that she would come here to him, knowing they were meant to be together, that one had to wait for love at first sight, wait to be changed forever like this, because such a love overruled all work, all patience, all plans, all vows, all war.

All of her heart.

Mariana did not notice the pews, the statues, the tiles, the reredos behind the altar, the nuns. They parted to let her through.

She was not walking but being led. She could see one of the nuns elbowing another. Why? She was merely walking, about to speak to him, broken Portuguese, bits of French, as the rest of them were doing.

He was of a strong build, and she could see whiskers beginning on the side of his face, and she closed her eyes; this close sight of him spoke of haste in leaving camp to come here, it spoke of his body heating up fast and sweating out hair for her face to brush against and mark her, to let her wear signs of him—

What utter madness!

She held out her hand as a proper noblewoman and smiled. He was fair but his eyes were dark and shiny.

"Mariana," he said.

"Noel," she said. As if he had introduced himself as her, and she was returning the favor.

"You know mine?"

They smiled. He was still holding her hand. He inclined his head to her, and his stiff uniform creaked and groaned. The other nuns backed away, Mariana could hear a murmur, but what did she care? God was telling her to be here, and she could not imagine disobeying.

"So crowded here," he said.

There is an ocean in me, pouring out of me, she thought. "Why are you here, when the whole world out there is yours?" she said.

"Death is out there, and life is in here," he said, bowing.

He was indeed a gentleman! "Life is in here," she agreed.

On the third night of his telling stories for the nuns in the locutory, Mariana waited in glorious agony for them to finish their endless questions. She had only one, which was, *I am correct, aren't I, that you are here for me?*

At last the others trudged off for bed, glanced at Mariana silently, paused, then shook their heads and went on. Workmen were pounding tiles with hammers to break up the worn ones and install new ones. Through the din of hammering she said to him, "I can hear them working all the way over in my room in the New Dormitory, the seventh room down the eastern corridor on the second floor."

"That far?" he said.

"That close," she said. "The whole night long the men go through the corridors working on floor repairs."

And she ran away, because Sister Genebra had stopped to stare back and time how long Mariana lingered alone to speak to a man.

At the mouth of the locutory, she looked back over her shoulder and saw that he had turned to face her squarely, fully.

When he stood in her doorway, wearing a mason's cape, she did not say, "How is it possible that no one saw you, caught you?" Since he was meant to be here, of course no one would catch him. Instead, she asked, "Is is true that in France people meet at dances?"

"It's true," he said, and without bothering to take off his cape, he held out his arms and she had no trouble going to him and resting her head on his shoulder, with her hands in his. "We have no music," he said.

"Play it loudly in your head, and I'll hear it," she said softly, and shivering in nothing but her long white nightgown, bareheaded, they danced around her room. He was breathing and moving heavily and she was light, light, and could smell his powder. He said, "This music is in your head, dear love. I can hear it."

Dear love! His dancing was so fine, so courtly.

"What is this music in my head saying?" she teased.

"That you are the most beautiful woman in the world, and I am the most blessed of men."

She was the one who first kissed him, and in his register of shock she found herself swept up, feet off the floor, and her arms and legs flew around him. *Most beautiful, most blessed.* Hold nothing back, nothing in reserve, or you will die in your greatest hour.

Perhaps others in the world, a few of them, had felt like this, but none had ever felt it more powerfully, more rightly, than she did.

Bleary-eyed, reciting Matins. Useless! Her lips moving not in words but in trying to relive what kissing him was like. How could she survive until tonight? What if he did not come to visit again?

He had to! Her ribs still ached from the weight of him, her insides still hurt so much that she could not tell if it was from his passion or hers. It did not surprise her that love caused great pain at first.

132

Sister Brites said, "Mariana? Are you awake? You think you're special, don't you?"

Mariana ignored her. What did it matter, what anyone said? About anything?

"Oh!" she said, sitting up naked in bed. "I was afraid you would not come to me!"

He threw off his cape. "What if we're caught?" he said.

"Let them catch us."

"You delightful creature," he said, amazed, running to her bed to kiss her. "You —" and framed her face in his hands, and all of her, every measure of feeling, all blood, every particle of the force of who she was, rushed to those points he touched. She did not lose her nerve or seek the relief of glancing away. "You elegant woman," he said, and laughed. "And ferocious. I've never met a soldier as ferocious as you."

"Thank you," she said. *One thousand times I thank you.*

He never called her a nun. His Portuguese was very good. He had been in her country for three years, fighting. He mixed in French. She did as well. Paint this word French, that one Portuguese. Fling them over one another, roll around in dabs of talk. The French word for heart sounded so close to the Portuguese word for color. She stroked his throat. He was not wearing his gorget. Baltazar had reported to her that Noel was never without his military dress, and she thought, "You expose yourself to all the dangers with me? For me? I'll never, never hurt you." And kissed his neck, paler than his face from living under protective metal.

He was not afraid to clutch her hand to his chest. He pressed it there so hard that she imagined he was trying to plunge her hand through to touch his heart as she touched the rest of him. Surely such a closeness would leave, trailing off her fingertips, a wake of golden leaf. Illuminating his insides.

Tonight he stayed immobile on her so long that his forehead wore the imprint of the sacred heart carved onto the headboard of her bed. She ran her hand over his bare back.

"You are bold and tireless," he said. "Where did you learn so much?"

"I was born knowing it," she said.

"Will you come to me tomorrow?" she asked as he dressed back into the workman's clothing he used to sneak to her room. It would be terrible if they were found out.

No! Every risk was worth it!

If they punished her as the laws of her country demanded, with a decade of imprisonment (his punishment would be a fine), she would scream and cry until she melted into water that ran below the door. She would flow to the battlefield, to the Count of Chamilly, and he would drink her. She would endure as the sea inside him.

If they were put in the stocks, she would starve herself to the size of an iron filing, and saw off her chains, and when she found him, he would keep her in his belt. Baltazar would comment to his friend that he always knew his sister would enjoy being transformed into a weapon.

Noel looked amusing in his mason's rumpled cape. She laughed behind her hands. Look at him smiling at her, her alone.

"Tomorrow?" she repeated.

"Only tomorrow?" he teased.

"Every tomorrow, every today," she said. "I'll die without you."

"Then we'll have to find a way for you to live forever, Mariana," he whispered.

Through the rest of the night, lovely night, she stayed alert, refusing to murder the night with sleep. A faraway owl sang to her. Wisps of roots of the cork trees tickled the red muscle of the clay of the ground: She could hear that, too — tiny, underground harps.

During daylight, she treasured her soreness, the lingering proof that he desired her. He was absent, but she could feel that he wanted her as much as her body wanted him.

At a dinner hour, they were served small cooked birds. Manuel, the procurer, must have arranged a good business deal. Their pelvises lay flat on the plates. Mariana was delighted by the chill bumps standing up on the cooked flesh. She was amused to picture Sister Angelica de Noronha in the kitchen, taking the blade of a big knife and going smack! on every little bird to flatten its tailbone. Crack! All of them magically opened up.

The nuns ate in silence in the crowded refectory.

A hair floated onto her plate. Noel's, from last night. Had he been clinging to her collarbone? Wonderful! Shed evidence of him, of the night, everywhere. Daytime was nothing but worthless pale padding stitched to the underside of night.

Sister Brites de Freire was glaring at her. She gestured at Mariana as if to say, "What is going on with you?"

What on earth?

"You're irritating me. Wake up! What is going on with you?" signaled Brites.

Sisters Brites de Brito and Maria de Castro were also staring at her. Mariana ate the hair dropped onto her plate along with some of the bird, and decided she must use whatever was at her disposal — silence, work, waiting for darkness — to shut out the rest of the pointless world.

When she glided along, gladly faint from lack of sleep, the blues, greens, and yellows of the tiles blurred as she passed. That was how she kept Noel without her as well as within her — a storm of colors. Her drowsiness made them whirl around her in the corridor.

Noel! This is joy. If you will permit it, this is joy everlasting.

Sister Francisca Freire was reading Mariana's totaling of costs for the month's meat and fish. She set the paper down on the table in the scriptorium and said, "Sister Mariana. Explain yourself."

"Sister? I beg your pardon?"

She with the Dove's Heart held up the sums. They were correct. Mariana had triple-checked them. "May I inquire, Sister Mariana, as to your impressions when you were next to Sister Beatriz Maria de Resende as she sang herself into blindness during the Battle of Montes Claros?"

"I felt as if – I'm not sure, Sister. I've never been asked to describe it. I felt as if human beings were being declared better than the sum of their actions. Yes. That was why Sister Beatriz was ruining her sight. To say that."

Sister Francisca Freire nodded sadly. "I would agree that what she did was noble. It also occurred to me that history would record the ugliness that day at Montes Claros, so many deaths, while ignoring her beautiful sacrifice. Why do you think that happens?"

Mariana was trying to leap ahead, to guess what this would have to do with her sums. "I don't know, Sister."

"I suspect you do. To record beauty is to frighten people in a way more perplexing than if you were to record a massacre. Beauty, every offering of extreme beauty, thrusts itself forward until it hits up against very bad pain. I am not certain why this is one of its laws. But at a young age, I learned that it was. I suppose if beauty has not yet encountered resistance, it knows it can go farther. May I trouble you with a story of my own? One day, my parents and I were invited to a fancy dinner at the house of friends. I was small, and the estate was swarming with people. I panicked, and wanted to find my mother and father. I looked up and saw everyone so sour, so tense, despite it being a nice event. Perhaps everyone knew the war was coming. I was concerned merely with finding my parents. I understood that they were considered strange because they were in love, that they were regarded with hostility, especially my father, since he was rich and she was common, and he had dared undercut his fortunes when he married her. You know all that. What I have not told you is that during this party, I came up with the idea of locating them by detecting sensations of affection. I found my parents at once. My father looked as if he had recently bathed, and he was radiant, and though my mother was a distance away, chatting with someone else, it was as if a string of light connected her to my father. A stranger could have walked in and known they were together. I thought this was amazing. I still do. When she moved, another string of light spun itself with the next string of light that he emanated when he moved, and their love crisscrossed itself round about the air and turned the room into their own massive, private web.

"This is what I wish to tell you, Sister Mariana. It broke me to pieces and made me call out tearfully later on, because it was the bravest spectacle I had ever seen, to construct a web so light and invisible but brazen, to do it for each other despite knowing that it would serve to increase their sorrow when one of them died. Beauty that would not relent until it met the worst final resistance. I am not ordinarily morbid. My parents rushed to console me, and I cried even harder. The web of love was now around me, and I knew that whenever I saw the slightest suggestion of it, I would hurt. I hurt whenever I suspect I see traces of such a web from anyone, Sister."

She turned Mariana's work face down, and pushed it aside on the table. She declared that they should take the rest of the hour off. Besides, Mariana shone with exhaustion.

Mariana waited for Sister Francisca Freire to say something else, tie the fragments sensibly together. But she did not. She did nothing more than to pause before leaving the scriptorium and say, "Be careful, my friend. And whether or not you wish it, I shall be there to comfort you."

In the hallways, the nuns bent their heads and gossiped, tittered. Shook their heads. One or two crossed their arms over themselves, hugging themselves, and walked to their room feeling wounded with awful wonder.

"Is this another one of your jokes, Baltazar? Why can't he come tonight?" said Mariana. Her tone was low in a corner of the locutory. Sister Michaella dos Anjos was observing her. On the thin breastplate of Baltazar's uniform was a carved unicorn. She did not know which alarmed her more, the skull engraved on the handle of his Swiss dagger, or the maidens and ribbons making such nonchalant prettiness of his helmet.

"Because," Baltazar hissed back, "we're cleaning out a Spanish encampment at midnight. North."

"If he cared about me, he wouldn't go."

"He cares enough to send me with a message. Have some respect for messenger-boy, your old pal."

"I thought the war was over."

"It is, sort of," said Baltazar, and grinned. "The Spanish are having trouble believing that."

"Still?"

"Still," said Baltazar. He had argued with their father that morning, which put him in a pleasant mood. They had been walking through the marketplace, and a few people blew kisses at them. Hushed comments rippled the air. When his father asked why everyone was behaving like jackals, Baltazar laughed, gratified to know about some goings-on when his father apparently did not. Part of Baltazar longed to shout that he was ecstatic to have done what he could to help Mariana lash out at their father's rules. At everyone's rules. When Captain Noel Bouton talked a while ago in camp about a nun he saw on the balcony of the convent at Conceição and said she was sublime, Baltazar knew it had to be Mariana, and it made perfect sense to tell Noel that she was magnificent and deserved every attention. It was not as if he went up to his friend, a soldier he admired, and begged him to go enchant his sister, the nun. For fate on its own, however, to take such a twist was entirely pleasing, and Baltazar was a facilitator, hardly that. Besides, she wasn't a nun; she was Mariana. She was entitled to some happiness. If her happiness managed to damage the arrogance of Francisco da Costa Alcoforado, then so much the better. It infuriated Baltazar that although his father had signed the proper papers making him, as the eldest son, the proper inheritor of the *morgadio*, he continued to speak to him as if he were not to be trusted and lacked the ability to make forceful decisions. Wasn't it a strong decision to defy his father, leave the priory, and join the army? Wasn't it forceful to have coerced his father into agreeing to this change, to the wisdom of Baltazar determining his own destiny? And what could be more forceful than to welcome any link to the great French cavalryman? What better act, above all, than to let Mariana triumph?

"If he loved me," Mariana was saying, "he wouldn't go to war. He wouldn't put himself in peril. It's thoughtless. Tell him that."

He sat back, looked at her. Her face was flushed and wet. "What about me, Mariana? I thought I'd hear you begging *me* not to go."

"Tell him, please. Please, Baltazar," she said, and clamped down on his sleeve so hard that he had to pull away from her abruptly. He wondered if she even heard him say goodbye.

She leaned into the silence, as Catarina taught her. She could not decide if that distant hum like a scale ascending and descending was Noel, or her fears rising up and then falling down.

In the "little house" next to Mariana's, where Sister Ignez de São José lived with Peregrina Alcoforado, the Vanity Doll sitting against their wall looked odd, as if caked with colored salts.

"Have you been playing with it, Peregrina?" asked Sister Ignez.

"Yes. Catarina's orange tree has its first baby branch. I asked Dolly to sit on the branch, because I wanted to but didn't want to break it."

"How did Dolly get covered with colors like this?"

Peregrina shrugged. "Maybe Catarina dressed her up for me."

Sister Ignez de São José had been debating going next door and asking Mariana what were those noises sometimes in the night, and if she wouldn't mind coming over now and again to visit her own sister. Sister Juliana de Matos was circulating a lot of vicious nonsense about devils in the Alcoforado wing. Sister Ignez de São José heard sighs that made her clutch her Vanity Doll and not know whether to wish them away or wish them hers. "Do you miss your sister?" asked Sister Ignez de São José.

"Which one? Catarina promised she would talk with me, and she does. I miss Mariana more," said Peregrina.

"Noel? Noel!"

"Mariana."

In his arms, she said, "I was so worried."

"About me?" He pried her off him to look at her, his gaze steady.

"About us. About this."

He reassured her once again that it was no problem to get past Sister Genebra Nogueira at the front door. Even if the portress were not so lax, plenty of workmen, soldiers, and refugees arrived in darkness to flit like moths through the locutory or chapel. The difficulty, he admitted it, was in slipping undetected through the portal that led inside the cloister, and then praying that no one was in the corridors or stumbling down to the cistern as he raced down the hallway, up the stairs, through the second-story quadra forming the southern face of the new wing, and rounded the corner to the eastern face, to Mariana.

"But don't worry," he said, grinning. "I rather like the excitement. Some of the nuns are so old I assume they'll think I'm just a huge bat."

"Noel! Please be serious. Promise me I won't have to worry."

"I can fight armies, I think I can get past a few nuns."

She tried to laugh.

"There, there's my sweetheart," he said, kissing her face.

"Be here always," she said. Would he speak so romantically, if he did not feel it?

"Always? You'll tire of me. You'll get in trouble."

"I'm already in the most trouble I can imagine."

"Shh. Your voice."

"Are you really twenty-nine?" she said.

"Yes, I'm an old man."

"No, it's just that I can't imagine you this old and still unmarried."

"I haven't met the right girl, I suppose," he said, and when he saw her face fall, he said, "Mariana! It's a joke. It's a wonder you don't die of your anxieties."

"I don't care if I die of them."

"I shall care, then."

"You?"

"Don't you see how much I love you?" His hands were on her scalp, holding her entire pounding head. He delivered the words against her temple. Who had ever claimed such radiance?

"I love you more than life," she said.

She truly did not understand how any woman could walk past him without their flesh melting as hers always did, without the invisible and implacable pull that made it impossible for her not to yield, not to touch him, not to touch the air for the need to possess him even when he was not there, the way hummingbirds frantically poked their beaks in empty air, stitching furiously, knitting unseen stamens, the need to disappear into flowers when no flowers were to be found.

At Nones, in the chapel, Mariana burst out with a laugh. Sister Dolores frowned. Sister Leonor Henriques was visibly embarrassed. So were Brites de Freire and Maria de Santiago. The others hugged their distress to themselves.

What did she care that they knew of her love!

When Noel next visited, she would report what struck her: his surname meant "button." Her Mama had sewn buttons to the insides of her sleeves. Even as a child, Mariana had been preparing for him. Had been learning from the start about the love and comfort and the thrilling bumpy sensation of being swept up in arms of buttons. As if Mama had given her the first dream of him, and Noel was giving sainted Mama, dreamed new, back to Mariana.

How ludicrous this chanting was! She should be doing nothing but chanting his name, into his ear, because he was her faith and her country.

In her white nightdress, she waited in the Grand Silence. Sometimes he was late. She played a game. It was no effort to wait for a minute. She could count the seconds easily. Therefore, she told

140

herself, she could last through two minutes. In this manner, she could slip past an hour – controlled torture. This method had helped her survive her twenty-six years of life, twenty-six years of war.

During that afternoon's meeting in the Chapter Room about Our Spiritual and Temporal Business, the Abbess suffered an awful moment. Sister Joana Veloso de Bulhão wanted an explanation of the passage in Saint Teresa's work, *The Interior Castle*, which said that the devil was incapable of joining pain to the spiritual quiet and delight of the soul. That was how one could judge whether a rapture was blessed or not. The devil *incapable* of joining pain to spiritual delight? "Is she saying that pain is the sign of the presence of God? How can that be?" Sister Joana Veloso de Bulhão asked, dismayed, and the Abbess, caught unawares, murmured that she must go and find out, and stumbled from the room.

No one was clear about an answer. Mariana wanted to assert, Yes, it is the holiest, purest agony to desire the beloved, and to have to wait to have him again. A painless rapture was full of the devil's indifference.

Then the terror of everything in reverse when he left.

Tonight, her stomach raging with dread, she prepared a speech. This is dangerous. Take me body and soul away with you. What use do I have for the hours as they are, for anyone who is not you. No heaven can compare to the bliss of you. When you stand before me, I am utterly powerless to stop from clutching you to me, and when you are not here, everything I do and think somehow embraces you. I am equal to the loss of tranquility to my grave.

Noel suddenly entered, and her speech vanished. She flew and he caught her and when she begged him to make love to her all over her room, change every space of these wretched quarters with the two of them joined, he chanted yes, chanted her name, and they might have been in a ballroom in France, with her dismissing with contempt the costly finery and farthingales and coy beating of fans around her as she glided barefoot down a staircase, wearing nothing but a rough white nightdress and bellowing out to her lover, before the scandalized assembly, *That night? Remember that night? There is no choice but to possess that without end.* In front of everyone he would do as he was now, almost crush her in his arms as he carried her with her legs around him from one corner to the next, no one and nothing else existing, the crowd clucking,

"Disgrace! Disgrace!" and when she shouted, "My God, Noel, I love you so much," there was the magnificent fright of owning, both of them, she fully sensed it: a perfect moment. A perfect moment. You lifted me up, our souls floated, you saved me. Complete grace.

When he set her down, she could feel him quaking. He reached into a pocket of his clothing, drew out two bracelets, and wordlessly slipped them onto her wrist.

This is my marriage, she thought, barely breathing.

He gave her a portrait of himself, a small oval, an etching on enamel.

"Why are you crying?" he said. "Why is my angel crying?"

Because of how you're touching my short hair, as if it were as sumptuous as the longest hairpiece on the most stunning woman ever born. Because I want a perfect moment at once, again. Because I never want to be subjected any more to such excruciating pleasure, because now every other moment must be defined as wanting. Because my room is converted, the air different. Now I have no choice but to breathe us. Because no one has ever inflamed me with the praise you have bestowed upon me. Because these bracelets impart to our love a weight, even as they begin to declare it a memory needing a souvenir. Because I keep attaching my spirit to my corporeal hungers, which I never knew so deeply existed, and wonder if I am a fool. It is my desire, my mouth and limbs, some odd ember within, not my spirit, that I truly suspect I am in service of. Because you make me abhor calmness. Because everyone speaks so well of you, because you are a friend to my brother, and because your bravery inspires men, which makes you triply, expansively beloved. Because I am going mad as an animal. Because I love you so much that every drop of death I carry within — and I have a belly of it — and every claim upon life surges up to glorious extremes.

"Because I can't imagine anything better than keeping you with me always," she said, pressing his portrait to her exposed, quaking chest.

That he should bend down and kiss the tears off her face made her give more of them to him.

*

"Darling! Please! I wouldn't have told you at all — but come, be sensible," said Noel. "You persisted in asking me." He added, "Shouldn't you keep your voice down?"

"I don't care if the whole convent hears me. I can't see how it's possible," said Mariana. "I *won't* see it." It was irritating that when he was finished with her, it afforded him no grief to change into his clothes and say, "a week, or longer. We're riding to the border," as if that were not eternity. As if he might not get captured or killed, as if he could conceive of anything but celebrating their ardor. It was true that she had been pressing him to tell her whether he ever loved anyone else. What she meant to remark was, "Isn't it pleasing that no one else ever stood a chance of meaning as much to you as I do? Isn't it a relief, to have found a love truer than most people ever contemplate? Isn't love at first sight the best of all?" But it came out as, "You've never loved another woman, have you?"

She was not looking to quarrel, but she wanted to understand how he could expect her not to react after the casualness with which he said that he had loved a woman in France. Clearly she was not requesting this flat honesty he was offering, but a higher truth.

"I met her before I met you," he said. "Come, dear. Be reasonable."

"I won't be reasonable. You should see any past affairs in a new light, and know that you're no longer able to call them love."

It exasperated her when he pretended not to comprehend, to be incapable of peering over the barrier of their different languages.

"Would you like to put on a uniform, and assist us? We could use you on the front, Mariana. You are the fiercest love a man could hope to find. There! Now will you please not destroy tonight? Will you be happy?"

Wrapping her arms around herself, she sank down and rocked at the edge of her bed. She was being ridiculous. Now she was dying to explain that whatever love was, she was not certain it had much to do with happiness, and then thought, For God's sake, Mariana, enough of the fevered mind; stop it! She giggled.

"There," he said. "There's my Mariana." He was fastening the clasp at the neck of his cape. Since it had a hood, he had not bothered to wear his wig. He had once been faintly annoyed when she had put it on her own head, and declared what wouldn't she give for a good look at herself.

When he kissed her hair at its crown, she gripped both sides of his cape. "It's just that I'm afraid of you leaving me. I can't bear it when you're gone as it is. How will I stand it when you leave me?" She had not meant to speak, but the words were pins in her lungs, and hurtled out.

"I'm here right now. I won't let you spoil our time, Mariana. I'm going to be careful, I'm going to fight, and then I'm coming back. You'll see I'm not leaving. Sweet girl. You are a sweet girl, you know."

"You won't leave me?"

"How can I? You won't let go of my cape."

She laughed, and rested her head against his middle. He brushed his palm up and down the back of her neck. Even that − rapturous enough to die for. Even in the midst of a thousand fears, one hundred cursed hauntings, this was a divine instant. Kneeling, he looked into her face, raised her chin with a finger, and said, "This I can swear to you. Never before and never again in my life, I know this, will I encounter anyone with your passion."

When the French cavalry left its lodgings in Beja the next morning under the joint command of Field Commander Schomberg and General Diogo Gomes de Figueiredo, Mariana did not attend Low Mass. She stood on the balcony outside the Mértola window and watched the Count of Chamilly ride away. Halberds and cannons, shields and banners, dust, red and green jerkins; wheellock guns, some matchlock muskets with their scent of sulfur − through the gates of the city, the battalions poured, but she had no trouble spotting Noel, tall and stout on his horse, his wig past his shoulders. He swerved around, and raised a rapier using the hand that had blessed the back of her neck.

Was he signaling her? Was he only shouting to his men? Look, he almost charged into the person in front of him. Was he thinking of her?

She had no idea.

Sister Brites de Brito strolled past in the corridor and said, "Taking an interest in military affairs these days, Sister?"

"Captain Bouton! Forgive me."

"My mistake," said Noel, quickly reining his horse, taking a short, repairing canter left. He had knocked into the soldier in front of him. He knew better than to let down his guard, court danger. A stupid error, to blunder into someone. He believed in admitting a mistake, even to a lower ranked officer. Not because he was humble. Because it was the right thing to do. His men respected that.

He had seen the nun on the balcony. What was it about women that drove them to claw love to pieces? Squeeze the contentment out of it. A man tried to do the right thing, bring them gifts, but nothing was ever enough. She had deceived him. Most girls were much more coy, but not eager for love. She certainly was. She was unaware that she touched him in ways that did not occur to most women. He thought that meant she knew what she was doing, could control herself. He had allowed himself to be flattered that she noticed him. If women could see him in combat, they might admire him to the degree that his men did. But women didn't. Except perhaps Mariana. He was honest when he swore he would never encounter anyone with such passion. He was overwhelmed by it, but it was dangerous. It never came to any good. It could kill someone.

This brooding wasn't like him. Neither was not watching where he was going. It could get an innocent man killed. The truth was, she was the first beautiful woman to pay him such fervent attention. He had become fond of her. Quite fond. That was dangerous.

"Onward!" he roared to his men, and they galloped towards battle.

She saw him in music. When Sister Dolores asked who could recite the three main categories of Gregorian chants, Mariana bowed and said to the mistress of the choir, "There is the syllabic, with one musical note for each syllable of the text; the pneumatic, in which several note groups are sung within one syllable; the melismatic, in which long note groups are absorbed in each syllable."

"Excellent, Sister," said Sister Dolores. "I was thinking you were half-asleep! What is the effect of the melismatic?"

"To make words exultant," said Sister Mariana. "To make them richer. To open them up, make them explode."

She saw him in the color of the vestments. When the celebrant offered Mass, wearing a green chasuble to designate Ordinary Time, Mariana thought jubilantly, Green? Greenness should be banished. Time can never be ordinary again.

She found him in the vast sorrow of the night, when she took out his portrait and the Saint Christopher medal, and spoke his name.

In the scriptorium, in her sums, in her numbers. Aroused by accounting. Flames licked up from the parchment. Sister Francisca Freire dropped one of Mariana's pages as though it had burnt her. "Sister Mariana," she said. "Is there anything you wish to tell me?"

Sister Maria de São Francisco, furious that dinner was not the pork loins that the kitchen had promised, threw her tray of stew onto the floor. A few of the postulants followed her example. No one was in control. The Abbess, Dona Joana de Lacerda, had passed away. Another noblewoman, Dona Isabel Pereira, doddering and older than her predecessor, stepped in to fill out the rest of the term when everyone else refused the job, but she was usually too sick to sit at the head table.

"Not the worst thing happening around here," trumpeted Sister Juliana de Matos, sniffing. "Not the worst hysterics."

Sister Brites de Noronha pointed out, in manual language, that Sister Juliana's sundering of the silence was itself an offense, though a venial one.

"Don't flap your hands at me," snapped Sister Juliana de Matos.

"A sin to waste food," growled Sister Michaella dos Anjos, cleaning up the remains of Sister Maria de São Francisco's portion. "Men are dying, and you act like a queen who wants servants to dance attendance on her!"

"I know someone who gets lots of attendance danced on her," said Sister Maria de Santiago.

An awkward shock gripped the refectory, reducing those present to conformity with the rules of silence. The discomfort abated when it was noted that Sister Mariana was not among them. Of course, why did she need to leave her room? Why come out to be their sister, to sing, labor, eat?

While doing Mariana's laundry, Sister Maria de Castro scrutinized the linens for spots of blood. She never found any, but the cloth was consistently saturated with a man's perfume. What was inexplicable was that even when the French troops were on the frontier, Mariana's sheets came to the laundry with a redoubled amount of that scent, as if she had sweated him in when he was with her, and was now sweating him out, to let him lie damply, invisibly beside her. Maria de Castro was impressed. This was so much more miraculous than the boring usual laundry stuff of the other nun-bell-heads!

When she slipped out of her dormitory that night and went to Mariana's "little house," it wounded Maria de Castro that Mariana's face collapsed with disappointment upon throwing open the door.

"It's only me," said Maria de Castro, plaintively.

"You can't sleep either?" asked Mariana.

"No," said Maria de Castro. "May I sleep on your linens tonight? I'd like to wrap them around me, if you don't object. Just this once?"

In the courtyard, around the well, some nuns were prattling about Mariana. Sister Ignez de São José went to them and said, "Why don't you take that kind of pig-slop to your confessor? Can't you see her baby sister is right over there?"

"Baby sister?" said Sister Cecília Sebastiana. "I don't think that stuck-up Mariana has said two words to Peregrina since she got here. She might as well be a perfect stranger."

"Peregrina is still an Alcoforado," said Sister Ignez de São José. "You should assume that means she understands more than you think."

Sister Brites de Freire brought a hen pie and some bacon-and-hare soup from the kitchen to Mariana's "little house." Mariana was curled up on her bed, but sat up when Brites came in.

"I've been worried about you," said Brites. She wanted to visit, to prevent herself from hating Mariana for being such an inattentive friend.

"I'm incredibly happy."

"You hardly look it. You must be starving." Brites offered the bowl of soup and plate of pie, and watched Mariana devour it.

"Oh! Forgive me!"said Mariana. "May I offer you some?"

I'm wrong, concluded Brites. Look how her skin glows. The irises of her eyes are emeralds, and the heat she's emanating makes me feel like I'm standing naked on the plains.

Brites de Freire bit her lip to keep from crying. "You've gone away from me," she said.

"I'm right here, you silly."

"Don't call me silly." Brites snatched back the empty plate. "At least —" and she dropped her stare. "At least tell me what it feels like."

It was Mariana who had to lower her head, to keep from weeping. "If I could, I'd tell you, of all people. You more than anyone else. But that's the curse of it, Brites. It won't let itself be described as any one exact thing." Later on, it occurred to her she might have said: You know those ex-votos we throw into the fire, Brites? The wax leg when an aunt has a broken shin, a wax baby when a child is sick, a wax arm when someone has had one chopped off at war? We think it's a leg, an arm, a baby. A wax heart, when a man leaves. We throw our wax wishes into the furnace to make our prayer, and the fire says, "You presumed to know what they were? Then where's the leg, the arm, the heart? It's all mine. All fire."

At last! At last! Though he looked terribly tired, she could not stop herself from saying, "Can't you end this war?"

"Then I'll be out of work and have to suffer French society." He collapsed onto her bed.

"I'll keep you busy." She threw herself onto him. How could he sleep?

"You'll be the death of me."

She sat up. "What a thing to say!"

He covered his face with his hand. "Why do I have to watch every word? Every word, around you."

"What do you mean?"

"You see? Every word requires caution. Exhausting."

"Noel." Caution? When nothing about them had anything to do with caution?

"Yes?" His eyes were shut.

"It's so simple, really."

"It isn't, but let's not quarrel."

He fell asleep. She did not comprehend how he could, but she thought, *Love is going to teach me everything on earth.* As he slept, she held one of his hands, studied the lines in it, tried to read them, soothed the nails, loved him lying there, scolded herself: *At the threshold of dead sleep, still he found a way to you.*

*

Sister Francisca Freire was doing her best to read the neumes and marks, like scrambling lice, on pages of organ music for Sister Beatriz Maria de Resende, directing the blind nun's fingers over the keyboard. Most of the convent was asleep. Sister Francisca Freire lacked any musical training and had to count the treble and bass staff lines to determine every note — chords took her entire minutes to figure out — but she feared that Sister Beatriz Maria de Resende might die if someone did not attempt to help her learn new compositions.

"Shall we stop? You're hoarse tonight," said Sister Beatriz.

"I'm a woeful musician, sorry," said Sister Francisca Freire.

"It's not that," said Sister Beatriz. "Since I lost my sight, my hearing has become hideously good, I'm afraid. You sound anxious."

Sister Francisca Freire conceded that she was, but did not elaborate. She was glimpsing broken tendrils of web, like spun-out love scattered around the convent. She must stay ready, for when Mariana needed her.

Sister Leonor Henriques wrote a letter, though this was a prohibited activity, to her brother Rui, saying that she might more favorably consider his bid to inherit her property in Viana d'Alvito if he took better care of his wife and her family. They undoubtedly needed that now. She did not go into detail. She was certain Rui would have heard the rumors. When she finished her letter, she strolled to the new wing. A sun-yellow light was spearing itself outward through the cracks in the door of Mariana's room. Sister Leonor Henriques knocked, and broke the Grand Silence by saying to Mariana, "I'm afraid for you. Are you well?"

A lantern was iridescent beside her bed. A response burst out from Mariana, "No, I'm immensely ill."

"My unfortunate membership in the Lôbo clan has trained me for many things," said Sister Leonor Henriques. "Here's a secret. Rui, Cristóvão, and Bartolomeu used to have paralyzing headaches when they were children. I'd order them to sit with me and concentrate on the contents of their heads until those thoughts spilled out into my hands, so that I could catch what was bothering them and throw it away. This worked in that it got rid of their headaches. It did not work in that I sensed that my brothers were going to grow up full of ideas that would lead to mayhem, and I failed to drain any of that out of them."

"I would like to try it," said Sister Mariana. "As much for your company as to see if it works."

With her head cradled in the hands of Sister Leonor Henriques, Mariana watched torments fly like ravens out of her mind. She discovered today that she would not be having a baby. A disappointment. She would have rejoiced in one shame more. It might have compelled Noel to take her without further delay to France. Why had he never managed that, never set forth a strategy, though he was a genius at strategies? He had acquired two Portuguese servants, Manuel and Francisco, and planned to return with them to France. Why did he always say to her, Wait, the English diplomats are doing what they can in Madrid, but the treaty is not signed.

Shouldn't love disdain any schedule but its own? Oh, she was the patron saint of the Alcoforado curse, which was to plan so far ahead that the rest of the world had not yet learned that it was expected to cooperate! Why did he not complain of her and say, Prove your much-vaunted love, leave your family and country and this convent where you were thrust against your will, denounce all but love's tyranny, ride into battle with me, and at the last toll rung at the end of war, I shall sweep you into my saddle, facing me, and proclaim, hold me, hold fast, I'll carry you alone, you alone.

Was she really to go to France?

Love devised its own reasons, forced its own solutions. With love such as theirs, anything was possible. He might stay here! She had not pondered that, but it made sense! He had been here for years. He played cards and went hunting with the local men. They were in awe of him.

It was not imaginable — no, not for a moment! — that he could exist without this passion. Yes, that should be her reassurance!

When agonized thoughts arose — Might she say goodbye to Papa, Ana Maria, Brites de Freire? Sister Francisca Freire? Sister Leonor Henriques, Maria de Castro, and the others? Would she be able to bear the gossip in France? — she poured these into the hands of Sister Leonor Henriques, who could hardly muffle a lament. "My prized child," she said. "Your skull is pounding worse than ever. My hands are shivering. Will you stop now? Can you stop?"

"No, I can't," said Mariana. "I'm so awfully sorry."

Who has ever thrown herself with such hate, such love, upon a man? When Noel arrived as she was hovering at the brink of despair, she pounded her fists on him. He said he couldn't stay long. A gambling tournament was going on in town, to celebrate their success on the frontier. It took him an hour to calm her. He, spoke of his brother, Hérard, writing to him of the war expanding to the Low Countries for the French. He spoke of Rui thwarting capture, Cristóvão fighting like a legion, and Baltazar showing infantrymen how to wrap cloth around a comb and blow stupid music out of it. Noel did an imitation of this until she relented, amused.

Lying with her beneath a blanket, he told her what Paris looked like, what Spain looked like, what Flemish aqueducts, English tapestries, and French beauty marks looked like. Did she know the theory that if a woman was too breathtaking, she would offend God, and therefore she should stick a small dark blotch somewhere on her face?

Mariana had not heard of this marvel! This was exciting, him knocking down the walls of her confinement and letting the world flow in.

Did Mariana know that these women sometimes used the beauty patches in certain configurations to convey a secret message, perhaps to a lover across a room? Although the patches were also used, more mundanely, to cover blemishes.

"I can see how a wrong message might get sent when all a woman is trying to do is hide the places where nature has betrayed her," said Mariana.

They laughed together at this.

"You should have a beauty mark," he said. "You are so lovely that I am sure you offend God."

"I am sure I don't. God made me this way and I think He likes it fine," she said. "But I would enjoy wearing a beauty patch, if that is what women do in France."

He kissed her cheek. "There," he said. "There's a beauty patch." He kissed her chin. "One there." He kissed all over her face. "All of it beautiful," he said.

She told him about how Papa used to set her on his shoulders, saying, "Slap the sky, Mariana! Higher, come on, you can do it!" She talked about Ana Maria's children, and Mama's proud stomach rounded out like a globe. About walnut trees, shrines, her blue bedspread from Macau. Vovó. Adventures. Mother Maria de Mendonça. She wept all of a sudden about Catarina and Mama, until he said, Shh. Shh, Mariana, I love you. About the shrine to Our Lady of the Upper Veranda, about some spectacles from Italy that Sister Francisca Freire was starting to perch on her nose for reading. She told him anything she could think of, and therefore contained, and therefore could give him as a gift.

She was beginning to feel that this was how they might love each other when they were in their real home — gently talking away the night with simple stories, jokes, and unknown facts, not everything perpetually staggering, ornate, lacerating — that they might be the first lovers in the history of the earth to domesticate ecstasy. To rise to the challenge of happiness and bring passion into a house, where it increased rather than slackened. Unheard-of feat! She would do it! They would do it. As she envisioned this, Noel said, "I must get to that card match, dear." She curbed the old urge to protest. Quietness, deafening love, comings and goings — all must exist for them, and none would diminish their love.

"If you see Baltazar, tell him I'm glad he's safe," she said, mildly.

He looked astonished at how well she was taking his leaving. A relief. She was going to stay friends with him, when they parted. She was using good sense.

After Noel left, Mariana danced in her room. She was embarked on an endless voyage with him, and would discover affection wild, affection domesticated. Every byway of it. Loud and raucous, and gentle and undemanding, like tonight. The whole dark night one beauty patch.

Good God, Mariana, Good God. He thought the last time he was here, matters had become nicely settled. Women did this. Had to finish with nightmare. He was taken aback at how she was ripping at his clothes, talking — where was her dignity? about her thighs. That she was burning up for him. Him? An idiot could see that whatever this was about, it had nothing to do with him.

She was a writhing mess. Her arms could not hold him tightly enough, her tongue not disappear far enough past the lips shrinking from her, her back not arch enough to snap in two and put her out of this misery because holy gracious mother Mary if she wasn't in a constant fire.

Ana Maria shrieked at her children to stop running and calm down. She was dabbing the blood from her brother Miguel's nose. He had been in a fight in town.

"Explain yourself! Explain!" Papa was thundering. As he approached seventy, he was becoming easily infuriated at the dawning notion that even if he lived to see peace, he was getting too elderly to do much with it. This seventeen-year-old son of his, on the other hand, groused about the war not lasting long enough for him to join it. "I won't have one of my children fighting improperly, using his fists like a ruffian. I won't stand for such commonness!"

"You know I'm not the common one," Miguel said to his father. "Why don't you go say that to Mariana?"

"Shut up, Miguel,'"said Ana Maria.

Francisco da Costa stared at him. His thirteen-year-old son, Francisco, and two granddaughters, Caetana and Inês, stopped their fussing to regard his stone-cold fury. Bastiana, the maid, brought a fresh basin of cold water so that Ana Maria could finish tending to Miguel's bleeding, and removed the one full of pink water.

Rui swaggered in and said, "The hero is home."

Ana Maria screamed at her husband, "What are you doing here? Are the whores in town busy?" She threw the bloody cloth into the water, said to Miguel, "Take care of yourself, why don't you?" and to her father said, "Papa? Where are you going? Say something."

"Christ! What's happening?" said Rui. He followed Ana Maria to their room, where she wailed that the children were misbehaving, not that he cared, that Miguel was surly, that one would think he would have enough respect not to lash out at Papa – but why was she explaining this to a drunk, a gambler, a whore-chaser like Rui? He and his temper and obstinacy were doing their part to push her father into his tomb. She jabbed an accusing finger at him. "You probably bet that Frenchman that he couldn't seduce my sister. That sounds like something you'd do."

"You think that?" Rui shouted. "That I'd do that to her? Jesus. Jesus. You don't know who's responsible for him getting to her? Christ. Never mind. You don't know me at all."

She covered her face with her hands; she hated for Rui to see her cry.

He put his hand on her elbow. "Ana Maria," he said.

"Don't speak to me," she said. "Don't touch me. I'm fat."

"Don't talk that way. You're my wife. You're the mother of my children." Rui's tone lowered. "I would never harm a woman. I wouldn't chance hurting a woman shut away in a convent. Especially not Mariana."

"Yes, how deranged of me, the Lôbos are so honorable."

"More than you give us credit for. We're more honorable than the young layabouts I see these days."

"God help us."

"God help us indeed."

"You harm me."

"What? Never. I don't."

"All those other women. All your drinking."

"That? Who cares about any of that?"

"I do."

He sighed. "Aw. Well. If it's any comfort, I'm getting old. Going on fifty. Look at me." He paused. "I mean, please. Look at me."

She glanced at him, then quickly away. "There. I've looked at you."

"I wasn't going to bother to tell you, but if you want to know, I tracked down this fellow, even though he's a friend of mine, and said he'd have to fight a duel with me, but I was a bit drunk, and he said I should go sleep it off, and then we got sent to the frontier, and I lost track of him. By the way, if anyone cares, we're about to get to be our own country. Freedom, you know? We'll have a treaty within a year."

She sniffled and nodded for lack of knowing what else to do. "Who helped him get to her?" she asked softly.

"Never mind. It's not important."

"I don't want Papa to find out about Mariana," she said. "By the way, if you care, I'm going to have another baby."

"Ana Maria," said Rui. "Your father knows about Mariana. He may not be ready to believe it yet, but he knows."

*

Sitting at the bedside of Maria Alves, who did not stir from her profound dreaming, Francisco da Costa said, "Speak to me, you old fox. With Leonor gone, there's no one to talk any sense. You and I should be arguing about what peace will mean." He scolded her for absenting herself for the last fifteen years. For not helping raise this tribe of grandchildren, who mystified him. His own offspring mystified him. He had not trained them to be so aimless. Baltazar in particular. That nonsense he was spouting about seeing to it that the legal demands of the convent at Santa Clara were concluded, that tired argument about Francisco's pressuring them to sell their property. The terms had been considered harsh but fair back when the convent was desperate. No reason for him to sell his purchases back. These days no one honored a deal that should have been set for life. He should not have to explain such a concept to his own son. Baltazar was supposed to be preparing to inherit a *morgadio,* but the coming era would have to be prosperous enough to compensate for his son's weaknesses. It hardly mattered to Baltazar that his father had given his life to throw off the yoke of Spain and create a free country.

His servant, Luís, found him. Ignoring that Francisco was muttering to the immobile Maria Alves, he pulled up her eyelids to check the glassiness beneath them. He would not humiliate his master by asking why he was conversing with a comatose woman, but if anyone came by, he would think of an excuse for what his master was doing. People were snickering about Francisco da Costa Alcoforado. Luís was failing at his job to care for him. He didn't know which he hated more, his own failure, or the ingratitude of the mob amusing itself at the expense of this man who had built the mint that produced the rebel coins — what would soon be the coins of weary freedom – filling their pockets. Boys in the cavalry had survived because Francisco da Costa set up farms to breed better war horses. The shortness of people's memories was disgusting.

"Ah. Sir?" said Luís, as Francisco's ranting at Maria Alves grew louder.

"I know she's not hearing me, Luís," said Francisco da Costa. "Can you guess why my mother-in-law and I liked fighting? It was a game, that business about whether the merchants or the nobles would inherit the earth. None of us is going to."

He ordered Luís to ride to the Rua do Touro in town and draw the blinds over the windows of their vacant manor facing the convent of Conceição, to close the eyes of the place of Mariana's birth. The blinds were to stay down in perpetuity.

In his solarium, he wrote a succinct note to the throne of Portugal. The French quartered in and around Beja, especially the cavalry, were a vexation to the entire innocent populace. As the retired alderman of the city, and as the chief engineer in the past in getting foreign troops in, he was the best judge of when they should go. Schomberg should be commanded to withdraw to different ground.

A man of will and vision should define his power by the extent to which he might write a letter that could alter the course of history.

He placed his seal on the letter, and found a walking stick. He was in need of some air. Luís went to saddle a horse and deliver the letter. As Francisco stood in the doorway, clutching the griffin's head of the walking stick, he was convulsed with a shudder of missing Leonor. He was not afraid of anything. Not death. Death meant joining her. He had waited to receive the dagger of the Spanish King. But he could not stand the stabbing in his heart from his own daughter. He could face squadrons of the enemy, but not her. He would never see her again, nor would he speak of her.

When Luís brought the horse around, he noticed Ana Maria trying to persuade her father to come inside. Francisco's mouth was open, and tears curved down his wrinkled face, but at first no noise was coming from him. Then he bellowed, "Mariana! Mariana!" Already breaking his vow. Never to speak of her? Never to claim Mariana? Luís saw how frightened Ana Maria was. They both knew that since they had found Francisco da Costa like this, he would turn vehement and angry, to wipe away their pity.

"Noel?"

"Almost caught. Almost didn't make it to you this time."

Her head against his chest, she listened to his heart racing, the sound of proof that he loved her, had rushed to her.

"I must hear yours," said Noel, putting his head on her chest.

How her heart was storming! Like his. Did he know the term *mouvement*? No? He must be enjoying himself at her expense. The word was French!

"I've never heard it before," he said. "Define it for me."

The standard definition was not full enough, because it did not include him. She considered telling him that her dead day had been resurrected, because of now. She said, "*Mouvement:* This. Here. You, my One More Than Everything."

And yet the next night when he visited, and they made love too fiercely and swiftly, and he was resting by her side and staring at the ceiling, she said, "Noel? I can feel that you're not here, so why don't you leave?"

The following night, he smuggled in wild flowers off the plains, hard purple thistles, and he said, "Forgive me."

She refused to let go of the flowers as he undressed her. He said, "How have I deserved you? What shall become of me? You've ruined me, angel."

The nights were running together, the mass of them, and the refrain at the end, no matter how long he lingered in the doorway, was, "Goodbye, Mariana. Goodbye," until she said, "I love you with all my heart and all my soul. Go, hurry, someone will see you."

When he disappeared, she was still clutching the flowers. The feeling in her room was that it was not a room. He had made it oceans, plains, everywhere. In the center of it was his portrait, his gift to her, hidden. She could wait past the end of the war. She could wait beyond whatever he needed to do to make arrangements. She could wait into dotage, and hobble out into his arms after decades of him being gone, if that was how long it should take, and say, "I never doubted you. My ardor has not lessened; it has increased."

She would be patient, even if it meant her temperature fluctuating as insanely as it did the subsequent morning, switching from hot to cold and driving her to the infirmary, until her twitching prompted Sister Juliana de Matos to murmur, "Poor Mariana. Rest. Forgive me for hating you."

As midnight approached, she crawled off the cot in the infirmary, and dragged herself back to her "little house," since nothing would be worse than to miss him. Upon finding her shaking, he said, "What have I done to you? You're not yourself."

"I'm more myself than I've ever been," she said.

*

"You could not!" he said, amused.

"I could!"

"I once picked some apples during a harvest when I was a boy," he said, "and I think that oranges would be no different. I could pick more in an hour than you."

"You could not!" she shouted.

"Shh."

"I know how to climb trees," she said. Her swiftness with orange trees would come from her wish to seize fruits that reminded her of Catarina, but she did not say this.

"You know how to do everything wonderful," he said. "Don't you?"

He kissed her so that their laughing would stay swallowed, low.

When they broke apart, she said, "Baltazar taught me how to wear a cloth tied around my neck and waist and how to collect oranges fast. He's a friend of yours – maybe he'll teach you, too."

"He's a friend for talking to me about you. We haven't had a chance to climb trees."

He told her a funny story about a man at camp who coughed and coughed and then pretended to pull long colored ribbons out of his mouth. He had them tucked somehow into his collar. It was such a stupid magic trick that everyone always was reduced to merriment.

Mariana laughed again. She coughed and pulled at the air, pretending she had produced ribbons, and they laughed until they were definitely in danger of being caught.

"It sounds like something Baltazar would do," she said. "Are you sure you're not referring to Baltazar?"

"It does sound like him, but no," said Noel.

When he left her that night, her fears were quieted. They could speak not of love, but of nonsense. They could venture into passion so profound that it could forget itself.

"Goodnight, my Mariana," he said, and his embrace, as he said farewell, was warm. Yes, love could forget itself and be light and amusing!

She made a coughing sound.

Be with me, stay with me.

Sharp intake of her breath, her eyes open, staring into his.

She could will this moment forever.

158

Don't say, *Remember this,* she told herself. Don't think or say anything.

"Mariana," he said, his arms tightening around her.

A thin ocean of sweat was between them.

Yes. He was also saying not *I shall remember,* but *I am this, this now, this with you alone.*

Noel Bouton tried to calm himself. Never before in his military career had a commanding officer been furious with him. To have been personally sought out by General Schomberg was as close as Noel had ever come to disgrace. When the General had shouted, "My God, man, don't you know who her father is?" Noel had been shocked.

But Schomberg was a decent fellow. He promised to see to it that Captain Bouton received the title of the Marquis of Chamilly, Count of Saint-Léger, for his considerable services, and would arrange for a carriage south. A ship was leaving in a week from the southern coast of the Algarve and would convey him back to France. To dispense with any suspicions that his early departure was dishonorable, Schomberg would leave the date blank on Bouton's papers, to be filled in later should a face-saving adjustment be necessary.

Bouton thanked his General, and added that in fact he had recently received letters from his brother and from the French King, asking if Noel would not mind commanding a cavalry force in the Low Countries.

He asked his servant Manuel to arrange for a carriage to arrive within five days, and his other servant, Francisco, to deliver a letter to the convent. Noel wrote a few lines telling Mariana that duty was calling him elsewhere. He apologized for this abruptness, but it was in keeping with his line of work. As she — as they both — well knew. She must promise not to forget him.

He did not go to the convent that night and sent Mariana another note the following morning. When not on the front, he was accustomed to conversing with her daily. On the third evening, two days before the carriage would come to transport him south, he chided himself. He must do the honorable thing and say goodbye to her face.

When he finished his speech to her that night, she was sitting calmly in a nest of a thin blanket, and said, "I don't believe you. I can't believe you."

"In time you'll think of me fondly," he said. He had been braced for a firestorm. She was a smart girl, and would release him, perhaps relieved − grateful − that her anxieties could be ended.

"Why would I reduce my love for you to a fondness? Nothing but a future thought? Why not love me always?"

He did not have a reply. He supposed it was too much to hope that she would appreciate how difficult it was for him to come here and do this in person. "In my country, we say, *au revoir*, Mariana. That isn't a final goodbye. It means 'until we meet again.'"

"Coward! Liar! I don't want a language lesson! Tell me that you love me! There isn't a reason on the earth that would ever rip me from your side! How can you stand there like that?"

"Mariana." He knelt at her bed. He must do this quickly. He kissed the tops of her knees through her black scapular. She had removed her veil. "I love you."

"Oh!" she said, disgusted, in a jolt of pain. "Don't say what I tell you to say! Don't say it because I say it! Say what's in your own heart." Her hands were around his head, and slipped away as he stood.

"I'll write to you," he said.

"Don't write to me. Oh, my love − come to me. Come stay with me. You *have* to. How can you think we have any other choice?"

As he headed for her doorway, she went after him, to throw her arms around him. If she held on, he would not leave. Such agony to feel his back, the huge flesh shield of a man's back, like the canopy of himself that a woman held onto when she made love to him. He was talking nonsense, her touch would give him the courage to tell her that the war was not over but when it was he would sail back, having prepared a place for her in the world, the easiest thing to do once a place was installed in the heart, simply a matter of arrangements, luggage, schedules, goods that meant nothing; she wanted no jewels, no finery, no mausoleum of a house, she wanted only him, forsaking family, honor, and title. He was not giving her an appointed day for fear of disappointing her, yes, that was it, that was how things went in war, and she should know this, because there had not been peace for a single day since her birth. I love you, I love you forever, she was saying in her heart because it was her heart that could best speak, and she could feel beneath her tightened embrace that he was waiting for her to let go. That he was not being a lover but a gentleman, waiting for her to be finished, and he was murmuring his reasons for leaving again, coldly and in order, but his hand was stroking her hair and that was enough to shatter her soul, and when he said, again, Think of me, she thought: What else will be left to me? If I cannot see you ever again – no, impossible! – I shall not have eyes. Not to hear you? I shall cease to have ears. Never again to hold you in my room with the fire that consumed us together? What good then is my worthless touch?

"No!" she said. "No, no! No!"

"Mariana," he said, and stepped back.

She was scalding. If she tried to speak, it would be like spitting out brittle pieces of her shattered skeleton. Tears were pouring without sound out of her, her open mouth could not speak, all sorrow and speech were gone out of her body as she watched him leave.

As he hurried away down the corridor, his mind was saying, Do not look back, it's more loving if you don't look back, no matter how much you want to. In a while, this will be fine and fond, a memory. As it was meant to be all along.

He had handed her a last letter.

She did not chase after him. Even in this, she was strong enough. Let no love come to me that does not on its own accord come.

But within the hour, she wished she had run after him, put on a disguise and gone to ride beside him, sail off, no more awful waiting. Instead, there was nothing to do but go to the window and pray, I love you. I love you still. I love you always. I esteem every joy and every sorrow your love bestows on me.

Every anniversary of this day as long as I must wait for your return, I shall come to my window and repeat this prayer. I shall add one line every year, to offer that time in summary, until I hold you again.

She opened the last letter he handed her, and read it. More of the same. No promises. Excuses.

Because she could not extinguish the fire she had made of herself, she feared being reduced to ash. She could not see with her eyes, she lost the feeling in her skin, and the only melody apparent was the echo inside as she shrieked in an anguish that contained every anguish she had ever known.

*

"Oh, child, what have you done?"

Mariana heard this indistinctly as she tried to swim upward, out of gray ashes. She was flailing, on hands and knees on the floor, making love to the air. Who was here? Who was speaking? Her ears were slowly loosening. Some feeling was returning. Someone's hand was on her wrist, grasping the bracelet from Noel that she kept hidden up her wide sleeve, and this person was pulling her by the arm up out of a howl. Mariana heard the last choked coda emerge from herself.

"Child, what have you done?" She heard this again. A woman's voice. Someone holding the precious bracelet, and saying this.

"Sister Mariana, do you hear me?"

It was Sister Francisca Freire. "There's a noise stuck in you, and I'm going to squeeze your jaw because I want it to come out, or it's going to kill you. All right? All right, Sister Mariana?"

A last broken measure was forced out of her. The screech of it was awful, final. She went cold and rigid, and curled up like a dead cat in Sister Francisca Freire's lap. She could vaguely distinguish Brites offering her some water, and settled into a blue agony, washed over by a sense of a light blue color wrapping around her, the sky carrying her away. She recognized the lullaby that Sister Francisca Freire was singing. When Brites held up like a mirror a gold paten stolen from the chapel, she said, "Look, Mariana. Why is your face covered with red spots?"

Because my heart is useless. Because my heart has exploded and is pushing the pieces of itself out of my body. Go away. What kind of a friend are you? I don't want to look at myself.

Her blotched reflection shone in the paten's gold, round as a halo.

When Sister Ignez de São José brought her Vanity Doll to Mariana, Mariana stared at its spots of color and could not remember if she had painted it this way, the colors of her love needing to find some spare body to adorn, or if the Doll was changed from leaning against their adjacent wall, madly drinking up whatever leaked out of this room when Noel was in it.

Had been in it. No, impossible.

Sister Francisca Freire slept on the floor of Mariana's room.

"Don't, Sister," Mariana said. "Don't, you'll make yourself sick."

"Then I shall take some of the sickness off you, I hope, Sister Mariana. Go to sleep now. I've sent for Baltazar. I think he can comfort you better than anyone."

Mariana awoke to find Peregrina in her bed, with her small arms around her. Mariana screamed and cried, "Mama!" and had to stay in the infirmary until Baltazar at last arrived.

Someone knelt at her bedside. She had no notion of how long she had been here. Her dreams were disemboweled by Noel's absence, and from rereading his last letters with their rationalizations. The truth of his being gone was biting at her arms and legs. Her brother was whispering, "What is it, Mariana? What's happened to you?" He did not care that Sister Juliana de Matos was staring. He had seen men dead on the battlefield who had fewer red wounds than were now marring his sister's skin. She was muttering about Noel.

He tried to distract her. He told her about Field Commander General Frederic Schomberg sending a letter addressed to "Whomever Is In Charge in Lisbon," stating that it was inconvenient to be so far out of Beja, and the hell with this. He was returning to the camps closer to Beja, whether they liked it or not.

Wasn't that hilarious?

She wasn't listening. Baltazar gripped her hand. He was in tears. "It wasn't supposed to happen like this, Mariana. It wasn't, I swear it. Mariana, tell me what to do. Tell me what I can do for you. It's killing me to see you like this. I'll do anything."

"I need to write him," she said.

"Yes, you know what, Mariana, I can get him a letter, if that's what you want. I'll find a way of getting it to him. The French travel back and forth all the time. I'll find a way."

She was suddenly excited. By now Noel was probably safely in France, engaged in a new life. But that would not matter! Her brother was giving her a chance to change all that, to save herself. He found a quill pen and some paper.

She hesitated. "I hardly know what to say," she said.

"Start the way you start everything, Mariana," said Baltazar, working to keep his voice level and sturdy. "Start by talking to your heart."

Head bowed towards the paper, pen held over it, she waited, as Papa used to do, for God to send an urgent message. She addressed her heart, and fast as a miracle, fast as a wish, the words poured out:

LOOK, LOVING HEART, how profoundly you have lacked any vision! Oh, ill-adventuring heart! Your fervor was betrayed, and with your false hopes I was seduced.

A passion that once promised me such unfolding pleasures now bestows nothing but mortal despair, as cruel as what causes it: the separation from my beloved. My sorrow looks with all its ingenuity upon his absence and does not know how to give it a sad enough name. Am I to be forever prevented from beholding that gaze where I once drank in so much love, that taught me incomparable rapture, that was my everything, was all I had been awaiting to suffice me to the end of my days? Listen, my love: My eyes, alas! have lost the sole light that gave them life. They are enlivened now only by tears; no other task can be put to them but to have them endlessly weep, ever since I realized that you were set upon a departure that I find so unbearable that surely I cannot long survive it.

And yet the misfortunes you have wrought exert such a hold on me that I cling to them gladly: I anointed my life yours from the first moment I saw you, and I take pride in making such a sacrifice. One thousand times a day I send out my sighs that search for you everywhere, but the only reply to my disquietude is a prudent warning voice, faithful to my sad fate and inhuman enough to forbid me the slightest delusion as it admonishes me at every turn: "Stop, unhappy Mariana! Stop consuming yourself in vain, wishing for a lover you will never see again, who crossed the seas to flee from you and is now in France, surrounded by gaiety, who hardly recalls your anguish, a lover who finds new ecstasies without the least remembrance of the ones he shared with you."

But no, I cannot bring myself to judge you so harshly; I am too intent upon absolving you. I refuse to believe that you have forgotten me. Am I not bereft enough, without tormenting myself with untrue suspicions? Such fine pains you took to convince me of your affection and lavish it upon me — why should I wear myself away, trying to dislodge that from my memory? So enchanted was I that I would be ungrateful if I did not still want you with the same abandon that my passion instilled in me when you first declared your love.

How can such sweet moments turn so bitter? Must they defy their own nature and now serve merely to lacerate my heart? Alas, poor heart! Your last letter forced it to yield to such a singular state! My chest was ready to crack open from the boundless leaping of a heart battling to free itself and take wing to your embrace.

Seized with these collisions inside me, I spent three hours adrift from the world, prostrate and senseless. I barely strove to return to an existence that by rights I should lose for you, since I am forbidden to devote it to you. Finally, though much against my wish, I revived, having flattered myself that I was dying of love, and there was some comfort in not being shattered in every instant by your absence.

Since that disturbance, various chronic ills have claimed me. But how shall I ever be free of them, if I am never to see you again? These tremors I shall bear without argument, because they come from you alone: Therein lies the sum of it. Is this the payment due me, for wanting you so extremely?

No, no, I must quit this! I am resolved to cherish you past eternity, and to have eyes for no one else. You, too, would not be amiss if you never noticed any other woman. Could any passion less fervent than mine content you? You might encounter beauty elsewhere — though there was a time when you told me that I was very beautiful — but you will never find anyone who loves you as vastly as I do, and the rest, all of it, is nothing.

Do not fill your letters with apologies, nor fall back upon exhorting me to remember you. I am unable to forget you. Neither can I relinquish the hope that you might come to spend some time with me. Oh, my love, why not have it be for the rest of our lives? If I could leave this accursed cloister, believe me that I would not be standing watchful here in Portugal for the fulfillment of your promises. Without so much as a sideways glance, I would strike out and begin the march *that would allow me to find you, embrace you, and love you always, everywhere.*

I am not so foolish as to imagine that this will ever truly come about, nor do I seek to nourish myself with wayward hopes, for these might grant me some relief, and it is solely to the heartbreak of my misfortune that I can dream of consecrating myself. I confess, however, that when my brother offered me the chance to write to you, I was surprised to feel some flutters of happiness, and for a while it has checked my agony.

I beg of you, tell me what drove you to charm me as you did, knowing full well that you would soon forsake me. My God, what possessed you to enrapture me so fiercely, only to leave me wretched? Why not let me alone in the peace of my cloister? What harm had I done you?

Forgive me; I blame you for nothing, nor am I in any condition to think of vengeances. I blame everything on the rigors of Destiny. It appears that in dividing us, Destiny has already done the worst we had to fear, but it shall not follow from this that our hearts need be separated. Love, stronger than Destiny, united them beyond all time. Look: If you feel for me some tenderness, write to me often. I am worthy of your taking some care to disclose to me how you are faring. Above all, I implore you . . . come see me.

Farewell: I can scarcely force myself to let go of this paper, to allow it to fly to you and fall into your hands: Oh, my precious love, what I would give if such a bliss were mine! What insanity — as if I didn't fathom how impossible that is!

Farewell: My spirit fails me.

Farewell: Love me always, and I shall endure still more.

*

Dona Maria Madelena Pereira could not believe she was stuck with the job of Abbess again. This was the doomed term! No one could undertake it and survive! First Abbess Joana de Lacerda had died, and now so had Abbess Isabel Pereira, Maria Madelena's sister. No one wanted the miserable job, and a group of nuns, led by Sister Brites dos Serafins, surrounded Maria Madelena and said that since she was Isabel's sister, she should do everyone the favor of taking over until the proper time for the election later that year. When Maria Madelena suggested that they could as easily hold the election that week, Sister Brites dos Serafins almost collapsed in horror. Never before had the election period been violated. Enough was going wrong in this convent without upsetting the clockwork.

Sister Michaella dos Anjos added that Maria Madelena could commence her duties by addressing the complaints of several of the nuns against Sister Mariana, who, as everyone was aware, had committed a very serious crime. Or was Maria Madelena afraid to punish an Alcoforado?

Maria Madelena retorted that there was so much unrest that she merely had to select any starting point. It did not necessarily have to involve a girl who had spent the last few weeks vomiting in the infirmary.

During choir practice, Sister Dolores announced that Abbess Maria Madelena was instituting a policy of rearranging everyone's regular position in the loft, to reduce the gossiping and the tendency to develop friendships that did not heed the rules of the Order about treating one another with equal degrees of closeness.

Sister Genebra Nogueira declared that since Sister Mariana had not bothered to come to practice, she would not stay here either.

Sister Angelica de Noronha, upon losing her place next to Sister Beatriz Maria de Resende, deprived of her one thrill in life now that Catarina Alcoforado was gone, wept furiously.

Sister Maria de São Francisco, who was losing her place on the other side of the world's most glorious singer, pitched her songbook over the railing, to strike the floor of the chapel below. "Why am I being punished?" she yelled.

Peregrina clung to Sister Ignez de São José.

Sister Maria de Castro thought, Bell-heads chiming.

"Sisters!" said Sister Dolores.

Sister Brites de Freire was ashamed to find herself rejoicing in an outcry that could be blamed on Mariana as much as on how exceedingly on edge everyone was to hear of a peace treaty. What was this mysterious feeling, to find ticklings of comfort in a friend's distress?

Abbess Maria Madelena headed for Sister Mariana's "little house." Her own special apartment in a building commissioned by her rich daddy. The nuns were right. That spoiled brat. Five times already she had refused to see the father confessor, saying that she had nothing to be sorry for! At some point, when Mariana's condition improved, the Abbess would force her to speak to him, and then she would be punished as she deserved.

Bursting into Mariana's room, the Abbess found her lying down, her chest heaving as if she had used up her tears. "For the love of God, Mother Mary, and Saint Clare, Sister Mariana! You are an abomination," she said. "You have upset everyone!"

Mariana babbled at her like a madwoman.

"Speak clearly! What do you have to say for yourself?" said the Abbess.

To the Abbess's bewilderment, Mariana gasped out pieces of sentences, saying that she was dying to wish her body away, that she was tortured by daydreams of hordes of women swarming over the mountainous body of the man she loved, that she could not cure herself and preferred to perish of sorrow, that news of her father's fury was afflicting her, that winged monkeys flew into her quarters at night to jeer, "Never again, never again." That she had received a few dashed-off notes from her Captain that were clearly meant to dismiss her and remove his guilt.

"I see that you're contrite, then," said the Abbess.

"No," said Mariana. "No, never. I want him still."

The Abbess tucked her blanket around her. Look at this girl. How could the Abbess be so harsh? Cysts disfigured Mariana's face. "Darling girl," said the Abbess, placing a cool hand on Mariana's mottled forehead. "If you were to turn to God with this intensity, I believe He would claim you as the queen of His heaven."

Sister Angelica de Noronha, out of respect for how Catarina had loved her sister, brought Mariana the first sprouting orange leaves mixed with honey and walnuts. She said to Mariana, "Eat this, dear. It's a taste of Catarina. She'll help you."

Sister Maria de Castro read Mariana a letter written by her thirteen-year-old brother, Francisco Alcoforado. He said that although he did not know her well, he grieved to hear of her illnesses. She must allow him to amend whatever was wrong. Sister Maria de Castro folded the letter and said, "Mariana, you're so far away, it's cruel to leave me behind."

Sister Brites de Brito brought Mariana the book of the Forty Hours, and said that perhaps it would help her to work. Mariana's weeping was renewed; she would have no choice but to record, "My One More Than Everything" for forty hours, until her hand dissolved into pure ink.

When Sister Maria dos Serafins reported to Mariana that on her behalf, she had stayed awake praying through the night until Prime, Mariana doubled over with grief — those were the hours for Noel.

When Sister Francisca Freire was not running the scriptorium by herself, or was not being the interpretive musical eyes for Sister Beatriz Maria de Resende, she was sitting in a chair beside Mariana in silence, refusing to fill the maw of time with inadequate words.

Finally relenting to Sister Brites de Freire's insistence that she leave her "little house" and breathe some air on the veranda, Mariana tottered out, blinking in the sunlight, only to buckle under the memory of being here when the course of her destiny awakened at the vision of her love riding through the square. She ran back to her room, to cry and claw at her skin. She wished to be rid of any encasement of body or thought. Months had passed, with no word from him. Not a single letter. Brites de Freire, seeing her friend's torment, asked her to tell her all, every detail of him. And hated herself, because shimmering within her sympathy was a pleasure that Mariana, accustomed to special treatment and privileges her whole life, could actually lose something.

Peregrina demonstrated how well her tutoring was going by leaving dead walnut tree leaves outside Mariana's neighboring "little house" with a note that read, See how sad everyting is for you. Don't cry, sister.

Sister Ignez de São José pointed out that although Peregrina misspelled "everything," it was frightening to see such a wise eight-year-old.

Their half-brother, Father José da Costa of Our Lady of the Snows, was informed at the front portals by Sister Genebra Nogueira that Mariana refused to see visitors. Obviously Father José had come quite a distance, and she was sorry it would have to be for nothing.

"The time and distance are insignificant. I love my sister," said Father José, handing over a patch he had woven of whatever he could find — blue string, a speck of blue flower, a piece of twig bark that he painted blue. "If you would please make sure she receives this." Not much in the way of extra cloth existed at his priory, and he had hunted up what he could to produce a miniature replica of her blue silk bedspread, where they had danced long ago with their bare feet. He had heard of her skin condition, and if she put a patch of blue over her inflammations, they might be cured.

Father José had gone to pay a call upon his father, Francisco da Costa, but the patriarch had called him a bastard. It had taken most of Father José's charity not to yell back. You made me that. You made all of us what we are.

On the tiring journey back to his priory, Father José da Costa asked God to enlighten him as to how he could prevent Mariana from being killed in the minds of the people of Beja, since their father was warning that her name must not be uttered. Miguel, her own brother, was denouncing Mariana. Already the work of annihilating her had begun.

Ana Maria did not care that the townspeople were glaring at the shame of a pregnant woman appearing in the streets. She stared right back at them — a small courage, compared to Mariana's. Ana Maria was going to pound on the convent's door and hope that this time her sister would not refuse to see her. Part of her wish was selfish, she freely admitted. Mariana would not disapprove of a selfish motive. Ana Maria needed to escape from home. Papa sat in his solarium, hardly moving. When the Marquês de Niza or Dom Joaquim Ferreira de Fontes came by, he shouted at them to get out. Even worse was having Rui underfoot. He was more trouble than the children, and his vile brother, Cristóvão, kept dropping by. They had shone through three decades of warfare, and peacetime and freedom meant not having a single notion of what to do with themselves.

The portress took Ana Maria's message to Mariana's room, while Ana Maria waited at the ogival-arched door. She was surprised to see Rui approach her. Good Lord, he truly had nothing to do anymore.

"Has Papa run you out of the house again?" she asked.

"He's too morose."

"You may not speak of my father like that. Don't you have a battle to finish somewhere, Rui?"

She was appalled to feel his paw gently land on her shoulder. Normally their contact was at night, when he was drunk and thought he should burden her with another child instead of taking his base wants elsewhere. Nothing that had anything to do with love figured into what they did. Only things that made her ancient.

The truth was that she wished to comfort Mariana, but she also wanted to say, I'm an old married woman, and I'm dying to know, you've been the one I've asked for answers, Mariana: What is it like? If love afflicts us as much as it's tormenting you, then why do we want it so much?

"My gorgeous Ana Maria," said Rui.

"Go home, Rui," she said.

"Come spend some time with me."

"Have you lost your mind? No. Besides, I want to see my sister."

To her astonishment, he got down onto his knees and kissed her hand and said, "Kick me if you wish, dear lady, but do not send me away. Nothing compares to being with you."

"You ridiculous liar," said Ana Maria, but she giggled. She did touch the side of his scarred face, full knowing that this was as close as she might ever come to having a moment of affection with her husband. It was not grand. But it was hers.

When the portress reported back that Mariana was not well enough to see anyone, Ana Maria said, "Tell her I know that she came to visit me just now." She went home with Rui, who promptly ran off to a card game with Cristóvão. Leaving Ana Maria to feel herself joined to the sorrows of Mariana, in that love could strike unexpectedly, but it was forever brief.

Worse than no love, worse than silence! A letter from him had been delivered that morning: "How are you, Mariana. I am well. The war will almost be over and I will go on a long vacation." That was all! Worse than the other absurd half-page of trivial nonsense that had arrived last week: "Miss you. Take care!" Mariana scratched her face until she drew blood, as if to ventilate herself, give the outrage a vent to escape! How could he be "well" – how not sick with the nightmare of this separation?

Each day was surely bringing her closer to the day he realized that their love was like none other.

One morning she awoke and said aloud, "Months. The time has turned into months since he was here with me, in my bed, in my room, night after night." She said to herself, "Years. If I can wait a single moment without him, I can wait years, since it will never be as if he has not left me half a moment ago."

One breezy morning, the conscience of a Lieutenant Foucault brought him to the royal convent of Conceição. Months had passed since Captain Bouton's departure from the war front, but the ship carrying him and the Lieutenant had been wrecked along the southern coast. The men on board survived, but they were languishing while waiting for the ship to be repaired and the seas to permit a voyage. Bouton spoke at camp about a nun, and showed the Lieutenant a letter from her. Her forlorn, heated words haunted Bouton, but they also affected the Lieutenant.

Foucault had recently broken his engagement with his fiancée in France. They had come to their decision in their own exchange of letters. His sweetheart had not seemed more than mildly upset at losing him, and when he read this Sister Mariana's words, he was intrigued. What must such a woman look like, sound like? He was going to be traveling into Beja the next day before returning to board the ship. His excuse to visit her would be that he would make every effort to carry a message to Noel, who was still in the country, though not for much longer.

He regretted this curiosity when he beheld the nun, worn and with ravages on her skin, in the locutory. She was overjoyed out of proportion to what he was saying, and overeager to practice her French with him, mentioning something about months and a length of water being meaningless in separating two people who were joined. She drew more details from him about the shipwreck and Bouton than Foucault was comfortable in giving, and she burst into an angry tirade when he said he had no letters to present to her. She was sweating as she ran off to find paper to write a letter, and he urged her to be quick about it; he really could not stay.

"He's fine, fine," said the Lieutenant. "He had a grand time playing cards during the voyage. Does that cheer you, to hear that his spirits were good during the trip?"

"Were they?" said Mariana. "I see."

Mariana told herself, Speak, wrecked heart, as if this is the last day of your hard beating, and she wrote:

YOUR LIEUTENANT has just informed me that a tempest has forced you to take refuge in a port in the kingdom of the Algarve. I fear you must have suffered at sea, and so vividly has this haunted me that I am no longer concerned with my own distress. Do you imagine that your lieutenant has more of an interest than I do in what befalls you? Why was he better informed? Why did you not write me?

I would be upset if no occasion has presented itself for you to write since your departure, but I am surpassingly more tormented indeed if a chance arose, and you did not seize it. Your injustice and ingratitude are pronounced, but I would be horribly afflicted were they to bring you any misfortune, for I would rather you thrive unpunished than to witness my hurts avenged. I resist every sign that ought to persuade me that you do not love me; I succumb to the stronger urge to marry myself blindly to my desires rather than to the reasons whereby I might deplore your neglect.

You might have spared me many griefs had you been as listless in our first encounters as you have now been for quite some time. But who would not allow herself to be as entranced as I was by such an outpouring of devotion, who would not judge it sincere? What a payment it exacts, and how reluctant we are to convince ourselves that we should doubt the honor of those we adore!

How clear it becomes that the least excuse serves your purposes, but even when you do not trouble to offer me one, I love you so immensely that I cannot assign you any faults, except for the exquisite joy of examining them and, despite all evidence, proclaiming you guiltless.

You devoured me through the perseverance of your wooing, you set me afire with your ecstasies, you enticed me with your sweet courting, your vows gave me assurance . . . but it was my own raging nature that seduced me, and out of my own violence, my wildness, so glorious and blessed, there is left but tears, but moans, but death in its gloom, without any chance of healing.

Our love brought me the most startling pleasures, but now I am shocked at the inexpressible pain: the emotions you stir in me always run to extremes. Had I obstinately resisted your advances, had I provoked your jealousies to increase your attentions, had you detected in me any artifice — had I, in short, used the ordinary weapons of flirtation and reason instead of falling within my natural attraction to you (though doubtless my effort to have reason prevail over passion would have been useless), you might have had license to wield with some justice the power you hold over me. But I deemed you worthy of my arms, before you ever mentioned that you loved me; you swore the highest ardor for me, and I was so elated that I delivered myself up to loving you without restraint.

You were not as blinded as I; why then did you allow me to fall into this quandary? How could you have craved my affections, which must have been bothersome? You knew you would not stay in Portugal; oh, love, why choose me for this sentence? In my country, you could certainly have found another more enticing woman, with whom you would have had as much pleasure, since it was only the baser kind you were pursuing. She would have loved you faithfully for as long as you were in sight, and following your absence, time would have easily comforted her. You could have left her without treachery or cruelty. Your conduct, instead, befits the tyrant set upon persecuting, rather than the lover who should dwell upon searching for ways to delight.

Why do you treat with such contempt a heart so entirely yours? Clearly you let yourself be persuaded against me as readily as I have let myself be persuaded in your favor.

Without the faintest idea that I was doing anything demanding, without summoning the aid of so much as a particle of the fierceness of my love, I could have easily withstood much more forceful reasons than the ones that compelled you to leave me. They would have seemed thin and weak to me; not one of them would have stood a chance of tearing me from your side. But you wanted to grasp at any pretext to return to France. A ship was leaving. Why not let it sail? . . . Your family had written. Are you unaware of the outcries that I have suffered from mine? . . . Your honor obliged you to give me up. Have I minded at all about my own honor? . . . You needed to go serve your King. If what they say of him is true, he little needs anyone's help, and would have absolved you.

I would have been blissful beyond measure if we could have spent our whole lives together. But since we were fated to be apart, I think I ought to be a little satisfied that I was never unfaithful; not for anything on earth would I have committed such a treachery. And you? How could you have swum to the bottom of my soul and to the height of my tenderness and still be capable of deserting me, exposing me to my nightmare that you will no longer think of me, or will recall me only for the sake of making yourself feel all the more a conqueror in some new affair?

I know that I ache for you like a woman who has lost her senses, but I do not complain of my tumultuous longings. I am becoming accustomed to the oppression of my emotions, and I could not live without this joy that I discover amidst uncountable sorrows: that I love you still. I love you more than all the strength of the world allows.

But what mortifies me without end is the nausea and aversion I feel for everything . . . My family, my friends, this convent are tedious to me. All that I am obliged to observe, everything I am made to do, is odious. So envious am I of my passion that it seems all my duties, all my actions, are declarations of you. Yes, I am uneasy if I do not find you within the center of my every moment. Oh, what would I do, without such great hate and such great love to fill me? How might I survive what occupies me continually, in order to live a dull, peaceful life? No! . . . Such soullessness, such an emotional void — I despise all that. It could never suit me!

Everyone notices the utter change in my temperament, in my manners, and in my person. My Mother Superior spoke to me about this, at first angrily, and then with some kindness. I scarcely know what I replied. I believe I confessed everything to her. The strictest of the nuns pity my condition, and show a certain regard and gentleness towards me. They are all touched by how rawly my love has overflowed . . . you alone remain indifferent, writing me nothing but cold letters full of tired banalities. Half the paper arrives blank, making it rudely plain how dying of impatience you are to conclude.

Dona Brites has been coaxing me for some days lately to leave my room. Hoping to distract me, she took me for a walk along the balcony, from which one sees the gateway set in the direction of Mértola. I followed her, but once there I was struck by a crushing memory that drove me to tears for the remainder of the day. She led me back to my room, where I immediately cast myself onto my bed and was assaulted by reflections on how little chance I stand of being tranquil. Whatever the nuns do to comfort me somehow aggravates my torment, and in their gracious gestures I find private reasons that end up magnifying my anguish. It was from that balcony that I saw you ride by many times with an elegance and grace that swept over me, and it was there that I found myself on the fatal day when I first began to feel the effects of my unfortunate yearnings.

It seemed you fell in love at first sight, before even meeting me. I was certain that you singled me out among all others; I imagined that when you stopped or pivoted your horse, it was because it excited you that I might see you better and admire the skill and pomp with which you then galloped your horse. I was surprised by the scare it gave me when you led him in a perilous maneuver; truly, I was secretly enjoined with your every move, and I sensed that you, too, were under the same spell . . . that whatever you did, you did for me.

You well know what followed these beginnings; though I am beyond acting cautiously now, I had best not refer so much to those early days of our rapture, for fear it directs a brighter light upon your guilt, were that possible, than presently exists, and for fear of incriminating myself as the wellspring of so many futile attempts to oblige you to be faithful — for faithful you will never be, never! How can I expect my letters and my laments to conquer your lack of response, when my soul and my lovemaking could not? Your coldness leaves me without the barest reason to doubt my fate. I should give in to fearing the worst, since the truth is that you have abandoned me.

Could your charms have dominion over me alone? How could you not appeal to other women? I clamor for evidence of their feelings, that I might justify my own. I wish that every woman in France might be attracted to you, but that none love you, and likewise you find no one pleasing. This fantasy is ridiculous, impossible — aside from how thoroughly I know from my own experience that you are little capable of a lasting affection, and that to forget me you do not need the incentive of a new lover. Perhaps I am wishing that you could offer some reasonable explanation as to why you vanished. Though that would make me still more unhappy, it might lessen your guilt.

Obviously you will stay in France — without rich passion, but in full liberty. The fatigue of the long journey, your petty notions concerning propriety, and your shame in not knowing how to respond to my desire, shall keep you there . . . Ah! Fear nothing from me. I would be content to see you from time to time, to know merely that we dwelled under the same sky.

Maybe I deceive myself; the hard dispassion of another woman might move you more than my tenderness. Is it possible that disdain excites you more? But before you yield to any tyrannies of love, consider the excess of my afflictions, the uncertainty of all my plans, the jumbled poundings of my emotions, the extravagance of my letters; consider my trust, my despair, my unquenchable longings, my jealousy . . . Guard yourself against such a plight as this. Pay heed to my folly, learn from my afflictions, so that at least what I suffer now for you will not be in vain.

Five or six months ago, you confessed, in a disturbing confidence, that you had loved a woman in your country. If it is she who prevents your return, tell me so frankly and at once, so that my wondering if you will come back to me may be put to rest. A remnant of hope still sustains me, but if this is eventually to be dashed, I would rather lose it now in one fell blow, and myself with it. Send me her portrait, and some of her letters. Tell me all she says to you: I might find in such truths some consolation, at the risk of letting them afflict me more. I understand only that I can no longer endure this dilemma in which I am confined; any change is *preferable. I would also treasure portraits of your brother and sister-in-law; whatever is dear to you is therefore precious to me. My devotions extend to every reach of your heart. Of myself, there is nothing left that can be of use to me. Occasionally I wonder if I could submit to waiting upon a woman you loved. So low has your disdain debased me that sometimes I actually consider myself the guilty one, for voicing jealousies that might annoy you; that I am the wrong one for reproaching you. I ought not to reveal, with the fever that I do, these uncontrollable feelings that you disavow.*

The officer who must take my letter to you has been waiting a long time for it. I had planned to write something that might give you unconditional delight upon receiving it, but you see how it has gone awry. I must conclude it — alas! I lack the strength for that. It seems I speak with you when I write, and that I can feel your presence. The next letter will be neither so lengthy nor so tiresome; I promise you will be able to open and read it and see that this is so. I should cease railing upon a passion that you find dismissible, and I shall speak of it no more.

In a few days, it will be nearly one year since I first surrendered myself to you without reserve or a sense of propriety or moderation. Your loving was so all-consuming I would never have dreamed, not by the remotest chance, that my fondness might engender a disgust that would drive you to go 500 leagues away, risking shipwreck, just to get away from me: Who would expect such treatment? You may reminisce about my chastity, my shyness, and my perplexity, but you find nothing in your memories that prompt you to love me.

The officer is telling me for the fourth time that he wishes to leave. Such a hurry! He, too, is probably fleeing some lonely woman in my country.

Farewell: It wounds me more to finish this letter than it wounded you to depart from me, perhaps forever.

Farewell: I dare not call you by a thousand tender names that could give voice to my desire, nor surrender without restraint to the tempest of passions in my heart's possession. I love you a thousand times more than life itself, a thousand times more than imagination can conjure. How dear you are to me! How cruel! You never write — I have not been able to silence this refrain — I am beginning to write this letter all over again, and the officer will leave . . . What does it matter? Let him go!

I write more for myself than I do for you.

I seek to unburden and console myself; I search in writing for ways to alleviate the weight of my own heart.

Certainly the length of this letter will frighten you, and you will not read it.

What did I do to be this star-crossed? And why did you enter my life, only to embitter it?

Oh, love, why was I not born in another country?

Farewell: Forgive me! I dare not beg you now to love me. Behold in what depths fate imprisons me!

Farewell!

*

She had marked it forever inside herself: One year since surrendering herself to Noel. What did it matter that a letter had burst out of her only a few days before today? She wrote another one, held it in her hands, waited, soaking the envelope, paced in the locutory.

Oh, it was meant to be, this day was meant to be marked, this anniversary, because there was Baltazar, coming to see her! The messenger!

She threw herself at him, crying, "Where is he? Where is he? Take this to him. Get him for me. *Please,* Baltazar."

"Mariana," said her brother. "Stop this now."

"Please, Baltazar."

Tears ran over her distorted features. She could not stand up straight, and her nails were digging into his arm.

He grabbed her and said, pulling her up, "Look at me. It's Baltazar. Can you see me at all? Can you say hello, can you ask me how I am, for a change? Mariana?"

She might as well be deaf. He could be bleeding wounded on the floor, and she would step over his body to get to that oaf who was supposed to be his friend.

"Get him back for me," she said, clutching him.

"Mariana." He was horrified, and shoved her away. "Where's the old Mariana?"

"I despise the old Mariana," she said.

"Tell you what," he said. "When she's back, let me know, since she's the one who remembers me."

He left before he could prevent her from giving her letter to a French soldier at the chapel's altar rail, who took pity on her and said that most people knew the Bouton family of Dijon, though the Captain would be residing in Paris if he survived the campaign in the Low Countries. A mail carriage was leaving soon. He would see to it that the nun's message was put in transit, since it seemed she would tear him apart if he refused.

WHAT WILL BECOME OF ME; what would you have me do? I am so far from my every plan and dream! I hoped you would write me from the places you traveled through, that your letters would be extensive, that you would feed my passion with the promise of seeing you again, that an utter trust in your fidelity would afford me tolerable repose. I even devised a feeble plan of bringing all the force I could bear upon a cure for myself, if by chance I could convince myself that you have quite forgotten me. Your absence, my aspirations towards prayerful devotion, my fear of ruining through my sleepless nights and vigils the little health remaining to me, the scant likelihood of your return, the coldness of your passion and last goodbye, your departure founded upon frivolous reasons that remain as unrelenting as they are worthless, all seemed a refuge built of truth, there should I need it. I have never had anyone to contend with other than myself: How could I have guessed at my unwillingness to enter that refuge? How could I have predicted what I suffer today?

Oh, this sadness! Do I not deserve compassion, for having no means of dividing my sorrows with you? Why must I be solitary, so completely solitary in this agony? This is what is killing me.

I die, as well, at the thought that if you are now indifferent to my despair, you were perhaps never fully seized to the depths of your soul by the pleasures we shared. Alas, yes, I now see the false face of your raptures: You were deceiving me whenever you repeated that your supreme joy was to be alone with me. Your ecstasies sprang merely from my importunities; you formulated a cold-blooded plan to entrap me; you looked at my passion as a conquest, without allowing it to penetrate your heart. It is you who should be pitied, for having so little delicacy that you cannot imagine how to put our ardor to fonder use than this. How is it conceivable that a love limitless as mine could not make you the most blessed of men? I mourn, purely out of love for you, the innumerable transports you have lost; how could you not wish to steal them with me? Had you genuinely felt them, surely you would find them of infinitely more lasting worth than the poor vainglory of seducing me, and you would sense how much more exalted it is to love vehemently than it is to be loved.

I know not what I am, nor what I do, nor what I yearn for: a thousand contrary torments tear at me . . . Who could design such an awful fix? How desperately I love you, and yet my consideration for you is such that I control myself sufficiently to dare not wish the same emotions to flood over you. I should kill myself or die of grief if I thought that you never had a minute's rest from this type of affliction, that you lived shedding tears, that all was repugnant to you. I can not stand my own suffering; how could I endure the pain that yours would cause me, infinitely more hurtful to me than my own?

Yet I cannot bring myself to wish that you not think of me; in all honesty, I am terribly jealous of anything that might gratify or touch you or bring you pleasure in France. I hardly know why I write you: You will only feel sorry for me, and it is not your pity that I want.

I am furious with myself when I reflect on how much I sacrificed for you: I lost my good name; I exposed myself to the wrath of my family, to the severity of the laws of this country regarding nuns, and to your ingratitude, the most fearsome of all disasters. Nevertheless I well know that this remorse is hollow — for I wish with all my heart that I had faced still worse dangers for love of you, and I nurse a searing pride in having risked my life and my honor. Should I not have offered you my every last esteemed possession?

Should I not be glad that I offered them — everything — as I did?

But I do not live content with the pangs of my wounds, nor with the excess of my passion, for in spite of flattering myself that I cannot go on without you . . . I live — holy God! Alas! — Faithless as I am, I expend as much effort to preserve my life as to lose it. I die of shame for that: Perhaps my torment exists only in my letters? If I loved you to the length and depth that a thousand times I have professed to you, would I not be for a long time now already gone? I have deceived you: Complain of me! Protest! I watched you leave, I lost the hope of having you again — and yet I live! Though I ask your pardon for misleading you, do not grant it; treat me without mercy. Declare my passion less monumental than I have portrayed it. Request that I die of love! Oh! Assist me in this, that I might conquer the weakness of my sex and cut short my wavering by a true act of despair!

A tragic end would doubtless tie me to your memory. The thought of me, and my extraordinary end, might become dear. Is a large death not preferable to this reduction of me? Farewell: If only I had never met you! Ah — this, too, is an empty sentiment: I know, even as I write, that I much prefer the anguish of loving you than never to have known you at all.

I resign myself without murmuring to my ill-starred destiny, because it is the one you have determined not to make better. Farewell! Promise that you will regard me fondly, should I die from pain; promise that at least my stormy emotions will produce in you a disgust for the earth and its ways and goods. This consolation suffices me: If it is written that I leave you for always, I wish that no one else in a distasteful world satisfies you. Would it not be unspeakable if you used my despair to make yourself more attractive, to demonstrate that you have inspired in me the greatest passion in the world?

Farewell, and farewell once more.

The letters I write are far too long; I show a lack of concern for you. I ask your pardon. Please indulge a poor, maddened soul who was not thus agitated, as well you know, before she loved you.

Farewell! I speak too much to you of my unrest, and yet I thank you from the depths of my heart for the disquiet you cause me, and I detest the tranquility in which I lived before loving you.

Farewell! My passion increases with each moment, with each day. Oh, love! What a host of things I still have to tell you!

*

Sister Francisca Freire took the Italian glasses off her nose and said, "Try, Sister Mariana."

A quill pen in hand, her arm shaking and splattering ink, Mariana was forcing herself to undertake the accounting on the year's expenditures for candles. Tears were sliding over her face from the effort, and her quivering nose was running. Sister Francisca Freire had gone to Mariana's room and said that the time had come to repair herself with work. As Mariana wrote "I," her hand was riddled with exhaustion.

Sister Francisca Freire took the quill from Mariana, who had slumped over at the table. "Good girl, there's a start," said Sister Francisca Freire. "That's all for now."

She used her own scapular to wipe off Mariana's face, and took her back to her "little house." She then paid a visit to Abbess Maria Madelena, and said that Sister Genebra Nogueira should be fired as portress, and Mariana assigned the job.

The Abbess indicated that she did not care one way or another, but it was not right to give someone of Mariana's rank such a lowly job. Her father might be outraged.

"I don't think we need to worry about that," said Sister Francisca Freire. "My idea is that she should do something simple and get some air until she's ready to come back to work with me." She did not add aloud that Mariana badly needed some contact with the outside.

When Mariana stood at the portals, as townspeople or soldiers walked by, murmuring, she scanned them for traces of Noel. She stared at the ones with letters in their hands, hoping that they would be coming her way. During attempts to cure herself, she forced herself to imagine him with another woman, but the effect of that was to have her shake, her shoulders droop. Sister Francisca Freire would appear and make Mariana lift her chin and straighten her spine. "Pride," Sister Francisca Freire would say.

The last particle of unforgiveness, lingering on one of the hairs of Maria Alves in a coma on her bed, detached itself from her short, corpulent body, and abandoned her to a state of delight, melancholy, and panic. It had been longer than she could recall to feel this unresentful, and the sensation was not entirely comfortable. "I am succumbing to death by forgiveness," she proclaimed, hoping that her dead husband could hear.

He answered, "Then join me."

"I'd rather be with Leonor. I assume you're in hell."

"Tsk, darling, I got absolved. I thought you'd forgiven me."

"I have forgiven you. I got a bit nostalgic for familiar feelings. The way everyone in this house shouts, it's no wonder they've awakened the dead. I have to present one of my great-granddaughters with my leaf pin of pearls," she said, "and I need to steal a key and go find Mariana. I owe her the answer to a riddle."

"Mariana would do better to find out that not every riddle gets answered."

"Do you know what we kiss, but never adore?"

"No," said her husband. "Is it our spouses, after decades of marriage?"

"No. Aren't you a chuckle," she said. "If we end up in the next world as nothing but flimsier versions of ourselves, I'm going to be outraged."

"Come," he said. "The man who died after opening those chests from India is here. Hurry. So many dead soldiers flocking around, it's difficult to fight through the crowd."

"Leave that to me, lover boy," said Maria Alves, and thumped her enormous breasts. "I'll work us to the front of the line. But first I must say my prayers."

Her soul said, Listen, God, I've been storing up rest so that you'll have extra to give Mariana, my companion. Grant her peace. Tell her that I will be doing whatever I can, dead or alive, to lead her to happier adventures. Here I come, God, and I'm going to give You an earful about repairing her wounds.

*

On February 13, 1668, eight-year-old King Carlos II of Spain signed a treaty with Dom Afonso VI, though he no longer possessed the throne, giving Portugal her freedom and ending the twenty-eight-year-long War of Independence. To celebrate this affirmation of peace between a deposed madman and an incompetent child, the nuns at Conceição threw a party to say goodbye to the refugees who would be leaving them. Everyone was in a calm but depleted mood, politely passing around salvers of caramel eggs and debating how Manuel might have managed to land them a shipment of pineapples from the Azores. Sister Beatriz Maria de Resende offered a rendition of the anthem under the new flag, and there was light applause.

"Sorry about your grandmother," said the Marquêsa Dona Fernandes, handing Mariana a gift.

"Thank you," said Mariana. "I thought she'd be around forever."

"I thought we'd be around *here* forever, too," said the Marquêsa, then stopped. "Oh. Sorry."

"That's all right," said Mariana. "If my Vovó isn't coming to kidnap me, there isn't anywhere for me to go." She unwrapped a new quill pen.

"I hear you're quite a writer," said the Marquêsa. She whispered, "I know I can persuade you to break the rules and write to me!"

Mariana frowned, but nodded, to be courteous. How trivial and frivolous everything sounded. To reduce the writing of precious letters to a girlish violation! The Marquêsa, of course, would never write back.

When Peregrina brought them a tray of lemon tarts, Mariana smiled and said, "Thank you."

A round of goodbye kisses and embraces was continuing at the door. Young girls, whooping with excitement, were being collected by relatives and parents. Sister Maria de Castro was sleeping in a pew, and Sister Brites de Freire sat biting her nails before coming to Mariana and saying, "This much fun is killing me. Have you ordered your new party dresses?"

When Mariana took up her post at the front entrance, Sister Maria de São Francisco said, "If war was in the past and this is peace, then why is nothing different? Shouldn't the feeling be different?"

"It feels like every feeling ever invented should be different from what it is right now," said Mariana.

It was a relief to be alone that night, and look out into the unchanged landscape, and to pretend that the whirling dust was Vovó going to haunt the houses of those celebrating peace, that she was the dust reading the lips of what everyone was saying, Vovó climbing into bed with everyone now drunk and free.

Go see and feel the whole world for me, Vovó, whispered Mariana.

And be the dust that settles on my ear during my sleepless nights, and recite to me all you discover about the places you enliven with your presence. Even when you were in a coma, you were more alive than most people.

I miss you so.

When a soldier passed by, she held out some of the pastries left over from their freedom party, and she begged him please to put them for her in a roadside shrine. Vovó would probably be at rest, but if she were not, Mariana wanted some trace of herself to be out there, telling her grandmother to come, please. That was the only celebration right now that might have meaning.

"You crying, Sister? You lose someone?" he said.

Sister Francisca Freire — that uncanny pest! — came by, and pushed Mariana's chin up to say, "Pride."

And so Mariana merely smiled at the soldier, and did not give in to the temptation to say, At this hour of our victory, I realize I have lost everything, dear man.

When Sister Brites de Noronha was elected the new Abbess for a regular three-year term, in accordance with the prescribed methods of balloting, and announced that she would continue Maria Madalena's policy of instituting changes to remind them of who and where they were, Sister Francisca Freire said to Mariana, "Start taking notes on what to do and not to do. I want you to be the Abbess here one day."

Mariana had the best laugh she had known in a long while, and figured that her friend was doing her best to cheer her up.

Now that there was peace, her waiting for Noel was reawakened, to torture her again full force. Now more than ever, he must look to his heart, and rescue her; her pulse was throbbing, My love, my love. When the loud warning voice scolded her, she said to it, "Leave me to my dreams."

When Sister Maria de Castro was punished for speaking in the refectory, she hid the psalm books in revenge.

When Sister Maria de Santiago was told to surrender a diamond pin, she screamed that her brother who had died in the war had presented it to her when she was five, and the Abbess would have to rip it off her.

A French soldier came to the front door and chatted for an entire morning with Sister Mariana about Noel Bouton, and mentioned that France had declared peace in the Low Countries through the treaty of Aix la Chapelle. She risked punishment by the Abbess for neglecting her duties as she wrote, standing up and holding page after page against the door while the officer waited to take and deliver her letter:

SURELY I am committing the worst possible wrong to the feelings of my heart in the futile attempt to clarify them to you in my writing. How happy I should be, were you to know them through the vehemence of your own feelings! But I can not expect this from you; neither can I cease declaring — though less sharply than it possesses me — that you should not humiliate me with a forgetfulness that unnerves me and even brings shame upon you. It is only fair that you tolerate my cries that come from a desolation that began to engulf me once I understood that you would leave. I deluded myself into thinking — how obvious it is now — that you would stay more loyal towards me than usually happens in these affairs. I felt that the grandeur of my love made me soar above the ordinary, above all the normal suspicions, and in return would merit a fidelity equally extraordinary. But your inclination for betrayal is greater than your sense of justice towards all I meant to you.

I would be no less miserable if you loved me only because I forced you into it. I want nothing that does not come unrehearsed from your affections — but this is so far from being the case that six months have passed without a letter from you! I blame my dismay on the blindness with which I insisted upon loving you. Should I not have guessed that our embraces would end sooner than my love? Did I dare imagine that you might spend your whole life in

Portugal, renouncing your fortune and country, only to care about me? My agony has no solace, and remembering how I once took pleasure in you now makes me distraught. Is my every craving to be frustrated? Shall I never again hold you here in my room, with the surpassing rapture you used to show? Alas for my delusion, even now; I know painfully well that those ecstasies that intoxicated my mind and heart were for you nothing more than thrills that came and burned out with the moment.

In those flashes of supreme joy, I should have called upon reason to temper the fatal excess of my delight and so forestall my present suffering. But I gave myself to you without reservation; I was in no condition to envision anything that might poison my enjoyment of the fiery displays of your longing. I was too captivated in feeling you near me to consider that one day you might be gone.

I recall, though, that now and then I voiced the fear that you might leave me unhappy, but these terrors rapidly vanished when you protested that no such thing would occur. I would be relieved, and willing to ignore everything for the sake of surrendering to the enchantment.

The remedy for my woes is obvious: I would be free of them if I stopped loving you. Oh, what a cure! No! I prefer to suffer still more rather than forget you. And must this task depend upon me alone? How can I chastise myself for not being able to contemplate a single moment in which I do not love you!

You are more to be pitied than I am. It is worth more to ache on the heights as I do than to wallow in the tepid diversions that your mistresses in France provide for you. I do not envy your indifference; I have contempt for it. I defy you to forget me completely. I cling to my dignity by telling myself that without me you must settle for less than perfect pleasures.

And I am happier because I am more occupied. Recently they made me portress of this convent. Everyone who speaks with me thinks I am mad. I have no notion of how I respond to them; the nuns must be as crazy as I am to think me capable of any job.

Oh, how I covet the good fortune of Manuel and Francisco! Why can't I be always with you, as they are? I would have followed and cared for you more splendidly than they.

I want nothing more in this world than to see you. Do at least remember me! I might be content with a place in your thoughts, but I can be certain of nothing anymore, not even that. I never dreamed when I was seeing you every day that I might be forced to limit my hopes this narrowly, but the cruelty of your will is such that I am left no choice.

But I do nor regret adoring you. I rejoice in your seducing me, and am even glad you have betrayed me. I pass the harsh test of your absence, perhaps for eternity, and discover that not for an instant does it diminish the strength of my love. I want the whole world to know of it; I do not wish it cloaked in mystery. I am proud of absolutely everything I have done for you, in defiance of every sense of decorum. My honor and my religion consist of nothing more than loving you to my grave, throughout my life, a course set from the first awakening of the love within me.

I mention none of this to oblige you to write to me; you need not worry. I want nothing from you that is not freely given: What is possible to withhold or control in love does not interest me. Should you be pleased to be spared the inconvenience of writing to me, I shall take pleasure in excusing you; that is how huge my desire is to forgive you your faults.

A French officer was kind enough to speak with me about you for over three hours this morning. He told me that France has finally achieved peace. If this is true, could you not come see me, and take me with you to France? But I do not deserve that. Do as you will. My love no longer depends upon the manner in which you treat me. Since your departure, I have not known any sound health; my sole relief is to repeat your name throughout the hours. Some nuns who know of the sad state into which you have thrust me speak about you frequently. I seldom leave my room, where you so often came to me, and I am always contemplating your portrait, which is countless times dearer to me than life itself. This

provides some comfort, but also much heartache, when I
realize that I shall never see you again.

How is it possible that I cannot simply turn my gaze, and
hold you? Have you indeed deserted me forever? The very idea
destroys me! Your poor Mariana can do no more; she grows
faint as she approaches the end of her writing: Farewell.
Farewell! Have compassion for me.

*

A letter arrived from Captain Noel Bouton, addressed to a "Sister Alcoforado."

It was exceedingly short, but at first she could not read it completely through. She forced herself to finish it.

She reread it over the next few days, to be certain that she was not mistaking what was on the page, and then she removed both bracelets from their hiding place up her sleeve. Saying goodbye to the Saint Christopher medal and the portrait was much harder, and she stared at the likeness of him until she trusted herself to have engraved it onto her memory — as if he were not already irrevocably tucked within her. She gathered these things along with his other letters. She would keep this final one, along with another brief note that she now saw he had hoped would be his final letter to her. They would remind her that he was helping her to be strong. Thank goodness her country did not pass about letters for general entertainment at parties — she would die of humiliation to show his pitiful scrawlings!

While walking through the corridor and carrying her treasures to Brites's room, she had to steady herself against the wall a few times. She passed Sister Joana Veloso de Bulhão, who was seething about the Abbess making her lie face down in the chapel to atone for her lateness at Nones.

Mariana drifted into Brites's arms, handed her the bracelets, medal, and portrait, and said, "You must help me. Sit with me while I write a letter, and do not allow me to rise until I finish it."

I AM WRITING TO YOU for the last time, and I hope you
will perceive by the different tone and content of this letter
that I am finally persuaded that you no longer love me, and
I have no recourse but to stop loving you.

At the first opportunity, I shall return whatever I still have of yours. Do not fear that I might resort to writing again; I shall even refrain from using my script to put your name on the package. I have entrusted everything to Dona Brites, who has long been my confidante, though in matters much different from this. I can depend upon her more than myself to take care of these details. She will take all necessary steps so that I may be assured that you will receive the portrait and bracelets you gave me.

For several days now, I have felt tempted to burn or destroy all pledges of your love, though once they were so dear to me. I have already exhibited such weakness that you might judge me incapable of such firm amends. I shall withstand the sorrow, however, of parting with these trifles. Perhaps your receipt of them will cause you some chagrin. I confess, to your shame and mine, that I found myself more attached to these baubles than I care to relate, and for each one of them in turn I had to summon my latest resolve, despite how much I was congratulating myself on being finished with you. But when a design is built upon reasons as clear as the ones I possess, one may always reach the sought-after end.

I have placed everything in the hands of Dona Brites. What tears this decision cost me! You can hardly fathom my endless hesitations — and I shall certainly not provide you with an account. I instructed her never to speak again of these sweet treasures, nor give them back, though I might beg to see them one last time. She is to handle them without my knowing anything further.

I faced the strongest powers of my love only when I had to muster every effort to be rid of it. If I could have predicted how difficult this would be, I do not believe I would have undertaken it. It would certainly be a lesser torment to continue loving you in vain, cold as you are, than to have done with you forever. But I saw that it was not to you but to my own passion that I was more attached; I am astounded how hard I had to fight with it, even after your behavior was plainly despicable. The natural pride of my sex did not help me take a stand against you. I suffered, alas, your contempt; I would have borne your hate and even the jealousy that your love for another woman might have aroused in me. At least in those cases I would have a real passion to battle with, but your indifference appalls me. Your impertinent protests of friendship and the ludicrous niceties of your last letter made me see that you received all that I wrote, and — heaven knows how — none of it made any impression on you. Heartless man! I am absurd enough to grieve for the loss of any illusions that came from thinking that my letters might not have reached you.

You with your "rank talk"— how I detest it! Did I ask you to pronounce the truth for me? Could you not leave me to my dreams? It would have been enough that you not write; I would not have looked to be undeceived. Am I not made more unhappy that you took so few pains to leave my errant passion to fool me? I might still be seeking to find you blameless, were your dubious qualities not so abundantly spelled out.

If all I have done for you deserves some respect, grant me a small favor: I implore you not to write me anymore; help me forget you entirely. Were you to show, even slightly, that this letter caused you some grief, I might believe in you; your repentant words might stir fresh ire within me . . . and the fire would again be kindled. Do not respond, nor intervene in my life; you would unsettle my plans however you chose to enter into them. I do not wish to know the outcome of this letter. Do not disturb the state into which I must commend myself. Content yourself with the harm you have already caused. Whatever you intended as I fell to misery, leave me now to my uncertainty. In time, I hope to change it to a relative peace. I shall not hate you. I dare not, having seen the cost of strong sentiments.

I should attempt to find a more faithful lover, but who could ever dare me to love again? Could passion for another absorb me, when I have witnessed what little power mine exerted over you? Have I not proven that a tender heart is never more deeply moved than when it is led out of innocence and into the raptures it scarcely knew itself capable of? That such stirrings are bound to that idol that first love creates for itself? First wounds can never be healed, never *effaced. The quickenings that fly to the heart's summons thereafter and try to satisfy it and make it rejoice will never recapture that initial profundity of emotions, and serve only to remind the heart that through all the pleasures it burns to find anew, nothing is as cherished as the remembrance of love past.*

Why must it be from you that I learn of the imperfection and disenchantment of a bond not meant to last, the whole bitter litany of a driven love that is not shared? What blind, malicious fate is it that propels us towards those who are fond of someone else? Even if I could hope for the distraction of a new love, and were I to find a man whose faithfulness I trusted, such is my awareness of what I am now that I would hesitate, lest I inflict this condition to which I am currently reduced upon even the lowest creature in the world. Were I by some chance to be in a position to bring you to where you have brought me, and though I owe you no such restraint, I could never have the heart, never, to devastate you so.

I seek to forgive you. I understand that a nun is generally not considered suitable for love, but if one used good sense in choosing a lover, nuns are preferable to other women, and more deserving. Nothing stops a nun from secluding herself incessantly with her passion; the many things that occupy and disturb the world do not trouble her. It seems to me that it can not be pleasant for a man to see his lover always distracted by a myriad of trivialities, and he must be quite superficial, if not on the verge of exasperation, to put up with her talking at every juncture of parties and shops, or adornments and strolls. The petty details and jealousies never stop when it comes to women who are bound to social conventions and courtesies, and idle conversations with everyone. Who can ever be sure that they are not in the midst of some love affair, and are not suffering with distaste the affections of their husbands? These women should distrust a lover who does not require of them a strict account of what they are about, who nonchalantly believes everything he is told and tranquilly watches them attend to their every empty obligation.

It is not my intention to prove to you, through a construction of reasons, that you ought to love me. Reason provides the shallowest means of persuasion; I tried much better ones, to no avail. I am too aware of my destiny to surmount it. I shall sorrow for the rest of my life. Was I not already tormented when I was seeing you every day? I was afraid you would be unfaithful; I craved seeing you continually, and that was not possible. The danger that you risked entering the convent tortured me; I died when you were away at war; I despaired that I was not more beautiful, more worthy of you. I bemoaned the lowliness of my rank. I feared that your love for me would bring you to harm, or that I did not love you enough. The anger of my family filled me with concern for your safety — I had, in a word, already entered the heartache in which I now firmly dwell.

Had you conveyed to me, even once since leaving Portugal, the slightest sign of affection, I would have perished in the effort to escape from here; I would have disguised myself, to flee to you. Oh, what would have become of me, had you abandoned me after my arrival in France! What a predicament! What madness! What inestimable shame for my family, dearer to me now that I have left off loving you!

I see, quite soberly, how much more miserable I could have been: Yes, at least this once I am speaking reasonably to you. No doubt this moderation pleases you — but whether it does or not, I have no interest in hearing. I repeat my urgent plea that you not write to me again.

Have you never reflected even a little upon the way you have treated me? Has it not occurred to you that you are more obligated towards me than anyone else alive? I loved you mightily, scorning all else. But your conduct was never that of an honorable man. You must have had some aversion towards me, since you did not love me madly in return. I allowed myself to be seduced by mediocrity. How did you bewitch me? What sacrifice did you ever make? Did you not pursue other diversions — gambling, hunting? When did you give anything up? Were you not the first to march off to war, and the last to return? No matter how much I begged you to save yourself for love of me, you recklessly exposed yourself to danger. You never tried to establish yourself in Portugal, where you were esteemed. A letter from your brother was enough for you to leave at once. And did I not hear from many people later that you were in the highest of spirits during your journey?

You must agree I have every right to despise you mortally. Oh, I admit I brought this misery upon myself! Right from the beginning, I made you aware of my great passion, too openly, with too much good faith. One needs more subtlety and artifice in wooing. Love by itself, alas, does not arouse love. Your plan was for me to make love to you; and once you formulated this design, you would try anything to fulfill it. You would even have resorted to loving me, were it necessary to seduce me. But you quickly saw that you could achieve your purpose without loving me . . . What baseness! Did you think I could be so tricked, and never the wiser? I declare to you, if by chance you ever again set foot in my country, I shall personally deliver you over to the vengeance of my family.

For too long I have submitted to an idolatry that now makes me shudder, and remorse persecutes me. I am thoroughly ashamed of the crimes that I was obliged to commit with you; now, alas, the love that prevented me from recognizing the enormity of my actions is gone. When shall my heart ever heal? When shall I be free of unrest? Please believe that I harbor no ill will; I might be persuaded to wish you happiness — though how could you feel such a thing, if you lack a true heart?

I would like to write you another letter to show that in time I have become more at peace. When I am no longer deeply hurt, I might take pleasure in throwing your ingratitude in your face and displaying my scorn, speaking indifferently of your deception, and saying that I have forgotten my joys and sorrows, and that I remember you only when I decide to remember.

I shall always acknowledge that you held great sway over me, and inspired in me a passion that turned me inside out, but you need not boast. I was young; I was gullible; they *locked me away in this convent when I was a child; I had never before met with any agreeable responses in love. I never heard the phrases you constantly wreathed around me. It seemed I owed to you the charms and the beauty that you admired in me, of which you were the first to make me conscious. People said grand things about you; everyone praised you. You did everything you could to awaken love in me, but at last I have broken the spell. You have assisted me invaluably in this; I should not bother to conceal that I was sadly in need of such help.*

Though I am returning your letters, I shall keep the last two, and reread them more than I ever read the first ones, to guard against falling into my previous weakness. Oh, how dearly I paid for these! How ecstatic I should have been, had you allowed me to love you forever. Ah — I remain too occupied with my laments. As I have said, I have vowed to bring myself to a more restful state, and I shall, or shall use some desperate measure against myself in the attempt — this will not trouble you much, should you hear of it. But I want nothing more of you. I am a fool to repeat the same things. I must quit you; I must not brood on you longer. No, I must not. I think it best not to write to you again. To write no more. Am I to give you an account of all that transpires within and without me?

*

The rebellion of the nuns at Conceição began with an object dashed. Less than four months after the signing of the peace treaty, Sister Maria de São Francisco, upon hearing the bell rung to awaken them to serve the Lord, ran into the corridor, tore the bell out of the grip of Sister Inês de São José, and threw it as far as she could manage. The peacetime night and peacetime day fell apart. Sister Maria de Castro, sick of the laundry, kicked over a pail of chalky white disinfectant. It dried like stale moonlight between the cobblestones. A postulant assigned to clean the baronial shields in the Escutcheon Room refused, stating that her parents had told her that nobles were no better than she was. Some novices got into the refuse heap to reclaim their cut-off hair, and stretched a rope of their braided manes across the Quadra of Saint John the Baptist to trip the mistress of novices, Sister Ana Henriques. Sister Angelica de Noronha, bothered by thoughts that were bat-shaped, was burning the meals, which triggered discontent in the refectory. Sister Brites de Freire, confused about Mariana — she did not want her to be aggrieved, but neither did she want her in ecstasy — was poor assistance in preventing disasters in the kitchen.

The new Abbess, Brites de Noronha, walked up and down the passageway that connected the convent's upper choir loft to the adjacent Founder's Palace, where the Duke of Beja was a recluse. She studied the red ceramic and brick Arabic designs, as if they might hold an answer. Although she was young, her daughters must learn to respect her. She prayed for strength. Whatever she did would involve them hating her. It would also involve her puzzling through why the aura of peace, the much-desired, the longed-for peace and freedom and independence, should prompt this buckling of emotions. Once, during her childhood, a bull had pursued her father through a field. He outraced it while she watched, helpless. Fear, outrage, and watery knees struck them many hours later, only when the terror was over.

Sister Maria de São Francisco's battle cry was the loudest: *Why does nothing feel any different?*

If this is what we've desired most of our lives — some of us, our entire lives — why does the notion of freedom threaten to suffocate us?

Mariana did not participate in the uprising, but because of her stillness, the unrest seemed to be radiating outward from her. She stood mutely as the portress at the front entrance at the proper times, and then spent the rest of the day and night in her "little house." She racked her mind for what she should think, and found nothing but a wise sadness that weighed upon her every motion and step. Nothing else was left. Everything had been poured into her letters, and now everything was gone forever, sent away. She recognized the kind of closed-off creature she had been told she had to be in this world, whether that world was at war or at peace. She would live this but refuse to accept it, and would wait for him to arrive — he would say that she had forbidden a letter and there-fore he was here in person to save her.

Sister Francisca Freire visited and said, "Sister Mariana. Sit up. Straight back! Pride! You must save yourself."

"Myself?" she would say, as her friend insisted that she eat.

"And me in the process," said Sister Francisca Freire. "You are a part of me."

"We should be thanking God for peace," said Sister Leonor Henriques.

"Thank you, thank you, thank you, God!" clamored the novices, and threw their hymnals into the air, and the older nuns joined in or fled the loft, and missed dinner, and kicked balls through the cloisters and said it was the head of the deposed King, poor bastard. (Evil word! Long live evil words!) Girls chased one another with buckets of water, and when veils got wet, they were draped over the heads of statues. Sister Angelica de Noronha could not stop her fellow sisters from eating the pastries meant to be sold to families in the city who were continuing to celebrate the peace treaty. Troublemakers peeked into Mariana's room, to see what she would do next. Sister Juliana Matos paced in the infirmary, rewinding bandages. Into the night, dice were rolled. The Abbess, worn out from running here and there to end the nonsense, caught two postulants having a sword-fight with silver candlesticks, confiscated them, and asked the girls if they wanted to leave. Mariana watched at her post as the Abbess pushed the combatants out the front door. She waited. The wailing rang out, "Mother, Mother! We're sorry! Our families won't take us back!" She allowed them to return inside, and instructed them to polish the silver with ashes. The candlesticks would have to be sold to meet that month's food bill.

In hallways across Beja, the shallow dishes to receive calling cards were showing many with a bent corner, meaning that money was owed. Many nobles were having to indicate that they could not pay their bills.

On the third day of the revolt, Abbess Brites de Noronha considered calling in the prefects, but that would establish that she could not handle a crisis. Those girls sparring with the silver gave her an idea. To those gathered at Collation, the Abbess announced that any nun who wished to leave was free — no, was encouraged — to do so. She said it over the chatter, and did not repeat it as the talkative ones said, "What? What now?" She stayed up most of the night, listening as several nuns walked through the cloisters with their light bundles of goods, and crossed the locutory and stood at the egress, and could not cross over. They had nowhere to go. Sister Maria de São Francisco lay in the doorway and cried.

One by one, those who stood at the threshold trudged to the door of Abbess Brites de Noronha, and said, "Mother? You're cruel."

Then they returned to their cells. By the end of the night, the Abbess was distraught, as she had predicted she would be. She had known that most of them would not be equal to the task of blaming themselves.

Eight-year-old Peregrina wrote down, during her tutoring with Sister Ignez de São José, that an enormous bird flew over the convent and ordered Peregrina to describe its wings and write, "a bird flew over." Out of nowhere, there now existed flight, bird, wings, her imagination.

Peregrina thought that everyone must help her decide if this was the Holy Spirit come to inspire them, or a bird of doom. She traveled from the cells of the Old Dormitory to the "little houses," some vacant now that the refugees were gone, of the New Dormitory. The nuns each looked at Peregrina and said, in turn, "It might be better to say it was the Holy Spirit."

It might be better to say it was the Holy Spirit.

Peregrina, you funny child, serious child. We'll call it the Holy Spirit, will that satisfy you? Such mirages you see.

She ended her journey at the Alcoforado wing of "little houses." Mariana's room was the last before she would be back home. To her surprise, Mariana did not tell her to leave. When Peregrina, her brown eyes earnest, asked if the bird she had dreamed up was the Paraclete or a grim shadow, Mariana was the only nun to insist upon getting the solution from Peregrina. "You tell me," said Mariana. "What was it?"

"I don't know. I wrote down that it might be both."

"Then your dream isn't afraid to see good and bad in the same thing. Your dream has everything in it."

Peregrina smiled. She had been waiting for years to win Mariana. She could wait years more. She did not know why her older sister, old enough to be her Mama, was so quiet, like someone who had been running and running with sand in her fists and had arrived at the end of long, long running and the sand was gone.

Mariana said, "I hear you're clever at your lessons, Peregrina. Is this true?"

Peregrina demurred. She stood drinking in her sister. Controlling her wish to fidget.

At the end of the three-day revolt, the hours jolted back into place and proceeded to move forward with the slowness and smoothness of the plains. Everyone would say that it took a child's journey to their dwelling places, the astute prodding of an Alcoforado child, to remind them that dreams remained possible, if they would raise up their heads and look.

Or lower their heads, to write the dreams down.

Sister Brites de Freire had received something she had awaited since meeting Mariana (though she could not have identified at the outset that she might want such distasteful reassurance). She was stronger than Mariana. Mariana had needed her. Had come to her with those bracelets, that portrait. Months had passed. Clearly her friend was in agony. Why, then, did it recently give Brites pleasure to have Mariana ask her, "You did send everything?" obviously hunting for an opening so that she could converse about that man, and for Brites to have replied, "I told you I would not allow you to speak any more on it?"

Though Mariana had not spoken further, an obstinate want radiated from her. Brites found herself vexed. Even in silence, some drive in Mariana imposed itself. She was still indignant about Mariana handing the items over and commanding Brites that even should she yell like Ulysses tied to the mast as he sailed past the sirens, Brites must not listen, just as Ulysses's crew had ignored him.

Who was Ulysses? Why did Mariana need to show off that she had grown up being taught to read like a rich boy?

She could not refrain today from saying to Mariana, "You look relaxed. How nice to see! I guess you're over — ah, you-know-who. That phantom."

Cool as the hour of the rooster's crow, Mariana said, "Not a phantom."

"Might as well be, eh? I mean, do you see him?"

Mariana lightly answered, "Yes, I see him. Everywhere. But we're not to speak of him, remember?"

Brites de Freire cried later in her room about how unjustly gifts were distributed. Mariana had a famous father. She got a Captain to love her grandly. Brites's sole gift, if it could be called that, was the revelation that she was jealous of her best friend on more accounts than she could add up.

In her "little house," standing at her window at the one-year anniversary of Noel's abandonment, Mariana prayed, I love you. I love you still. I love you always. I esteem every joy and every sorrow your love bestows on me.

I do not want a cure that makes me stop loving you. I am strong enough to learn how to love you though I might never have you again.

Shall I ever be able to be gladdened at the thought of you traveling, dining, flirting, marrying, finding bliss without me?

Someday I'll picture that without wincing.

I'll picture that, my love.

But not today, this day when I must also bear the envy of my friend. God in heaven, what could anyone possibly envy about me?

Captain Noel Bouton, newly appointed Count of Saint-Léger and Marquis of Chamilly, disliked parties. He liked dressing for them, but the small talk was excruciating. The Parisian salons, including the literary salons of the Montespans and Maintenons, were having dances or gatherings to welcome home the victorious troops. He was included on most invitation lists, for serving in Portugal and the Low Countries and for his promotions from General Schomberg, though the moment he began to tell about any military campaign, listeners edged away, leaving him to study his drink.

He considered with disbelief that Mariana had accused him of being a womanizer, a dissipate. She should look around here, and apologize to him. Corseted females with their ermine petticoats and appointments with sash makers, all exhibiting a disagreeable lack of clarity in who they might be and what they might want. Mariana could not avoid plainness, since she wore a religious habit, and confirmed in his mind that fineness could dispense with adornments. Her railing at him was inexplicable. As she herself pointed out, there was never any real possibility that he would live in some dry farmland in a poor country. If he occasionally said that she needn't worry, he would do everything for her, it was because she wanted to hear it, and he wanted her to be happy. He wrote her friendly letters as evidence that he had cared, and what she did was scorn them. It was her fault that he was forced to write that final letter spelling out the truth she was so hysterically determined not to face. Another kindness in the long run, but like a spoiled child, she had thrown his presents back at him.

His Portuguese servants, Francisco and Manuel, had aided him in translating her letters, though their message, even at a glance, was unmistakable. One of the main problems with women was that they did not have sufficient things to do, and made endless romantic demands of men who did not have time to waste. He was willing to forgive her, because her letters provided him with proof that he was not the sluggish, awkward lover that tiresome women at every party insisted that he was. These women passed around letters from their husbands or lovers who went abroad, and the men who had gone off to war or on business showed off the sugary notes from their wives or mistresses, with everyone's voice getting that phony tremor in those garbled, high-flown passages that he found impossible to digest. Another problem with women — they liked music and floweriness, even when they were false. At least that nun had been blunt. Honest. He admired that, though he wished that she had resorted to salon language so that he could pass her letters around as other people did with theirs.

A woman with a green taffeta dress and a large bustle cooed, "Noel! Who's persuaded you to come out tonight?"

He bowed abruptly, stiffly, and controlled himself enough not to redden when she snapped open a fan to conceal her smirk. "I would not miss the festivities, Mademoiselle Bourbon," he said.

"Certainly not! Not a wild man like you!" she said, laughing.

Another woman passed a tray of petit-fours below his nose as if he were a horse, and said, "Uh, uh, Noel. Marquis, I mean. I don't suppose you can resist these?"

He bowed again, and both women convulsed in laughter.

"Sweets from the sweet," he said, furiously trying to guess what they expected from him. Gallantry was harder than killing a man.

"Now that the fighting is over, you'll have to watch your waistline," said Mademoiselle Bourbon.

"I am watching it, Mademoiselle," said the Marquis, "and it appears to be expanding. The good life has been kind to me. Or should I say unkind?" He breathed hard from the effort of his speech.

Women liked a man's self-deprecation, another reason why dealing with soldiers was less degrading.

"If I were you, Noel, I shouldn't say anything at all," said the woman with the pastries. "Just stand there and look nice and military for us."

Another explosion of laughter accompanied the women as they linked arms and disappeared towards the orchestra beginning a gavotte. All the rage now. Noel Bouton, the Marquis of Chamilly, walked out onto the balcony, where he could be alone. The strains of the regimented music followed him. He was not given to day-dreaming, the refuge of the unambitious, but he allowed himself some nostalgia for the battlefields of the Alentejo, where he had been in his glory. That nun preserved some of that for him, when she commented upon how well he rode his horse. He liked the violent way she had loved him. He admired the violence of her writing, her lack of subterfuge, and that was why he carried her letters with him. When he gave her those bracelets, it was to thank her for her fierceness, to reward her plain fineness, though now he was glad to have the bracelets back. Everything to its proper owner.

He heard Mademoiselle Bourbon describing her encounter with him to another group of women, and before he could hear their assessment of him as a potential lover, he used the curtains as a shield, stalked the perimeter of the party, and departed.

It did not cost him much debate to bring versions of the love letters from the nun, which his servants had helped him copy into French, the next evening to a party at which Mademoiselle Bourbon was present. A pity that Mariana was not refined with social talk. He risked them ridiculing her flat, provincial diction, or her lack of skill in dressing matters up in pretty phrases. These men and women surrounding him were accustomed to reading each other's roman-tic letters, not documents about dying of love. On the other hand, this might make them shut up for good.

One or two of the women were sharing their own love letters, and Noel handed Mariana's to a woman who had mocked him once by saying that he should think of paying an escort to accompany him to the salons. In fact, it pleased him immeasurably to see that Mariana's letters were killing the festivities. This woman read the first letter, glanced up at him, back down at the paper. She handed a page to another woman who came over, demanding to be in on the secret. Dancers wandered away from the music. Butlers could not persuade anyone to sample the hors d'oeuvres. Women slumped against the brocade wallpaper, reading. One woman who had been showing letters from her husband in the Netherlands went to claim and hide them, suddenly outdone. Noel stifled a smile when Mademoiselle Bourbon herself exclaimed that one could almost feel the hot sun of that little country right there on the paper. Such torrid people. Such anger! Such anger, Noel, you beast! When someone teased the Marquis that he had invented these love letters himself, just to impress them, he had to accept another woman's hasty rejoinder that neither Noel Bouton nor any other man could get inside a female skin like this, and that she must have a copy to store in her dressing table, to refer to when she was melancholy.

In the ensuing weeks, Noel Bouton entertained reports that many salons were clamoring for copies of his love letters. Women were said to be in a faint as they read them and had to be fanned by their servants. Especially popular, apparently, was Mariana's assertion that she pitied Noel because he was not possessed by the sorrows of love. Noel was willing to suffer snide comments in exchange for the glances he now received from women on the streets of Paris or Versailles. He was moderately amused by the notes from women begging him to be their lover. The choicest incident was when Mademoiselle Bourbon said at a fancy dinner that she was perhaps wrong about him being nothing but a soldier. It was with pleasure that he rebuffed her advance.

Mariana. Such were her powers that she could make him appealing. He found himself grateful to her.

Copies of the letters continued flying around France. When Claude Barbin, a bookseller in Paris, contacted him and said that the wording of the Portuguese letters was nothing short of revolutionary, so devoid were they of the sickly, sentimental prose that passed for romance in every current book, Noel Bouton was pleased, but cautious. Barbin insisted that these had the scent of a woman's naked body, they were scandalous, they were raw with fury. The climate was right, with French society so stuffy and demure, for a hint of extremity, some heat from the south. They would be able to make some good money from their publication. Bizarre to have a woman talk about love with the sensibility of her sex but with the directness of a man. Barbin found that more striking and salable than the fact that she was a nun. Everyone understood that the convents of Portugal were as full of girls without vocations as they were in France.

Barbin said that they would have to act swiftly. Other publishers were trying to assert some ownership of copies of the letters. A Dutch editor, while visiting Paris, heard a woman reciting certain passages, and he wished to persuade his superiors that the people of Holland, having taken over many of the Portuguese trade routes, would view any Portuguese phenomenon as in vogue. Some English and Italian publishers were sniffing around. Barbin proposed that with the permission of the Marquis of Chamilly, he would obtain a Royal Privilege, giving himself the copyright for exclusive publishing in Paris for a five-year period, and Bouton would receive an agreed-upon percentage of the royalties.

Noel considered the letters his to do with as he pleased, but objections darted in and out of his thinking. Publication was a larger-scale version of the practice of everyone showing love letters to everyone else, was it not? Mariana, whose family was far away, would not be unduly hurt. Though when he married, this might return to haunt him. He voiced this last thought aloud.

Claude Barbin waved aside his concerns. "You wish to be protected?" He chuckled. "Some future angry wife or father-in-law to contend with?" He explained that it would be even better to publish them anonymously, with a teaser about a translator, which there would have to be for the sake of authenticity. No salutations named Bouton. Everyone would know to whom the letters were written, but legally, technically, he could deny it. Barbin offered to ask Gabriel Lavergne de Guilleragues, the director of the *Gazette de France,* to lend his name. "Do you know him? Gadabout. Rather full of himself, but he's written a few items. People will recognize him as the fellow who never leaves their buffet table."

Noel agreed that this was an honorable means of arranging matters. He was scheduled to leave on an expedition to Crete, to fight the Turks, and would not be around when the book was released. His absence would be a method of allowing production without the direct guilt of putting it into motion, though he would regret not seeing Mademoiselle Bourbon's face when she discovered the words written to him printed and irrefutable.

The truth was that he could not bring himself to reread the letters. He was trained to look upon suffering; his job was to negotiate the least possible amount of it for men under his command. The anguish of Mariana was a type of suffering that perplexed him, cried out perhaps to be diffused by being taken in by many readers, who would agree with him that naturally she was wrong to deprecate him for an inevitable departure.

Deprecate! It was the nun who once told him that the word could also mean trying to avert something through prayer.

The Portuguese heaped so many honors upon General Schomberg and King Louis XIV that a number of French citizens looked out at the dampness of Paris and decided upon an early retirement. The Portuguese were reportedly welcoming even humble Frenchmen as heroes. As a new country, Portugal was glad to receive anyone with money to spend. French families entering Portugal brought copies of the *Portuguese Letters*, in French, with them. The books trickled across the border, flowed into the port city of Lisbon, dispersed from there. Some of the newcomers tucked copies of the *Portuguese Letters* deep in their suitcases. One never knew about censorship. Talk had it that the Index of Forbidden Books would at any moment list the scandalous letters.

Portuguese nobles who elected to set up *morgadios* in rural areas rather than try to penetrate the labyrinth of the Lisbon courts set out to build impressive libraries. French and English books were sought to fill the shelves. It was fashionable to own foreign works, and to claim a few volumes considered risqué.

Baltazar, wandering through Beja, unsure of what to do now that the army no longer needed him, noticed the townspeople snickering at him. At first, he assumed it was because he was turning out to be a terrible estate master, good for nothing but reviving a legal action against his own father. He lacked his father's ability and desire to stare into the future, and he heartily despised ordering people around. He suggested at one point that he would be glad to step aside and allow Miguel to take the reins, but his father yelled that he had adjusted his will to name Baltazar as the heir apparent, and now, by God, Baltazar had better act the part. His sole comfort was that he was not alone. Most of the soldiers home from the war had no idea what to do next, since work was scarce. Look how pathetic Rui was, trading livestock for his father-in-law, selling sheep and cows, arguing with people attempting to complete the transactions on credit. Baltazar's father was pulling strings to get Rui accepted into the Military Order of Christ — more badges, more titles, more of the old world. The War Council finally absolved Rui and his brothers of blame for the 1662 riot against the English garrisons, though everyone said that the Council's long, ambivalent silence proved how questionable any notion of innocence was when connected to the Lôbos. Rui's approval for the Military Order of Christ was being held up because of his family's tainted reputation — even Francisco da Costa, the grand master, was not securing appointments with his former splendor.

Cristóvão Pantoja Lôbo, meanwhile, rejected the position of overseas governor in Pernambuco, complaining that the fight was drained out of him. He moved his wife, two sons, and one daughter to the edge of the country estate in Viana d'Alvito, the property held in abeyance by his sister, Leonor Henriques. Some gamesmanship remained in Cristóvão to set himself up near the estate he hoped his family would inherit from her. Another daughter was left behind in the convent of Santa Clara, as if to torment Francisco da Costa by putting a Lôbo on watch during the legal quarrel. Baltazar debated contacting Santa Clara and insisting that he had made a mistake in waging war against his own father. But if he caved in, he would be as ridiculed for that brand of weakness as for the rest of his behavior nowadays. He was not going to win.

One day in town, a drunk yelled an insult about Mariana, and Baltazar got into a fight and cut the man's arm so severely that he lost the use of it. Baltazar could not say if that made him into his father, defending his family's honor, or a Lôbo, fighting first and sorting the mess out later.

"Oh, why not take me to France with you? Why not take me to France?" sang the butcher and his wife as Baltazar entered their shop.

"What is to become of me? Oh, oh!" said the candlemaker, cackling as he stirred a cauldron of tallow.

"Farewell, and farewell once more!" sang a girl on the street to a dazed Baltazar.

When he went to the house of his friend, Humberto Soma, his inquiry about what was going on was cut short. Humberto poured him a glass of port, and insisted that Baltazar drink it.

"I can't believe you don't know," said Humberto.

Baltazar felt his blood galloping. He was aware that what had happened between Mariana and the Count of Chamilly was in the public domain. But for the sake of discreetness, out of respect for Francisco da Costa — Baltazar was not above calling upon such freight, when it was needed — why wouldn't people lower their heads knowingly, turn aside? Baltazar had had a wholly different reaction in mind from the one that was being manifest. The public was supposed to look upon Mariana and him with awe, and call them the creators of a new order — what they did would be judged every bit as exalted and defiant as the building of a mint. Let their father be the patron of national freedom; Baltazar and Mariana were to be viewed as the patrons of personal freedom. Nothing was turning out right. His last visit to her had been horrifying. She was miserable, ill, desperate, pleading that he must do something. He could not get that image of her out of his mind.

There was nothing, nothing he could do for her.

When his friend set a book written in French before him, he cursed himself for not studying his lessons, though he could sift through some of the phrases that wailed from the pages. There was no mistaking his sister's voice, nor any mistaking — Humberto pointed him to it, in case he missed it — that he was mentioned as delivering a part of her over to this man who had plunged her into anguish. Baltazar had reviled her at their last visit, and this was his payment. He covered his ears. Her screaming and crying, her broken heart, were more than he could stand. He closed the book, and still heard her agony reaching him from her prison.

"I'm sorry," said Humberto. "These books are all over town. I thought you knew. I wasn't going to tell you, Baltazar, but I figured better me than someone else."

"Better none of this."

Humberto hesitated. "You should tell your father. Sooner or later —"

"He doesn't leave his study anymore."

"This will find him anyway. It's in the air. I truly am sorry."

Baltazar rose without a word and ran through town. People's heads seemed swollen into grotesque shapes. Their speech was demonic. He arrived at the convent to discover that it was not the hour for Mariana to be at her post as the portress. He would have to speak to her through the grate. The locutory was empty, and the door to the cloister was sealed. The Abbess was dedicated to putting the life of the convent aright. He screamed, "Mariana!"

My dear Baltazar,

Your visit, after your prolonged absence, remains with me. Take it as a mark of my affection for you that I can write at all.

I still bear the mark of the grate upon my cheek, where I pressed my face in order to touch yours. We nuns have, of late, become entirely closed off. My brother, my tormented brother, I am troubled by how unwell you appeared. Such two sad ghosts we seem. I shall follow your advice and apply cold well-water to the boils plaguing my left wrist. I promise to live a long while, and offer this vow as an inspiration for you to do the same. It was wrong to tease you and say that you go out hunting and amusing yourself too often, instead of coming to see me. Travel far and wide. Only come to me and tell me of it, send me letters describing what you have seen, and I shall be content in my convent.

I must trouble you to speak no more of the past, nor to blame yourself for helping me set aside all decorum. I thank you eternally for the taste of everything you may have caused. I can imagine no finer triumph in my life than what has issued from the souls of you and me. Such terrible beauty we have dared to claim!

Be thunderously healthy, be well. Be unspeakably happy, Baltazar.

With one thousand embraces,

Your Mariana

Officials representing the convent of Santa Clara called upon Baltazar to thank him for turning over his father's private papers. In them was the proof they needed to show that the original agreement, signed by both parties, granted the Alcoforado estate temporary ownership of Santa Clara's properties. The word "temporary" was the key. Such scurrilously inexact wording could be attributed to no one being able to predict when the war might return business to normal. The convent's poor management in the past had caused their copies of the agreement to be lost. When the officials emphasized that this provided them with a good case to present to the local magistrate to effect the return of the lands surrounding the convent and several of the buildings on that property for the original purchase price, Baltazar shouted, "I've changed my mind!"

The officials squinted as Baltazar launched into a wild discourse on how his father's mind worked. To Francisco da Costa, the word "temporary" did not mean what it meant to everyone else. In his will, he had purposefully used the clause, "these methods shall ensure the proper running of my *morgadio* for as long as the world shall last." This was a man to whom "temporary" could mean ten generations.

The officials replied that "temporary" to the anxious people at Santa Clara meant that they had a right to reclaim and rebuy their property, and now they had a signed document in hand, thanks to Baltazar, to demonstrate that Francisco da Costa had not agreed to anything permanent. Opinions about time were a matter for the magistrate.

Baltazar staggered like a wounded man to confront his father, and skipped over the body of his confession and warning about what was to come from the Santa Clara. Terror ate the lengthy speech he intended, in which his culpability was to have figured, and instead he blurted out what was to have been the final, summary line — that he was going to rejoin the priory. He was not fit to live in the normal world, could not stand commerce and human society. His father, stunned at this incoherent idiocy, summoned up the energy to remind Baltazar that he was to run the *morgadio*. That was final.

"I am doomed," said Baltazar.

"Stop this infantile nonsense," said Francisco. "Start acting like a son of mine."

Baltazar said, "I am a son of yours. I'm a ripe bastard. Your other bastard is in a priory, and so should I be."

He packed very little, and left at once. When the servant Luís caught him and said that his father would not forgive him if he did nor come to his senses, Baltazar remarked that he did not wish to be forgiven, and there was not much likelihood of returning to his senses.

He did not often leave his cell at the priory at Beringel. The Duke of Sidónia rarely persuaded him to come out hunting, but on those few ventures into the woods, Baltazar found some tranquility. He would point at his reflection in puddles, and describe what kind of monster he looked like on that day. He liked to joke when he brought some rabbits or pigeons back to the monks that he was the killer but not the cleaner, and would hand his catch to Brother António, the cook, to pluck and dress. He would say, Once I was a real soldier, and now I am a soldier of the forest!

He earned a reputation as a practical joker by putting his sandals on his hands and performing dance numbers on the tables. The brothers loved to be around his childlike wistfulness. But at night, the wind whistled at him, "When my brother offered me the chance to write to you, it checked for a while my despair," and the water boiling for porridge in the morning uttered as it rolled, "Oh, why was I not born in another country?"

The spirit of reform eventually gripped Baltazar and his brother monks, and they were not allowed to leave the priory with the indulged frequency of the past. Isolation allowed a glimmer to return to his eye, and he permitted himself to pretend that he was a proud outlaw. In these days of lackeys, sycophants, and merciless landowners, there should be more rebels like him. But then he would be visited by memories of the grief of his sister, or the thunderstruck gaze of his old father, and Baltazar would have to sit down and marvel that this was what the freedom he had fought for should be like for him. He would violate the rules once more to go to Mariana if he could be convinced that it would make any difference or rewrite history — but he could not fathom how any of that could come to pass.

Francisco da Costa sensed that one of his goals, to live to the age of one hundred, might not be reached. One hundred was a memorable number. The first numeral was a line that stood alone, representing a single man beside two symbols of infinity. He wished to be depicted as a man of a century — an impressive achievement. Perhaps this was what it meant to be old: Thirty more years seemed a penance.

He wanted his will changed to disinherit Baltazar so that Miguel could be officially in charge of the *morgadio,* but a solicitor informed him that not even an Alcoforado could bend the rules governing probate. Francisco drew his sword and threatened the solicitor, and then reviled his actions. A Lôbo would have behaved no better. A will that could be too easily amended could also facilitate the swindling of proper heirs. The *morgadio* could not transfer to Miguel until Baltazar's death. Baltazar was cooperating enough to sign deeds where necessary, but he was not actively making the estate prosper from his cell. Francisco da Costa and Miguel were doing what they could, but a crisis of authority was bad for business.

One afternoon, Francisco da Costa began to reel with the conviction that Rui was keeping back some of the money he was supposed to collect from the sale of Alcoforado livestock. Francisco dressed, despite the glare of the sunlight, in a heavy jerkin, cloak, and concertinaed boots, and ordered Luís to saddle his horse. Luís labored over this task; he, too, was older.

Francisco rode to the tavern that Rui frequented in town, passing the mint along the way and glaring at the rubbish heaped near the front door. The foreman would receive a lecture from him about the workers having more respect. The shopkeepers sweeping the cobblestones or setting out crates of vegetables were glancing at Francisco and swallowing their laughter, strangling on it, though he robustly called out good morning to them from his horse. They did not make a proper response. Fools. The economic woes engulfing them could be solved if everyone were not so empty-headed.

Rui was slouched at a round table in a darkened corner of the tavern, half-asleep, his shirt unlaced. His brother Bartolomeu sprawled beside him, with an overturned bottle by his elbow. Francisco recognized a group of men that included his friend Dom Joaquim, who had lately turned to drinking away his financial worries. Dom Joaquim grew nervous as his companions snorted derision at Francisco's elaborate costume, loudly enough to be heard but sufficiently quiet so that they would have a chance of denying it. Dom Joaquim was ashamed of the satisfaction he had felt reading the *Portuguese Letters* — Francisco could save a nation, but could not keep his children in line — but also felt honor-bound to protect his friend for as long as possible from any knowledge of the letters.

"Stand up!" shouted Francisco to Rui.

Rui's red hair was rumpled into errant flames. He gazed at his father-in-law. Bartolomeu woke up and scratched at his whiskers as if he were a large, dull cat.

"You've been cheating me out of money for my horses, you live in my house without paying me anything, and I want my due!" said Francisco.

"Calm yourself," said Rui, bored. "I haven't stolen anything from you. Nobody has any real money to pay, that's all. I'll croak soon, and your grandchildren will get their hands on my property. Now have the decency to go away and leave me in peace, sir."

"That's right," said Bartolomeu.

"Shut up, you moron," said Rui to his brother. "I'm surrounded by morons." He let his head fall back onto his arm stretched out on the table. He looked like a man killed while reaching for something.

"You will pay me. Now," said Francisco, and in the dreadful silence, as Rui raised his head, one of the men sitting with Dom Joaquim anointed the air with a kissing noise. Out floated a comment about Francisco needing to consult his daughter in the convent for advice on how to get things out of men.

Francisco turned to face the man who said this, drew his sword, and said, "I am an old man, and I plan to kill you where you stand."

"This is crazy," said Dom Joaquim, leaping up to arrest Francisco's arm, but Francisco had kicked over the offender's chair and pushed him against the wall. The man was fumbling for a dagger, and Francisco pinned him by the neck, contemptuously; these young men nowadays were all talk but never knew how to act quickly.

"Before I kill you," said Francisco, "apologize to me on behalf of my daughter."

Dom Joaquim, two of his other companions, the tavern owner, and Rui and Bartolomeu attempted without success to pull Francisco off his victim. Dom Joaquim was pleading for Francisco to excuse the comment. A few words were not cause to take a man's life.

"A single wrong word is just cause," said Francisco, and lifted his sword.

"The one who needs to apologize is your own son! Your own son! If you need to make someone pay, he's the one!" shouted the man pinned to the wall. "He's the one who assisted your daughter in sin! Your own son! It's written in her book for everyone to see!"

"Book?" said Francisco, and the arm with the sword dropped. His thinning white hair framed his face like a scythed halo, and his eyes would not relax. His mouth opened and froze.

Rui grabbed his father-in-law's arm as his hand relaxed its grip on the weapon.

"Go on home, Francisco," said Dom Joaquim.

"This isn't a good place for you to be, sir. Too many morons who don't know what they're saying," said Rui, drawing Francisco away. Rui kicked the man against the wall in his groin, buckling him over. "I'll have to come back and explain more of what I think of you," Rui added, leaning over to hiss in the man's ear.

Rui, as he led his father-in-law home, refused to unearth a copy of this book that the man had been talking about, despite Francisco's pleading that he should not be kept from anything that was true.

Francisco persisted in asking everyone he knew that they not forget that he had always taken immense pride in knowing everything.

The Marquês de Niza, the ambassador to France, handed over a copy of the French translation of the *Portuguese Letters*, and Francisco's unerring instincts allowed him to find rather swiftly the passage implicating Baltazar. The rest was unendurable to read, as if Francisco were seeing one of his daughters undressing, and he slammed the book shut and dashed it onto the floor.

This was someone's idea of a joke in these undignified times, and that person would pay.

And then with a chill in his spine, Francisco realized that if the affair were true, as he knew it was, then the recording of it by her hand could also be genuine.

He picked up the wretched book again, and his glance settled upon one other passage — Mariana telling this cad that he was her honor and her religion. Who but his Mariana could have the strength of such convictions, disgraceful though they were? The words sprang out like swords aimed for his eyes. She had stabbed him in the heart, and now she was slashing away his vision. He did not need to read further. He burned the book in the fireplace and ordered the Marquês de Niza to assist him in going from door to door to hunt copies out and burn those as well. The Marquês was moved by his friend's grief, but pointed out that it would be impossible to cover the whole country.

"We will start at once," said Francisco. "We will make the time, and then we will do the same in France."

Because the Marquês refused to accompany him, Francisco went alone. He bashed his fists on the doors of the homes in town. Some people felt sorry for him, and offered him a drink, which he refused. Women pretended that they did not understand his request — they were not about to surrender their books of love letters. When Francisco, having covered almost one hundred houses, fainted in a doorway from exhaustion, Rui was summoned. He brought the carriage to transport his father-in-law home, and consoled him by saying that nowhere in these books was the name Alcoforado printed. The letters would drift into the ether of history. "Cheer up, old fellow," said Rui, and hurried the horses. Things were bad enough without anyone seeing that Francisco was muttering in delirium.

"Papa," said Ana Maria, getting out of her childbed to greet his return, "you must stay quiet now."

He returned to his solarium. His son Francisco assisted the servants in bringing him his morning coffee, and sipped it with him, and silently removed the tray afterwards. Francisco da Costa found it the most decent communion he had experienced in a while – filial duty, without having to contend with words.

One afternoon as he was dozing, his granddaughter, Inês, covered him with a blanket and jumped back when he sat up with a start and exclaimed, "Mariana? Mariana!"

"No, Vovô," said Inês. "No, Grandpa. It's Inês."

"Inês the Beautiful?"

She smiled. "If you say so, Vovô."

He did not want to frighten the child by telling her — as he told Mariana when she had been much smaller than this girl — that Inês was loved so much that Pedro dug her from the ground and put her on the throne, where she could be adored beyond death. In his mind, he went to the plot where he had buried all his memories of Mariana. He found a throne empty within himself, and there he put his daughter, though he called her dead. Leonor would not mind. Leonor was beseeching him to love Mariana, even if he could not discover how to forgive her. Oh, Mariana! Betrayer! But she was the precious one of his heart. He looked upon where she was enthroned in him, and pictured himself kneeling to kiss her soiled hand. The genuflection would have to remain this and nothing more, because he refused to see her in the flesh ever again.

After that, it was a minor defeat to learn that Baltazar had betrayed him as well, by turning over private papers regarding the sale of properties of the convent of Santa Clara. He conceded to the representative from the convent that he could not argue with what was plainly written on the page in front of him. He would return the required buildings and land to their trust upon payment of the original amount. The notary bringing the petition on behalf of the convent was disappointed. Francisco da Costa was supposed to be a swashbuckler. Instead, the notary was shoving papers at a man with a lap robe and a shaking hand, and was moved to compassion.

"Sir," he said, folding the signed papers and putting them into a leather parcel. "It may interest you that although your son provided us with the evidence that has brought us to this juncture, he also sent us a letter withdrawing his complaint against your impropriety. Of course, we could not do that, not with the document we needed already in hand. You understand. But it might be a comfort to you that Friar Baltazar made clear at the last minute that he regretted his actions."

Francisco sighed. The last minute. How typical. Even taking Holy Orders would not giv

Baltazar any foresight. He said, "I have no son named Baltazar."

Because his father lacked the power to fight, it was left to his son Miguel to defend the family. When someone commented about Mariana, Miguel beat him without mercy. The people in this pathetic town should read his mind and see that he thought they were laughing at nothing, because he considered her a dead whore. No one uttered the words "love letters" more than once around Miguel.

Father José Trindade, the confessor, debated whether he should ask Sister Mariana Alcoforado if she knew that copies of her love letters were circulating in a whirlwind throughout Europe. He had glanced through a French edition prior to his interview with her but could not force himself to read it completely. The letters were far too personal. Whether she was aware of her words infiltrating foreign countries had nothing to do with the fact that she was accused of a serious crime. Several nuns had written to him blaming her for the recent three-day rebellion. He wondered if she knew that her story had spurred King Dom Pedro II to issue a crackdown on the scandals and disorder within religious orders.

Imagine having a love of such far-reaching proportions that it was affecting matters of state.

Under the heading in his notebook, "An Investigation into the Crimes of Sister Mariana Alcoforado of the Royal Convent of Conceição in Beja," Father José Trindade wrote, "The Issue of Penitence."

"Are you sorry for what you have done, Sister?" His tone was rote.

"Oh, no, Father."

"Pardon me?" He looked up at her.

"I regret that nothing worked out as I hoped. I'm sorry that my family is upset. Do you know how my father is? Have you heard about his health? Could you persuade him to come and see me?"

The confessor was stunned for a moment before saying, "What do you mean you're not sorry?"

"I would gladly fall into hell rather than regret that I know the height and depths of the universe. Why not? I am in hell right now, and no escape is permitted to me."

"Repentance will bring relief, Sister," said the priest. "You don't plan to make this easy for me, and for yourself?"

"Easy?" Sister Mariana shook her head. "Never, never."

Father José Trindade did not record that he was struck helpless at the sight of tears marking the neck of her wimple, their trail making sorrow take the shape of watery claws. He wanted to write, "This girl is beautiful, shockingly beautiful. Why have I been sent to make her cry?" When he mentioned the prescribed ten-year sentence − confinement in a cell without any outside communication − for any nun caught in illicit liaisons, she did not flinch.

"I love forever," was all she said.

"Sister Mariana," he said. "I have seen the room meant for incarceration in this convent. The walls are seething with vermin. It is damp, You don't appear well to me, and I cannot in good conscience allow you to be placed there. Will you at least repent of your actions so that I may offer absolution?"

"If you had met love itself, God Himself, would you repent of it?"

"I can look at you and see that you're going to punish yourself more than I or anyone else could inflict. I do wish you wouldn't. God is loving. Will you allow me to absolve you?"

"To say I'm sorry about love? To erase it, wipe it away?"

"I would never ask anyone to be sorry about love. I ask you to be sorry that you broke your vow."

"I broke a vow that was imposed on me. The vow that was my own, sprung out of my heart, I never broke. Never, never."

"King Dom Pedro is irate about − about scandals."

"Dom Pedro? The man who stole his crippled brother's wife and then grabbed the throne?"

"I must ask you to check the boldness of your speech," he said, though for the first time today he was grinning. "You would have made a good scholar, Sister Mariana. Scholars have to know how to argue, and hold to their convictions even to their detriment."

"I am a scholar."

"True," he said. "Sister Francisca Freire has told me as much. She's worried about you."

"I'm sorry to cause her any discomfort. I'm sorry that you appear so pained, Father."

"Sorry for that much?" he said. "That is sufficient for me. I shall absolve you, though you do not accept it." He raised his hand in blessing and recited the "Te Absolvo," and for her penance, he said, "Consider life precious. Do not become bitter. I am not going to recommend that you be imprisoned. The others will have to learn to live with you, and you with them. We've suffered enough in this country without filing reports against one another."

Mariana said, "Father, Saint Teresa of Avila endured penances and illnesses for thirty years before God sent ecstasy to her. I received my ecstasy ahead of the trials, that's all. Thirty years of penance is nothing to me. I shall give myself three times the sentence that you've been sent to deliver, and then God will have to give me a glimpse of heaven, a miracle."

"Sister Mariana," he said, "God need do nothing of the kind. God does not strike such bargains."

"He shall not be able to resist me, Father," said Sister Mariana. "You see, I have forfeited my right to quiescence, and I say farewell to it, and good riddance."

Father José Trindade closed his notebook. Even if Sister Mariana did not know how people were clinging to her letters, her force brought them alive, through love and will, to breathe and stamp across the earth, their shout rolling far because she would have it so.

Mariana's self-imposed sentence of thirty years of penance began at once. A diet of vinegar and water on some days almost drowned her in hunger. Her arm, without the bracelet from her love, would feel mercilessly weightless and would suddenly fly out to strike solid pillars. She would walk on her knees up and down her room, but that would only increase memory, sweet pain, the pleasure of her flesh refusing to die.

Sometimes she awakened with her sister sleeping on her out-stretched arm, and under Peregrina's weight, Mariana's arm went bloodless, buzzing like a live snake that could not move.

She denied herself pastries from the kitchen, cakes of aniseed and fire-water, until craving made bumps stand on her skin.

Her attendance at the divine hours was exemplary. In her "little house" she held her arms outstretched until they were in spasms from the torture and waiting. When God sent her a miracle, her embrace would be wide to receive it. She lay her belly upon the thorns of roses. She wore the hairshirt of her enemy, Sister Michaella dos Anjos.

And still she loved. When Peregrina steeped tea from the leaves of Catarina's orange tree and insisted that Mariana try it, Mariana loved the taste, smell, the heat of the water, the memory of Catarina.

She spoke with joy through the grate with Ana Maria, who visited with her new son, Gomes Freire de Andrade Pantoja. "Poor thing! He's my runt, my end of the line. He's not very quick, but he'll be my special one," said Ana Maria of the sickly child. Here, too, was love — touch, hearing. Mariana brushed her fingers on the baby's skin through the iron grating, and clenched Ana Maria's hand with a lattice of metal in the middle of their grip.

Papa would not come to see Mariana. That was the largest penance.

In addition to the task of being portress, Mariana ordered herself to learn how to apply gold leaf to moroccan leather book covers,

219

but instead of labor and sleeplessness erasing the pangs of love, the love within her increased.

When Sister Joana Veloso de Bulhão, Sister Cecília Sebastiana, or Sister António Sofia Baptista d'Almeida complained of her, she did not point out the obvious ways in which they were wrong. When Sister Brites de Freire made a remark that clearly hid an envious spirit, Mariana held her tongue until she imagined herself chewing on fire, and swallowing, and letting her gut burn about the loneliness of all men and women.

Always, always, she whispered, Oh love, feeling your absence is the cruelest punishment of all. Do not mistake my sorrows for a means of ridding myself of you. To possess the greatest love, I must embrace everything about it, including its opposite, the greatest sadness.

She realized she was not whispering to Noel, but to the mysteries of formless love, pure love, love that gives a reason to live even as it drains away all reason.

Out in the middle of nowhere, Cristóvão Pantoja Lôbo dozed under the sky. It was three years since freedom, but peace had not ceased causing him fatigue. He was full of wine and roasted goat. His wife, Dona Mécia de Sousa, swept dead flies out of a pantry. She was tired of begging her husband to move them to Miranda, near her family. She lost this fight, as she lost every fight with Cristóvão. Their eldest son, José de Melo, who wished to be named guardian of the estate and had his eye on his aunt Leonor Henrique's adjacent property, lurked in the orchard. He continued scheming of ways to circumvent his father's sloth.

A servant crept behind Cristóvão's chair, though he could have ridden up to him on a roaring lion and the man would not have stirred. The servant took courage by reminding himself of the many instances of Cristóvão beating and insulting him. Raising a knife and then striking with one deep plunge, he sent to judgment the man who once boasted that no king or field general ever born could subdue him.

No kings, no field generals; the act was reserved for a servant.

The servant was released from custody when no one could disprove the rumor that he was originally contracted by Cristóvão to murder Mécia, his wife, to end her nagging about moving, and

220

that she and her eldest son discovered the plot and persuaded the servant that to murder his tyrannical master would be more honorable than if he were to kill a woman.

During one of her penances, Mariana became so hungry that she thought death was there to rescue her, but then the urge not to die overpowered her, and she tried to conquer hunger by scaling up her wall and out the window. The room felt like her stomach, unfilled, and above her shone an open mouth, and if she climbed to it, she could escape from her empty insides. She could not later conceive how she had managed to climb up a high wall, using only her bare hands and desire to escape, but she had grasped the window and shouted, frightening some postulants in the courtyard below. One of her palms was scraped to the muscle.

The Abbess ordered bars placed across Sister Mariana's windows, and the nuns could not decide if it was to protect or punish her. When she lay on her bed, the shadows draped a lovely black lace across her skin.

To cure her scraped hands, Sister Leonor Henriques took Mariana to choir, where Sister Beatriz Maria de Resende was at the organ, with Sister Francisca Freire helping her hands blindly locate the correct tonic and dominant chords. Sister Leonor Henriques placed Mariana's hands on Sister Beatriz Maria de Resende's throat when she began to sing, and the rumble of perfect music was a wonder in soothing the wounds, until Mariana said, No, stop. Sister Leonor Henriques has lost her brother Cristóvão. She is the one who needs to feel the music of the world's most beautiful singer. Nothing could be worse than losing a brother.

Abbess Brites de Noronha, having confiscated a copy of *Lettres Portugaises* from a postulant who had attempted to smuggle it into the convent, glanced through the book, shut it, and hid it in her desk. She wrote a letter to her sister, making inquiries as to the extent to which this publication was available on the outside.

Her sister reported that twenty editions of the love letters of the nun, in about three or four different languages, existed across Europe, but that Francisco da Costa Alcoforado and his allies had warned that they would ruin any publisher who released them in Portuguese.

The Abbess went into the chapel and knelt at the altar rail. At the end of three hours of prayer, no advice descended upon her. Sister Mariana had a right to know what was happening to her voice. On the other hand, what would that change? It might increase her shame, and bring more shame upon everyone. One did things in the world, and was never the wiser in determining how they bloomed; one had no control over what the outside chose to do with one's dreams.

Being of noble blood herself, the Abbess made the decision that those of a certain birth must protect one another from scandal. No girl would be admitted without her belongings thoroughly searched, and she would be excommunicated should she resort to gossip. Penalties would be discreetly issued against nuns who spread news of the book, should they receive any from visitors. Eventually the excitement would die down. She would inform the next elected Abbess of her policy. She extracted the copy from her desk and burned it in her fireplace. The cover was stubborn. At last it exploded, permanently charring the bricks.

Not much outside word leaked in, but one year came the notice that the King of France, Louis XIV, had outlawed a color.

The Protestants, the Huguenots, were being driven out of France, a quarter-million of them. The King was reaching the end of his life, and decided that his sins would be excused if he terrorized the ones he decided were not chosen by God. He declared his enmity with William of Orange, who had taken up the Protestant cause.

Orange was banned in France — the fruit, the dye, the paint. Nothing orange was to be allowed.

Mariana, standing as the portress at the door, mourned that Noel should be denied a color. She could see his mistresses sadly putting away their topazes, wrapping their orange skirts in heavy paper. Were orange trees to be draped with mourning cloth? Never more to dine and talk long into the night, elbows resting and wine spilling on an orange embroidered tablecloth? What of orange blossoms decorating fans? Walking sticks of orangewood? Would books with orange-gold covers have to be destroyed? Never to see orange ribbons? What paintings would have to be stored in attics for fear of the wrath of the King? Hearths must be cold in France, to prevent the leaping of orange fire, and no blankets with orange threads brought out to warm the children. A landscape drained of color! No party with orange coconut oil from Brazil leaking onto a serviette.

Noel might look across the length and breadth of his country, and say, What is missing? I miss the color denied to me. I miss it so much that no other color exists.

Mariana, looking into the evening sky, thought, The King shall smile about his decree, and go out of his palace to see no orange flowers, no orange clothing upon the gardeners, no orange on the tea tray brought at his command.

But then, as night approaches, he shall lift up his head and see the unconquerable orange wash of the sky and setting sun above, a canopy he cannot pull down, and this orange will bathe the skin of the French, sanctify their clothing, redouble their desire for what they have been told they may not have; it shall seep through windows, and the King will know (though he will probably not admit it) that it will return the next evening, and the next, as long as for ever lasts. Noel would wander through forbidden orange, no matter where he went.

Mariana curved her neck backward to receive the caress of the orange sky. The same here as there, refusing to obey a king. Deny anything, even a color, and the color floods in, announcing, I am everywhere, the heat of the forbidden dying sun. Wear me on your skin, if being told you cannot have me makes you want me more.

I love you. I love you still. I love you always. I esteem every joy and every sorrow your love bestows on me.

During the first decade of her penances, Sister Mariana did not fail to keep her vow to offer this prayer at her window every year on the anniversary of Noel Bouton leaving her, but she did not always mention him by name in her recitations.

One year, she added, This is the fifth year I have not seen Baltazar, but sometimes I stop, as if I'm hearing a child asking me to protect him from the night, and I know it is my defeated brother. I write to him, though he does not write back.

Another year, she added, My sister Ana Maria and my youngest brother, Francisco, visit frequently. Francisco is grown-up, about to go to the University at Coimbra, to study to be a judge.

Another year — I have begun to write my sums again. I help Sister Francisca Freire during the recreation hours.

Another year — Not long ago, as I was standing at the front door, I saw my father happen past, on his way to the marketplace. He looked old and weak. I disobeyed all orders and shouted, "Papa!" when I saw that he had spotted me but intended to ignore me. "Papa!" I shouted again, and was preparing to run to him. But then he turned, and smiled at me so sadly that I was reminded that I still have a heart that can be broken again. And he blew me a kiss. I pretended to catch it in my hand. I blew one back. He pretended to catch it, but quickly, before someone saw him. He went on.

And another year — Brites and I have long conversations, but it pains me how cautious we both are with what we say, as if one or the other of us will sift through the conversation and find the reasons we have been seeking to mistrust the other.

And another — I am thirty-six. How did I get to be this old! My sister Peregrina is about to turn sixteen. Sometimes, Noel, I think: I share all of this with you. At other times, I think: The massive book of my life keeps writing itself, whether or not you care to sit with me by a fireside and read it, whether or not you care that so much of it continues to be colored by my love.

Sister Peregrina Alcoforado imagined herself standing in a bower among cordate leaves, though the convent lacked the room for lush vegetation. The party to welcome her to the Franciscan community of Poor Clares was subdued because of a shortage of funds, but Sister Angelica de Noronha had taken pains to prepare a modestly lavish table. The Bishop had proclaimed, during the ceremony, that God was today in His heaven, and Sister Peregrina felt her first joyful tinge of dissension — No, no! The Bishop was wrong. God was right here, on the ground, next to everyone.

Two postulants flung spoonfuls of rice pudding at each other, and Sister Angelica reprimanded them, though not severely. Peregrina was pleased. Even the daring sin of wasting food seemed exuberant. She fingered the new flax cordon around her waist. She had discarded the rope belt of novices.

Paper flowers hanging from the trees in the courtyard swayed back and forth like clapperless bells. The garden on the confined property was the best that she and Sister Ignez de São José could make it, though it left much to be desired. The vegetable patch would be less straggly if the nuns would be more careful to walk around it. Catarina's orange tree flourished in the corner, its branches like a girl's arms, its trunk solid, its fruit full and textured and plentiful, like a defiance of the prohibitions of France.

The nuns filed by to congratulate Peregrina, and she was clutching an envelope and anxiously awaiting Mariana, who was sitting off by herself. Peregrina worried; her sister was in the eighth year of penances, and often needed to rest.

Mariana, trembling, was having trouble facing Peregrina, not because she looked like a sixteen-year-old version of Mama, but because she looked like Mariana twenty years ago, taking her own vows. To embrace Peregrina as a nun would be tantamount to embracing the truth of who she herself was. Odd that she had never quite believed it, had been waiting, even now, decades later, for someone to release her and say that what she had planned for the fulfillment of her life could now commence: time remained. She recalled thinking on the day of her profession that she was going through with some play-acting that the nuns and her parents had decided was necessary in order to justify caring for her during the war. When her better dreams were allowed to flourish, she would leave and find the reward for her patience. At the party — like this one — to welcome her as a bride of Christ, Mariana had eaten Angels' Tummies with brittle stamens of caramelized sugar floating over them. Her gown had been a much-handled white. Because of the shortages during wartime, Mother Maria de Mendonça had sewn it for her out of the curtains from the office of the Abbess. Her dress smelled of the breath of requests from those who called upon the Abbesses over the last century, and of the *memento mori* skull that had rested near the curtains. To entertain her friend, Brites de Freire, Mariana had pretended to be a dead person and walked with exaggerated wooden steps in the gown up the chapel's nave.

She lay before the Bishop, who covered her with a white cloth to represent that she had died to the world.

When she knelt on the white silk of the prie-dieux, he asked if she would be obedient, poor, and chaste.

Mariana said, Yes, yes, yes.

Did she understand that she was to sacrifice the right of proprietorship, rendering her incapable of receiving any gifts, legacies, and inheritance, or personal goods not shared with the community?

Yes.

Did Dona Mariana understand that sin could be exterior, or interior, such as an unvoiced criticism of a superior?

Yes. Her response was disembodied; why not; this was not her.

Did Dona Mariana understand that she must guard against interior thoughts or seductive representations in her imagination, and against too tender affections and friendships?

She had said yes. This was wartime waiting, nothing to do with the life of the heart that she had chosen. How could any affection be too tender?

Did she understand that her eyes must avoid unhealthy reading and curiosities, her ears must resist flattery, and her tongue loose from itself words of double meaning, or worldly song?

Yes. But how could there exist such a thing as dangerous reading or songs?

The Bishop slipped a band of white gold onto the ring finger of her right hand, and the nuns sang the "Regina Coelis." She then found herself smashed against the bosoms of well-wishers, her cheek wounded against the brooch, a boiling of diamonds and rubies, of some rich refugee.

Later she exchanged her novice's white tunic for the scapular of estamin, the rough woolen cloth of her new black habit. Her forehead, throat, and neck were covered with a white, cap-like swathing, and her black veil floated to her shoulders.

Today when she had heard and seen it again, enacted by Peregrina, it was as if Peregrina were proclaiming, This was you, Mariana. This *is* you. Your life is here, like this, like me. Will you embrace that or do you intend to continue fooling yourself?

Mariana walked up to Sister Peregrina and kissed her. Peregrina handed her an envelope and told her to read the note inside.

The note was a summary of Papa's dowry arrangements for Peregrina. The amount was the same as it had been for Mariana, except that upon Peregrina's death, the parcel of land and the wheat thereon were to revert not to the convent, but to the person or institution of Peregrina's choice, ". . . because she was placed in this convent when she was scarcely more than an infant, and missed a decade more of the outside. Therefore I, Francisco da Costa Alcoforado, in consideration of this and in commendation for the outstanding reports concerning her progress in her studies, do decree that she be given a modicum more of outside dealings."

Below this, Peregrina had written, "I hereby will that upon my demise, all my property and any amounts that may accrue shall be turned over to my sister Mariana, to do with as her wisdom demands, in gratitude for her raising me in this convent since I was a child of three."

Mariana stared at the paper, waiting for it to make sense. It did not. "No," she said. "This isn't right."

"It is what I want, and perfectly right. This is my day, and you can't refuse me," said Sister Peregrina, gripping Mariana's hands and pushing the testament closer to her.

"I've done nothing for you. Give this to Sister Ignez."

"I've given it to you. I told Sister Ignez what I wanted to do, and she agreed with me."

Mariana knew she must say something funny, or perish on the spot. "You're planning to die before me, Peregrina? Planning to die even though you could be my daughter?" she said, her eyebrows arching.

Peregrina smiled. "I'll do as you tell me. Unless I don't care for your orders, of course."

"I've just decided that I'm going to be the Abbess someday, and I'll forbid your predeceasing me," said Mariana.

"Any other commandments?"

"Yes. You must find out the answer to a riddle that Vovó once asked me. She died before she could tell me. Do you remember Vovó?"

"I remember that she never got out of bed. I never heard her speak. The riddle?"

"What is it that we kiss, but never adore?"

"I shall see what I can do to find out. And I'll vote for you, when you stand for Abbess. Mariana? If Vovó never told you the answer, how will we know if what I come up with is right or not?"

"I think we'll know. We'll both say, 'That's it! *Duende*! Magic!'"

Peregrina laughed. "You haven't commented on how I look."

Mariana stood back, took her in. "You look like a nun," she said. "You look beautiful."

*

Francisco da Costa Alcoforado had taught his grandchildren, including the girls, how to play chess. He was always faced with deciding whether to use the full force of his skill and score a sure victory, the better to train them, or to let them defeat him occasionally, so they would remain eager. He alternated both methods, though in either case, he was the one in control. So it was with surprise during a match with Caetana that he heard her say, "Sorry, Vovô. Checkmate." The opposing bishop and queen had boxed him into a corner, with a knight positioned to seal his doom. He laid his king carved from ivory down on the board, and was pleased to find that as old as he was, there were new sensations to experience. This was the first rime he had lost without intending to, and he was moved to see that Caetana was afraid that she had hurt him.

"Well done!" he said.

She took the ivory king and set him back upright.

"No, dear," said Francisco, and placed him down again, where he wobbled on his back. "He's finished. Don't delude him with false hopes."

"Shall I brush your hair now, Grandpa?"

"You Godsend, you."

Caetana used the silver-backed brush that had belonged to her grandmother Leonor, who died when Caetana was three. Her grandfather's hair was long, thick, and white, like something shed from the ghost of a lion. They played a game of seeing how short a time it took her to lull him to sleep, with the bristles plowing upward, neck to scalp, across skin that flashed here and there bare and pink and spotted, up one side, down the other.

He fought against drifting off to sleep, to prolong the soothing feel of his granddaughter's hand through his hair, the pleasure in the hard teeth of the brush sweeping in tight lines. The nicest moment was in knowing that wonderful oblivion was soon to come. His hands tightened on the lap robe, the same one that Leonor used after each of her babies had been born, and it still bore the milky smell of her, and of all their children. She would drowse in this same chair, with an infant against her, and he would peer in and have a sense that the world was self-created and abundant; and he would leave her, quietly closing the door, so as not to disturb anything. He disagreed with those who dismissed him as a harsh father. Times were dangerous. His job was to teach them lessons.

He recalled that once while out with Ana Maria and Mariana when they were children, he pointed out a thicket of blackberry bushes and mentioned that the fruit was miraculously sweet. He waited to see what they would do. Ana Maria tried to pluck a few berries close to the edge of an outer bush, and reacted with alarm when the thorns stabbed her. Mariana, though, went in search of a fallen branch, and came back wielding it, smashing down the thorny vines and forcing a path into an inner clearing of the thicket, where it was swollen with quarry. She made the branch hold the brambles flat against the ground at the entranceway. Mariana led her older sister along, and then realized that the oozing fruit was so desirable that she would not be able to steal as much as would content her. She forced her sister to remain in the clearing, where they could eat until their hands were stained a deep purple. All at once the branch bracing open their exit sprang up and flew out of reach, trapping them, and he heard Mariana crying, "Papa! Come rescue us!"

He sat up with a start in the chair. Caetana was no longer brushing his hair. He was alone; he must have fallen asleep.

Mariana had called for him. He stood up and became dizzy. He remembered that she had disgraced the family, had concocted a diary of some private shame, that somehow it had gone into other people's homes, like secret agents, and he had to finish collecting anything that might cause anyone to laugh at her. It was his mission as a father to go from door to door from here to the ocean. Not because of disgrace, but because she was calling him. How long had he been dozing? The sound of Mariana was deafening. He vaguely recalled a vow that he must treat her as dead, but it was confused with thinking that she was standing in a blackberry patch, where he, after all, to be fair about it, had sent her.

"I'm on my way, Mariana! Wait a moment more!" he shouted. "Wait for me! Watch!"

It occurred to him that he should dress himself in such a way that people would understand that they must get out of his path. He took his sword in its scabbard, in case he had to cut through thorns. As he prepared to leave the house, he saw Caetana, and said, "Have I taught you to count angels when you cannot sleep?"

"Yes, Vovô. I count angels, and I count stars, and I sleep very well. Why are you dressed like that?"

"I'm being called. I'm going out."

"Why don't you go back to your room, Vovô, and I'll have Bastiana bring you some cake. Would you like to have a tea party with me?"

"Ah! So you can gloat about your victory at chess?"

"You told me that only people without manners gloat."

He leaned down and kissed the top of her head. "So I did. I've said and done a lot of things, wouldn't you say? Will you remember me?"

"Why are you talking like that, Vovô?" She lightly held the rich fabric of his sleeves.

"Because it's a strange world, my dear, and I'm tired of trying to make it otherwise. Forgive me — but won't you excuse me now?"

When Francisco da Costa Alcoforado reached the edge of his property, where it melded in an invisible line with the rambling expanse of the plains, he faced the center of town. Mariana was somewhere in there. That was where he had to travel. But he was tired. He should rest. She would wait, and when he saw her, he would explain that he had been out collecting love letters into a bouquet. He forgot what this had to do with his daughter, but a sense of duty was flaring up, mixed incomprehensibly with love, and he was trying to figure out the task at hand. In the meantime, it was good to lie down on the ground, until the answer came to him.

Another portion of unfinished business was that he had spent many hours holding a brush over a page, asking God to send him an automatic picture, and nothing ever came. But the sky above him was a hot, clear white, blank as paper, and he thought, "Then you've been waiting for me to tell You, God? My memories are the paintings, to be splashed across the sky? Is it my task to astonish You?"

He heard Mariana shriek, "Papa!"

"Yes, dear!" he called back. "I'm on my way!"

How strange that the land should be falling away beneath him. He had come down from the mountains of his youth to storm into the plains and tell them not to be complacent — they must give their lives for independence, for freedom. To die free! Free forever! One's children, whether they understood it or not — free! He had envisioned that at some point the men who keenly constructed their lives would be allowed to cling to the frame of what they had done, holding on to some part of the skeleton of history. He had thought there would be a solidness to one's completed destiny, with rigidity, impetus, solidity; a thing of horses, mill-stones, coins, saddles, crops. Not this air and memory, not this floating above the ground.

He held his arms straight up and said, "Leonor, my darling, I have kept you waiting."

His servant Luís found him like this, with his arms stretched rigidly towards the sky. It was clear that his master had dressed in the outfit described in his will as the one in which he would be buried, with full military dress, red toque, high-laced buskins, so that no one would look upon his nakedness, and he had had the grace and decency to leave his room, so that the children would not peek in on him and be frightened. The plaque stating that 400 Masses were to be said for the cleansing of his soul as he lay in his sepulcher at the São Francisco Monastery had been forged long ago. Luís sensed that his stern but generous master had positioned himself so that half of him lay squarely on his own property, and the other half on the land of the nation he loved.

Luís, kneeling to close his master's eyes, could not guess at first why both the arms of Francisco da Costa Alcoforado were frozen heavenward. They could not be moved or lowered. The explanation that came to Luís was that the founder of the incomparable house and destiny of the Alcoforados was not a man who would be content to depart docilely. He must have commanded God to pick him up, to take him now, and be quick about it.

Across the province of the Alentejo, as everyone debated why this free era should be the worst economic time in memory, as citizens discussed how to manage their holidays in light of the shortages, there arose many conversations as to why Baltazar Vaz Alcoforado, scarcely over the age of thirty and in generally good health, though increasingly given, as reports had it, to juvenile oddness, should have contracted paludism like a soldier in the tropics, and taken to his bed at the priory in Beringel with alternating fits of hotness and coldness, to die burning and shivering on Christmas Day in the exact same year that his father had ceased to exist.

Baltazar's last words had been, "I am the greatest sinner in the world!"

A sizable faction believed that Baltazar chose the day of the birth of the Son to enact the death of the son, proving himself to be of a fundamentally contrary nature. His final statement was a boast — perhaps made in the throes of delirium, but a boast nonetheless — that he was a rebel in his last gasp, proud to have played a role in outlaw love.

Others disagreed. Baltazar was a tortured soul. Why else had he withdrawn to a cell, why else cried out at the end in what could well be remorse?

No one knew with any certainty. His inflection had given nothing away, according to the monks who were with him.

At the convent of Conceição, Christmas Day in 1676 was as fine as the nuns could manage. Sister Angelica de Noronha and Sister Brites de Freire cooked vats of mutton stew with fava beans and prepared trays of burnt caramelized eggs, figs with wild honey, conserves of pears, and citron with sugar crystals. Some monks living in the Hospice of Saint Anthony, near the front of the convent, sent over the turtle doves and golden plovers they had hunted. People in Beja were generous, though few could afford it, delivering scented candles, thimbles packed with saffron, sandalwood boxes, ribbon-tied bunches of rosemary, and a Chinese lacquered chair.

The nuns used their minimal allowances to buy one another handkerchiefs or miraculous medals. The poorer nuns dispensed Spiritual Bouquets — promises to say certain prayers on behalf of the recipient of such a bouquet cost nothing but time. Sister Mariana had scraped together her percentage of the proceeds, severely diminished this year, from the wheat field given to the convent as part of her dowry, and arranged for a shipment of *lampa* — fruit collected on a midsummer's night. She had thought ahead, and put Manuel, the procurer, in charge of collecting figs and peaches one summer evening in the plains, and had them dried and preserved to offer as Christmas gifts. She liked the idea of everyone tasting something deliberately chosen when it was soaked in starlight.

The Abbess that year, Mother Constança Evangelista, upon receiving the message about the death of Mariana's brother and his last words, asked Sister Leonor Henriques and Sister Francisca Freire to assist her in delivering the tragic news to Mariana, who did not seem to have recovered yet from the death of her father, though it was difficult to ascertain what was going on with her.

To the nervous surprise of the three nuns delivering the sad word, Mariana merely remarked that it made a certain amount of sense that her brother should die too hot, too cold — death by extremes.

"We're so, so, hideously sorry, my dear," said Sister Leonor Henriques.

"Yes," said Mariana.

"Will you be all right?" said the Abbess. "We'll have his name put on the altar for Mass in the morning."

"That would be nice," said Mariana. She was very calm. Her expression did not change. "May I be excused, Mother?"

Mariana remained serene. She kept to her job as portress. She greeted her fellow sisters when that was appropriate, and was silent when it was time to be silent. She continued to increase the hours spent in the scriptorium with Sister Francisca Freire. The nuns were kind. They were wary around her. At one point, she noticed that she was moving like someone wearing heavy clothing in water. Sometimes she was extraordinarily aware of every motion. For instance, getting out of bed. She could break that down into separate acts. Lifting up her head. Moving aside the blanket. Putting feet to floor. Standing. It was amusing. Imagine getting out of bed being this complicated.

Sister Michaella dos Anjos asked her bluntly, "Do you think he meant to be arrogant at the end, or sorry?"

"Baltazar? I know that if I had been there, I would be able to decipher the feeling behind what he said."

"You act as if you hardly care. You're a strange one, Sister."

"You'd like to see me weeping?"

"No."

"I think you would. Would you excuse me?"

Mariana went about her chores. She well knew that a cry of pain and a cry of triumph could sound alike, and therefore she had not told Sister Michaella dos Anjos the precise truth, which was that she was waiting for Baltazar to explain to her what he had meant, since he understood how to get messages to her, but that was no one else's business. She had never felt so quiet and slow before. Put on veil. Put on left shoe. Put on right shoe. It was as if she had stepped backward, and was falling down a dark tunnel that extended through the center of the globe, but she was not falling fast, not plummeting; she was drifting down, farther and farther, and though there was no light and little air, she could discern that she was still alive, because the falling was going on. Sometimes it was as if she were at the top of the chasm, watching herself. That was so funny that really she should shriek with laughter, but in the middle of such falling no one would be able to hear her, so what was the point?

Moreau & Zwick, a French and German poultry company that set up their business in Portugal after the war, complained of a receipt she presented to them. Instead of writing "balance" at the end, she had written "Baltazar."

She thanked Sister Ignez de São José for being such a longtime guardian of Peregrina. Her final words trailed off, because she realized that she was falling, and she was already too far away to be heard.

Falling like snow — something she had never seen — lace fragment here, lace fragment there.

When Sister Francisca Freire said, "Sister Mariana, what penances are you performing? You seem faint," Mariana offered that her mortifications were not so demanding.

"I do not like the practice of mortifications, Sister," said Sister Francisca Freire. "You look shocked at my heresy? I think that they should indeed be offered up as they inevitably befall us, but I do not believe we should deliberately injure any of creation, including ourselves."

"Yes, Sister," said Mariana, but her words were weak, because they had to travel a long way up the tunnel.

"You wish to continue with your thirty years of penance? I have one for you, more demanding than anything you have attempted thus far. Are you equal to the task?" asked Sister Francisca Freire.

"Yes," said Mariana, half-dreamily. "Maybe."

"It is far more difficult to love than to suffer. To love simply, without facing trials, is good. But to love after tragedy is heroic. You must go inside love and feel it again, Sister Mariana."

"I do."

"You don't. Your pain is stored inside your mind like a book on a high shelf. Take that book down and open it, because your loved ones are written into the center of it."

234

"No."

Sister Francisca Freire, She with the Dove's Heart, was not afraid to cry. "Yes. I'm sorry, but yes, you have to. Come back to the world, and love it, and love us."

"No."

But it was beyond Mariana's powers to disobey her. In her "little house" that night, while falling, drifting downward, she reached out and plucked the book about Noel off a shelf stuck on the inside of the bottomless tunnel. She threw back the book's cover. Searing jabs spun her around; she had never, never stopped loving him, despite how the nuns conferred sagely about the passage of time healing everything. He should have forsaken home, family, country, as she was still ready to do. She would never accept it as right that this would never come to pass. She only accepted it as true, permanently true, that he wanted imperfect pleasure, which could never harm him.

In that moment it was as if he had left her yesterday, and she could feel his face pressed wet against hers and him muttering, I love you so, and her saying, Yes.

The memory had her shaking. The tunnel she had been drifting down was the endless chasm of her own heart.

A decade since I have held you, and my empty arms are still in agony, clutching at nothing, and the taunt comes to me: Never again. I am meant, it seems, in the confines of my room, to become acquainted with every manner and permutation of love, and the death of love, and death itself.

I am strong enough to live it all. Love gives me the wings I need to fly to the grave of my father, and say that I cannot imagine he lived in vain.

Love gives me the wings I need to open the book of my brother, and go to him.

I can see you on your bed, Baltazar, in your cell. I am wiping your forehead as you go hot, then cold. Fellow monks, your friends, are around as I pick up your fevered head. Amidst the smell of sickness, they tell me funny stories about you. One says that you stored tadpoles in ceramic jugs, hoping the Abbot would drink from them. Another says that you never combed your hair. A third says that you would perform rope tricks with stolen cinctures. Others said that you would spend too much of money you did not have on gifts for them, that you would hoe the garden and do plain tasks, not like some of the other noblemen who wanted to try on asceticism like a fine new set of clothing and considered themselves above work. Are you gone, Baltazar? I would bounce you on my knee when you were a baby, and hug you when Rui brought you and Miguel to visit when I was put in my convent. Being older than you, I had such an earnest death scene of my own devised, with you by my side!

I lean forward, into the silence, straining for the pitch of the notes of your last words. You're grinning at me. I say sternly, You can't die. We lost Papa. This is an absurd family detail, to lose a father and a brother in the same year. You say, He's gone to a higher ground, and I have to move up there, if I want to finish our arguments. I shake you and reply, No more fighting! It's peacetime! No more arguments, Baltazar. I can't tell if you're joking now or not.

Is it your notion that dying on Christmas Day is a death that outdoes his? What nonsense. I order you to stop it.

You say, Haven't I always done as you asked, Mariana? Even if it led to daring sorrow?

I say, You promised to care for me always.

Your response is that you care enough to die from what love can do.

I scream that you must not take on the project of dying of love in order to spare me the need to do it, but I know you are leaving me, and I hold you so that the last words will enter me as close as I can get to you, Baltazar, and you say, "I am the greatest sinner in the world!"

And brother of my heart, I listen with full body, full mind, full soul, with my memories of our brief childhood together, I listen past my broken dreams that we might have lived much differently: And I do not know exactly what you mean. I cannot tell absolutely whether you are defiant and proud, or distressed.

I simply cannot divine it.

Therefore I have no choice but to call you hot, cold, forlorn, triumphant. What does a final statement matter? Since you were everything to me, it is right that I decide that you contained every possible coloration, nuance, range.

Farewell, my Baltazar.

And farewell to you, my father.

*

Spiteful, unpredictable, mutable love! Such unfairness, to lose so many, so much! The moment that reason says that love must not be trusted — says to live without sentiment — love comes pouring in. Mariana felt it flooding into her, alive, making her writhe in a starry heat, with Noel and her beloved departed ones embracing her. She moaned aloud. Ah, Noel, you, in my arms! Here! All her loved ones were dreamed real. The challenge of joy was not only allowing them to be constantly present, but to know and feel that they were also gone forever. Her moan grew into a crescendo of a howl, and she pulled herself out of the tunnel of her heart and stared out to see love as formless as sidereal glare waiting to see what she would make of it next. In the blinding of that, and in the midst of her roaring cry of assent and protest, into her room ran the nun who looked like her mother but was young enough to be her daughter. Mariana's sister, whose skills in studying were so stellar, who shone in the garden she tended as best she could. The star pupil. Into Mariana's room rushed Peregrina, who was strong enough to raise up her sprawled, tortured sister, and soothe her, and say, "I'll be with you now, Mariana, and I promise I won't ever leave you."

Part 4

THE PATIENTS rolled their heads until their sights rested upon the angelic face of Sister Mariana. Sisters Peregrina, Brites de Freire, Francisca Freire, and Juliana de Matos, other seraphic ministers, walked from bed to bed in the infirmary, pressing wet towels onto the suffering nuns and wiping away the black streams flowing from their mouths, occasionally stopping to help Sister Mariana to her feet and set beneath her arm the walking stick she used as a crutch. Her three decades of penance had ended some years before, but damage was sustained. Kneeling on grass mats in the Chapel of the Holy Crucified had worn one of her knees to nothing. Her prayer was for God to maintain the racking feel of love that had never left her, that she never wanted to leave her. Her precision with the financial accounts and bookkeeping and her tutoring of Peregrina had sanded down the sharpness of her eyesight. An erratic diet of salt had not desiccated her longings, but had imparted to her a sense of being crystalline, gloriously thirsty, and sparkling, and gave her a radiance in her old age, a sign of her having subscribed to Sister Francisca Freire's mandate that she rise to the defiance of finding joy, ineffable joy, despite everything that had or could be done to her. Now that she was sixty, she attributed her serenity to spending so much time raising Peregrina. Being a mother was something that Mariana never fathomed could bring such elation. The sick nuns wanted to bathe in the almost supernatural love pouring from her like sunlight, and called for Sister Mariana to aid them in their last hour.

The Abbess, Dona Mariana dos Serafins, screamed that the skin was burning off her scalp. She had recently received viaticum, the

Eucharist given to the dying, and was endeavoring to ignore her agony, lest her complaints work against her when she stood before the peace of heaven. Sister Mariana limped quickly to the bedside of the Abbess.

"Mother! We with the same name must help each other. Can you press some of your heat onto me? It is terrible to be on fire," Mariana said, and held out both hands for the Abbess to clench.

The Abbess groaned that she had failed as guardian of the nuns. Had she formed an inviolate community, the plague that was ravaging Beja and much of the country would never have infected the cloisters.

"Are we to claim ourselves untouched by the world?" said Sister Mariana.

"Am I to die holding the hands of a sinner?" shrieked the Abbess.

Sister Mariana grinned. "You flatter me, Mother. Jesus befriended sinners, and loved them better than the rest."

Peregrina glanced over at her sister. It bothered her that Mariana freely touched fevered hands and changed soiled linens. Mariana's hands were glowing red, from the hotness seeping into them from the dying Abbess.

Sister Joana Veloso de Bulhão and Sister Ignez de São José brought meals from the refectory into the infirmary, though no one was interested in eating. Sister Caetana and Sister Inêz, the daughters of Ana Maria and Rui, assisted with feeding the patients, though they were frightened. Sister Francisca Freire, old as crackled parchment, might wish to close the final chapter of her long life with corporal works of mercy, but they were two women barely into their forties. When Sister Caetana revealed this to her aunt, Sister Mariana, she was ashamed when Mariana replied that any thought or action that did not entertain risk was merely a point of rest before the challenge of some other risk arrived. Instead of being a soothing hiding place, a cloister intensified the emotional demands of humanity.

Also in the convent was Leonor Jacoba, the daughter of Mariana's youngest brother, Francisco. Her being here was a vote of affection from Francisco, who traveled in his work as a judge but visited his daughter and sisters whenever he could. In contrast, Miguel had placed his two daughters, quite pointedly, in the Convent of Esperança. Once Mariana got over being hurt, she was bemused that Miguel preferred to expose them to byways echoing with the raptures of Sister Mariana de Purificação, who died in 1695 and whose visions of sleeping with her redeemer remained under discussion. Reports from the Vatican hinted that Sister Mariana de Purificação was to be proclaimed an innocent given to flights of fancy.

Sister Leonor Jacoba and Sister Maria de Castro shared the task of cleaning the voluminous amount of laundry.

After the death of the Abbess, Sister Josefa Maria de Jesús ranted, her mind splicing onto the wartime past, that she was the Queen and wished to reunite her troops. She received Viaticum from one of the monks who slept in the Duke of Beja's Founder's Palace or the Hospice of Saint Anthony and remained on call to offer Extreme Unction to the dying.

They lost Sister Inês dos Serafins, who had caused an oratory to be built in the courtyard because she said that two angels hovered there. Mariana placed her in the convent's Book of Miracles, despite the objections of some of the nuns.

They lost Sister Genebra Nogueira, Sister Cecilia Sebastiana, and Sister Brites de Brito.

Sister Peregrina and Sister Joana Veloso de Bulhão undertook to drag into the central courtyard and set on fire the furniture and belongings of the victims. If only that sulky Sister Inês de Melo, the daughter of Bartolomeu Lôbo, and the lazy Sister Antónia Sofia Baptista d'Almeida would do their part. Like a number of the others, they were cowering in their cells, refusing to emerge until the danger passed. Since the plague had started in the year before the turn of the century and was now into its second year, they were getting fat and brusque, like hibernating animals. Sister Caetana left food outside their doors, trying to pretend that their taciturnity was a sign of their contemplation of sadness.

Sister Peregrina looked at the stockpile of clothing, writing desks, bed frames, and personal items from the rooms of the sick, and told Sister Joana to light it. They blessed themselves as fire swallowed the remnants. A section of Peregrina's and Ignez's garden was permanently scorched. Though the proper way to dispose of the holy items such as breviaries, scapulars, crucifixes, and cards of the saints was to consign them to fire, it was difficult to watch the contents of a life being reduced to ashes. One of Peregrina's hobbies was the constructing of Hortae Conclusae, little enclosed gardens that she created from paper, twine, ribbons, and saints' pictures in framed, covered boxes. Hortae Conclusae compensated for the smallness of the convent's actual garden and allowed Peregrina to decorate the rooms of her friends. Now many of her handiworks had to be destroyed. The cinders drove the nuns in hiding to stick cloth into their door jambs. Sister Peregrina wearily placed an arm around Sister Joana. The desk of the Abbess had been heavy with papers and books, now piled loosely as tinder among the chests and blankets.

"Happy birthday," said Sister Joana. "We'll celebrate when we have a chance."

"My birthday was last month, Sister," said Peregrina, who had turned forty-one. "We'll celebrate next year."

"We'll survive that long?"

"I shall, yes," said Peregrina. "I promised Mariana I would not die before her. I am glad to see that all signs point to her lasting forever."

"When I perish, you must write my obituary. I'd take it as my one chance at immortality," said Sister Joana.

Bits of singed paper wafted partial sentences from the Abbess's books over the cloister wall. Words powerful enough to resist fire! Peregrina considered it an impromptu tribute to her years of learning how to write from Mariana, who preached, *Outwrite the elements of earth, air, water, fire. Write living words. Bleed upon the page.* They spent many sessions in which Mariana impressed upon Peregrina the importance of writing each numeral as if it contained the sum total of memory and history.

When Sister Francisca Freire was elected Abbess in 1681, her first official act had been to remove Mariana from the shame of being portress and appoint her as head of the scriptorium. Mariana gathered Peregrina into her care and after lessons in history, Latin, and philosophy trained her to write the Forty Hours and to record the obituaries, the dowry donations, and the professions. When Mariana was named Vice-Abbess in 1693, Peregrina was put in charge of the scriptorium, though she was very young for such an honor. Her obituaries — all of her writings — were revolutions. Instead of the customary few lines listing a nun's birthdate, birth-place, date of entry into the convent, amount of donation, date of profession, and date of death, Sister Peregrina wrote massive stories. When Sister Maria de Sâo Francisco died of plague, Peregrina wrote seven pages detailing how the deceased had been an instigator in a past rebellion, but had been converted one day by an inner sensation. Peregrina was intransigent about compiling every woman's life as if it were from the Book of Saints, and Mariana rearranged the finances to bring in more paper, gold leaf, brushes, and shelves to accommodate Peregrina's wonders. The obituary for Sister Leonor Henriques, who died in 1696, covered ten pages, with two whole pages given over to a lament that she had not decided who would inherit her property in Viana d'Alvito, leaving Rui and Ana Maria to be at war against Cristóvão's greedy son. Peregrina and Mariana wrote letters to various magistrates on behalf of Ana Maria and her children. Thus far, no one wanted to make a decision.

The plague killed thirty nuns, and therefore Peregrina was continuously at work, weeping. One afternoon, while sitting alone in the courtyard, writing an obituary while another desk was burning, she noticed a book tumble from the fiery heap. She went to kick it back into the flames, but something prompted her to bend and turn the half-charred pages, not caring that it was injuring her fingers. The writing was French, a language that Mariana and Sister Ignez de Sâo José had taught her. Much of the book was devastated, but Peregrina had no trouble identifying what it was. Ages ago, Mariana had confessed to her about an affair with a man during the war. Their love had played itself out right next door to Peregrina, who had noticed none of it. With the incoming postulants pointing at Mariana and whispering, with the gossiping of some of the older nuns, it would have been impossible for Peregrina not to learn about her sister's *gravia delicta.* Mariana even admitted to sending five letters to the Frenchman, a Count and a cavalry captain. But she had not told her that they were a book. How many copies were there? Peregrina glanced at a line about the heart that threatened to split open her sister's chest, to fly to this man's embrace. The paper's edges were like black lichens from the bonfire. Maybe Mariana had not told her about the publication of the letters because she wished her privacy.

Or because she did not know about this. Was that possible? Shouldn't Peregrina, who told her sister everything, mention finding this burning book? Since the age of three she had seen very few men, and they did not stir anything more for her than a dismissible curiosity. She liked not having to listen to them. Instead of tucking the book of love letters back into the fire, she hid it under a loose tile in the floor of her "little house," thinking that when the timing seemed right, she might ask Mariana to explain about love, and to ask if she knew she had created a book.

First there came interruptions from the infirmary. Sister Juliana de Matos received the sacraments and said that she had borne a lifetime of sicknesses from everyone, and this was her chance to be ill. This was as close as she had ever come to a joke, and she died with a magnificent smile.

Sister Dolores expressed the desire to see her family, now in heaven on account of the plague. She had not seen any of them for years. Nor had she seen the Chapel of Bones in Évora. After the monks in residence died, their bones were used to fashion a house of prayer. Skulls without the bottom jaws to form walls, femurs in the pillars. Sister Dolores had always wanted to see it, but her father put her into the convent. She wrote letters begging her older brother to go to the Chapel of Bones and describe it, in order to remove the fear of death from her. He never wrote. Some nuns could speak of the ossuary to her. They said that a person could sourly assume that life was nothing but an accumulation of bones, or could applaud the good-naturedness of the monks who consented to be part of a building after their deaths. Yes, the bones appeared to cackle, We shall stand on each other's shoulders like children, and our bones will dance at night naughtily, clack-clacking. We can laugh at anyone who looks at us and thinks, Not I! Not I! Only the ancients die!

That was why there was a legend across the doorway leading into the Chapel of Bones: *Our bones here are waiting for yours.*

To the fevered recital of Sister Dolores about the chapel, Sister Caetana replied, "You are too modest to bare your bones like that, Sister."

Sister Dolores laughed. "I am!" she said, and her delirium forced her to repeat, "I am, I am," until the other patients begged her to lie quietly.

Blind Sister Beatriz Maria de Resende sang the mistress of the choir to her rest.

A pity, thought Sister Caetana, brushing the straggling hair that remained on the skull of Sister Dolores. The skeletons of monks are allowed to dance through the night. We must lie beneath flagstones. She pretended she was brushing the white mane of Francisco da Costa Alcoforado, her grandfather. She missed feeling that she could lull to sleep the eminence radiating from that man.

When Sister Angelica de Noronha took ill, the supervision of the kitchen was surrendered to Sister Brites de Freire, who cooked and then set plates of food, broths of crushed wheat and pork stews, outside the cells of the nuns who were trusting that plague could not seep through their doors.

"Catarina!" cried Sister Angelica de Noronha when Peregrina brought her water. "Oh, Catarina! I must be in heaven."

"Yes, Sister," said Peregrina. Mariana was in a corner of the infirmary, pouring disinfectant around the cot where another nun had died. They would soon need to carry the dead woman to the cemetery in the Quadra of the Rosary, where a vacant space and lime awaited. Peregrina had not looked directly at her sister since rescuing the book of letters from that outdoor pyre.

"You aren't Catarina!" said Sister Angelica de Noronha. "Where is she?"

"Just a moment," said Peregrina, and went out to Catarina's orange tree, which bulged with thick-skinned, bright fruit. The leaves exuded a strong oil, and the branches grew like the many arms of an Indian goddess against the restraint of the wall. She picked an orange for Sister Angelica.

"Here she is," said Peregrina, bringing the fruit to the dying nun.

Sister Angelica said, grasping the orange globe, that this was like holding all she knew of love.

When Sister Ignez de São José collapsed, Peregrina rushed to her, put her to bed, and conducted a hurried treasure hunt in the unburned patches of the garden to give her a bouquet of her years:

For the childhood of Ignez — fennel. Peregrina stuck a sprig of the licorice-smelling herb in the fist of her sick friend. Fennel signified the demanding of compliments. How like a child! Could Ignez recall her childhood before the convent, wearing dresses with fancy bows? No doubt her father doted on her. When he was trying to address business, did Ignez stamp her feet and demand that he pay attention to her?

Call fennel the first decade of life.

Peregrina gave Ignez an apple — fruit of passion, fruit of wishes. To be a young woman! Thinking that one could take a bite out of the world, could feel its juice running down one's neck.

Peregrina could not find an oak leaf, and asked Ignez to imagine it. Oak was the plant of freedom. Of the end of the war. Of Ignez in her thirties.

What other plant should Peregrina give to Ignez? An orange leaf, because its scent permeated everything, and so did Ignez's lessons, her teaching, her comforting. "Because you were a splendid instructor and guide," whispered Peregrina, putting the orange leaf into the hand of Ignez.

Did Ignez know that orange blossoms are the plant of brides?

Could they call it the plant for brides of Christ?

If only Peregrina could bring her a rose, if only the garden of the convent were grand enough! She asked Ignez to imagine a rose. She would call that Ignez's fifties — full-colored, full-bodied. Fragrant.

For the sixties of her dying friend — a clove. Peregrina stole it from the kitchen. Pungent. The plant of dignity. Star-shaped. For now, her seventies, her end — Peregrina held out a dipper of water and said, Water, the substance that nourishes plants, absorbed into what it touches. The water of you that poured into me. You took me in and let me go without jealousy. You let Mariana and me find each other.

"Clever, clever girl. You went through my decades with me," said Ignez, glowing through her fever, and she touched Peregrina's face, as she did when Peregrina had been the size of a doll and came to the convent to stay. "Thank you," said Sister Ignez de Sâo José, and shut her eyes.

Sister Peregrina Alcoforado's hand went into prolonged spasms by the time she finished the obituary of Sister Ignez de Sâo José.

By the time the plague wore out, towards the spring of 1701, only one hundred and fifty-five nuns survived. Few girls were knocking on the door to be postulants, even if theirs was the rare family that could afford a decent donation. Girls were being made to stay at home and care for households ruined by sickness.

*

Mariana and Peregrina sat in the courtyard's patio, peering up at the second-story Terrace of the Little Birds.

"Define *Molinismo*," said Mariana.

Peregrina grinned. She took Mariana's hand in hers. The sun was unrelenting on them. Whenever they played this game, Peregrina was transported to her late teenage years and her twenties, when Mariana was especially earnest about lessons. Peregrina had learned from her about Brazil, elementary accounting, Chinese myths, the lore of the Alcoforado family, and monthly bleeding. She was taught the two categories of infused prayer — consolations, or prayers that began in human nature and ended in God, and spiritual delights, which originated with God and overflowed into human nature. Back in those years, she and Mariana moved their beds to their respective sides of the common wall of their "little houses" so that their nightly dreaming could imbed itself in the same mud and stone. She never tired of Mariana's maternal drive to teach her everything. "Molinismo is a philosophical quandary given particular study by a Spaniard who lived in Évora, and centers upon the problem of reconciling free will and divine prescience," said Peregrina.

"And your position?"

"I have faith that God may be aware in advance of what our free will might cause."

"I like that answer," said Sister Mariana. "Let's see. Why is it that the Japanese have a dish called tempura?"

"It is an effect of the Portuguese presence in that country in the past century. When the missionaries would switch from meat to fish, the Japanese could see that it was related to a time of the week or season of the year. And the missionaries had a taste for frying their food, a process requiring careful timing. Tempura is a word derived from our word *tempo,* a length of time, or *temporada,* a season."

"What other effects have our countrymen had upon Asia?"

"The destruction of art and interference with a religion that they did not understand." She lowered her voice. "Excuse the heresy."

"Sister Peregrina, can you name the Four Waters of Saint Teresa?"

"I can, with pleasure. The First Water is the state in which the sum effect of a person's will is evident. The Second Water is the guidance of inspiration, a slight loosing of the individual will. The

Third Water is possession, the complete loss of one's own will. The Fourth Water is the ecstasy of heaven."

"What is the Latin or Greek root for the word ecstasy?"

"The Latin *ecstasis*, or the Greek *ekstasis*. Both indicate a being put out of place, removed from stasis."

"To where do you dream of being removed?"

"I do not dream of being anywhere but here."

"Do you remember Catarina?"

"Very little, I'm sorry. I was a baby when she died."

"You're like her. Very much like her."

"That's good," said Peregrina.

"Name an irony of history."

They both laughed.

"Where should I begin!" said Peregrina. "It is an irony of history that General Schomberg, commissioned by France to fight for us, should now have turned against France, owing to that country's campaign against Protestants."

"Who is the finest scribe in Beja? No. Wait. Who is the finest scribe in our free nation?"

"Oh, Mariana. Don't embarrass me."

"Wrong answer. When shall this finest scribe in our free nation be Abbess, so that her older sister may feel that together they have achieved the height of what may be won?"

They had to let go of one another's hands, to cover their mouths and giggle like teenagers.

"You're the one, Mariana, who should run for Abbess."

"I cannot. I think you know that."

Swallows and hummingbirds swooped near the well, pecked at the sparse ferns, flew away. Peregrina considered that this would be a good instant to ask Mariana if she knew that there could exist, in some unknown quantity, copies of her letters. But the moment passed.

"I cannot," said Mariana. "For one thing, I don't know enough. I have no idea what we kiss but never adore. Have you figured it out for me?"

"Is it our past histories?"

They considered this.

"No, that doesn't sound right," said Mariana. Sister Francisca Freire once said that she knew the answer to this riddle, having been told it by her mother when she was a child. She would share it with Mariana and Peregrina when they stopped wanting to guess it themselves, but warned that they would be disappointed by the absurdity.

"Ask me something I can answer," said Peregrina.

"Have we survived the plague?"

"For the moment, yes. Next question."

"Define the style of architecture referred to as Manueline."

"The style of the end of the fifteenth and early sixteen centuries, during the reign of King Dom Manuel, that featured the dominance of nautical themes and celebration of open spaces, height, and elaborate decor to induce a feeling of airiness and optimism. Meant to suggest that all of us are staring at a distant horizon."

"What do you see on that horizon?" asked Mariana.

"The convent's outer wall."

"No, tell me the truth."

"That is my answer."

"What would you see if you imagined yourself sailing on a ship?"

"I never imagine that."

"Try."

Peregrina pretended to furrow her brow, then shrugged.

"My greatest desire is to take you everywhere," said Mariana. "To Évora, to Lisbon, to the ocean. Don't you want to see the ocean?"

"The ocean? No, I don't really think about it," said Peregrina.

"You must."

Peregrina laughed. "Because you say I must?"

"Because in the last thirty-eight years, you've never walked outside the gate here. Close your eyes, and tell me how far you can travel."

Peregrina did as Mariana asked. When she opened her eyes, she said, "Do you see the wall near Catarina's tree? It's a far wall, because — well, it's far. That's where I went."

Mariana asked her to lean into the silence and let her thoughts take her anywhere she pleased, to Spain, to England. To France. To go wherever she was transported, but to make sure that it was as far as she could manage. When Peregrina reported that going to that wall was wearisome enough, that surely Mariana could see that it was the opposite end of the world, Mariana said, "Island fever. Dear God in heaven, what you teach me. *Island fever!*" How long ago was it when Mother Maria de Mendoça counseled Mariana it might take a while for her to comprehend? She had figured that island fever meant the wish of those who were confined to range far afield, but it was not. It described, instead, how the imagination of those who were confined shrank to the size of a room, a convent. This fevered condition could cause an islander to exist near the sea but never see the water, to judge it a journey too overwhelming. Island fever was not the lust to go over the rim of the planet and fall into nothing, because anything mysterious, including the possibility of nothingness, was perceived at hand.

Certainly her room contained countless mysteries. It had never lost those mysteries of love that made it as gigantic as sky, plains, ocean, France, and her own country, everywhere, gigantic as all thought and feeling.

My love continues to visit me in revelations, thought Mariana. Bless you, my love.

She did not pronounce this aloud. Instead, she asked Peregrina to try to travel as far as the Founders' Palace next door, and Peregrina said that she recognized that it was there, but it might as well be in heaven. She did not see how she could stretch that mightily.

"You would call it heaven?"

Peregrina nodded. "Absolutely. So far and unknown and such a distant garden that I would have to name it heaven."

Sister Mariana's knee bothered her as she walked through the Quadra da Portaria on the lower floor and crossed the sparse southwestern garden area at the base of the New Wing dormitory of "little houses" commissioned decades ago by her father. She slowly proceeded north, stopping when she needed to revive her breath, to the patio area on the opposite side of the Escutcheon Room. The ground was damp from the morning air, and Peregrina's herb garden was bravely attempting to flourish. Moss inflamed the cistern with a green rash. In one corner was the pen that Mariana and Brites de Freire had constructed with wooden fences to hold the flock of ten geese donated from the poultry firm of Moreau & Zwick. The geese had been intended for feastday dinners, but Brites could not face slaughtering them. Mariana agreed that although money was a problem and being tenderhearted was a luxury, they had all tasted enough death to last for the time being. They would eat vegetables and soups, at least for a while. The ungrateful geese were a nasty, spitting, slippery-boweled lot, and Mariana had struck up an enjoyable enmity with them. Their skinny, rigid necks shot through the openings in the fence as she limped past.

With mock-fury, she shook a fist at them and yelled, "Monsters! I helped spare your lives, and this is how you repay me!"

They squawked and brandished the pinions in their stiff wings. Knobbed red faces twisted and craned. She sensed that the geese looked forward as gleefully as she did to their daily exchanges.

"Behave now! I have work to do!" said Mariana, though before leaving she tossed grain into their pen.

With honking and the scratching of webbed feet behind her, she entered the Escutcheon Room, passed through it, and began to climb the stairs leading from the lower choir to the upper choir. She needed to pause with her good leg planted on each step, use her hands to lift her ailing leg onto it, catch her breath, reposition the walking stick that served as her crutch, and then repeat the process for the next step. Her wet handprint left an ornate trail up the banister. She gasped and collected herself on the landing, and said to Our Lady of the Milk, "If it's no trouble, would you mind teaching me how to fly?"

She continued up the flight of stairs, through the choir, and down the passageway connecting the convent to the Duke of Beja's palace and land. His name was António Luís Leão de Atouguia, and though it was rumored that he wanted to move to the countryside and be cared for by a niece, he was cantankerous about anything requiring exertion. Despite repeated efforts by various abbesses over the last century to buy the property, the occupants of the Founders' Palace traditionally resisted, asserting that their noble legacy was not for sale. Many generations had lived without budging from the palace. Duke António was the last heir of the convent's founders and would soon die childless, but this had so far not proved incentive for him to face the inevitable end.

Mariana tapped her walking stick on the thick, bolted door separating the passageway and convent from the Duke's quarters. When there was no reply, she pounded on the door with her fist. When that failed as well, she threw her body full-force on it, both her fists flailing for several minutes. When no answer came, she waited to regather her strength, and then threw herself several times more at the locked portal.

"For the love of God!" came the voice of an old man.

"There you are! My fists are quite bruised, but not as bruised as they'll be when I see you!"

"Are you threatening me?" said the Duke, not opening the door.

"Yes."

"I see." The old man chuckled. "With whom do I have the pleasure of speaking?"

"I'm Sister Mariana."

"Is this the Sister Mariana who should know better than to be caught speaking with a man?"

"May we talk business instead of nonsense, Your Excellency? Since you refuse to unlock the door, I am breaking no rules. We are not, strictly speaking, in the same room."

"True. How might I assist you, Sister Mariana?"

"You must sell me the Founders' Palace and the adjoining property, including your hillside at the back."

The Duke's response was an unleashing of mirth. "This again?"

"Pardon me for pointing this out, Your Excellency, but upon your death, may God postpone it many years, your property will be auctioned because you have no heirs. Someone will buy it. Why not your neighbors? I want your garden. You've done very poorly by it, shame on you. It could be heaven to someone who cared for it properly."

"Why has the Abbess not come with this request?"

"Abbess Filipa has only recently been elected, and she's busy."

"You have no chores yourself, Sister Mariana?"

"I have many chores. This is one of them. This is one of the last gifts of my heart for someone I love."

"Not much of a gift, if you ask me. My garden is an unholy mess."

"In the proper hands, as I said, it could be heaven. May I have your answer?"

"The answer is no. I don't have any interest in moving."

"Very well," said Sister Mariana. "I shall return tomorrow at this time and expect a different answer."

"Come if you like. I don't talk to many people, and I'll anticipate your arrival. But my answer will be the same."

Sister Mariana smiled, though he could not see her. "My price is 650,000 *réis.*"

"What? Such impudence! Goodbye until tomorrow, Sister," said the Duke of Beja.

"*Au revoir,*" said Sister Mariana.

Over the next nine days, Mariana undertook the same arduous journey through the bare gardens of the convent, up the staircase, through the upper choir, and down the passageway to the sealed door leading to the Duke's residence. She would stop at the geese pen to exchange insults with them, throw them food, and revel in their strangeness, the contortions of their necks, their incessant, blaring demands. Each day, the Duke awaited Mariana and complimented her unearthly punctuality. On one visit, they debated the merits of *The Morals of Saint Gregory* and the most suitable preparation for a proper jugged rabbit (Mariana was feeling the strain of the regimen of vegetarian dishes that Brites de Freire was producing in the kitchen). They discussed the works of the playwright Gil Vicente, which gave Mariana such pangs of nostalgia for her Papa's library that she had to sink to the floor of the passageway, and the Duke did likewise, on his side of the lock, to keep their voices on the same level. They grew fond of one another's disembodied company, but their conversations always ended with Mariana persisting in asking if the Duke was convinced of the wisdom of selling his property, and the answer remained no.

One morning on her way to chat with the Duke, Mariana ran into Brites de Freire carrying a basin of currants. She admitted that as the new head of the kitchen, she was having a problem managing what should be consumed before it spoiled. The currants were old and oozed an acrid juice, and Brites needed assistance in deciding whether she should serve them.

Mariana almost fainted from their pungency. "We could give the geese a treat," she said. They threw the aged currants into the pen, and Mariana whooped with delight as the geese dived beaks down to gorge themselves. Their white feathered bodies writhed in a circle, looking altogether like fluttering lotus petals. "That's right, garbage-eaters! Noisemakers!" said Mariana, and Brites commented that this was the most enthusiasm any savory from her kitchen had ever received.

Neither of them pondered further about the currants and the famished geese. Brites de Freire returned to her tasks, and Mariana conducted her daily struggle to climb the staircase, conquer the brick-and-ceramic passageway, and make her demands of the old man at the gateway to heaven, invisible from where she stood. He persisted in denying her petition, but Mariana detected that somewhere in his loneliness, he did not lack sympathy for her pleas.

The next day, Brites de Freire, horrified, reported to Mariana that they had committed a serious miscalculation. She hurried Mariana to the geese's pen to show that every one of the birds was sprawled warmly on the earth, with wings retracted and eyes shut. Not one was standing. The breathing holes in their beaks did not vibrate. Brites prodded one with her foot, and it did not respond. "We killed them," she said, and burst into tears.

"We didn't mean to," said Mariana. "Look, I don't think it would be safe to eat them, but we should pluck their feathers for pillows."

"This is awful," said Brites. She was generally taken aback by the pronounced practical side of Mariana.

"It is a bit awful," said Mariana. "But it's done. Go fetch Sister Leonor Jacoba and Sister Caetana and Sister Inês, and let's get to work. See if Sister Maria de Castro wants a break from the laundry."

The nuns plucked the white feathers, and when they finished, no one wanted to bury the remains. The geese were vulnerable red sacs and bare red necks, all of it freckled with frightened, bumpy skin. Sister Maria de Castro said that as laundress for decades, she had dealt with many disgusting things, but this could be the prize. The geese looked like giant newborn rats. Disposing of the remains of Moreau & Zwick's gift was, they agreed, a grim enterprise that could be left for another day. The bodies were replaced in the pen, so that if geese owned spirits, they would not be alarmed by unfamiliar surroundings.

The following morning, on her journey to harass the Duke, Mariana was shocked to a standstill to see ten naked, pink-and-red featherless geese wobbling in their pen, bumping into each other, stumbling, sometimes knocking another bird down, where they lay like plucked roses and honked with mooning, flute-like verve. Some of the geese spun onto their backs and stared straight into the sun, and then rolled, beady eyes whirling, onto their bare stomachs. Two wound their necks together and gazed up at infinity.

256

"Geese in ecstasy," said Mariana. She had lived long enough to witness geese in ecstasy! The currants must have been fermented. Eating them must have pushed the geese past drunkenness and the appearance of death and into rapture. "Geese in ecstasy!" she proclaimed.

Insatiable world! Drunken world! Mariana bowed as if invisible hands were twisting her, doubling her over with shots of blue pain and red sleep, for she was feeling what it was like to be naked and sunstruck. This was replaced with her sense of being all at once buoyed upward as if the air were a bowl of feathers containing her, telling her, *Rise off your feet. Claim the properties of love, claim the properties of light.*

When the Duke of Beja said that he had been worried, she was never tardy, he had been waiting on his side of the door for half an hour and was going out of his mind with praying that she was unharmed, she said, "Your Excellency! Sir! We have geese in ecstasy in our possession."

When the Duke said, politely, that she needed to explain, Mariana detailed for him what had occurred, and added, "I believe, Your Excellency, that the least of us should fall down in wonder under the immensity of what is above us." Tears streamed down her face. "And I believe, sir, that love is the mightiest surprise and immensity of all, and it is only right that the least of us fall down and honor how stunning it is."

The Duke was silent, waiting for the boiling forth of her emotions to halt before he said, "Your voice is majestic, Sister Mariana." He hesitated. "Are you crying because you think it will sway me?"

"No!" she thundered. "Never! Trust me that I have had sufficient sorrow in my life to value it. I never, not once, not ever, I promise you, cry when I do not feel it. I have no patience with duplicity and wiles."

"I beg your pardon," he said. "Sister Mariana?"

"Yes."

"I shall miss you and your fruitful conversation. I swear that I shall think of you while I sun my decayed flesh in the countryside. I agree to your purchase and will settle for 650,000 *réis* for my property — you robber — on the condition that I am allowed to take with me an ecstatic goose, so that I can look at it and know that God loves naked, squawking fools and therefore might look kindly upon me and my wasted career. I should have thought to love someone. I should have thought to love so greatly that I surrendered everything."

Sister Maria de Castro pointed out that the geese would get cruelly baked by the sun if left unclothed. Sisters Peregrina, Mariana, Brites de Freire, Leonor Jacoba, Caetana, and Inês cut out blocks from the discarded white veils of novices, and spent their recreation hours stitching capes, hats, and tunics for the geese. The red birds, crotchety now that the currant liquor was exacting its payment, snapped with their beaks as they were measured for their new wardrobe. Mariana detested basting, blundered through it impatiently, and got exasperated when haste compelled her to rip out a seam and redo it. Peregrina, stitching with calmness, would beam at her and say, teasing, "Rushing off somewhere?"

In the mess of Mariana's sewing, there was the swiftness of God: uneven, whipped stitches, ragged piles; tempestuousness, unrest.

In the beauty of Peregrina's sewing, there was the slowness of God: measured and careful, with edges matching edges; precision, immobility.

At night, a bizarre angel entered Mariana's room — a goose dressed in white. Mariana recognized it as one of hers, owing to the bunched unevenness of the seams. "How did you escape from your pen?" she asked. The force of wanting to find more currant juice had driven it here, and Mariana admonished it, "Everything for you from now on will be a disappointment, if you allow that to be so. By the way, you're lucky you didn't die of that potion."

Scars cross-hatched the backs of Mariana's hands. She was aligning her additions and subtractions cautiously, doing so many totals so strenuously that numbers were crowding into her palms and fingers, waiting their turn to be released in writing, swelling her hands until she had to scratch them for relief. Bloodied, she wrote columns of purchases and columns of debits. One detail she had not mentioned to the Duke was that she had no idea where she would get the money to buy his garden. Gold had been discovered in Brazil, and sometimes, tilting back her head, she sniffed to see if any of it might be drifting towards them on the air.

In the middle of the night, Sister Francisca Freire would hobble into the scriptorium and say, "Heavens, Sister Mariana! Rest!"

"I can do plenty of that when I'm dead," Mariana would respond.

She was accustomed to a certain monthly allowance from the wheatlands that Papa had offered to the convent in her name, but since her brother Miguel had stepped in to run the *morgadio,* Mariana was seeing precious little of it. He required that she pay a portion of the mortgage on the land though she did not actually own it, telling her, in his blunt notes, that she would have to be more careful in dispensing the money delivered to the convent on her behalf from the property's wheat sales. She would have to abide by her arrangement to turn over the usual monthly donation to the convent's treasury. Then she would have to take the remainder and forward the necessary proceeds to assist with the mortgage. If nothing was left over for her personal use, so be it. It would teach her how to be thrifty.

She wrote back explaining to Miguel that with wheat sales down, with no one entirely recovered from the high taxes and bad times that had lingered for decades since the end of the war, and with his own cutback on working hours for laborers in that wheat field, she was not receiving much of a portion. Certainly not enough to contribute towards the mortgage — which Papa had never intended for her to do. She was barely able to pay her monthly stipend to the convent, and there was nothing in reserve for the minimal spending ration that was supposed to be hers. The vow of poverty meant that the nuns must not submit to extravagance or hoard money, but they needed a trifle of it for candles, feastday parties, donations to the priests for Masses for the dead, maintenance emergencies, or loans to a sister in need. Her letters were strictly factual, devoid of any emotional drama that might displease Miguel, but he did not reply.

Mariana went begging. Using her position on the convent's finance committee, she delivered a speech at the quarterly meeting, detailing why they should not let a chance they had been awaiting for centuries to slip past. When Sister Michaella dos Anjos complained that the population of the convent was smaller than ever and expansion was ridiculous, Mariana said, "May I put you down for one thousand *réis,* Sister?"

She walked among the "little houses," knocking on doors, and to the cells and rooms of the dormitories, pleading for contributions.

Towards the end of her campaign, exhausted, she fell and had to be helped to her feet by Sister Constança, who said, "Rest, Mariana,"

"No," said Mariana. "How much can I put you down for, Sister Constança?"

Because she believed that it was not enough to give everything that one had, that one should give more than what one had, she arranged a secret second mortgage on her wheat field, and let Miguel fulminate at her. She made deals with townspeople for bulk goods to lessen everyone's burden of operating costs, and she led a contingent in fasting to save money on food.

She showed up at Abbess Filipa's office every day for ten days until the Abbess agreed to draft a contract, if only because she did not want Mariana's collapse on her conscience. The Abbess would seek contributions from local patrons, and the convent's administration would put up two-thirds of the 650,000 *réis* payment. She agreed it was a price that was hard to forego. The general community of nuns would offer up the last third.

An ecstatic goose was delivered to Duke Antónío in 1703, and the deed to the Founders' Palace and adjoining land with its maté plants, trellises, laurel trees, and belvedere on the apex of the gentle hillside facing the plains was signed over to "Abbess Filipa Freire de Andrade and various nuns acting as silent partners." There was no ceremony, no celebration. No one had any leftover money. Even if someone had thrown a quiet thanksgiving on the day the deed was signed, Sister Mariana would not have attended, not merely because she was fatigued within a paper's breadth of her life but because she had an appointment that day, and went to stand below the window in her room and said, "I love you. I love you still. I love you always. I esteem every joy and every sorrow that your love bestows upon me."

It was the thirty-fifth anniversary of his departure.

What could she offer as this year's summary? "I have less than no money, if one could imagine such a thing! But I am exquisitely happy. And you, dearest? I hope you married and had children and prospered.

"I would say it is as if you left me yesterday — but you have never left me, not ever, my dear love."

*

"Come," said Sister Mariana to Sister Peregrina, guiding her past the sisters calling out with excitement as they ranged through the unlocked door at the magical end of the passageway, into the empty rooms of the former palace of the Duke, and out into the huge, walled yard. They took their time climbing the slope leading to the belvedere. Peregrina chatted with animation about the flowers she would sow around it, azaleas, lilies, agapanthi, and the vegetables she could plant in the open spaces, and enough garlic to make the earth smell like broth. Citrus trees and almond

trees could fit in, giving a new scent to the air.

"Come," said Mariana. "It's the view we've bought."

"You shouldn't have done this," said Peregrina. "Where did you get the money?"

I clawed it out of my books. I clawed it out of the air, thought Mariana, I would claw it out of the lining of my own skin for you, daughter, but she said only, "The view came free. It's all yours."

In the belvedere they located the plaque that Sister Francisca Freire had prepared at Mariana's request. It said "Peregrina's Garden." Not a single wall was in sight. Peregrina was trembling at the sight of such vastness. Mariana pointed at the mist billowing along the plains, which they could see from their high perch.

"Can you spot King Sebastião, the Longed-For?" said Peregrina, her voice fine and high.

Mariana shook her head. "He's a famous coward, and he'll never return. The Long-Dead, I say. But it's a lovely story that he might some day ride through the mist and save us, and makes for lovely hours of pretending."

It was the first hilltop on which they had stood since childhood. Mariana indulged in the fantasy that her father might be proud of her at last, to have claimed some manner of mountain in the center of the plains of their birth. Not only can you claim heaven, Mariana wanted to say to Peregrina, but do you see? Can you see? You can climb up high and gaze far beyond it, beyond heaven, far over the boundaries of where you dwell.

Father Jerónimo, sent to inspect the works of the religious at Conceição, was mystified by the obituary entries in the books of Sister Peregrina. She devoted pages of anecdotes to every nun. As she sat before him, he hardly knew what to remark, since he had never seen anything like this. "You go on at some length, Sister?" he said.

"Oh, yes, Father," she said.

"May I ask why?"

"I would go on forever if I could for each one. I'm sorry I have to stop."

"No one writes like this, Sister. Are you aware that no one writes like this?"

"I've seen the entries of the scribes who had this job before me," said Peregrina. "I think maybe they lacked the time?"

They lacked a good deal more than time, thought the astonished Father Jerónimo. For his report, he wrote, "Sister Peregrina Alcoforado exhibits a literary fondness beyond the ordinary. Her calligraphy and diction are more correct than what is offered by most scribes. She is obviously intelligent. She writes with confidence, with distinction. She knows her Latin. She produces whole citations correctly, as the result of her thorough education, and yet she also displays an extraordinary individuality. She is smarter and more generous than her years. She must have had a genius for a teacher."

To Sister Peregrina, sitting at attention, he said, "It is traditional that I give you a criticism, but I am at a loss." He squinted, tried to think. "I have an idea. You don't leave any white space between the entries."

"White space?"

"It's supposed to be the width of three fingers."

"I try to leave a blank space, but then I think of the next thing to say. But you're right, Father. I should give their spirits room to breathe."

Mariana negotiated the acquisitions of holy-wood, new missals, golden chalices, and white damask covers for Peregrina's books of records. She wrote letters to tradesmen and arranged for yellow and black leaves as ornaments for the pages. She lit candles in oratories around the convent and in the new extension that she had caused to be purchased. Lanterns glowed at the shrines that Mariana set up to Our Lady of the Mirror, Saint Francis of the Stairs, Our Lord of the Steps, Our Lord of the Courtyard, The Saints of the Future Garden, and Our Lady of the Veranda. She was laughing when she anointed the shrine to Our Lord of the Prison Room, the place of confinement she had been spared. Every corner, every object was a shrine, a light, a guardian. It must all be honored as the home, clean and perfect, that Peregrina would inherit when she rose to being Abbess some day, when the totality of it became hers.

At night, the fire in the sanctuaries flickered in the darkness. When Mariana sat in the upper veranda, her home appeared to be a city of stars wrenched down to the earth. Sister Beatriz Maria de Resende and Sister Francisca Freire, one blind and the other's eyesight about to desert her, rested together outdoors as if they were in a mansion floating in the midst of constellations that they could feel and did not need to see.

"Baltazar, Papa," whispered Sister Mariana, aching with exhaustion, "can you see the dazzling city we've built?"

When the bill for her share of the mortgage on her wheat field came due, she cried aloud at whatever gold was being smuggled into her country from Brazil to float to her assistance, to fall from the sky. She beseeched the golden light from the candles to turn into real coins, so that she would not be punished for wanting a garden beyond heaven for Peregrina.

The golden lights flared when she spoke to them.

Abbess Filipa informed Sister Mariana that week that her brother Francisco had sent 300,000 *réis* on her behalf. According to his note, he felt a sudden compulsion to share his good fortunes as a judge with her. A notary also visited the convent, bearing a signed document from Father José da Costa, her half-brother at Our Lady of the Snows, that read: ". . . for my sister Mariana of Conceição, so that she not suffer unduly in the religious life." Enclosed was 240,000 *réis*.

She wrote back that it was shrewd of him to send a notary, so that she would be less likely to refuse his generosity. She suspected Caetana, Inês, and Leonor Jacoba, her nieces, of spreading the news that she was destitute. When Ana Maria showed up and tried to push money through the grate in the locutory, Mariana shoved it back, saying that she should save it for herself. How did Ana Maria survive in that house with Miguel and his wife? They laughed about old Rui. Who would have ventured to suggest that he would still be alive, though ailing and hunched over, as he lurched towards his eighties?

Mariana met her obligation for her wheat field and made the appropriate donation to the treasury. She used the remainder to buy saplings for Peregrina's garden, to replenish the pantry in Brites' kitchen, and to restore the vellum and the bindings of the books in the scriptorium.

In this climate of golden messages arriving from the outside, it happened one day, out of the blue, without the barest hint from any of the other nuns, young or old, about what they may or may not have known all along, that a postulant beginning her studies at the convent came to Mariana's "little house," held out a book, and said, "May I have your autograph?"

"Whatever are you talking about?" said Sister Mariana, and took from the girl a thin volume written in French. She did not linger over the pages. She knew them as deeply as she would know a child who might have been taken from her when it was a baby and that she did not see again until it came back as an adult. She knew each letter of every word. Each was etched on her soul, with blood seeping out of every letter. Mariana's pulse thumped with amazement and outrage that the outside should be better acquainted with her own secrets than she was herself. "Where did you get this?" she asked.

"I stole it from its hiding place in my mother's credenza. I wanted to come here, so that I could meet you," said the girl.

Mariana handed the book back to her. She did not need a copy when the original was within her. "It's all my signature and autograph, every word," she said. "Would you mind leaving me in peace for a moment?"

Alone, curled up on the floor of her room, Mariana put her hands over her chest to prevent her heart from exploding out. Although in one sense she knew every letter of every word, if she tried to recite right then the letters she had sent Noel, she would be speechless. Inarticulate. Love letters began without any idea of what they were to say, and finished without the writer understanding what was proclaimed. She was unaware then and she was unaware now of precisely what she had said. Love was not a recital. Her bad leg smarted beneath her. Was this book merely in French? How many people in Portugal knew about it? She would never be able to look into anyone's face without wondering if that person knew! How much did her fellow sisters know? Did Peregrina? Why had no one told her? Was it her lifelong fate never to be informed of what mattered to her the most? Ah, Mariana! she thought. He loved you that much, that he printed your words so that you would never die. So that your love would be arrested young and urgent, for mankind to see.

Sweet delusion. No, the book of her letters — she had seen it, a real item made out of her emotions, with print and a cover, real the way a tree or a military battle was discernible — had nothing to do with him loving her. He had sold her, thought so little of her torments that he had offered them up for the amusement of others. Or was he proclaiming love, was this the best he could do, even while he profited from it? She could not decide; eternal unknowing. Love, in its merciless complications, a real force and not a memory, was killing her again. Of all the records, Forty Hours, and histories she had labored over throughout her life, should there exist far and wide the few documents she wrote with anguished speed, the speed of love, almost forty years ago, when she had been twenty-six?

What did it matter? Who could ever total up the extent to which the love that one threw at the world was absorbed or discarded by the world? The extent to which it was forgotten or remembered?

Her mind resounded with, At last, love, you have given me reason to rejoice in you. I shall say, despite evidence to the contrary, that you wished me to live forever, that you could not keep our love to yourself and had to let it ring out so that I — and us, and love — might survive. I rejoice in your carrying my cry farther than I could cast it by myself.

And at last, love, I can pardon you the inexcusable fault of tossing my words and the very soundings of my innocent, desperate, wild heart into the public without a care. I can forgive you everything. I can forgive anyone anything, since I forgive you this.

Mariana was swallowed by a violent, almighty bliss that was not blue, as she dreamed bliss would be, but blue and red, yellow and the white of geese feathers. Wrapped in a multicolored shroud, she cascaded within a moment that contained everything and all the contradictions of everything and then rose above all of that, into blessing. In such a moment, one could discover the weight of light, the coolness of fire, the water that did not melt within sky. One could know everything, which was to see that one knew nothing. One could feel everything, and therein find that all of one's requests — once the will stopped determining what these should be — had already received manifold answers.

I asked to be sent grand love that would feel like forever, said Mariana, and I have had it for quite some time. It's just that I didn't accept that it would be mine in a way I had not imagined.

She arose from the floor and sat at her writing desk. She wrote a letter to her brother Francisco, asking that he do her the inestimable favor of going to the family manor. Without Ana Maria's knowledge, and even if Miguel or his wife protested, he must dig up a statue of Saint Anthony buried beneath the largest walnut tree and bring it to the convent. Saint Anthony had long ago fulfilled one of her requests, and she fretted that he might be furious that she had been so slow to realize it.

Her crutch below her arm, Mariana waited an epoch for Peregrina to return from her day's work in the adjacent garden. After missing her going to the kitchen, Mariana circled the cloisters, searching. She waited outside the scriptorium; Peregrina was not there. This was the most confounded mission of Mariana's career! She would go insane with anticipation! Where was her sister? She checked the washing area, she rounded back to the New Wing of "little houses," she searched the terraces.

She had to find her before the Grand Silence sounded. She checked the infirmary, the belvedere again. She asked Brites and Maria de Castro, "Peregrina! Have you seen Peregrina?"

They told her to calm down. What was wrong?

"Absolutely nothing wrong, nothing," said Mariana.

When she found Peregrina in the chapel seconds before the bell for the Grand Silence was to sound, she knelt beside her. Sweat dripped from Mariana's veil.

"Mariana?" whispered Peregrina. "You look like you're about to burst."

The bell sounded for the Grand Silence.

Mariana could not bear the length of the night, limped through the cloisters as her sister walked with her, patting her to say, Shh, shh, we'll be able to speak soon, dawn is almost here, what are you killing yourself to say?

Mariana's game was to keep repeating to herself, I survived that minute. Now one minute more. One more. Her knee wobbled, her nerves danced.

Dawn arrived. Bells, God's music, God exploding with consent. Full into the roar of the bells calling everyone to let loose the sounds they had trapped within themselves in homage to the night, Mariana said, "It's you. You, Peregrina."

"Mariana?"

"I should have told you long before this," said Mariana, and the beauty of it pained her, to have been given the gift of a sister, mother, and friend to cherish, and that this was a type of love that was in itself chaste but monumental, that wanted itself called best of all. "Do you know, Peregrina,"she said, "that you are the love of my life?"

Francisco, the younger of the two surviving Alcoforado sons, often returned to his native Alentejo. Being in demand as a judge required him to go from town to town, but he stayed whenever he could at the home he kept in Beringel. He would call at the convent of Conceição and the family estate, though it seemed unimaginable to have Miguel and not their father running it. Francisco never bothered with the house with its sealed shutters on the Rua do Touro, though the family still owned it. He had no memories of it. It was not his job to be involved in some debate as to its disposal. He believed in honorable, fair dealings, and in enjoying the passing days. He and his wife had friends in every province; he played the guitar; he was considered a hard worker and a seeker of truth. He prided himself on having enough matter-of-factness to have done a venerable job in Porto in a post called, in an equally straightforward manner, The One in Charge of Righting Wrongs, followed by an appointment to the position of The Supreme One in Charge of Righting Wrongs. Northerners, to his mind, tended to aver that every case had an ultimate right and wrong, which afforded him a keen insight into the sensibility of his northern father.

He was nearing fifty, his hair was whitening, and he was still in love with his wife, Catarina Arcângela. Their daughter, Leonor Jacoba, was well enough, if a bit pale, at the convent. He was proud of his son, Francisco, who was married to Maria Lopes Pita and lived in Beringel with their children, including an eldest boy named Francisco: like an echo of the patriarch into the future. He was also pleased that his other son, José da Cunha, had followed in his footsteps and attended the University of Coimbra and then moved back to Beja, to marry Ursula Rose Pereira de Campos. Everyone had survived the plague. Having his offspring settled gave Francisco the sense that he had done what fate had determined for him. It was obvious to everyone but Miguel that Francisco and his sons wanted nothing to do with the Alcoforado *morgadio,* had in fact constructed their lives to avoid it. As a joke with his friends, Francisco would ask them to pray for the health of Miguel's one son, so that Francisco's branch of the family could remain free of inheritance of the estate.

Francisco could also admit that he himself would be less competent than Miguel, and it was easy to look down from his seat of judgment on a job that he would do more poorly than his brother.

One reason that Francisco wanted to keep the *morgadio*'s concerns away from his own personal family was that being in charge of the Alcoforado estate involved invective against publishers who wanted to print Mariana's letters in Portugal. Not that he didn't find them embarrassing. Not that he didn't have to put up with comments. But a more basic issue was at stake. They were a part of his sister, and he loved Mariana. Not many people knew their own minds and hearts as well as she knew hers, and he often found himself, in court, when he had to make a decision, asking himself what she might recommend.

He never wavered about her, never refused her. It had been a welcome adventure to follow her request that he go to the homestead, find the walnut tree, and dig until he found Saint Anthony. Apparently she and Ana Maria had buried him half a century ago. The saint was caked with dirt, worm-bitten, with chunks of his robe worn away. Francisco grimaced and laughed when he held the statue. Ai, the mysteries of sisters. What had they been up to? Francisco had to endure Miguel's wife holding a parasol over her head but not his, protesting about Mariana reaching out from behind her walls to annoy them some more, and Francisco told her, remaining as much a gentleman as he could, to mind her own business. To Saint Anthony, Francisco remarked that he looked pleased to be out in the fresh air at last.

When he delivered the statue, Francisco had to speak to Mariana through the iron grate. "You don't look well. Do you need more money, Mariana?" he asked.

"I have Saint Anthony now," she said, "and I have you here. I don't need anything more."

"Neither Saint Anthony nor I look too wonderful," he said.

"He looks chewed up. You look fine."

"May I ask why you buried him?"

"Because I'm an Alcoforado, and I want everything at once."

Since she was telling everyone that she had a book in print — hearts were far too secretive, didn't he think? — she asked if he knew about it. He said that he did, and had to wait while she scolded him for not informing her. When she wanted to hear if it existed anywhere in Portuguese, he could not bear to mention how many people wanted to cover up every trace of her. He said that as far as he knew, she had traveled to France and England and Holland and Italy and Spain. She looked astonished. He added that she was not in Portugal, and before she could ask why, he said, "Just tell yourself that you've sprung past the whole nation and gone to live in France, as you dreamed."

"Dreamed long ago," she said. "When did my baby brother get to be old?"

He leaned over and kissed her forehead through the grate, a rosette of metal against his lips. They leaned the sides of their heads together, warming the metal patterns that were separating them. He asked again if she needed money, because his daughter, Leonor Jacoba, was advising him that once more the tireless Sister Mariana was in debt. "I'm one of the faithful," he said, "and if you're going to be old, then I shall be old with you, Mariana."

The ceremony to declare Noel Bouton, the Marquis of Chamilly, as a Marshal of France was moderately attended. Saint-Simon, Noel's friend, could not assess how the new Marshal was viewing the proceedings. If he was angry that it had taken the French crown until 1703 to confer the title, he was not showing it. It was difficult to guess anything of what Bouton felt on practically any subject, which put Saint-Simon, as Noel's biographer, in a strange position. Noel was continuing to put on weight, and now in his late sixties had become increasingly doddering. Though being a Marshal entitled Bouton to be a supreme commander of the French Army, it was clear that his war record was a bright spot in the distant center of his life.

Saint-Simon remarked to Noel's wife that she seemed well, and she shrugged. She shared her husband's distaste for social events. The daughter of Jean Jacques de Bouchet of Villefix, she was reasonably pleasant, and had married Noel back in 1677, when he was forty-one and his military career was ending. Bouton was regarded as a dutiful husband to a plain wife, and if they did not seem enthralled by one another's company, they certainly were devoted to their marriage and to each other.

Two legends had sprung up around Noel Bouton. The first arose towards the end of the seventeenth century, when King Louis XIV prevailed upon Bouton to visit the royal court and receive a special commendation from his grateful country. His inspiring leadership, his regard for his troops, and the repeated risk of his welfare on the battlefield were prominently known.

King Louis XIV looked down from his throne and asked the Marquis of Chamilly what he might deem a suitable reward.

Noel Bouton replied that it had come to his attention that Colonel Briquemault, his superior during the War of Independence in Portugal, had quarreled with Minister Louvois, and the King had ordered the Colonel to be incarcerated in the Bastille. The Marquis boldly told the King that whatever offense the Colonel had committed must be judged in light of his exemplary service. Bouton could imagine no finer reward than to hear that Briquemault was released from confinement and his disgrace curtailed. That was the sole honor that Bouton would accept.

The King agreed at once.

The mythical quality of this event grew when Bouton did not remain long at the fête that the court arranged for the evening. It was decided that his premature departure was to spare himself the unchivalrous acceptance of accolades for doing what he merely judged to be right.

The second legend, of course, was that he was the inspiration for the *Portuguese Love Letters*, which Saint-Simon, though he recognized this as genuine, could scarcely comprehend. Bouton was the best kind of man of the world, honorable and honest, but he was also dull and cumbersome, which age was unfortunately accentuating. How he had possessed such a talent for war, much less for love? The puzzle was not solved by observing him with his wife, to whom he seemed faithful, He treated her gently, but as one might handle an elderly mother.

"Congratulations," said Saint-Simon, standing near Bouton and observing with him the couples on the dance floor.

"For what?" said Bouton.

"For being named a Marshal," said Saint-Simon, and right as he was about to conclude that this was yet another proof that Bouton was declining into an imbecile, Bouton leaned over and said, "I won't be able to hang that anywhere but my tombstone, my friend." With that he saw a chance to leave his party early.

Noel and his wife sat together quietly as their phaeton transported them through the streets. As often happened when they dozed by the fire at this same time every evening, she was speaking and his mind was wandering. She never got angry when he did not reply, and he realized that in one sense their mutual consent to this mild disconnection was a reason they had married. Tired of resistance, tired of war, he determined that he had earned the right to let his brain go soft and bland, if that was the natural direction in which it yearned to go.

In the early years of their marriage, it had been a relief to discover that her womb was barren. Children would have been far too troubling a commotion. Sitting by their fire together every evening was his greatest pleasure, and it did no harm if his wife prattled on.

When the phaeton arrived at their house, on a street with the center of Paris accessible but at a decent distance, he helped her adjust her cloak as she dismounted. He then committed a grievous error. A combination of details had, over the course of the evening, become mixed up in his mind — with talk about that war in Portugal, with his observation that plain fineness was devoutly to be sought, with his wife's habit-like black cloak and the headiness of being out and about instead of by the fire where he usually would be — and he said, "Welcome home, Mariana," instead of saying, as he often did, "Welcome home, Madame."

She either did not hear him or was pretending not to have heard, but he was mortified and did not speak to her for the rest of the night, nor for the entire subsequent day.

Just as he was beginning to think that any possible unpleasantness was averted, the biannual royalty payment arrived from Barbin.

His wife had, in the earlier days, made a good show of being some-what proud of having captured the notorious Count of Chamilly, and sometimes she even remarked that she wished he had made a smarter deal with the publishers. It was not fair that they were getting rich off the sentiments that her Noel had aroused and that rightly belonged to him. Certainly it was unfair that some Italian, or Englishman, or someone Dutch could print them and Noel not receive a *sou*.

Today, however, she said, "I think you've been lying to me for years. Everyone says that Guilleragues wrote those things."

"Whatever you say," he said, wishing to close the subject.

"I mean," his wife persisted, her tone sharp, "those letters couldn't be about you, Noel. I mean —" and she broke off in a snorted laugh.

"Fine," he said.

Why did women *persist?*

"That shrill little bitch who wrote those hysterical things sounds dangerous. Any man confronting such an irrational, demanding, *possessive* woman would be glad to have escaped with his life," she said.

"What nonsense!" he exploded. "You have no idea what you're talking about."

As luck had it, Saint-Simon arrived at their house with the uncanny timing of a savior. They ushered him in, and the exchange of normal pleasantries smoothed out their fight, soundless waves on rough sand. In the clatter of collecting spoons for tea and arranging cakes on a plate, Noel and his wife fell into a rhythm that was like an apology. Sitting in the drawing room, directing Saint-Simon to help himself, Bouton smiled at his wife. She smiled back. While looking directly at her, Bouton asked Saint-Simon if he did not agree that marriage was a happy state of affairs.

Saint-Simon replied, "Yours is as happy a marriage as I have seen." He noted that Noel did not detect the studied neutrality of this cynical response. The newest Marshal of France asked his wife if she would not prefer a better pillow for her head, another cup of tea. Perhaps there was a sweetness in growing old together, in sharing chores, in gestures of caring, and Bouton and his wife had stepped into that sphere.

Sitting in their usual chairs by the fire that night, Noel was dozing off when he felt the shock of a hand on his. His wife was reaching over to touch him. She had not done so in a long time, and paused a moment before she withdrew her hand. This brief, surprising warmth had the effect of making him fall into a deep sleep in his chair, and it was therefore beyond his control when Mariana came to him and he watched himself embracing her and burying his weary head against her ferocious breast. He was young again and running under the starry night, running to have her cast herself upon him, and whether he was about to change his mind and flee from her, or carry her away, or utter some form of apology, he would never be able to say, because he woke with a start, before the dream careened on to reveal its imaginary outcome.

"What is it, dear?" said his wife. She mentioned that if he was distressed by anything connected to their contretemps, they must not speak of it again.

"I —" and he stopped. A man was not responsible for what went on in his dreams.

He fell back asleep, and when he awoke, he was alone in the middle of the night. But someone had tucked a thick cover over him, so that he would not grow completely cold.

In somnolent Beja, a voice undulated in on the waves of heat, *Sleep, Mariana. Enough. You've turned sixty-seven. Sleep.* Sister Mariana awoke from her dozing, and said with fury, "God? God? Is that You? No, I won't sleep! I have more to do!"

She and Peregrina returned to their campaign of writing letters to magistrates about deceased Sister Leonor Henriques' land in Viana d'Alvito. They requested that the property be bound over to Ana Maria and her children. Now that Rui was dead — wonder of wonders, he had perished in his bed one day of nothing more than old age — Cristóvão's son was living on the property without a deed, daring the authorities to drive him out.

"I suspect he's laughing at us," said Mariana, "that rotten little pig."

Peregrina said, "Well, another round of letters to the magistrates won't hurt. Shall we get started?"

"I have a new idea," said Mariana. Terrific glee brought a freshness to her skin. "I think we can safely say that with Rui gone, and having it a choice between Cristóvão's miserable brat and Ana Maria, Sister Leonor Henriques would not hesitate to pick Ana Maria."

"But she isn't here to do that," said Peregrina.

"No, but we're here to do it for her," said Mariana.

They drew up a false document, with red and green inked borders, a colossal capital letter to introduce each paragraph, and fish sailing through openings in words. Mariana lit a candle and singed the edges to make the paper look old. They faked the signature of Sister Leonor Henriques. The note stated that her property was to go to Ana Maria. Mariana added a note stating that this document had been discovered in Sister Leonor Henrique's old cell, and should be acted upon accordingly.

"Here we are!" said Mariana, holding up the document, its edges still hot from the candle's fire. "The official deed."

"You think Leonor Henriques would approve? Do you think she's watching?"

Mariana declared that she would not want any part of a heaven that would not allow a saintly nun like Sister Leonor Henriques to be amused by a glimpse of mischief on her behalf.

"Shall we send it to the local magistrate?" said Peregrina.

"This time we'll send it to Francisco," said Mariana. "I don't know why we haven't thought of our own brother. He's the district judge in the north, but I'm wagering that he knows the district judge for the Alentejo, and will persuade him to do what we ask."

Ana Maria was stunned at the news that in this winter of 1707, she had at last been awarded a comfortable place to retire, the first tangible thing that had ever been hers alone. She could weep with her desire for solitude. Before Rui's death, three of their sons had gone to seek their fortunes in India and had written only once, to report that one of them, Gil Vaz Lôbo Freire, had not survived the voyage. Her oldest boy, Luís, had married and moved to Alcácer do Sal, and was not much in contact. Ana Maria had become heavier. Her eyes vexed her, causing the landscape to look splashed in milk. Wrinkles made her skin look like the fatigued glaze on Asian pottery.

She took indecent satisfaction in the shock of Miguel and his wife, Brites da Costa, when they heard that the lawsuit was settled, that a document had been found in the convent and Francisco had used his authority as a judge to have Cristóvão's son removed. Ana Maria announced that she was moving to Viana d'Alvito with her youngest son, Gomes. Miguel was furious, and his wife's mouth jutted out as if her lower jaw had been fitted with a horseshoe. Ana Maria had no idea why they should care. She was going to be seventy in a year, and was not of much use.

A soothing new life awaited, and she had an image of herself on a raft woven from the field grass of Viana d'Alvito, with her son Gomes waving as she paddled away. She had not dared much in her life (though sometimes she told herself that raising eight children counted), so she was pleased to find that she was not afraid of an unknown place or of dying. She did not believe in self-praise but judged this as the most daring passion of her existence — a lack of fear of infinity.

Her son Gomes was slow-witted, large, and incompetent, but sweet. It would be nice to take him where no one could make fun of him. He wanted to know if they could take his father with them.

"No, dear, but we're going to stay on land that belonged to his family and now belongs to us, and we'll make the best of that," she said.

When he peered at her suspiciously, she said that they could visit Rui's grave and say goodbye. Gomes, who had his father's red hair, insisted on bringing flowers. She herself brought along a bottle of wine, and poured its contents on her husband's grave. She thought he would prefer a drink to some flowers. Gomes giggled and said, "Mama, are you drowning him?" Although Rui had been almost twice Ana Maria's age when they married, the chasm between their ages had magically narrowed. Her years with Rui taught her to detest easy sentimentality, but with him she had known a certain type of love. He had given her a chance to claim that she could live in a lion's den for her entire adulthood, and then calmly walk out, and onward.

She saved the last swallow from the wine bottle for herself, and said simply, without tears, "Here's to you, Rui." Then she turned and walked away, linking arms with her son, and she never returned.

She took one part of her husband into her retirement. He had foreseen that one day she would own some Lôbo property. The efforts of Francisco da Costa Alcoforado to claim everything were too powerful. Rui's sole request before his demise had been that he be allowed to name the land or villa for her. He presented her with a plaque wrapped in paper, though he forbade her to open it until this inevitable fortune came to pass.

She now carried this package with her. Upon her arrival at her new property, she tore away the paper around the plaque. Her eyesight was blurry, but there was no mistaking that the lettering spelled out *Namorada*. My Beloved. That was all, except for Rui's signature, with the initial of his name entwined with the initial of hers, a thorny-looking embellishment.

She discovered another package waiting for her, unwrapped it, and laughed until she was sobbing. It was a moldy statue of Saint Anthony, his robes dabbed with fresh gilt. He was bringing her a letter from Mariana.

Dear Ana Maria,

Do be so kind as to adopt this wastrel. I have, as you can observe, attempted to make amends with him for forgetting that we buried him by giving him a new suit of clothes.

I am sorry to hear that your eyesight has become such that I can no longer receive a letter from you, and that Gomes cannot write well enough to take your dictation. I know you are straining your eyes to read this. I shall attempt to curtail my long-winded ways. Leonor Jacoba and your daughters, Caetana and Inês, are well. Peregrina is the delight of my soul. She continues to look like Mama, though she is now older than Mama lived to be. When I see Peregrina, I feel that the portion of our mother's life that was missing is now being gorgeously fulfilled.

I have always loved you, my sister. I know I shall not see you again. I know that when strangers see you or me, they see old women. But what is seventy, eighty years, or two hundred and eighty? At what point do we become dismissible, unworthy of our desires?

Did Saint Anthony cause enough love to be directed your way? I believe that he has answered you and me richly, though not as we might have schemed, and we should have thanked him before now. I have hardly any hair any more – though Caetana brushes the little bit that remains. I hope the shedding of my locks evens the score with that episode when I cut yours off. (Forgive me, but I still don't regret that at all.)

This will be the final letter I write for the rest of my life, so that my last one can be said to have been dedicated to you. I shall embrace you in heaven, Ana Maria.

Your loving sister,
Mariana

"I see that I must remind you that I expect you to stand for Abbess," said Sister Francisca Freire, She with the Heart of a Dove, flushed from the effort of walking from her room, where she was often confined by infirmities. It was 1709. She was almost ninety, and Mariana was almost seventy. When Francisca Freire visited Mariana, they would discuss the latest financial meetings, or the garden at what used to be the Founders' Palace. Sometimes they would sit in the scriptorium and do nothing but page through the decades of volumes. In the years since the end of the plague, Sister Mariana and Sister Peregrina had opened each book a leaf at a time, to cleanse the pages with air.

"I cannot stand for Abbess," said Mariana. "I suspect the authorities would not approve."

"Nonsense. Your thirty years of penance are over," said Sister Francisca Freire. "Are you sorry for your past?"

"No," said Sister Mariana. "It's the only past I have, after all, isn't it, Sister?"

Sister Francisca grinned. "You're never disappointing. Do you regret so many years of penance?"

"No," said Sister Mariana. "I wanted to feel sorrow as deeply as I feel love."

"Listen to me, Sister Mariana," said Sister Francisca Freire. "You helped expand our holdings a while ago. I am certain that you can bring such wisdom and expansiveness to your rule. Will you stand?"

Mariana was partly chagrined, partly delighted, as if she had been waiting for the command of her friend. "Have I ever refused you?"

The campaign of Sisters Francisca, Peregrina, Caetana, Inês, Leonor Jacoba, Maria de Castro, and Brites de Freire to advance the cause of Mariana as Abbess was met with a contrary vendetta — as Sister Francisca had known would occur but did not suggest to Mariana — waged by the Franciscan provincials in charge of overseeing the activities of the royal convent. Though they could not veto or control elections, they were in charge of presiding over them. Three of these priests took up residence in the monks' quarters at the Hospice of Saint Anthony upon hearing that Sister Mariana Alcoforado of the notorious Love Letters was standing for election. Citing the King's 1671 decree against religious scandals, they informed Sister Francisca that though everyone respected her influence and saintliness, no official could stand by and allow her to promote a sinner to such an elevated post as Abbess. One of the provincials was not much older than the number of years that Sister Mariana had performed penances. He certainly was not born until after the War of Independence.

Sister Francisca informed him and the other two members of his frantic committee that she could not forbid their campaign against Mariana, nor could she censor the advice they were offering to the nuns seeking guidance on this matter in confession, but she would not stand for them putting themselves above God, who commanded His children to forgive one another.

"It is well known that she is not ashamed of herself," said Father Diogo de São José Baptista, the secretary who would be in charge of confirming the votes.

"She has suffered," replied Sister Francisca Freire.

The oldest provincial father answered that those impudent, so-called *Portuguese Letters*, doubtless the work of some profligate Frenchman, were spreading like a revisiting of the plague across their country, and what did she have to say to that? At least the Portuguese were self-respecting enough not to have translated them from French, English, or Italian, or heaven only knew what other languages they were in now. He himself had nominated them for the Index of Forbidden Books, and had joined the movement to attribute them to the French.

"If they are the invention of a Frenchman," said Sister Francisca Freire, "why punish Sister Mariana? If they are hers, why not allow her to make peace with God as she sees fit?"

"She is an old, lame woman, but she has an arrogance that is unsuitable," said Father Diogo de São José Baptista.

"Nothing is more humbling than taking upon the mantle of an Abbess. Will you excuse me, Father? It is my turn to set out the hymnals in the upper choir."

"You are an exemplary nun, Sister Francisca," said Father Diogo.

"I counsel you to continue your record of service, and vote for Sister Joana Veloso de Bulhão as your Abbess."

"I am fond of Sister Joana, but she can be stern merely for the sake of it, and this is not what our sisters need. Are you telling me that I shall be committing a sin of disobedience if I do not do as you say?"

"Yes."

Sister Francisca Freire knelt and kissed the priest's hand. "Thank you, Father, and bless you," she said. "I shall vote for Sister Mariana. I have waited close to a century of life to find the transcendence of following my heart in a way that is forbidden me, and you have presented me with that chance."

In the record book of the Forty Hours marked "30 July 1709," Sister Peregrina, the convent's chief scribe, wrote: "In the election for the three-year term of Abbess for the Royal Convent of Conceição, Sister Mariana Alcoforado, age 69, received 48 votes.

"Sister Joana Veloso de Bulhão, age 60, received 58 votes, and shall begin her term immediately.

"Sister Mariana Alcoforado's expression did not change when the results were announced in our meeting in the Chapter Room. Mariana is good and kind to everyone. Some of the nuns are so poorly acquainted with themselves that they appeared to be trying to remember why they had voted against her. They studied her, to detect how she was reacting to her loss. She kept them guessing. She warmly and sincerely embraced Sister Joana, and congratulated her. Abbess Joana will be decent and fair.

"Mariana lost the election, but the surprise — and she and I knew it — was that so many in our community voted with her, against all recommendations and in confrontation of the wrath of our superiors. In her defeat, it was rather a victory, though not the one that she and I and Sister Francisca Freire prayed for.

"Mariana confessed to me that she had felt her will roaring loudly, as if her sheer wishing could make what she desired come true. As I assisted her back to the New Wing, she informed me that she had very much coveted the fulfillment of being Abbess. Her mistake was to slip into the First Water of thinking that her will could achieve what she longed for. 'Therefore what I wanted was taken from me,' she said.

"I told my sister that I would someday stand for Abbess, that I understood that she had spent decades training me for such an elevation. I would wait until the moment came upon me telling me that my time was right, and I daresay, I humbly submit, that this made her smile with such power that she said, 'They will call us irrepressible.'

"I said, 'Yes. Irrepressible.'"

Sleep, Sister Mariana. Enough now; rest. Count angels, and sleep. Troops of angels no longer traipse in with holes where cannonballs violated their stomachs. Their gauze skirts are not torn by swords. They wear fancy silks, stolen from those who have become rich from the import and export trade with England. What exciting times, when one need not have been born into a certain family to have a chance at being rich!

Sleep. Rest your eyes during choir. Doze during Sext. Vespers. As the lives of saints are read during Collation, do not rein in your hallucinations.

Sleepwalk when Peregrina escorts you to the garden. Under the sun of the Alentejo, she has ordained flowers to riot. Dream of Michelangelo's controversial Sistine Chapel. Imagine the painting melting in the hot sun, its colors running and swirling. Puddles of the Creation.

Speak with the new generations of geese with their fresh white coats. They have not known ecstasy.

Do you recall, Mariana, those restless nights of your youth, and the nights when you were in love and never slept? When sleep was not to be thought of? Now your love of sleep approaches a passion, a commitment to pure time, time unsullied by action.

You are still waiting for God to send you a miracle, so that you can be inscribed in a book of the blessed.

In the scriptorium, your work saves Abbess Joana from financial despair. You advise. You call upon debtors. You thrill to promptness, exactness, a charting of growth and decline.

Peregrina, your sister and daughter, your mother and nurse, strolls with you and understands when you tire of talking. She says to you, *Sleep. Sleep, Mariana.*

Blue petals of sky filter through the iron grille over your window and settle onto your forehead, where sleep imprints in you so many artworks that you wake up and say, Come for me, unconsciousness, you delirious painter of minds.

Sister Antónia Sofia Baptista d'Almeida, the scribe-in-training, was careless and imprecise, and inflexible in asserting that her noble rank smoothed out any errors. When her superior, Sister Peregrina, requested that she rewrite something, it came back with some corrections made and some missed, and new mistakes. She argued with Peregrina's strictness. Every day was exactly the same. What difference did a number more or less make?

Sister Francisca Freire arrived at the choir loft. She had to start the walk from her cell fifteen minutes early in order to be in place by the appointed time. She stared at a gift honoring her ninetieth birthday from Sister Mariana, who must have done her usual magic with computations and money in order to squeeze money from the books to buy the finest gold ink in Europe. Sister Mariana had drawn doves from this gold, with a heart inside the sketch of every dove. She kept the doves small, so that she could use three hundred and sixty-five of them to spell out the name "Francisca." "Francisca" was repeated in this manner ninety times – in total, one dove with a golden heart for every day of her existence. Though Sister Francisca's sight was nearly gone, she could see the vibrancy of each dove, each with its heart, each forming some tally of herself and her long life. Never so beautifully had all her days been given wing and form.

Mariana, accountant and writer, with her sense of humor, remarked, I won't call you "She with the Heart of a Dove," but will have doves proclaim themselves "We Who Fly with the Golden Heart of Francisca."

Cristina Isabel Bettencourt, a novitiate, climbed the orange tree in the courtyard. A branch broke below her feet. She wanted the ripest, fattest orange hanging overhead. Stupid branch! Stupid orange, out of her reach! She kicked the tree trunk. A blot of bark fell into her eye.

Sister Ana Custódia glared at her pupils. They were not interested in their Latin and were unprepared about the classics. When she testified that this was one of the few places where they could dedicate themselves to true learning, that awful Bettencourt girl replied that only the insane could care for such dead things as Latin and the classics.

Sister Maria Carmo weeded the marsh mallow plants and grimaced at the plaque that said, "Peregrina's Garden." Typical nobility, claiming the highest vantage point. Naming it after themselves. Sister Maria Carmo was onto them. Just because her father was a chandler was no reason for them to make her do the dirty work and get none of the glory. Such swine slop they spread, the hypocrites, about what was fair and equal!

Sister Caetana brushed what remained of Mariana's hair. From the veins on Mariana's scalp, Caetana could see the pulsing of blueness. Sometimes the veins looked green. Coursing in Mariana's head were the colors of the ocean. The ocean that Caetana, like Mariana, had been told about but had never seen.

Sister Inês snorted impatiently at the Book of Miracles. The modern age was coming, and this sort of fairy-tale nonsense would be dumped out a window. She would sing and shout hurrah when her country learned to shake off wistfulness. Inês wanted a gospel based upon deciding that birth was an inflicted miracle, and every thought and action after that was a practical attempt to reject the innocence of that miracle. This would signal the end of her Aunt Mariana's era. It would be a new dawning of rationality, thank God.

Sister Beatriz Maria de Resende said, "Sister Mariana, I recognize your voice."

"Such two old ladies we've become," said Mariana.

"What do I look like?"

"Like the world's best singer."

Sister Beatriz Maria de Resende laughed. "Not any more," she said.

"I have counted twenty times since the war when your singing made me cry within myself, *Duende*!"

"Twenty? You flatter me."

Mariana indicated that she wished to ask something that might open the floodgates of a musical answer.

"Let me hear your question."

"Have you liked being a nun?" asked Sister Mariana.

"I have loved it," said Sister Beatriz Maria de Resende. "Shall I tell you why? Because it is courageous to sing night and day about mystery. It is good to pray for friends and even better to pray for strangers. Our chanting wraps mankind in the aspirations that every human shares. We send petitions into our shared atmosphere to act in the same way that a clear wood stain protects a plank from harm, rain, insects. To have our vocation is to study time, music, and the unknowable in their most concentrated forms. I have liked not being the slave of a man. To those who say that we do not participate in life, I say we rejoice in the most fundamental living principles, but not in life's objects and vanity. To those who say we do not assist mankind, I say that prayer is the finest assistance available. We are the invisible chorus wishing them well and moving the spirit in their direction. Do you like your profession, Sister Mariana?"

"I have loved it and hated it," said Sister Mariana, "but I have never been indifferent to it."

"What is that sound, Sister?"

"I'm afraid I don't hear what you're hearing," said Mariana, but led Sister Beatriz Maria de Resende outside, in search of the musical sounds that were imperceptible to anyone but her. So acute had the blind nun's register become that she could hear the swishing of rosary beads in the Quadra of the Eternal Father, and the sound of a worm being pulled from the ground by a bird, and the soprano glory of someone blowing on soup to cool it. When they walked over to Peregrina's garden, Mariana watched her friend cover her ears and bow from the impact of the wild symphony sent up by the constant growing of the plants.

Sister Maria de Castro's special fun was the convent's annual war between the Cult of Saint John the Baptist and the Cult of Saint John the Evangelist. The nuns would arrange flowers on the bier of their favored saint, taunt the drooping sprays on the bier toiled over by the opposing cult, and shout insults about the weaknesses of the opposing saint. Mariana was in the Baptista group, and so was Sister Maria de Castro.

In her youth, Maria de Castro looked forward with enthusiasm to these feastdays. One year, she raided the storeroom where the Evangelistas were storing their flowers, and pulled their bouquets askew. This struck her now as embarrassingly juvenile. More than that, it was beginning to feel like the centerpiece of her life — high spirits that never took a worthwhile shape. What had she done, except wash everyone's clothing? Where was the glory in performing a menial task over and over for years? In being the childish jester?

So wrenching was her sorrow that she wept into the tank containing the habits. The salt of her tears must have pulverized the harshness of the fabric. The following day, Sister Mariana ran into the courtyard, yelling, "Sister! What have you done, my friend? My veil feels like silk hair!"

Throughout the convent, the older nuns walked about in amazement, hands smoothing down veils, saying that their habits were smooth as infantile skin. They were young again! One by one, following the lead of Sister Mariana, they came to thank Sister Maria de Castro.

Sister Brites de Freire stacked kale leaves, rolled them tightly together, and demonstrated to a novice how to slice them into green threads. When she urged her understudy to be more precise with the knife, the girl said, "What difference does it make?" Sister Brites de Freire said, crabbily, "God lies within the stretch of that difference."

Being in charge of the young cooks was supposed to be the crowning epoch of her career. She wondered if these girls ever considered her with the same speechless, sudden happiness that she and Mariana used to find when they entered the kitchen and saw nuns in concert with clouds of flour rising and sifting around them.

So much about her lengthy friendship with Mariana was cluttered with ambiguity. In one sense, Brites was angry that Mariana should work so obviously to make the convent perfect for Peregrina. In another sense, everyone profited from that love. When had Mariana ever stinted on giving Brites anything she asked for? She understood the expression about loving someone to pieces; she loved Mariana to the point of wanting to turn fragments of her over and over in her hand, to understand them.

There was the time, as novices, when Mariana boasted, "My father built the mint in this town!" But there was another time when Mariana hid her last few *réis* for Brites to find, because Brites also did not have ehough.

Mariana once recited a poem and said, "Please tell me one yourself, Brites!"though Brites did not know any. But there was, as well, the occasion when Mariana said, "Brites, I'll bet you know how to waltz. Will you show me?" Brites did such a good job of inventing what she envisioned would be the steps of that dance that she and Mariana careened into the walls of a cell, grateful that they would never be apart.

Mariana never failed to admire the culinary work of Brites, never forgot her birthday. Brites once practiced the deceit of storing underneath her pillow that bracelet from Mariana's lover, for a few nights, just to pretend it was hers. Brites had needed back then to chisel her way through a regrettable phase of wishing that her friend would disappear.

Now Brites wanted Mariana to be eternal. Some nuns chose not to believe that the love letters had been printed. (Were they continuing to be printed?) Incoming postulants were not told. If they knew, they brought their knowledge with them. It was rumored that the letters existed in several countries, but not even Mariana could say how many. *What was the final number of copies? How many languages?* It had to be a torment for an accountant of Mariana's caliber to be forbidden to grasp such an essential number. It might as well be nothing, or infinity. Mariana did not speak about the letters, not anymore. Neither did Peregrina.

What numbers mattered to Brites? What was important was not the number of agreements and disagreements with Mariana.

Brites found Mariana and took the arm that did not need the crutch as they walked through the cloisters. They discussed whatever came into their minds. Brites said that with Mariana's brains, she should have been a man at the University of Coimbra, like her brother Francisco.

They pictured Coimbra in the north, where the male students wore black robes as they swept through the narrow streets where the Romans once drove their carts. The students lived by their own laws in their own walled city, and kindled their own traditions. One of these was that every time some inspiration came upon them, they ripped their black robes. Though originally a notion that some academic discovery should prompt the tearing, it quickly became the case that the men would rip their clothing whenever they felt a pang of love. The men roamed the streets in their torn garments, and the most impassioned of them were the most ruined and disheveled.

"They probably look like torn-up crows," said Brites, laughing.

"Shedding feathers," said Mariana. She stopped and quivered with a call to action. Taking the hem of her black habit, she ripped it near a loosened seam. Then, with a roar of laughter, she ripped part of her front scapular.

"Mariana!" said Brites. "What are you doing?"

"Something just occurred to me — an inspiration! After all this time, we do treasure one another, despite everything, don't we?"

Brites followed suit, ripping a loose side seam along its grain. She had done their friendship justice whenever her actions echoed any of Mariana's impulses. Was it so horrendous, to be a follower? Now she could show off the inspired tatters that announced that her dearest, most precious friend was then, now, always Mariana.

I love you. I love you still. I love you always. I esteem every joy and every sorrow that your love bestows upon me.

I see the sense of long, slow, constant mature love. But I see, as much as when I was young and held you in my arms, that no one can know the height of any variety of passion without believing in the kind that we had, Noel.

What is it like, Noel, for you to be old?

A surge of longing unnerved her, exhausted her, and she shouted, "No, I won't sleep! God? God?"

Sister Mariana asked for a miracle — for pure, perfect love. She yearned to contain the paradox of an abstraction that she could feel.

Relax, rest, Sister Mariana, a voice came. *Sleep now. Stop wanting.*

"No!" said Sister Mariana. "No! I won't rest, I won't sleep! There is more for me to do."

Sister Mariana Alcoforado commenced her self-taught musical education at once. She would continue it for over a decade more.

She learned the seven letters of the musical alphabet, the naming of the lines on the treble and bass staffs, and the distinctions of sharps and flats. She tapped a desk to measure out musical tempos. After several months of figuring out chords — tonic, dominant, subdominant, major and minor — she moved on to matching harmonies with melodies. When she understood what it meant to have a composition in the key of D minor, or A major, she drew a paper keyboard and practiced, filling her "little house" with meticulously redressed silence. Moving her fingers over a paper diagram of the white and black keys, she mastered a brief fugue, and thereby discovered the strict laws of counterpoint.

She went to Sister Beatriz Maria de Resende and said, "You've been in torment since Sister Francisca Freire stopped being able to read music for you. I've come to take over the job."

"Mariana," said Sister Beatriz. "I didn't know you could read music!"

"You've been in torment, and so have the rest of us, since we haven't been able to hear you sing or play the organ," said Mariana.

With the blind Sister Beatriz seated at the organ in the choir loft and the nearly-blind Sister Francisca Freire escorted to a place to the right of the keyboard, Mariana placed Sister Beatriz's hands in an outward fan from the middle C, showed her the immediate black keys, and moved with painstaking slowness through the "Toccata in E Minor for Organ" by Johann Pachelbel. As disjointed as this first effort was, Sister Beatriz Maria de Resende insisted that they try until it was perfect, and they worked until Prime. As Pachelbel filled the church, the townspeople crowded around the outer doors, pleased to discover that sounds could be so sumptuous that there was no recourse but to cry.

Mariana made a deal with the tradespeople and suppliers for the convent that no billable goods would be accepted unless they included a sheet of music. A grand influx of new melodies poured in. The poultry firm of Moreau & Zwick innocently handed over a sheet of a "Fugue in D Minor" by some new composer named Johann Sebastian Bach, which had come to the proprietors from their native Germany. Sister Mariana paused. She got out her paper keyboard to test Lutheran music. It did not look or feel different from other pieces.

She practiced the Bach on her silent keyboard for a week, and nothing terrible happened. Though she had no idea how to pronounce the composer's name, she brought the music to Sister Beatriz Maria de Resende, set her at the organ, said that a new musician had come to them, and moved her fingers over the notes. Contrapuntal magic blasted from the pipes. People in the marketplace of Beja dropped what they were doing and ran to the church. Nuns looked at their tasks, considered them, left them, went to the concert. To the excited whispers of "Who invented this?" came the scandalized reply, "Some German." The older citizens who remembered the war record of General Schomberg defended the music.

"Bach." The whisper coursed around.

"What's a Bach?" Some people used an Italianate *ch*.

"Shh!"

"Shh!"

Sister Francisca Freire, transfixed, thought that if heaven were like this, she was ready for it.

Sister Peregrina wiped the face of Sister Beatriz Maria de Resende. The work of this sensation from Germany was making her insides heat up, and she was boiling. Sister Brites de Freire comforted Sister Francisca Freire, who trembled with emotion. Listeners teemed in the chapel below. Sister Mariana watched the swiftness of Sister Beatriz's fingers, and marveled. If Sister Beatriz were to stop and rationally consider what she was producing, it might cease, turn flat. Then came flourish, coda. End. The tossing of the notes onto the audience continued until the finish, when Sister Beatriz slumped forward. Sister Mariana caught her, and no one spoke. The townspeople lingered, as if the music were still dripping off the pews and circling around the altar. The notes that had sailed up to collect in the indentations in the ceiling expanded and plunged downward. The echoing of the fugue wafted out the door, to coat the landscape in the same manner that a prayer hopes to fly from a church and insulate people from despair.

Bach the unknown had been welcomed to Beja.

Bach, ushered in by the demands of Mariana, and given to everyone.

To those who wanted Sister Beatriz to repeat the composition, the answer came, No, there is nothing like first love, first hearing, first gorgeous unveiling of new music, new musician.

The nuns in the choir remained quietly for an hour, until the last particle of the spell rose from them, to be claimed by the history of the hour. Peregrina said, "Music! Music is what we kiss, but never adore."

"I've adored it," said Sister Brites de Freire.

"Music," insisted Peregrina. "We kiss it by opening our mouths and letting it in, and we forget to adore it."

"Music," said Mariana. "That's it."

"You two will drive me insane with this business," said Sister Francisca Freire. "The answer to the riddle, as I've told you one thousand times, is stupid. It's a dumb, ridiculous trifle."

Sister Beatriz straightened up at the keyboard and said, "I surrender. What is it that we kiss, but never adore?"

"Shall I just tell you?" said Sister Francisca Freire.

"No! We have to guess!" said Sister Peregrina.

"Is it the work we do?" said Sister Maria de Castro.

"No," said Sister Francisca Freire.

"Is it the food we eat?" asked Sister Brites de Freire.

Sister Francisca Freire said, "You're close. I can't believe that none of you ever listened to your grandmothers."

"I listened to Vovó, but she wouldn't tell me," said Mariana.

"Shall I give you a hint?" said Sister Francisca Freire.

Mariana nodded.

"Go out to the well in the courtyard, and have some water. Go ahead, Sister Mariana. We'll all join you."

Mariana leapt to her feet, grabbed Peregrina's hand, and said that Vovó had been at a well with her long, long ago, out near the shrine to the souls-not-at-rest, when she first posed the riddle to Mariana.

"A *dipper*?"

"A dipper is what we kiss, but never adore?"

With the ladle at their lips, they drank the water that sprang from the center of the earth. They kissed metal, kissed water, but naturally did not stop to adore it.

"Do you mean that the answer I've been looking for since I was a girl," said Sister Mariana, "is nothing but inanity?"

"It isn't as if I didn't warn you," said Sister Francisca Freire.

"A dipper? Are you sure?" asked Sister Brites de Freire, crowding around the well with Sisters Maria de Castro and Peregrina.

"Would you like to leave your long-sought answer as foolishness, Sister Mariana, or can you do something else with it?" asked Sister Francisca Freire.

With her sister and friends around her, Mariana studied the water in the full ladle. On the pane was a shapeless sparkle of sunlight floating like a white hot flower. As she moved the dipper away from herself, the blurred reflection of Brites de Freire, Maria de Castro, Peregrina, Beatriz Maria de Resende, and Sister Francisca Freire jumped onto the pane, like a committee of well-wishers. They might as well have been standing in the middle of the immense sun; they might as well have been reduced to the size of a portion of water, to waver at her.

Mariana consumed the dipperful where all of them were held by the sunlight and the water. "I adore all of you, I adore this instant right now," she said after drinking in her friends. The others said the same when it was their turn to kiss the pane that held them alive, held them in a flower of sun and a small ocean of water, this moment that each of them adored.

"I've been looking for you, Sister Mariana," said Sister Francisca Freire.

Mariana froze, her pen in mid-air. She had been writing in the scriptorium but sensed her friend on the way. Without turning around, she said, "You've come to say goodbye?"

"How did you know?"

"We started out learning to read each other's works, and now that we're losing our eyes, we can read each other," said Mariana. She turned around, away from her work, but had trouble looking at her friend.

"And what do we kiss, but never adore?" said Sister Francisca Freire, grinning.

"Water, sun, metal, earth, what comes from the concealment of the earth, and whatever we hold in our hands." She began to cry. "Do you think I don't understand why you're here?"

"Can you kiss and adore death, Sister Mariana? Can you call it your friend? Can you call it your brother and sister, even as our model, Saint Francis, did? Sister Moon, Brother Wolf, Brother Death. Can you have affection for this most fearsome and dreaded part of life, and in doing so, possess and love everything of the world and beyond it?"

"No," said Mariana.

"Sister Mariana, I must tell you that I am quite exhausted. If I don't think you've learned this last lesson from me, I won't be at rest."

"I can tolerate death, because I have no choice," said Mariana.

"That's not good enough," said Sister Francisca.

"I'll take you to the infirmary," said Mariana.

"You'll do nothing of the sort," said Sister Francisca. "I wish to die in a beautiful room with one of my friends. Take me to the Chapter Room."

Mariana and Francisca Freire walked slowly through the cloisters, and settled with a creaking of bones onto the seating bank in the Chapel of the Sacred Heart within the Chapter Room.

"Sister Death, Brother Death. . ." said Mariana. "I can't." She covered her face with her shaking hand. "Listen, my dear old friend. Death does not do much that would have us love it."

"Oh, you are keeping me waiting!" said Sister Francisca.

"Forgive me," said Sister Mariana. "Death is an impossible entity to love."

Sister Francisca Freire turned to her and looked full into her eyes and said, "You must love it with all your soul, my dear, for I shall be in it."

"Brother Death," said Sister Mariana softly, "Sister Death. How generous of you not to take her for yourself before this. I would want to claim her much sooner than you have."

Sister Francisca Freire's head eased onto Mariana's shoulder. She murmured that her life had been exquisite, and she was grateful.

"I love you, Sister Mariana," said Sister Francisca Freire.

"I kiss you, I adore you," said Mariana. "Make a place ready for me. I won't be far behind."

She with the Heart of a Dove, she whose parents were scandalous enough to fall in love, she who felt that the only love that could be vaster than that would be to love God, she who wrote with the blood from her arteries and never ran dry, passed on, as gently as a loving mother folds cloth.

Mariana said, "Thank you, Brother Death, Sister Death, for gathering her painlessly."

To celebrate Sister Francisca Freire, Sisters Mariana, Caetana, Inês, Leonor Jacoba, Peregrina, Maria de Castro, and Brites de Freire met in the Chapter Room. Weeping blurred their eyes, and as they studied the *Mudéjar* tiles, the shapes and colors swam. The nuns described how uncanny it was that features of Sister Francisca Freire should be appearing before them – here the half curve of her heart, there the bluntness of a dove's wing, there a square that might be her jaw. Generous Sister Death, Brother Death, who did not clutch Francisca in greedy talons, but allowed those who survived to feel her encircling them until they were breathing as rapidly as the tempo of the heart of someone who had just fallen in love.

Sister Peregrina Alcoforado turned sixty-three in 1723, and still the inspired call to stand for Abbess did not come. She was regretting its lateness. She watched Mariana with her ruined knee at the altar rail. Mariana confessed that her leg was sending a flame straight through her spine and into her skull. Despite this, she was able to focus on the festivities to honor Mother Uganda, the first Abbess in the convent over two hundred years before. A chip of bone from Mother Uganda, a first-degree relic, had changed into a speck of black carbon and lay on a miniature round of red velvet, with a pregnant belly of glass over it. A starburst of silver formed a platform for the bone and velvet and glass.

A visiting priest held the remains of the first Abbess under Mariana's lips. She kissed the belly of glass. She venerated it. It pleased her to imagine that the skeleton of Inês the Beautiful might also have been a resplendent black, the shade of earth and night, after she was exhumed by her lover and the court was ordered to pay her homage.

Mariana feared that she might topple or fall. But she could not die yet. God had not provided her with a proper miracle, an apparition, a visitation of perfect love. He was running out of time, because she was running out of time.

On June 1, the date of a conference scheduled by Abbess Bernardina and the financial committee in the Chapter Room to review the accounts and finish out the year's second quarter, Mariana set out an hour early. She had to cross the entire convent, down the stairs of the New Wing, across the southern garden with the cistern, through the Quadra da Portaria and then the Quadra of

Saint John the Evangelist, to the Chapter Room. She touched her good foot onto the floor near her bed, waited until her footing was steady, and then tried to plant her bad foot and leg while reaching for her walking stick. With her free hand, she gathered the papers she had prepared for the meeting. She fell and sprawled on the floor. Her dizziness was so extreme that she spent a glorious minute thinking that she was in Papa's solarium, where the sun would squeeze the room until the objects inside it were coated with glare.

Wincing, she rolled over onto her opposite hip. She might have cracked the one she landed on. She crawled to the papers, and her hands turned them damp as she fixed them in order. Gripping them as tightly as she could, she reached for her walking stick. The knuckles of her hand blanched as she grasped it and attempted to use it as a prop to pull herself up. She managed to fight into a sitting, then a kneeling position. As she braced the walking stick to act as a lever against the floor, she stood, but her hip was in flames, her knees were quaking, and she fell again and had to collect a few fallen pages. She would have to crawl to the meeting.

Using her elbows, she dragged her body forward, moving one arm at a time, the pages of the report bunched in her hand. When she reached her door, she rested. Gasping for breath caused her insides to heave, and she fought to prevent herself from vomiting. God? her mind flashed.

God? Why this pain? Why such pain? Is this what I must endure to experience a blinding flash of pure, unknown love — purest of all, a pure unheard of?

She crawled a body's length through the corridor. Then another. One more. No one passed by, and she would not call for help. She bit her tongue so that she might have some control over where she was feeling pain. Using her elbows and forearms, she again dragged her torso forward. The agony in her hip spread into her back and gripped the scruff of her neck. She lost her veil as she proceeded, and did not retrieve it. She must not retrace any of her journey, or she would lose the song in her head caroling, On, on, on. When she reached the staircase, she was panting, and looked at the decline as a puzzle. There were a finite number of steps, and therefore if she could do one, she could take on them all. She swerved around so that her feet pointed downward, and with both heels on the second step, she told her body to fold up and go down to keep the feet company. On the second step, she again stretched out her feet, and repeated each stage for each step until she landed at the bottom. Her legs felt as if they had split open and someone had dipped a brush into sun and painted the exposed insides of her muscles.

At the bottom of the stairs, the pages again flew away from her. She winced and gasped "No" at them, and proceeded once more to gather them up. Some of the numbers were getting smudged.

After crawling through the first Quadra, she wondered how much time had elapsed, and why she was alone. It seemed that it was now getting close to an hour, and she was going to be late for her meeting. She wanted to file the report, smeared though it was, and demonstrate that the sums were in perfect order. Best of all, their suppliers were continuing to send over goods accompanied by sheets of music, as she had directed.

In the Quadra of Saint John the Evangelist, she knew that she should use the last of her strength to stand, so that she could enter the meeting properly. Mariana sat, knelt, braced the walking stick into her chest, and stood, and at least one of her ribs cracked.

With a broken hip and a broken ribcage, she placed one foot out, dragged her other foot to meet it, and continued. Several paces from the Chapter Room, Peregrina and Brites appeared, running through the cloister, crying that they had been to Mariana's room to find her. Just two minutes into the meeting, Sister Brites de Freire had screamed, "Sister Mariana! She hasn't been a second late to a meeting, not once, not in the last five decades that she's been keeping the books!" They had run from the Chapter Room and taken the opposite route, through the Quadra of the Rosary where the cemetery was, while Mariana had been crawling in the Quadra da Portaria. They had entered her room, found her missing, and retraced their steps, searching.

But now here she was, faithful to her obligation, and when they saw her ashen, holding out the sweat-soaked pages of her records, they hastened to either side to catch her.

Sister Mariana fainted into their arms.

They enlisted Joana Veloso de Bulhão and Maria de Castro to aid them in carrying Mariana to the infirmary, but she surfaced to shout, "No! My room." She wished to be in the room saturated with love. Peregrina knew her sister, and spent the remainder of that day, into the afternoon, long after completion of the meeting, pushing her back onto her pillow to prevent her from getting up and attempting to go to the Chapter Room. Even after each of the nuns on the committee came and told Mariana to stop crying out, to save her strength, that there would be the third quarter's get-together for her to attend, Mariana kept ordering herself to rise, to go where she was supposed to deliver the work of her hours, her mind, and her hands. It did not matter if the others had adjourned, if the meeting place was deserted. She must go, as she had promised. Into the night, Peregrina waited outside Mariana's door, and listened as her older sister fought to climb from bed. Peregrina would sweep in, collect Mariana, and tell her to stay, stay, please stay. Finally, Peregrina pled for mercy. She was old, too, she said to Mariana, and this would kill them both.

Only then did Mariana lie back in her bed.

She would never rise out of it again.

On June 12, 1723, the Feast of Saint John the Baptist, Mariana could not attend the festivities for the Baptista Cult, nor could she hear the organ music that she had negotiated for Sister Beatriz Maria de Resende. Peregrina grabbed fistfuls of air from the choir, and walked with clenched fists to Mariana's room, and opened her hands, palm upward, to release the trapped music, to soothe the air around Mariana.

On July 25, 1723, the Feast of Saint James, the pilgrim monks staying in the hospice received the urgent request of Abbess Bernardina to assist three nuns who had entered into torment. One of these was Sister Mariana Alcoforado.

Most startling to the monk bearing the last rites to Mariana was that it was clear that she was in extraordinary pain, but she was lying still, in perfect agony. Her green irises had neither aged nor discolored. She turned her burning face towards him, and he could tell that somehow − how remarkably bright she was, star-brilliant, sea-stirring − her reason was shining above what she was suffering, enough for her to ask, "Father, why pain? Why should this passage cause me pain?"

"I don't know, daughter," he said. "Perhaps because you are on the edge of vastness. Don't be frightened."

"Nothing frightens me," she said.

Mariana scratched out an order giving 600 *réis* for the excavation of a grave and for lime, so that the convent should not be burdened with the expense of burying her. She donated 1600 *réis* to the convent in order that eight Masses be said for the repose of her soul, and designated an extra 450 *réis* to the monks for their troubles and for being such good storytellers, and to cover the cost of their food and wine, plus 140 *réis* more for sugar and eggs to cook special desserts for them.

That was all the money she had left to her name.

Her wheat field was to go to the convent.

She was attended day and night by the monks, and by her nieces, Caetana, Inês, and Leonor Jacoba. She was sung to at the height of every hour by Sister Beatriz Maria de Resende. Sister Maria de Castro changed her linens. Brites de Freire held one hand, and Peregrina held the other.

On the first day of her agony, she said to Peregrina, "Sister, daughter, companion. Scribe. Leader. *Abbess.*"

Peregrina said, "Yes, you have to live. You have to see me become the Abbess."

But Mariana was listening to God — if that mysterious streaming in the back of our souls is God.

He said, "Is that you, Mariana? My cherished one? Come to Me now. I shall make you an angel."

"No," she said. "Anyone can be one of those fools. I won't be an angel. Send me a miracle! I have the strength to outlast you, God!"

God moaned enough to rattle the trees outside.

On the second day of her agony, Sister Mariana Alcoforado heard, "An angel? Will you not let Me love you — as I always have — as an angel?"

And Mariana shouted, "No!"

The nuns around her bed crooned to her, "Shh, Mariana. We're here."

God's moan rattled the trees and set the waters to buckling in streams.

On the night of the second day of her agony, God bellowed, "Mariana! Mariana! Mariana! Come to Me! I am the Word and contain the Word made flesh, and it is I who have been waiting since the dawn of creation to love a heart as foolish as yours! Come to Me and be my angel!"

And Mariana said, "No. Angels are stupid soldiers, and I won't be one. Where is my miracle, God?"

And God was so distraught that He came down to her bedside, saying, "Come to Me. You break the very heart of God."

She shouted, "No! I can't bear to leave the earth."

And God's moan rattled the trees and set the waters to buckling in streams and forced the wings of dragonflies to open and shut like wind-blown reeds.

On July 28, the third day of her agony, a song lit the insides of Mariana Alcoforado: Sister Death, Brother Death, I shall conquer this test, my insides are boiling out of me, and I ask, Sister Death, Brother Death, why suffering? For me, for anyone? If this is what I must undergo to own a miracle — for while I draw breath there is time — I can endure more. I think of you, my love, who entered my body and soul but did not let me love you with my might; the ardor of you has never left this room, and I do not regret that I was never cured of you, that I did not use time as a means to recover, and it is right that I leave this life from our bed. I cannot tell where I end and the hands of my friends begin, Brites, Peregrina, Maria de Castro, Beatriz Maria. I shall write on the underside of my unmarked grave, scratching out my words with the bones that stick through my decaying flesh until words carve my passage out, though I might emerge into a world that no longer knows me. Peregrina! Peregrina! She is begging me not to leave her, and I say with my eyes, my gestures, my hand that begins and ends with hers, never shall I leave you, you who will be Abbess, for my heart is as huge as the sky, as deep as the blue ocean of my dreams, and my sister, my sister, my friends, living and dead, Vovó, Mama, Papa, my departed brothers and sisters, listen to me, my beloved ones, and you who might never have met me but have loved your life and your dear ones: The sole eternity I shall accept will be if you take my memory, my life, the powers of my love, all of it, all of it, and my heart, and use them, for what I am is wholly yours.

That night God said, "If you will look at Me, I will hang you as a star between the earth you love and the heaven too small to hold you."

297

Mariana said, "Where is my miracle?"

And God burst out, "Why do you ask me for miracles? Why for this or that reward, that achievement, that finished thing? You are the miracle! You alone! I love as God should — idiotically, inexplicably. I am perfect for you! You ask why pain? Because I am perpetually unfinished! You on the earth, so proud of your tidy accomplishments. The art of creation is incompletion! Come to me, and know the pain of God."

And Mariana said, "Let me do one last thing, and then I shall look at the face of God and burn myself alive."

She lurched up in bed in front of her startled friends. She ripped the front part of her soul as a person might rip away a portion of skin, and held it out in her hand, passing this buzzing mantle of her spirit to her sister, and she said to Peregrina, "Take the last of my strength from me; it is too much for me to keep to myself. If you stand for Abbess in 1732, you will reverse this 23, this year of my death. It will serve as my last victory with books and accounts if I know that you are the one to spin the numbers of my death back into a living triumph."

Peregrina said, "I will not fail you."

On the night of the third day of her agony, Mariana Alcoforado said, "I love you. I love you still. I love you always. I esteem every joy and every sorrow that your love bestows upon me." And then she commanded God — if that mysterious streaming at the back of our souls is God — "Take — me into Your arms," and she reared her head back to gaze upon pure love, and it melted her eyes, peeled back the raw remains of her torn soul, exploded her like a seed thrown into fire, immolated her skin; and her skeleton rattled its protest before it, too, snapped into powder and her insides turned into an ocean of flames without cover or boundary, and she saw that she had become not someone beholding a reflection of God in the stars, but a star itself, to burn in the sky, seen from many countries. She writhed invisible through the day and was suspended raging at night in the only part of the earth that we also call the heavens.

In shedding starlight, she shed pieces of herself, and lovers could use such refulgence to paint her light upon their bodies as they entwined their limbs.

And whenever the man-made lights of the world went out, lovers separated from their beloved could find themselves drawn to their windows by the abundance of starlight — strange, blessed light! Alas, poor hearts! Ludicrous hearts! These lovers in their aloneness could use this beacon in the darkness and write love letters wrung out of sleeplessness and heat, all of them with this refrain:

My love, I must write this down, into the human record. The greatest miracle open to anyone is to love madly. Therefore I defy everything in order to stand thus joyfully undone before you, to trouble myself forever, to cast down all before the greatest passion in the world.

For there is something in my heart and the starlight this night that bleeds upon my page, that transports me, urges me on, and will never, never release me.

Glossary

Aguardente: A strong liquor, brandy, or firewater.

Alentejo: One of the southern provinces of Portugal; sometimes divided into Upper and Lower Alentejo, with Évora, the capital of the province, in the upper portion, and the city of Beja in the lower. Alentejan would be the suitable adjective.

Algarve, kingdom of the: The southernmost province of Portugal. The term "the kingdom of," used in the seventeenth century to designate this area, is a remnant from the times of Moorish occupation.

Anafaia: waste silk; the first thread spun out by a silk worm.

Assunção: Assumption. The bodily taking up into heaven. The Assunção of Our Lady, therefore, celebrates her corporal assumption into heaven.

Azores: (In Portuguese, spelled Açores): The archipelago of Portuguese islands (Terceira, Santa Maria, Corvo, Flores, São Jorge, Graciosa, Faial, São Miguel, Pico) in the mid-Atlantic.

Azulejos: glazed wall tiles. Since *azul* is blue, these tiles originally designated blue-and-white designs, though the term has become more all-encompassing and may now include tiles of any color.

Beja/Bejense: A small city 78 kilometers south from Évora, in the southern interior plains. Originally named "Pax Julia" to honor the peace between Portugal and Julius Caesar, the words were eventually elided and shortened to sound like "beja." A Bejense would be an inhabitant of Beja, or an adjective to indicate anything from that region.

Beringel: A small rural town about 10 kilometers from Beja.

Bicho-Papão: *Bicho* may mean any animal, except a fish or bird; it might mean a bug, worm, or someone completely repulsive. *Papão* is the large form of "papa," or pouch. Bicho-Papão is the legendary monster who sits on roofs and swings through windows at night and gobbles up children inside his enormous pouch.

Boca de mel, coração de fel: An old expression: Mouth of honey, heart of bile. In other words, don't trust sweet talkers.

Bragança (house of): The highest-ranking noble family in Portugal, from which the line of rulers commenced with the declaration of independence and appointment of João IV of Vila Viçosa in 1640, and continued unbroken until 1910, when Manuel II was assassinated.

Brites: A common nickname for Beatriz (Beatrice).

Caldo Verde: Green broth. A thick soup, often made with a potato base, with sausage and thinly-sliced chard and onions.

Câmara: City hall, or a chamber, stateroom, or room. (I have always liked that our word "camera" comes from the Latin root that means "room," because the early box-cameras were like little rooms that could, in a manner of speaking, contain people.)

Castile: A former kingdom in central Spain, with Madrid as its capital. Considered the old ruling province. Castilian Spanish is now the standard form of the language.

Catalonia: Formerly a province in northeastern Spain; it attempted to secede from the rest of the country in the seventeenth century. In Spanish: Cataluña.

Coimbra: Site of the murder of Inês the Beautiful. North of Lisbon (though south of Porto), and on the banks of the Mondego River, Coimbra is also the site of the university.

Conceição: Conception, specifically, the Immaculate Conception. Also a female name. O Real Mosteiro de Nossa Senhora da Conceição would be the Royal Convent of Our Lady of the Immaculate Conception.

Costa: A popular surname; also, coast or sea-shore, or the slope of a hill.

Cunha: Literally, "wedge." A common surname. It is also current slang for an influential person, or someone who can be used as a source of recommendation or advancement.

Dona/Dom: An honorific title. While used for the nobility, it is also a common title of respect prefacing a given name. Dona is the female term.

Duende: Literally, a gremlin or goblin. In Spanish, it indicates the spirit taking fire and consuming the dancer, musician, etc., engaged in the art form in an inspired moment.

Duenha: A chaperone for young girls; governess. *Duenna* in Spanish.

Encharcada: Literally, swampy, marshy, flooded. The name of a rich confection, traditionally from the Alentejo. A combination of egg yolks and sugar heated into a syrup, then poured onto a deep plate, baked until crisp, and sprinkled with cinnamon.

Entojo: A truly magical word: Nausea, or the bizarre fancies, wishes, and dreams peculiar to pregnancy.

Esperança: Hope (or wish). Since it also refers to one of the theological virtues, it may be used as the name of a religious site or place, such as the Convent of Esperança in Beja.

Estremadura: The province on the western coast of Portugal that includes the country's capital city of Lisbon.

Évora: The capital of the Alentejan province; a walled city.

Frei: A friar or monk. *Frei* may also be used as a title (Father).

Guadiana River: A river running along the southern border of Spain and Portugal.

Guerra de Restauração: The War of Restoration. In Portugal, it was the War of Independence to be free of Spanish rule, which began in 1580. The war lasted from about 1640-1668.

Infantes: Literally an infant or infantry soldier, but more commonly understood in Spain and Portugal to indicate any son of a king who is not an heir to the throne.

Janela: window.

João: The Portuguese version of John.

Lampa: Any type of fruit that is gathered during a midsummer's night.

Limeiro: Lemon tree. Could be a surname. The name of a famous Lisbon prison.

Lôbo: Literally, "wolf." A common surname.

Locutory: An English word used to indicate a room set aside for conversation or meeting, specifically in a monastery or convent.

Lusitania: The old Roman word for Portugal. Hence a Luso-American is the proper term for a Portuguese-American. Travelers to

Portugal or Portuguese-speaking countries will notice many journals or products that make use of a "Luso" prefix.

Mantua: a tunic, usually black.

Manueline: A particularly Lusitanian style of architecture meant to pay homage to the age of the great navigators. At its height in the late fifteenth through the early sixteenth centuries, during the rule of King Dom Manuel, the style encouraged maritime motifs, with entwined ropes and ships, and high embellishments, plus a sense that a viewer might be gazing at a far horizon.

Marquês/Marquêsa: Marquis, Marquise.

Menina: child (female). *Menino* means boy or lad. Considered a term of endearment.

Mértola: A small town in southern Portugal, near the Guadiana River. There was a now-famous "Mértola Window" at the Convent of Conceição in Beja, so-called not because one could see this town from the window or balcony, but because it looked out on the southern gates and road that led the fifty-four kilometers to Mértola. It was from this window that we are certain that Mariana first saw the Count of Chamilly.

Meu bem: My dear, my love, my darling: a term of affection. *Bem* also means happiness, goods, blessings.

Migas: A type of bread soup or porridge, or a mixture with a more stuffing-like consistency. Fats and possibly meat, seafood, or eggs may be mixed in with the crumbled bread.

Milu: A nickname for Maria Luisa.

Morgado/Morgadio: A *morgado* is the inheritor, often the first-born, of an estate; the *morgadio* refers to the majorat, entail, or estate.

Mosteiro: Monastery or convent. Place of monastic life.

Mouvement: A French term indicating a sweeping-over or possession by emotion not in control of the will.

Mudéjar: Properly speaking, the term used for one of Moorish descent who continued to live in Spain or Portugal after reconquest was achieved by Christian armies. *Mudéjur* commonly refers to any style of art or architecture (e.g., decorative tiles) that combine Arabic or Christian elements.

Namorada: The feminine form of sweetheart, beloved.

Néné: A nickname for Manuela.

Nogueira: The walnut tree, or its wood. A common surname.

Pão-de-ló: A type of spongecake. Literally "bread of gauze." *Pao* is the word for bread.

Pedro/Inês de Castro: The "Romeo and Juliet" of Portugal. Inês was the Castilian lady-in-waiting to the wife of Dom Pedro, prince and heir to the throne of Portugal. After the death of his wife, Dom Pedro fell in love with Inês and had several children with her. The couple were married in secret to legitimize their union. The King, Dom Afonso V, unaware of the marriage of his son to Inês but aware of his love for her, was persuaded against her by those who feared she was a Spanish spy, and her throat was cut in a garden in Coimbra. When Pedro ascended the throne in 1357, he tracked down her murderers and killed them. (Legends often add that he cut out and ate their hearts.) It is true, at least, that he ordered her body exhumed and the nobility to kiss her hand. Their sarcophagi in Alcobaça was vandalized by the troops of Napoleon.

Pequininha: The diminutive form of *pequeno*, meaning small or child. A term of affection for a little girl.

Peregrina: The pilgrim, traveler, wanderer. A common first name for girls and women.

Portaria: The principal door of a convent, or any entrance or portal.

Quadra: A square place, yard, or enclosure. In a convent, it would mean one of the four cloistered walkways that make up the square forming the courtyard.

Rasquilha branca: A pastry made of slightly curved and hardened dough, whitened by coats of sugar syrup. Red wine is traditionally poured into the pastry and drunk from it, which also serves to soften the sometimes tooth-threatening brittleness.

Real: Real or actual, but also royal.

Réis: A corruption of the plural *reais.* The singular form: *real.* A former Portuguese silver coin; also, a former unit of the Portuguese (and Brazilian) monetary system.

Rua do Touro: Street of the Bull.

Rui: A common male first name, short for Rodrigo.

Scriptorium: A writing room. In a monastery or cloister, the room where manuscripts are written, studied, or stored.

Sebastião & "Sebastianismo": Also called "O Encoberto," or the Hidden One, or The Longed-For, King Dom Sebastião led a misguided campaign against the Moors at Alácer-Quibir in 1578, using much of the national treasury. Thousands of Portuguese died, and the body of the King was never found, leading to a cult of *Sebastianismo* in which the King is supposed to return, riding back in the mist, to restore Portugal to prosperous days. His folly, however, caused Spain to seize its chance in 1580 to seize control of the Portuguese government in an attempt to unify the Iberian peninsula.

Senhor/Senhora: The equivalent to "Sir" or "Mister" and "Madame" or "Mrs." Interestingly enough, Portuguese seldom use the diminutive to address an unmarried woman or young girl (the Spanish equivalent of *señorita). Senhorinha* is not unheard of, but it is rare. *Senhora* is preferred, no matter a woman's marital status.

Sóror: The title "Sister," referring to a nun or lay sister. (*Irmã* is the word for a blood-relative sister.)

Talha: Literally, "carving" or "engraving." Specifically, the art form popular in the baroque period, extending from the seventeenth into the eighteenth century: carved wood painted with gilt. Highly ornate, with flowers, entwining flourishes, vines, etc.

Temporada: A period of time; season. (*Tempo* means period, length of time, epoch, seipon, etc., as well as "weather.")

Terceira/Terceirense: An island in the Azores, known for its fort and because it was the only area in all of Portugal to resist the Spanish takeover of Philip II in 1580. Terceirense are the inhabitants.

Tia/Titia: Aunt. Titia would be a child's term, or term of endearment.

Trás-Os-Montes: Literally, "behind the mountains." Refers to the northeasternmost province in Portugal.

Vasco da Gama: (c. 1469–1525): Portuguese navigator who discovered the maritime route to India from Europe. His great-grandson was the godfather to Mariana Alcoforado of Beja.

Vidrar: To coat with a glaze; to become dull; to make glass; to fall desperately in love.

Vigária: Vice-Abbess, or one who substitutes for her superior.

Vila Viçosa: A small town of the Alentejan province, not far from Beja. Once the home and seat of power for the House of Bragança.

Vovó/Vovô: The proper term for grandmother is *avó,* and for grandfather, *avô.* Vovó is an affectionate term, like "grandma," and Vovô would mean "grandpa."

About the Love Letters of a Nun:
A Word from the Author

Matisse drew portraits of her. So did Modigliani. Dozens of other artists painted representations, including Georges Braque. His cubism is as accurate a rendering as anyone else's, because what Sister Mariana Alcoforado looked like has long been a mystery. From the age of eleven, she lived in a cloister in provincial Portugal and endured the endless war in the seventeenth century when her country was fighting for independence from Spain. She had a love affair with a French captain who was part of the mercenary army that had come to Portugal's aid. She wrote him five love letters that went on to become famous (I shall leave it to the narrative to disclose how this came to pass) from the moment she wrote them up to our present time.

International societies exist to investigate "Marianista" issues. The writer Stendhal said of her, "It is necessary to love like the Portuguese nun, with that ardent soul whose fiery mark is left for us in her letters." The sculptor Rodin voiced his awe of what she embodied. No one was more rhapsodic about her than the poet Rainer Maria Rilke, who did a 1913 German translation of the letters *(Portugiesche Brieife)*. Jean Jacques Rousseau proclaimed that surely the love letters were a hoax, because no woman was capable of converting romantic feelings into art. She continues to be legendary across Europe. She is known in Asia, Africa, South America. Translations of her letters, hailed as "the most passionate documents in existence," have sold out in over two hundred and fifty editions around the world.

Why, then, is she virtually unknown in Great Britain and the United States of America? There is an on-going debate regarding the authenticity of the *Portuguese Love Letters*. Because they were first published in French (in Paris) and no originals in Portuguese have been found, many scholars have built a case that Mariana, her history, and her letters are entirely a work of fiction by a Frenchman. The primary works documenting her existence are out of print, have never been translated into English, and are obscure outside of Portugal. Despite their knowledge of such documentation, some French and North American writers (for whom French is more the language of discourse than Portuguese) continue to insist that the Love Letters belong exclusively in the canon of French literature. This viewpoint suffuses the increasing number of references to Mariana that I have seen in the USA, causing her to be dismissed as "alleged."

Bad enough that her letters should be taken from her. Unforgivable that anyone should attempt to brush her spirit aside. My conviction is that her life and authorship should be returned to her. Though the translation of the Love Letters is mine, the sentiments are Mariana's. I have fleshed out her story based upon my research in the original Portuguese sources. This novel relies on true events, including some that seem uncanny.

Several points are worth emphasizing. It was common practice in her time to put girls into convents whether or not they had vocations, to preserve the line of inheritance regarding an estate. Too many sons-in-law were seen as detrimental to the future of a man's holdings. The powers of state and church were inexorably connected; for reasons of piety (and sometimes for political gain), children were routinely given back to God. It should not be shocking that Mariana Alcoforado had trouble seeing herself as a nun in the sense we might view her today. She was a noblewoman, and lived in what by today's standards would be more of a spacious studio apartment (referred to as a "little house") than a dank cell. Because Mariana lived in wartime, conditions were extremely lax, with the convent as much as place of refuge as it was a bastion of devotion.

It has become the stock stuff of comedy routines to ridicule vows of chastity. No one mentions that in centuries past there were precious few places where a woman could use her talents for scholarship, music, and art other than a convent, and few places where she could construct a small city and make decisions that would affect its running.

It must be happily mentioned that men as well as women adore Mariana. I remember when my friend Leonel Borrela, one of the curators of the museum now housing the remains of the convent, said that only someone who understood nothing about love could fail to be enchanted by her. Mariana thrives within anyone who ever felt, or dreamed of feeling, that every thought and action must be drenched with transcendence – with a love beyond love itself.

Acknowledgments

This book would not exist were it not for my dear friend, the novelist Gwyneth Cravens, who first recommended the project to me. Gwyneth was kind enough to read through the manuscript and offer encouragement and many helpful insights and suggestions.

When I traveled to the convent in Beja, I arrived on a day when the museum now housing the remains of the convent was closed. Not content to wait a moment longer, I went to City Hall and the Tourist Office to see if I could gain admittance. I was put in contact with Senhor Leonel Borrela, one of the curators and a tireless "Marianalia" collector. He immediately met me at the convent to open the doors.

As an artist, he has produced a number of representations of the most famous nun in Portuguese history. He and his wife, Ermininha Glória, their children Silvia and José Miguel, and a family friend, Ermelinha, opened their extensive library and their hearts to me, and took me to visit the old Alcoforado estate. They asked for nothing in return for the gold-mine of information that they turned over. It was for love of Mariana and the wish to have her known at large that their generosity was boundless. I hope this novel pays back a small part of the debt of gratitude that I owe Leonel Borrela and his family.

The Norton Library Edition of the *Duino Elegies* of Rainer Maria Rilke, (translated by J. B. Leishman and Stephen Spender, W. W. Norton & Company, New York & London, 1939, copyright renewed by Leishman & Spender in 1967), whose Appendix I describes Mariana Alcoforado, was one of my first inspirations in writing this novel.

My appreciation to the staff of the Biblioteca Nacional in Lisbon, where I did some research, and to the staffs at the University of California at Berkeley, Irvine, and Santa Barbara. Thanks also to Bettina Soestwohner, who translated the French works by Deloffre and Rougeot regarding the arguments about authenticity for my use.

I could not have written this book without referring to *Soror Marianna: A Freira Portugueza* (sic), by Luciano Cordeiro (Lisbon: Livraria Ferin & Companhia, Second Edition, 1890). This is the seminal work (to the best of my knowledge, not available in English) on the existence of Mariana, and provided me with numerous facts about Mariana, her family, and Beja at the time of the Letters, including the names of some of the nuns in the convent during Mariana's era, citations of miraculous events recorded in the convent's history, the writings of Sister Mariana da Purificação of the convent of Esperança, the Alcoforado genealogy, and the military actions in the Alentejo during the War of Independence (or Restoration). The roster of nuns at the beginning of the second chapter is from his book as well, with a few fictitious additions of my own. I have used other details here and there from his remarkable volume. Likewise, an invaluable source was *Vida E Morte De Madre Mariana Alcoforado* by Manuel Ribeiro (Lisbon: Livraria Sá da Costa, Editora Lisboa, 1940). Most of the details about the actual life in the convent are from this volume, also out of print and not translated into English. I could not have written this novel without the research done by these two leading lights of Marianalia.